CALL OF THE KIWI

ALSO BY SARAH LARK

In the Land of the Long White Cloud

Song of the Spirits

CALL *of the* KIWI

SARAH LARK

TRANSLATED BY D. W. LOVETT

amazoncrossing

This is a work of fiction. Names, characters, organizations, places, events, and incidents are either products of the author's imagination or are used fictitiously.

Printed in the United States of America.

Call of the Kiwi was first published in 2008 in Germany by Verlagsgruppe Lübbe GmbH & Co. KG as *Der Ruf des Kiwis.* Translated from German by D. W. Lovett.

Published by AmazonCrossing, Seattle
www.apub.com

Cover design by Paul Barrett

ISBN-10: 1477820264
ISBN-13: 9781477820261

Library of Congress Control Number: 2013921788

In memory of Einstein and Marie Curie

Contents

PART ONE

Rearing: *Canterbury Plains, Greymouth, Christchurch, and Cambridge, 1907–1909*

PART TWO

Paradise Lost: *Canterbury Plains, Cambridge, Auckland, Cape Reinga, America, Australia, and Greymouth, 1914–1915*

PART THREE

War: *Canterbury Plains, Greymouth, Gallipoli, and Wellington, 1914–1916*

PART FOUR

A Long Road: *Greymouth, Canterbury Plains, and Auckland, 1915–1918*

PART FIVE

Peace: *Dunedin, Kiward Station, and Christchurch, 1917–1918*

Rearing

CANTERBURY PLAINS, GREYMOUTH, CHRISTCHURCH, AND CAMBRIDGE

1907–1909

1

"Come on, Jack, I'll race you to the circle of stone warriors!"

Not even waiting for Jack's answer, Gloria brought her pony into starting position next to his horse. When Jack nodded, Gloria lightly pressed her legs into the mare's sides and took off.

Jack McKenzie, a young man with curly red-brown hair and serene, green-brown eyes, likewise brought his horse to a gallop and followed Gloria over the seemingly endless grassland of Kiward Station. Jack had no chance of catching up to Gloria on his relatively slow cob gelding, but he let the girl have her fun. Gloria was awfully proud of her horse, which had been shipped from England. Swift as an arrow, she looked like a Thoroughbred in miniature. If Jack's memory served, it was the first birthday present from her parents that had made Gloria genuinely happy. The contents of the other packages that arrived for her at irregular intervals had not impressed her: a flouncy dress with fan and castanets from Seville, gold-lamé shoes from Milan, an ostrich leather purse from Paris . . . nothing of much use on a sheep farm in New Zealand and even much too extravagant for her occasional visits to Christchurch.

But Gloria's parents never considered such things—quite the opposite, in fact. William and Kura Martyn probably would have thought it amusing to shock the rather provincial society of the Canterbury Plains with a taste of the larger world. Shyness and restraint were foreign to both of them, and they took it for granted that their daughter felt as they did.

As Jack rushed at breakneck speed down the country road to keep the girl in sight, he thought about Gloria's mother. Kura-maro-tini, the daughter of his half brother Paul Warden, had been blessed with an exotic beauty and an exceptional voice. She owed her musicality to her mother Marama, a Maori singer, rather than to her white relations. From a young age Kura had nursed a desire to conquer the world of European opera. Jack had grown up with her on Kiward Station and still looked back with horror on the countless hours she'd spent banging away on the piano and practicing her singing exercises. Initially, it had looked as though she would have no opportunity to realize her dreams—until she met William Martyn, now her husband, who knew how to make good on her talents. The two had been touring through Europe with a group of Maori singers and dancers ever since. Kura was the star of the ensemble, which combined traditional Maori music and Western instrumentation in unique compositions.

"I win!" Gloria skillfully brought her pony to a halt in the middle of the rock formation known as the circle of stone warriors. "And the sheep are back there too!"

The small flock of ewes was the real reason for Jack and Gloria's ride. The animals were grazing near the stone circle, a piece of land sacred to the local Maori tribe. Though the land belonged to Kiward Station, Gwyneira McKenzie, who managed the farm, respected the religious feelings of the natives. There were enough pastures on the property that there was no need for the sheep and cattle to roam on Maori holy sites. Hence she had asked Jack at lunch to bring the sheep in, which had drawn energetic protests from Gloria.

"But I can do that, Grandmum! Nimue still has to learn!"

Ever since Gloria had begun training her first sheepdog, she had pushed for more responsibilities on the farm, much to Gwyneira's delight. She smiled at her great-granddaughter and nodded.

"Very well, but Jack will help out," she consented. She could not even say herself why she would not let the girl ride alone. In principle, there was no cause for concern: Gloria knew the farm like the back of her hand, and all the workers on Kiward Station knew and loved Gloria.

Gwyneira had not been nearly so cautious with her own children. Even as an eight-year-old, her daughter, Fleurette, had ridden four miles to the little school Gwyneira's friend Helen had run on a neighboring farm. But Gloria was different. All Gwyneira's hopes rested on the only recognized heiress of Kiward Station. Since Gloria's blood flowed with that of the Wardens—the founders of Kiward Station—and of the local Maori tribe, she was acknowledged to belong to both worlds. A strong rivalry had always existed between the Wardens and Tonga, the chieftain of the Ngai Tahu; Tonga hoped to bring the land more firmly into his control by means of a marriage between Gloria and a Maori of his tribe. This strategy had, however, already failed once with Gloria's mother, Kura. And thus far Gloria had demonstrated little interest in the life and culture of the tribes. Though she spoke fluent Maori and loved to listen to her grandmother Marama's tales of their people's past, her primary tie was to Gwyneira, Gwyneira's second husband, James McKenzie, and above all, their son, Jack.

A special connection had always existed between Jack and Gloria. Though he was a full fifteen years older than his half grandniece, he had always shielded Gloria from the caprices and disinterest of her parents. Jack had never cared for Kura or her music, but he had liked Gloria from first sight. Even as a baby, she had started crying as soon as Kura struck the first notes on the piano, and Jack understood completely; he took Gloria with him wherever he went like he might a puppy.

Gloria's border collie, Nimue, was panting when she reached the stone circle and looked up almost reproachfully at her mistress. She did not like it when Gloria took off ahead of her. The dog had been happier before the swift-as-an-arrow pony had arrived from England. Nevertheless, when Gloria whistled sharply, she set off for the sheep that were grazing among the rocks. After Nimue had herded the sheep together, Gloria deftly led the flock in the direction of home.

"See, I could have done it alone!" the girl said, beaming triumphantly at Jack. "Will you tell that to Grandmum?"

"Of course, Glory. She'll be proud of you. And of Nimue."

More than fifty years ago, Gwyneira McKenzie had brought the first border collies from Wales to New Zealand, where she bred and trained them. She was delighted to see Gloria interact so skillfully with the animals.

Andy McAran, the farm's old-as-dirt foreman, watched Jack and Gloria as they drove the sheep into the pen. It had been a long time since Andy actually had to work, but he liked to keep himself busy around the farm and still saddled his horse almost every day to ride from the village of Haldon to Kiward Station.

"Almost like the old days, Gwyn." The old man grinned knowingly when Gloria closed the gate behind the sheep. "The only thing missing is the red hair and . . ." Andy left the rest unspoken; after all, he did not want to annoy Gloria. But Jack had heard similar remarks too often not to be able to read Andy's thoughts: the old hand was sorry that Gloria had inherited neither her great-grandmother's delicate figure nor her narrow, pretty face—which was strange because Gwyneira had passed on her red locks and petite frame to almost all her other female offspring. With her angular face, close-set eyes, and tightly drawn mouth, Gloria took after the Wardens. Her lush, light-brown hair overwhelmed her face more than it framed it. Styling that wild luxuriance was so hopeless that she had cut it off in a fit of spite a year earlier. Although everyone had teased her, asking whether she just wanted to be a boy—she had already taken to pilfering the breeches her grandmother Marama sewed for the Maori youths—Jack thought Gloria's short hair looked wonderful on her and the loose riding pants suited her stocky frame better than dresses.

"She really didn't get anything from her mother," James McKenzie remarked as he observed Jack and Gloria from the bay window in Gwyneira's bedroom. Ever since James had turned eighty, his age had begun to cause him difficulties. He had been suffering from joint pain for a while, but he hated using a cane to get down the stairs to the salon. He claimed he could keep an eye on the goings-on of the farm better from his place at the bay window.

Gwyneira knew better: James had never really felt comfortable in Kiward Station's elegant salon. His world had always been the workers' quarters, and he had only acquiesced to living in the manor and raising his son there for Gwyneira's sake.

Gwyneira laid her hand on his shoulder, likewise looking down at Gloria and their son.

"She's beautiful," Gwyneira said. "If the right man ever turns up for her . . ."

James rolled his eyes. "Not again! Thank God the fellows aren't chasing her yet. When I think back on Kura and that Maori boy who gave you such a headache—how old was she then? Thirteen?"

"But she blossomed early," Gwyneira said, defending her granddaughter. She had always loved Kura. "I know you don't care for her. But her problem was simply that she didn't belong here."

Gwyneira brushed her hair before putting it up. It was still long and curly, but the red was increasingly shot through with white. Though her face was now lined with a few wrinkles—she had never protected her skin from the elements—she remained as slender and wiry as in her youth, and no one would have guessed that she was almost seventy-three years old.

"Kura's problem was that no one taught her the word 'no' when she could still learn," James grumbled. They had had this discussion about Kura a thousand times; it was the only subject that had ever given them any reason to fight.

Gwyneira shook her head disapprovingly. "You're making it sound like I was afraid of Kura," she said. That accusation was nothing new either, though it had originally come from Gwyneira's friend Helen O'Keefe, not James—and just the thought of Helen, who had died the year before, stung Gwyneira.

James raised his eyebrows. "Afraid of Kura? Never," he said. "That's why you've been pushing that letter Andy brought in this morning around the table for three hours. Open it, Gwyn. Eighteen thousand miles lie between you and Kura. She can't bite you."

Gwyneira's fingers trembled as she opened the letter—postmarked this time from London. Kura had never displayed any interest in her daughter, and Gwyneira prayed it would stay that way.

James could see by his wife's reaction that the letter contained upsetting news.

"They want to take Gloria to England," Gwyneira said tonelessly when she'd finished reading. "They"—Gwyneira sought the place in the letter—"they appreciate the work we've done raising her, but they're worried about whether Gloria's 'artistic-creative side' is being sufficiently developed here. James, Gloria doesn't have an 'artistic-creative side.'"

"And thank God for that. How exactly do those two plan to awaken this new Gloria? Is she supposed to join them on tour? Singing, dancing? Playing the flute?"

Kura's virtuosic mastery of the *putorino* flute was among her program's highlights, and so Gloria naturally possessed one of her own. To her grandmother Marama's dismay, however, the girl had not even been able to call forth one of the flute's "normal voices," let alone the famous *wairua*, "the spirit voice."

"No, she's to be sent to boarding school. Listen to this: 'We have chosen a small, idyllically situated school near Cambridge that boasts a multifaceted girls' education with a special focus in the intellectual-artistic field.'" Gwyneira paused. "Girls' education! What's that supposed to mean?"

James laughed. "Cooking, baking, sewing?" he suggested. "French? Piano playing?"

At Gwyneira's anguished expression, James stood up laboriously and took her in his arms.

"Come now, Gwyn, it won't be all that bad. With the steamships, the journey to England is a snap. Lots of people send their children to boarding school. It won't do Gloria any harm to see the world. She'll be with girls her own age and play field hockey or whatever it is they do there. She'll have to get used to a sidesaddle. A little more social polish wouldn't be the worst thing, given that the livestock barons here are only getting more sophisticated."

"I shouldn't have let her send the photo with the horse. But she just had to have it. She was so happy about the pony."

Gloria was photographed for her parents once a year. Though she generally wore a stiff Sunday dress, Gloria had insisted on having her latest photo taken on her new pony.

"I should at least have insisted on a sidesaddle and riding dress."

James took her hand and gently brushed his lips on it.

"You know how Kura and William are. Perhaps it's just time. They had to remember someday that they have a daughter."

"It's about time!" Gwyneira cursed. "But why didn't they consult with us? They don't even know Glory. And straight to boarding school! She's so young."

"English children go to boarding school at four," he reminded her. "And Glory is twelve. She'll manage. Maybe she'll even enjoy it."

"She'll get homesick."

"All the girls must get homesick at first. But they get over it."

Gwyneira flared up. "If their parents live twenty miles away, that's fine, but for Glory it'll be eighteen thousand. We're sending her half a world away to people she doesn't know or love!

"Can't we just pretend we never got the letter?" she asked, leaning against James.

"Gwyn, my love, this is probably all William's doing. He likely fancies the idea of marrying Gloria off to some earl."

"If only Gloria wouldn't be all alone," Gwyneira sighed. "The long passage by ship, so many foreigners."

"What if we were to send another girl along?" James considered. "Doesn't she have any Maori friends?"

Gwyneira shook her head. "You don't really believe that Tonga is going to send a girl from his tribe to England," she said. "Besides, I can't think of anyone Gloria is close to. But, yes"—Gwyneira's face brightened—"it's a possibility."

"Who?"

"Lilian. She's rather young, of course, but she got along well with Gloria when Elaine was here last year. And Tim went to school in England, so he might warm to the idea."

James smiled at the mention of Lilian's name. Gwyneira's great-granddaughter Lilian, Elaine and Tim's eldest, was redheaded, lively, and spirited, just like Gwyneira, Fleurette, and Elaine. Although Gloria had initially been a little shy when Lilian had come to visit the year before, Lilian had quickly broken the ice. She chattered about school, her friends, and her horses and dogs at home. She raced Gloria on horseback, and she made Gloria teach her Maori and take her to visit the tribe on Kiward Station. It was the first time Gwyneira had ever heard Gloria giggling with another girl.

"Lilian is so much younger than Gloria," James offered for consideration. "I can't imagine that Elaine will be ready to part with her. Regardless of what Tim thinks."

"It doesn't cost anything to ask," Gwyn said resolutely. "I'll write to them straightaway. What do you think: should we tell Gloria?"

James sighed and ran a hand through his scraggly hair—a gesture of his that Gwyneira had always loved. "Not right away," he said finally. "But soon. It'll be hard for her if she shows up midyear."

Gwyneira nodded. "But we have to tell Miss Bleachum. She'll have to look for a new position. Damn it, we finally have a tutor who actually earns her keep, and then this happens!"

Sarah Bleachum had been teaching Gloria for years, and the girl was very attached to her.

Miss Bleachum had attended the teaching academy in Wellington. She loved the natural sciences and had passed on her passion for New Zealand's flora and fauna to Gloria. They spent hours buried in books on the subject. Would Gloria's teachers and fellow students be able to appreciate her enthusiasm for insects and animals in an English girls' school?

2

"It's all right; I can get out on my own."

Although Timothy Lambert had just rejected the help of his servant, Roly, he found it especially difficult that day to swing his legs onto the gig's footboard, put his leg braces on, and then find solid footing on the ground with the help of his crutches. He felt stiff and irritable—which was almost always the case when the anniversary of the accident to which he owed his handicap approached. This would be the eleventh year since the collapse of the Lambert Mine, and like every year, the mine management would hold a small memorial on the anniversary. The victims' surviving relatives and the coal miners working in the mine appreciated the gesture, but Tim would be the center of attention as Roly O'Brien once again told the story of how the mine owner's son had rescued him. Tim always hated watching the expressions on people's faces, which alternated between hero worship and horror.

While Roly led the horse into the stable, Tim limped up to the house. As it did every time, the sight of the isolated white wood building lifted his spirits. He had had the simple structure built after marrying Elaine—despite the protests of his parents, who had advised him to build a more suitable residence. Their own villa closer to town was much more in keeping with the proper image of a mine owner's residence. But Elaine had not wanted to share Lambert Manor with Tim's parents, and the grand two-story estate, with its open staircases and bedrooms on the upper floor, hardly suited Tim's needs. Besides, he wasn't really a mine owner; most of his shares in the business belonged to the investor George Greenwood.

"Daddy!" Lilian threw open the door. Tim's oldest son, Rube, appeared behind Lilian, looking disappointed because Lilian had once again been the one to open the door for their father.

"Daddy! You have to hear what I was practicing today." Lilian loved to play the piano, though she did so with more enthusiasm than skill. "'Annabel Lee.' Do you know it? It's really sad. The woman is sooo pretty, and the prince loves her awfully, but then—"

"Girl stuff," Rube complained. Though he was only seven years old, he already knew what he was supposed to think was absurd. "Check out my train, Dad! I built the new engine all by myself."

"That's not true. Mummy helped you," Lilian said.

"I'm sorry, but I can't hear the word 'train' anymore today." He tousled his son's red-brown tuft. Though all four children had their mother's red hair, the three boys otherwise looked more like Tim.

Tim's countenance brightened when his wife appeared. She was still beautiful, with shining green eyes, pale skin, and untamable curly red locks. Her ancient dog Callie trotted behind her.

Elaine kissed Tim softly on the cheek. "What did she do this time?" she asked by way of greeting.

Tim furrowed his brow. "Are you a mind reader?" he asked, confused.

Elaine laughed. "Not exactly, but you only make that face when you're contemplating a new way of disposing of Florence Biller. And since you don't normally have anything against trains, it must have something to do with the new rail connection."

"Precisely. But let me get settled first. What are the little ones up to?"

Elaine snuggled up to her husband so that he could surreptitiously lean on her and helped him into the living room, where she removed his jacket before he sank down into one of the armchairs in front of the fireplace.

"Jeremy drew a sheep and wrote 'ship' underneath," Elaine explained. "It's hard to say whether he wrote or drew the wrong thing." Jeremy was six and learning his ABCs. "And Billy managed four steps at a go."

As if he wanted to prove it, the little boy waddled toward Tim, who picked him up, pulled him onto his lap, and tickled him.

"Just seven more steps and he can get married," Tim said, laughing and winking at Elaine. When he had relearned to walk after his accident, his first goal had been eleven steps—the distance from the church entrance to the altar.

"Don't read anything into that, Lily," Elaine said to her daughter, who was preparing a question. Lilian dreamed of fairy tale princes, and "wedding" was her favorite game. "Why don't you go to the piano and send 'Annabel Lee' to the angels one more time while Daddy tells me why he suddenly doesn't like trains anymore."

Elaine poured Tim a whiskey and sat down next to him. He rarely drank, but that day he looked so exhausted and aggravated that she figured a drink might do him good.

"Florence has been negotiating with the railroad company without bringing in the other mine owners. I found out accidentally from George Greenwood. He has his hands in rail construction too, which enables us to negotiate much better terms. But Florence seems to hope that everyone in Greymouth will just ignore the new tracks so that the Billers will be the only ones to enjoy improved coal transport. Matt and I have asked for a rail connection for the Lambert Mine as well, but I reckon that Florence will have her own depot in a matter of weeks." Tim sipped his whiskey.

Elaine shrugged. "She's a savvy businesswoman."

"She's a beast!" Tim moaned. Florence Biller ruled her husband's mine with an iron hand. Her foremen and secretaries trembled before her—although there were rumors that one young office employee was treated with favor. Over and over again, one of her employees played the favorite for a short time—three times altogether up until then. Tim and Elaine Lambert, who knew a few secrets about Caleb and Florence's marriage, had come to their own conclusions since Florence Biller had three children.

"I have no idea how Caleb can stand her." Tim set his glass on the table and began to relax.

"I think her machinations must sometimes be embarrassing to her husband," Elaine said. "But on the whole, he probably doesn't care. She leaves him alone as he does her—that was the agreement, after all."

Caleb Biller had no interest in managing his family's mine. He was a private scholar and expert in the field of Maori art and music. He had not wanted to marry, but, lacking the courage to live out his real desires, he had negotiated a marriage to Florence in which they could both be halfway happy. Though he was the nominal head of the Biller Mine, Florence let him pursue his Maori studies and he gave her the chance to be the businesswoman she had always wanted to be.

"I just wish she wouldn't manage her business like a pitched battle," Tim sighed. "I understand she wants to be taken seriously, but she's not the only one."

Early on, several suppliers had tried to use his handicap to deliver inferior goods, assuming that Tim couldn't oversee the deliveries. Tim, however, had eyes and ears outside of his office. His representative, Matt Gawain, kept a close eye on things, and though Roly had never set foot in a mine again after being buried in one for two days with Tim, he worked with the miners above ground whenever Tim didn't need him.

Tim had become a highly respected boss, and no one tried to take advantage of him anymore. Surely Florence Biller could have made peace with all her male competitors, but she instead continued to wage her war with undiminished energy. She wanted not only to make the Biller Mine the leading mine in Greymouth but also to rule the entire West Coast—if not the country.

"Is there anything to eat?" Tim asked his wife.

Elaine nodded. "In the oven. It'll be a little longer. I wanted to talk to you about something beforehand."

Tim noticed that her gaze flitted over to Lilian.

Elaine turned to the girl just as she was closing the piano.

"Very nice, Lily. We're all deeply moved by Annabel's fate. Could you and Rube set the table now?"

Once the children had left the room, Elaine pulled a letter from the folds of her housedress.

"Here, this came today. From my grandmum, Gwyn. She's rather beside herself. William and Kura want to take her Gloria away."

"Now? They've only ever cared about Kura's career and suddenly they want to be a family?"

"Not exactly," Elaine said. "They want to send her to boarding school in England, supposedly because my grandmother is letting Gloria's 'artistic-creative' side wither."

Tim laughed. "They're not entirely wrong there. Nothing against Kiward Station, but it's not exactly a bastion of art and culture."

"I didn't get the feeling Gloria was missing out on much. The girl seemed totally happy to me. A little shy, though. In that respect I can understand my grandmother. She's worried about sending the girl alone on such a journey."

"And?" Tim asked. "What does that have to do with us?"

Elaine handed him Gwyneira's letter. "She's asking if we wouldn't like to send Lilian with her. It *is* a renowned boarding school. And it would make it easier for Gloria."

Tim studied the letter carefully. "Cambridge is always a good address to have," he said. "But isn't she a little young? Besides, boarding school costs a fortune."

"The McKenzies would bear the costs," Elaine said. "If only it weren't so far away."

Lilian entered the room wearing an apron that was much too big for her. Though Lily's freckled face was impish, her eyes were dreamy. She wore her fine red hair in two long braids, and in her giant apron, she looked like a sprite playing at being a maid.

"The table's ready, Mummy. And I think the casserole is too."

"We'll talk more later," Tim said, letting Elaine help him out of his chair. "First we need to feed the hordes."

After setting her youngest down in his high chair, Elaine went into the kitchen to get the food. Just as she was about to call everyone in, Lilian appeared in the doorway. The girl's whole face was radiant, and she was waving Gwyneira's letter, which Tim had carelessly left on a table in the living room.

"Is it true?" she asked breathlessly. "Grandmum Gwyn is sending me to England? Where the princesses live? And to a boari . . . boarni . . . to the kind of school when you can annoy the teachers and throw midnight parties and things like that?"

Tim Lambert had described his boarding school days to his children as a series of escapades and adventures. Lily could hardly wait to follow her father's example.

"I may, mayn't I? Mummy? Daddy? When do we leave?"

"You don't want me here anymore?" Gloria's wounded look flitted from one adult to the other, and tears glimmered in her large, porcelain-blue eyes.

Gwyneira could not bear it. She could have cried herself as she embraced the child.

"Gloria, how can you say that?" James said, yearning for a whiskey. Gwyneira had decided to inform Gloria of her parents' decision after dinner.

"Everybody goes to school," Jack said, trying to placate the girl. "I was in Christchurch for a few years myself."

"But you came back every weekend!" Gloria sobbed. "Please, please, don't send me away! I don't want to go to England. Jack—"

The girl looked imploringly at her longtime protector. Jack sat uncomfortably in his chair. It wasn't his fault. On the contrary—Jack had spoken out unequivocally against sending Gloria away.

"Don't do anything right away," he had advised his mother. "A letter can go lost. And if they write again, tell them in no uncertain times that Glory is still too young for the long journey. If Kura insists, she should come and get her."

"But she wouldn't be able to, just like that," Gwyneira had objected. "She has concert obligations."

"Exactly," Jack had said. "Glory will have gained at least two years. She will be almost fifteen by then."

Gwyneira had seriously considered Jack's suggestion, but she wasn't as confident as he about what to do. Although Gloria was the heiress, Kiward Station nevertheless still belonged to Kura Martyn. If Gwyneira opposed her wishes, all it took was a signature on a deed of sale and Gloria along with the entire McKenzie family would have to leave the farm.

"Kura doesn't think that far ahead!" Jack had said, but James McKenzie could understand his wife's fears. Kura may not give a thought to the farm and who owned it, but William Martyn was more than capable of forcing their hand.

"You'll be back soon," she explained to Gloria. "The passage is very quick; you can be back here in just a few weeks."

"During vacations?" Gloria asked hopefully.

Gwyneira shook her head. She could not bring herself to lie to the girl. "No, the vacations are too short for the round-trip journey."

Gloria sniveled. "Can I at least take Nimue with me? Or Princess?"

Although it broke Gwyneira's heart, she shook her head again.

"No, love. They don't permit dogs there. As for horses, I don't know, but many schools in the countryside do. Isn't that right, James?" She looked at her husband imploringly as if the old shepherd were an expert on English boarding schools.

James shrugged and turned. "Miss Bleachum?"

Sarah Bleachum had, until then, kept quiet. She was a rather inconspicuous young woman who kept her hair up in a matronly bun and who seemed to keep her handsome light-green eyes always lowered.

"I think so, Mr. McKenzie," she said. Sarah Bleachum's family had emigrated when she was still a baby, so she could not speak from experience. "But it varies. And Oaks Garden is more artistically oriented. My cousin wrote me that they don't participate in sports much." Miss Bleachum turned beet red as she uttered the last sentence.

"Your cousin?" James teased her. "Are we missing something?"

Since she could hardly turn any redder, Miss Bleachum's skin grew mottled.

"I, well, my cousin Christopher has just begun his first rectorate in Cambridge. Oaks Garden belongs to his parish."

"Is he nice?" Gloria asked.

"He is very nice," Miss Bleachum assured her. James and Jack observed with fascination how she turned red once again.

"Regardless, you won't be alone," Gwyneira said, now playing her trump card. Elaine had confirmed to her that Lilian would be traveling to England as well. "Your cousin Lily will also be going. You like her, don't you, Glory? You'll have loads of fun together."

Gloria looked somewhat comforted.

"What exactly do you have in mind for the journey?" Jack asked. He knew he should not criticize in front of Gloria, but the entire plan felt wrong to him, and he could not hold himself back. "Are the two young girls supposed to board the ship alone? With a sign hung round their necks: To be delivered to Oaks Garden, Cambridge?"

Gwyneira glowered at her son, caught unawares. "Of course not. Kura and William will most certainly pick her up."

"Oh, really?" Jack asked. "According to their tour itinerary, they'll be in St. Petersburg in March."

"They're . . . ?" Gwyneira broke off. None of this should have been discussed in front of Gloria. "We'll have to find someone to accompany the girls."

Miss Bleachum seemed to be wrestling with herself. "If I, well, I would not want to impose, but I could." Once again the blood shot to her face.

"My, how times have changed," James noted. "Fifty years ago, people married in the other direction."

Miss Bleachum seemed close to fainting. "How, what . . . ?"

James smiled encouragingly. "Miss Bleachum, I'm old, not blind. If you'd like to be discreet, you're going to have to stop blushing every time a certain reverend is mentioned."

Miss Bleachum reddened again.

"Please don't think I . . ."

Gwyneira looked up, irritated. "Am I understanding this correctly? You would be willing to accompany the girls to England, Miss Bleachum? You understand that you'll spend at least three months traveling?"

Miss Bleachum did not know where to look, but Jack eventually took pity on her.

"Mother, Miss Bleachum is trying to tell us, as properly as possible, that she's contemplating taking on the vacant position of pastor's wife in Cambridge," he said, grinning. "So long as that affinity is affirmed, which, after several years of exchanging letters with her cousin Christopher, she believes both parties feel. Have I expressed the situation correctly, Miss Bleachum?"

The young woman nodded, relieved.

"You want to get married, Miss Bleachum?" Gloria asked.

"So you're in love?" Lilian asked.

Elaine arrived on Kiward Station with her daughter a week before the girls' departure for England.

After two days with the lively Lilian, Gloria had thawed, and the girls became the best of friends. During the day they roamed the farm; at night they curled up in Gloria's bed and exchanged secrets—which Lilian blabbed immediately the next day.

Miss Bleachum did not know how to keep from blushing when the girl mentioned her love life.

Lilian, on the other hand, found nothing embarrassing in it. "How exciting to cross the ocean because you love a man you've never seen," she prattled. "Just like in 'John Riley.' Do you know that one, Miss Bleachum? John Riley is at sea for seven years, and his true love waits for him. She loves him so much she says she'd die if something happened to him, but then she doesn't even recognize him when he returns. Do you have a photograph of your true love, er, of your cousin, Miss Bleachum?"

"Ever the bar pianist's daughter," James said, teasing his shocked granddaughter, Elaine, who blushed in turn. "She learns these songs from you."

Before marrying Tim, Elaine had played the piano for a few years at the Lucky Horse Inn. Lilian had a weakness for the stories behind the ballads and folk songs that Elaine had once entertained the coal miners with.

"Lily, we don't ask such questions." Elaine said. "Those are Miss Bleachum's private affairs. Please excuse her, Miss Bleachum."

"Lilian is right, of course. It's not a secret. My cousin Christopher and I have been writing to each other since we were children. Over the last few years, we've, well, become closer. And yes, I do have a picture of him, Lilian. I'll show it to you on the ship."

Gwyneira wished for nothing more than a happy rendezvous for Sarah and Christopher Bleachum. If it all turned out as they hoped, Gloria would have a trusted adult nearby.

When the girls finally climbed into the coach in which Jack would drive them to the ship, Gwyneira forced herself to smile. Elaine would accompany the group and then board the train in Christchurch to return to Greymouth.

"We're riding over the Bridle Path," Lilian said excitedly. Legions of New Zealanders had stumbled along the path, weary from the endless ocean passage and too poor to afford the mule transportation service. Gwyneira had told her about the magnificent sight that greeted them at the end of the climb: the Canterbury Plains in the sunlight, with the breathtaking panorama of mountains rising behind them. In that moment she had fallen in love with the land that was to be her country. But the girls' path now led them in the opposite direction.

3

Accompanying Gloria and Lilian to Christchurch was the hardest thing Jack had ever done. The group made good time with his powerful cob mares, but he would have given a great deal to slow the passage of time as they approached the ship.

He still thought it an awful mistake to deliver Gloria to her parents and their whims. He knew people did it all the time, but Gloria was different. Everything in him bristled against putting the girl in Kura's custody. He still recalled the many nights when he had taken a wailing Gloria out of her crib while her mother slept soundly in the next room. And Gloria's father had only cared about what to name her. "Gloria" was meant to symbolize his "triumph over this new land," whatever that was supposed to mean.

The travelers spent the night at a hotel in Christchurch then took the Bridle Path early the next morning. The ship was to weigh anchor at dawn, and Gloria and Lilian were still half-asleep as Jack directed his team through the mountains. Elaine held her daughter tightly. Gloria clambered onto the driving box and curled up next to Jack.

"If it's really bad, you'll come get me, right?" she whispered sleepily.

"It won't be so bad, Glory. Just think of Princess. She came from England. There are sheep and ponies there just like here."

Jack caught a look from Miss Bleachum, who was visibly biting her lip. She had made inquiries, and there were neither sheep nor horses at Oaks Garden. But she held her tongue. Sarah Bleachum, too, loved Gloria.

Shortly thereafter, Jack and Elaine were left waving on the pier as the gigantic steamship pulled out into the bay.

"I hope we're doing the right thing," Elaine sighed. "Tim and I are far from certain, but Lily wouldn't hear otherwise."

Jack did not answer. It was all he could do to hold back his tears. Fortunately, however, they had to leave to get Elaine to the train on time.

After dropping off Elaine, Jack directed his team toward the Avon River. George Greenwood and his wife had a house near the river. Although he would have preferred to brood silently on the drive back to Kiward Station, he was hoping to catch up on the latest news on the wool trade, and Elizabeth had invited him to spend the night.

Elizabeth Greenwood, a slightly corpulent matron with crisp features and friendly blue eyes, noticed his unhappy demeanor when she opened the door.

"My God, boy, you look like you sent little Gloria to the scaffold. We'll cheer you up a bit," she said and embraced Jack. Elizabeth Greenwood and Gwyneira McKenzie had traveled on the same ship from England to New Zealand, and Jack was like family to her. "She'll be happy in England. Our Charlotte didn't even want to come back." Elizabeth smiled and opened the door to their little parlor for Jack.

"That's not true, Mum."

She looked up and glared reproachfully at Elizabeth.

"I was always homesick for Canterbury, sometimes even dreaming of the view from above the plains toward the mountains. There's no place where the sky is as clear as here." Her voice was soft and musical.

Jack had heard that Charlotte, George and Elizabeth's youngest daughter, was back in Christchurch. As the girl stood up to greet Jack, he momentarily forgot the sharp pain of separation from Gloria.

Charlotte Greenwood was the prettiest girl Jack had ever seen. Her skin glowed, translucent and milk white like fine porcelain. Her hair was blonde like her mother's, and her ponytail fell in luxuriant locks over her shoulder. Her most riveting feature, however, was her large, chocolate brown eyes. The girl looked like a fairy—or like the magical being in that song, "Annabel Lee," that little Lilian was always singing.

"Allow me to introduce my daughter Charlotte. Charlotte, Jack McKenzie," Elizabeth Greenwood said, breaking through Jack's breathless silence.

When Charlotte reached out her hand to him, Jack responded unconsciously with a gesture he had practiced in his etiquette lessons but never performed for a woman from the Canterbury Plains: he kissed the girl's hand.

Charlotte smiled. "I remember you, Mr. McKenzie," she said amiably, "from that concert that your—cousin?—gave before she left for England. I traveled on the same ship, you know."

Jack nodded. He only had hazy memories of Kura-maro-tini's farewell concert in Christchurch.

"You were looking after that little girl, and I was a little jealous."

Jack looked at Charlotte incredulously. He had been almost eighteen at the time, and she . . .

"I would have preferred to be playing with that wood horse and building a toy village with the Maori children to sitting still and listening to the music," the girl admitted.

Jack smiled. "So you don't count yourself among the admirers of my . . . strictly speaking, she's my half niece."

Charlotte closed her eyes, revealing her long, honey-colored lashes. Jack was smitten.

"Then again, maybe I wasn't old enough," she said. She opened her eyes and abruptly transitioned from polite chitchat to her thoughts on artistic representation. "Mrs. Martyn's interpretation of her people's heritage is not exactly what comes to mind when I think of the preservation of cultural treasures. 'Ghost Whispers' only makes use of that element of the culture that seemed to be of use to the singer to—well, to increase her fame. While Maori music, as I understand it, generally has a more communicative dimension."

Although Jack understood little of what Charlotte had said, he could have listened to her for hours. Elizabeth Greenwood turned her eyes toward heaven.

"Enough, Charlotte, once again you're giving speeches while your listeners politely starve to death. Charlotte stayed in England to attend college, Jack. She studied something to do with history and literature."

"Colonial history and comparative literature, Mum," Charlotte gently corrected her. "I apologize if I've bored you, Mr. McKenzie."

"Just call me Jack," he managed. He just wanted to go on worshipping the girl silently. But then his mischievous spirit shone through again. "After all, we're among the few people in the entire world who don't revere Kura-maro-tini Martyn. It's a very exclusive club, Miss Greenwood."

"Charlotte," she said, smiling. "But I did not mean to diminish the accomplishments of your half niece. I had the pleasure of hearing her again in England, and she is certainly a gifted artist. As far as I can tell, that is. I'm not very musical. What bothers me is how myths are being taken out of context and the history of a people reduced to, well, banal love poetry."

"Charlotte, offer our guest a drink before we eat. George should be arriving soon, Jack. And perhaps our Charlotte will attempt somewhat more comprehensible conversation. If you keep ranting like that, my dear, you'll never find a husband."

Charlotte led her guest into the neighboring salon, and offered him some whiskey. He declined.

"Not before sundown," he remarked.

Charlotte smiled. "You do look like you could use something strong. Maybe some tea?"

When George Greenwood arrived a half hour later, he found his daughter and Jack McKenzie deep in animated conversation. At least that's how it looked at first glance. In reality, Jack was simply stirring his cup of tea and listening to Charlotte, who was telling him about her childhood in an English boarding school. If English boarding schools produced such angelic beings as Charlotte, nothing bad could happen to Gloria.

"And your 'artistic-creative' development?" Jack asked.

Charlotte furrowed her brow charmingly.

"We painted a little," she said. "And whoever wanted to could play piano or violin."

"I don't think the girls at Oaks Garden are denied a musical education," George Greenwood interjected. "I have no doubt that the Martyns will put a very different emphasis on their daughter's education than we did."

Jack looked at George Greenwood, confused. He made it sound as if English schoolgirls were forcibly dragged to the piano.

"These boarding schools aren't all alike, Jack," George continued. "Some are little more than finishing schools with a touch of literature and art. Others offer girls Latin and physics and chemistry, and the students don't automatically get married right after graduating. Some go on to college or university. Like our Charlotte, you see."

He winked at his daughter.

"It's true. I went off to college, and now I'm not even engaged. But you'd be happy if I were to get married, admit it. And Mum most of all."

George Greenwood sighed. "Naturally your mother and I would welcome it if you were to find a suitable husband, Charlotte, instead of parading around in blue stockings. Studies in Maori culture! What use is that?"

Jack's ears pricked up.

"You're interested in Maori culture, Charlotte?" Jack asked rather keenly. "Do you speak the language?"

George rolled his eyes. "Heavens no."

Just then, Elizabeth called them to dinner.

Elizabeth Greenwood dominated the conversation at dinner, mostly chatting about society in Christchurch and the Canterbury Plains. Jack only half listened, as he was making his own plans. Toward the end of dinner, the conversation returned to Charlotte's projects. The girl intended to ask a Maori named Reti, George's business manager for the wool trade, for lessons in Maori. George was energetically opposed.

"Reti has other things to do," he explained. "Besides, the language is complicated. It would take you years before you had enough of a command of it to understand their stories and get them down on paper."

"Oh, it's not all that complicated," Jack objected. "I speak fluent Maori."

"But you were partly raised in their village, Jack," George said.

"And the Maori on Kiward Station speak English just as fluently," Jack continued. "If you came to stay with us for a while, Charlotte, we could arrange something. My half stepmother, so to speak, Marama, is a *tohunga.* A singer, really. But she supposedly knows all the most important stories. And Rongo Rongo, the tribe's midwife and witch doctor, speaks English as well."

Charlotte's face brightened.

"You see, Daddy? Everything will work out."

"Gwyneira McKenzie has probably had enough of spoiled girls interested in culture beneath her roof for one lifetime."

"Not at all, not at all. My mother is . . ." He trailed off.

To depict Gwyneira as a patron of the fine arts would be an exaggeration. But Kiward Station, like all the farms in the plains, was a welcoming household. And Jack could not imagine his mother being anything but taken with this girl.

Elizabeth, however, broke in.

"But George, what are you thinking? Of course Gwyneira would support Charlotte's research. She's always been interested in Maori culture."

That was the first Jack had ever heard of it. Gwyneira got along well with the Maori. Many of their customs aligned with her practical nature, and she did not tend toward prejudice. But Jack's mother was more interested in animal husbandry and dog training than anything else.

Elizabeth smiled at Jack.

"Didn't Jenny work for a year on their farm?" Charlotte asked, turning to her mother.

Jack nodded fervently. He had forgotten that the older Greenwood daughter, Jennifer, had spent a year on Kiward Station teaching the children in the Maori village.

"Yes, of course," Elizabeth said. "Your sister got to know her husband there."

Elizabeth gave her own husband a meaningful look. When he still did not understand, she moved her eyes back and forth between Jack and Charlotte.

George finally seemed to understand.

"Naturally nothing at all stands in the way of Charlotte paying a visit to Kiward Station," he said. "I'll take you along the next time I have business in the plains."

Charlotte beamed at Jack. "I can't wait!"

"I'll be counting the days."

4

After the first few exciting days at sea, Lilian Lambert had grown bored. Though it was nice when dolphins accompanied the ship or the occasional giant barracuda or whale was spotted, Lilian was more interested in people, and the *Norfolk* had little to offer in that regard. There were only twenty passengers, primarily older people visiting their homeland and a few businessmen. The latter were not interested in children, and though the former found Lilian sweet, they had nothing to talk about.

Gloria, however, enjoyed the journey—as much as she could enjoy anything that was not Kiward Station. She often sat for hours on deck watching the dolphins at play. Miss Bleachum and Lilian were enough company for her. She listened enthusiastically when her teacher read to her about whales and ocean fish, and she attempted to figure out how the steamship's engine functioned. Her insatiable interest in the sea and the ship brought her into contact with the crew as well. The sailors attempted to bring her out of her shell by showing her sailors' knots and eventually let her help with minor tasks on deck. One day, the captain brought her onto the bridge, where she was allowed to hold the steering wheel of the giant ship for a few seconds. Navigation interested her as much as sea life.

Sarah Bleachum observed it all with growing concern. Her cousin—who had expressed his delight that Sarah was accompanying the girls to Canterbury—had arranged for her to receive a prospectus for Oaks Garden. The syllabus confirmed her worst fears. The natural sciences were hardly covered at all.

When the ship arrived in London, Gloria was at a loss for words for the first time in her life. She had never seen such large buildings, at least not so many at once. Although the cathedral in Christchurch could hold its own against its European counterparts, here there were just so many. Between the architecture and the incessant noise and the fast pace, the English capital oppressed her.

While Lilian blossomed—she was soon speaking just as quickly as the English and laughing with the girls selling flowers—Gloria only looked around her with big eyes, careful not to lose sight of Miss Bleachum.

Gloria could not even comprehend the musical performance for which Kura and William had reserved tickets—the only proof of their existence that they had left for their daughter before departing for Russia. She found the singers affected and the music too loud, and she did not feel comfortable in the clothes she had to wear in London.

Sarah Bleachum was not surprised. While Lilian looked lovely in her sailor's outfit, it looked like a costume on Gloria. The girl even burst into tears over her school uniform. She looked stocky in the knee-length skirt and long jacket, and the white blouse made her complexion look doughy. What was more, they would not hold up to the demands of Gloria's daily life. Gloria wanted to touch everything, and was accustomed to wiping her hands on her clothes, which wasn't a problem when she was in breeches on Kiward Station, but white blouses and light-blue blazers were not made for such treatment.

Sarah breathed a sigh of relief when they finally boarded the train to Cambridge. Country life would be more appealing to Gloria. According to Christopher, Sawston—the nearest town to Oaks Garden—was a rather idyllic little town. Sarah looked forward to meeting her cousin with a wildly beating heart. She had rented a room in the house of a widow who was said to be a pillar of the community, but she hoped to take a position at Oaks Garden. She had told the McKenzies nothing about applying for the job, to keep Gloria from getting her hopes up. But she wanted to get to know Christopher with the security of a solid position rather than as a more or less destitute relative. A school year would be an ideal way to reach a final decision about her possible future husband. And in the worst case, she could save the money she earned to return to New Zealand without admitting her failure to the McKenzies. It would be too embarrassing for her to accept Gwyneira's magnanimous offer of a return ticket if things didn't work out.

Sarah watched with bated breath as London gave way to suburbs and finally to the lovely landscape of the midlands. Gloria appeared happier when they spotted the first horses in the green pastures, and Lilian could hardly contain her excitement over Miss Bleachum's love life.

"It must be so thrilling to finally see your sweetheart. Do you know the song 'The Trees They Grow So High'? A girl marries the son of a lord, but he's much younger than she, and . . . How old is the reverend anyway?"

Sarah sighed and looked anxiously over at Gloria, who had grown silent as they approached Cambridge. Although the landscape looked quite like the Canterbury Plains, everything was on a smaller scale and more densely populated, with farms and cottages dotting the fields. Gloria chewed on her fingernails, a bad habit she had developed on the sea crossing, but Sarah did not want to admonish her. The girl was unhappy enough as it was.

"Will I be able to write letters at least, Miss Bleachum?" Gloria asked when the conductor announced that Cambridge was the next stop.

"Of course, Gloria. You know Christopher and I have been writing each other for years. It just takes a few weeks for them to arrive."

Gloria nodded and gnawed on a hangnail.

"It's so far," she said quietly. Her finger was bleeding. Sarah gave her a handkerchief.

Reverend Christopher Bleachum was waiting at the train station. He had borrowed a small chaise since he did not own a carriage of his own. He usually made his visits on horse, but if he were to get married, he supposed he would have to acquire a vehicle for himself. Christopher sighed. The changes would be enormous if he took a wife. He had never seriously considered the possibility before getting Sarah Bleachum's letter announcing her arrival. But there had been that incident with Mrs. Walker a few months before, and the girl before that during his theological seminar.

Not that Christopher could help that women chased after him. With his curly dark hair, his tan complexion, and his soulful, almost black eyes, he was simply too handsome for them to stay away. His dark, soft voice made him an exceptional singer, and he listened well. He seemed to look into people's very souls—as the parishioners were so fond of whispering to each other. Christopher had compassion for almost everyone. But he was also a man, and when a young woman needed more support than words could offer, the reverend could not exactly hold himself back.

He tried to be discreet, as did most of the women. But there had been talk about Mrs. Walker, a rather labile young wife whose husband was more inclined to visit the pub than her bed. The bishop himself learned of it after Christopher had been forced into a fight with the man one Sunday after service. Although the other fellow had started it, Christopher could not simply sit passively by. The witnesses were all on his side, but the bishop had left no doubt as to his opinion on the matter.

"You ought to marry, Reverend Bleachum. In fact, you are meant to marry. It will be pleasing to God and keep you from further temptation. Yes, yes, I know you are unaware of any wrongdoing. But it will also keep women from viewing you as fair game. Eve will give up tempting you."

From Christopher's perspective, that only meant having the serpent at his throat. The young ladies in his parish seemed to him more a damnation than a temptation. And the bishop would hardly give him a few months off to go to London to look for someone more suitable. His cousin Sarah's last letter arrived just in time. Christopher had been exchanging letters with Sarah since they were children, and he had always found her naïve reaction to his mild flirting and innuendos amusing. In the photograph she had sent him, she looked a little homespun, but attractive enough, and she was more than suited to the post of pastor's wife. When she had announced the news of a free crossing, Christopher decided to accept Sarah Bleachum as a godsend. He could only hope that God had demonstrated a happier hand in her creation than in that of the other unmarried girls in the area.

As Christopher sauntered across the platform, he once again drew looks from the women all around.

"Good day, Reverend."

"How do you do, Reverend?"

"That was a wonderful sermon on Sunday, Reverend. We'll have to go over the parable again more closely in our women's group."

Most of these ladies were far too old to lead Christopher into temptation. But the petite Mrs. Deamer now smiling at him and raving about his sermon could well have been to his liking. If only she were not already taken. Christopher had baptized her first child at Christmas.

As the train pulled into the station, Christopher could hardly keep still.

"You should put your glasses on, Miss Bleachum," Gloria advised solicitously.

"No! He might not find you pretty," squealed Lilian. "Miss Bleachum, I think I see the reverend. Oh my, he is good-looking!"

Sarah Bleachum, completely beside herself at the prospect of meeting her cousin, gathered their trunks and felt her way to the exit. She tripped over her hatbox and stumbled down the steep steps to the platform. As Gloria tried to help her, Lilian skipped onto the platform and began to wave.

"Reverend? Are you looking for us, Reverend?"

Christopher Bleachum looked around. There they were. The lively-looking redhead was quite pretty and would undoubtedly develop into an attractive young woman. The other girl seemed to be in an awkward stage, and she was hanging on her governess's skirt. Sarah Bleachum seemed not to have any radiance or personality at all. She was evidently one of those poor faceless goats who take other people's children for walks in the park because they were not blessed with any offspring of their own. Sarah was wearing a charcoal gray dress with an even darker shawl under which any physical form disappeared. She hid her austerely pulled-back dark hair under a hat like a nun, and her expression alternated between confusion and helplessness. At least her face was symmetrical. Christopher sighed with relief. Though Sarah Bleachum was featureless, she was not downright ugly.

"Put your glasses on," Gloria pressed her. It was true that her teacher was prettier without them, but stumbling aimlessly behind Lilian was not going to make a good impression.

Christopher decided to take the initiative. He approached the small group.

"Sarah? Sarah Bleachum?"

The young woman smiled vaguely in his direction.

She had pretty eyes. Sort of veiled, dreamy, a light green. Maybe his first impression had been wrong.

But then Sarah fished her glasses out of her pocket, and her most attractive feature disappeared behind the monstrous frames.

"Christopher." She beamed, raising her hands. Then she did not know what to do. Christopher smiled at her, but also seemed to be assessing her. Sarah lowered her eyes.

"Sarah, it's wonderful that you're all here. Did you have a difficult journey? And which one of these lovely ladies is Gloria?"

The reverend was gently patting Lilian on the head as he spoke. Gloria leaned against Miss Bleachum. She had already decided she did not like the reverend. He could act as friendly as he wanted, but she had seen the expression that had passed over his face when Miss Bleachum had put on her glasses—and now there was this exaggerated good cheer. Why did he call her lovely? Gloria was not lovely, and she knew it.

"This is Gloria Martyn," Sarah said, if only because it gave her an excuse to make conversation. "And the redhead is Lilian Lambert."

"And you're both bound for Oaks Garden? Then I have good news for you, girls. I was able to borrow a chaise for today. If you like, I can take you there straightaway."

"The school is sending a carriage," Sarah said. Everything was moving a little too quickly for her. If Christopher drove the girls to Oaks Garden, she would be alone with him on the return drive. Was that even proper?

"Oh, I took care of that. Miss Arrowstone knows I'm bringing the girls." Christopher smiled encouragingly, but Gloria looked close to tears.

"But Miss Bleachum, the students aren't expected until tomorrow. What are we supposed to do all alone there?"

Sarah drew her close. "You won't be all alone, love. A few girls always come early. And a few even stay during the holidays."

Sarah bit her lip. She should not have said that. After all, that was precisely what awaited Gloria and Lilian.

"Miss Arrowstone is looking forward to meeting you," the reverend explained. "Especially you, Gloria."

It was meant to be kind, but Gloria didn't believe it. Why should a headmistress in England be happy to meet Gloria Martyn of Kiward Station?

Distraught, the girl kept her silence as Christopher stowed the luggage in his carriage and ushered the three of them on board. As he gallantly helped Sarah into the chaise, she felt the gaze of several of Sawston's female inhabitants upon her. That evening she would be the talk of the town.

Lilian prattled contentedly about everything she observed the entire way.

"Does Oaks Garden look like that?" she inquired of one building.

The pastor shook his head. "Oaks Garden is a great deal bigger than that. It used to be a lord's manor, almost like a castle. It once belonged to a noble family, but the last owner died without descendants, and she specified that her house and fortune should serve to found a school. Lady Ermingarde loved the fine arts. That's the reason Oaks Garden specializes in the creative arts."

"Are there horses?" Gloria asked.

"Not for the students. I assume the caretaker keeps a team, but riding isn't included in the curriculum."

Gloria resumed her silence until the carriage rolled through an opulent stone gateway into a park enclosed by a wrought-iron fence. The grounds were beautifully designed, with rows of magnificent oaks bordering a wide approach that led to the main building.

Gloria felt overwhelmed. She kept an eye out for stables. There had to be some. Maybe in the back?

The reverend pulled to a stop in front of the imposing double doors, and everyone got out of the carriage. As they stepped into a large entrance hall, several girls were rushing about with their suitcases, giggling and making plans to room together. A few older girls glanced over at the new arrivals. Although Lilian smiled at them, Gloria gave the impression of wanting to crawl under Sarah's skirts.

The young governess gently pushed her away.

"Now, don't be so shy, Gloria. What will the other girls think of you?"

Gloria did not seem to care. But she took the opportunity to look around. A few parents were giving their daughters instructions on how to behave.

"You must work harder on your violin, Gabrielle, dear—" Gloria heard. The girl looked her age. Would they really expect her to play the violin?

The reverend smiled as he walked over to the reception desk.

"Good day, Miss Barnum. I've brought you the Kiwis. Isn't that what you call yourselves in New Zealand? The settlers nicknamed themselves after the bird, isn't that right, Sarah?"

Sarah Bleachum nodded, mortified. She would never have referred to herself as a Kiwi.

"They're almost blind," Gloria remarked, "and can't fly very well. But they can smell. You don't see them very often, but you hear them call—sometimes all night, except when there's a full moon. They're rather, hmm, fluffy."

A few of the girls giggled.

"Two blind birds," laughed the girl whose parents had just called her Gabrielle. "How did you ever find your way here?"

Gloria blushed. Lilian glared.

"We simply flew where we heard the worst violin playing," said Lilian.

Gabrielle looked annoyed when the other girls giggled.

"Welcome to Oaks Garden," Miss Barnum said to the girls. "I look forward to getting to know you. You in particular, Lilian, since you will be living in the west wing where I'm the housemother. You'll be staying in the Mozart Room. Suzanne Carruthers, one of your roommates, has just arrived. I'll introduce you in a moment."

Gloria's eyes widened. Lilian said aloud what she was thinking.

"Couldn't we room together, Miss Barnum? We are cousins, after all." Lilian assumed her most beguiling expression.

But Miss Barnum shook her head. "Gloria is much older than you. No doubt she would prefer to live with girls her own age. You'll like it better, too, once you've gotten to know the other girls."

"Could you not make an exception in this case?" inquired Miss Bleachum. She could almost feel Gloria closing herself off again. "The girls have never been away from home before."

"It's no different for any of the other students," Miss Barnum explained firmly. "I'm sorry, girls, but you'll adjust. Now it's time to meet Miss Arrowstone. She's expecting you in her office, Reverend. You know where that is, of course."

The headmistress's office was located on the second floor of the main building. Christopher knocked on her office door.

"Come in," announced a deep voice from within.

Sarah could not help stiffening, and Gloria tried to make herself invisible behind her. Only Lilian seemed unimpressed as she faced the corpulent headmistress, who sat enthroned behind an imposing oak desk.

"The queen," the pastor whispered to Sarah with a half smile. The girls were indeed reminded of Queen Victoria, who had died only a few years before. Miss Arrowstone's face was austere, her eyes a watery blue, her lips thin. She was smiling.

"Have I heard correctly? The students from New Zealand? With . . ." She looked questioningly back and forth from Sarah to the reverend.

Sarah was about to introduce herself when Christopher explained: "Miss Sarah Bleachum, Miss Arrowstone. My cousin. And my, well . . ." He blinked, embarrassed, at which Miss Arrowstone's smile became even more radiant.

It was hard for Sarah to maintain a friendly countenance. Christopher seemed to view their impending marriage as a fait accompli. What was worse, he had apparently announced the engagement to his entire social circle.

"I'm a teacher, Miss Arrowstone," she said. "Gloria Martyn has been my student, and as I have relatives in Europe"—she cast a brief glance at Christopher—"I've used the opportunity of accompanying the girls to England to renew family bonds."

Miss Arrowstone produced something like a giggle.

"Family bonds, aha," she said insinuatingly. "Well, we're all happy for the reverend, and the parish is in great need of a female hand." More giggling. "Surely you'll lend him a hand in the parish while you're here?"

Sarah wanted to object that she was thinking more of a new position as a teacher, but Miss Arrowstone had already turned her attention to the girls. An expression of bewilderment crossed her face.

Gloria turned away from her gaze.

"So you're Gloria Martyn," she remarked. "You certainly don't take after your mother."

Gloria nodded. This was hardly news to her.

"At least not at first sight," Miss Arrowstone said. "But your parents have suggested that you have some as of yet undiscovered musical talents."

Gloria looked confused. Maybe she should just tell the truth.

"I, I can't play the piano," she said.

Miss Arrowstone laughed. "Yes, so I've heard, child. It causes your mother much heartache. But you're not even thirteen. It's not too late to learn an instrument. Would you like to play the piano? Or would you prefer the violin? The cello?"

Gloria blushed. She didn't even know what a cello was. And she certainly did not want to play it.

Lilian helped her out.

"I play the piano!" she declared confidently.

Miss Arrowstone looked over at her severely. "We expect our pupils only to speak when spoken to," she said. "However, I'm quite pleased you feel yourself drawn to this instrument. You're Lilian Lambert, correct? A niece of Mrs. Martyn's?"

Kura-maro-tini had clearly made an impression.

"Mrs. Martyn visited our institution personally to register her daughter," she explained to Sarah and Christopher, "providing us with the pleasure of a little private concert when she did. The girls were all deeply impressed and look forward to meeting you, Gloria."

Gloria bit her lip.

"And you too, of course, Lilian. I'm sure our music teacher, Miss Taylor-Bennington, will appreciate your piano playing. Would you like some tea, Miss Bleachum? Reverend? The girls can make their way downstairs now. Miss Barnum will show them to their rooms."

"Oh right, I'll be living in the west wing," Lilian said. She had already forgotten that she was not to speak before being spoken to. "I'll be 'Lily of the West'!"

"Lilian!" Sarah admonished her, horrified, while the pastor burst out laughing. Miss Arrowstone frowned. Fortunately she did not seem to know the story of "Lily of the West," in which an unfaithful barmaid leads her sweetheart into ruin.

Gloria gave her teacher a desperate look.

"Go on, Glory," Sarah told her gently. "Miss Barnum will introduce you to your housemother. No doubt you'll feel right at home."

"Say good-bye to your teacher now," Miss Arrowstone added. "You'll see her again at Sunday service."

Gloria tried to maintain her composure, but her eyes overflowed with tears as she curtsied before Miss Bleachum. Sarah could not help herself. She pulled the girl to her and kissed her good-bye.

Miss Arrowstone observed this with pronounced disapproval.

"The girl is too attached to you," she noted once the girls had left the room. "It will do her good to spend some time away from you and develop friendships with others. And besides"—again this conspiratorial smile—"you will have your own children soon enough."

Sarah blushed deeply.

"In truth, I did not intend to give up my profession right away. On the contrary, I would love to remain active as a teacher for a few years yet and wanted, in this regard, to ask . . ."

"What do you have in mind, my dear?" Miss Arrowstone asked, sugar sweet, pouring Sarah some tea. "The reverend needs you at his side. I don't know how things are done on the other side of the globe, but in our schools, teachers are generally unmarried."

Sarah felt the trap spring under her feet. Miss Arrowstone would not hire her. Her only remaining option was to obtain a position as a tutor in the area. But from what she'd seen thus far, no one seemed particularly well-off. And the town matrons would probably not want to stand in the way of "the reverend's happiness." She would have to have a serious word with Christopher. Though it spoke well of him that he was so determined to marry Sarah, he had to give Sarah at least a few weeks to make up her mind. She cast a shy sidelong glance at the man next to her. Would a few weeks really suffice to get to know him?

Miss Coleridge, the east wing's gaunt and strict-looking housemother, was older than Miss Barnum, and appeared to be her exact opposite.

"You're Gloria Martyn? Why, you don't take after your mother at all." Miss Coleridge sounded markedly disapproving. Gloria was coming to expect this response.

Miss Coleridge cast a further, rather unmerciful look at her before looking at her notes.

"Martyn, Martyn, ah yes, here we are. The Titian Room. Gabrielle and Fiona are already there."

Gloria followed her housemother down the halls of the east wing, which were rather gloomy in the afternoon light. Though she tried to convince herself that there must be more than one Gabrielle in the school, she knew that was not likely. And, indeed, the girl who had been at the reception desk looked up when Miss Coleridge opened the door. Gabrielle was hanging up her school uniforms in one of the four narrow wardrobes. Another girl—Gloria recognized a petite blonde who had been with Gabrielle in the entrance hall—appeared to have already finished putting away her things. She was placing a few family pictures on her night table.

"Fiona, Gabrielle—this is your new roommate," Miss Coleridge said. "She's from . . ."

"New Zealand, we already know, Housemother," Gabrielle said, curtsying politely. "We met her when we arrived."

"Well, then you all already have something to talk about," Miss Coleridge said, clearly happy not to have to break the ice between the girls. "Please accompany Gloria to dinner."

With that, she left the room, shutting the door behind her. Gloria stood awkwardly at the entrance. Fiona and Gabrielle had already claimed the beds by the window, so she plopped down on the bed in the furthest corner, wishing she could simply pull a blanket over her head and hide. But the other girls did not intend to leave Gloria alone.

"Here we have our blind little bird," Gabrielle remarked nastily. "Though I've heard she can really sing. Isn't your mother that Maori singer?"

"Really? Her mother is a niiigger." Fiona dragged the last word out. "But she doesn't even look black," she added, looking Gloria over intently.

"Maybe a cuckoo's egg?" Gabrielle giggled.

Gloria gulped. "I . . . we . . . back home there aren't any cuckoos."

She had no idea what she had done to become the object of ridicule without cause. But she understood that she was stuck.

And there was no chance of escape.

5

Charlotte Greenwood arrived at Kiward Station with her parents a month after she had met Jack in Christchurch and following a formal invitation from Gwyneira McKenzie. The official occasion was a small celebration for successfully herding the sheep down from the highlands. Although this was a routine occurrence and not normally cause for celebration, Jack had hounded his mother to come up with a reason to invite the Greenwoods, and this was as good as any other.

Jack was beaming as Charlotte alighted from the coach. She was wearing a simple, dark-brown dress that highlighted her hair, and her huge brown eyes shone.

"Did you have a pleasant trip, Charlotte?" he asked.

Charlotte smiled, and dimples appeared in the corners of her mouth. Jack was once again smitten.

"The roads are much better than I remembered," Charlotte replied in her melodious voice.

Jack nodded. He yearned to say something intelligent, but he could not think clearly in Charlotte's presence. Everything in him wanted to hold this girl, protect her, bind her to him, but if he did not manage to say something intelligent, she would think of him as the village idiot.

Nevertheless, he managed to introduce the girl to his parents, at which point James McKenzie expressed precisely the gallantry that had escaped Jack.

"A boarding-school education in England suddenly strikes me as a very good idea," James remarked, "if it produces women as charming as you, Miss Greenwood. And you're interested in Maori culture, is that right?"

Charlotte nodded. "I'd really like to learn the language," she explained. "And since Jack speaks fluent Maori . . ." She gave Jack a quick look that James couldn't help but notice. He had already noticed the light in his son's eyes. But now he saw that Charlotte appeared to be interested too.

"He'll no doubt spend the next three months teaching you words like *Taumatawhatatangihangakoauauotamateaturipukakapikimaungahoroukupokaiwhenuakitanatahu.*" James winked at her.

Charlotte bit her lip. "They have words that long?"

She furrowed her brow in that manner that had charmed Jack when they first met.

He shook his head and reassured the girl. "That's a mountain on the North Island. And even the Maori think it's a tongue twister. It's best you begin with simpler words. *Kia ora*, for example."

"Which means hello!" Charlotte smiled.

"And *haere mai*?"

"Welcome!" Charlotte translated, apparently having gotten a head start. "Woman is *wahine*."

Jack smiled. "*Haere mai, wahine* Charlotte."

Charlotte wanted to reply, but was trying to think of a word. "And what's the word for man?" she asked.

"*Tane*," James said.

Charlotte turned back to Jack. "*Kia ora, tane* Jack."

James caught Gwyneira's gaze. She, too, had been closely observing the interaction between Jack and Charlotte.

"Looks like they don't need to make a detour by way of Irish stew," Gwyneira said, alluding to the first blush of her love for James.

"But bible verses might be important soon," James quipped. When Gwyneira had first come to New Zealand, the only book that had been translated into Maori was the Bible. Whenever she needed a specific word, she had to think about where she might find it in there. "For where you go, I will go."

While Gwyneira and James chatted with George and Elizabeth Greenwood, Jack gave Charlotte a tour of the farm, which was bustling now that the sheep had been herded down. All the stables were packed with sheep in their prime—well-nourished and healthy, with clean, thick wool that would keep them warm through the winter until shearing time. Talking about the sheep was easier for Jack than making polite conversation, and he gradually recovered his self-assurance. He and Charlotte wandered over to the Maori village, and Jack's easy interactions with the natives gave him a chance to impress Charlotte. She enjoyed the idyllic village on the lake and admired the carvings on the public buildings.

"If you want, we can ride over to O'Keefe Station tomorrow," Jack said. "Only the people who come to work at the farm every day live here. The tribe itself has moved to Howard O'Keefe's old farm. The Maori received that land as reparations for irregularities in the purchase of Kiward Station. Marama lives there. And Rongo, the herbalist. Both of them speak good English and know lots of *moteateas*."

"Those are songs that tell stories, right?" Charlotte asked.

"There are lamentations and lullabies, stories of revenge and of tribal feuds—just what you're looking for."

Charlotte looked up at him with a slight smile. "No love stories?"

"Of course there are love stories!" he said reassuringly. But then he understood. "Would you like to take down a love story?"

"If one presents itself," Charlotte said, embarrassed. "But, I mean, it may be too early to take anything down. I think first I need to, to experience more. I'd like to be better acquainted first."

Jack felt the blood rush to his face. "With the Maori? Or me?"

Charlotte blushed in turn. "Won't one lead to the other?"

Charlotte planned to stay on Kiward Station for three months to research Maori culture. Elizabeth and Gwyneira exchanged conspiratorial looks as the arrangements were made. It was clear to both of them what had sprung up between Jack and Charlotte, and both approved. Even if Gwyneira did not always grasp right away what Charlotte was talking about, she found the girl charming.

She rode around the farm with Jack, let Gwyneira explain the finer points of the wool trade to her, and laughed as she practiced the various shrill whistles the shepherds used to direct the collies. At first the shepherds and Maori treated her with reserve—the young lady just back from England with the latest fashions and perfect manners had an intimidating effect. But Charlotte knew how to break the ice. She attempted the *hongi*, the traditional Maori greeting, learning that here it did not involve the mutual rubbing of noses but rather a light touching of one's nose to the other's forehead. Her elegant riding dress soon looked worn, and she quickly turned in her sidesaddle for one of the more comfortable stock saddles.

Behind Charlotte's well-bred facade lurked a child of nature—and a feminist. With an astounded Gwyneira, she discussed the writings of Emmeline Pankhurst and seemed almost disappointed that women already had the right to vote in New Zealand. In England she had taken to the streets with other students and had obviously enjoyed herself royally. James teased her by offering her a cigar—smoking was considered a means of protest by the suffragettes—and Jack and Gwyneira laughed when she took a few puffs on one. Everyone agreed that Charlotte enriched life on Kiward Station, and even Jack managed to converse normally in her presence. One night, Charlotte lured him outside in the moonlight, insisting on seeing to the horses once more. Cautiously she placed her hand in his.

"Is it true that the Maori don't kiss each other?" she asked quietly.

"I'm not sure," Jack replied.

"You might think the Maori would have learned to kiss from us *pakeha* by now," Charlotte whispered. "Don't you think one could learn?"

Jack swallowed. "Without a doubt," he said. "If you found the right teacher."

"I've never done it before."

Jack smiled. Then he tentatively took her in his arms.

"Should we start by rubbing noses?" he asked teasingly, trying to downplay his own nervousness.

But Charlotte had already opened her lips. There was nothing for her to learn. Jack and Charlotte were made for each other.

Love did not distract Charlotte from her studies. She had fun flirting with Jack in Maori, and found in James McKenzie a patient teacher. After three months on Kiward Station, she could not only pronounce the old tongue twister but had written down her first Maori myths in English and in their original language. Time flew, and her parents soon arrived to fetch her.

"Naturally I would like to stay longer," she explained to her parents. "But I'm afraid it wouldn't be proper."

At which point she blushed and smiled over at Jack, who almost dropped his fork. He had just been about to help himself to a piece of roast lamb but suddenly seemed to have lost his appetite.

The young man coughed. "Yes, well, the Maori see things differently, of course, but we want to stick to the old *pakeha* customs. And so, well, when a girl is engaged, it's not proper for her to share a roof with her future husband." Charlotte caressed Jack's hands, which were nervously playing with his napkin. "Jack, you wanted to do it right," she said, softly chiding him. "You were supposed to request a tête-à-tête with my father now and formally ask for my hand."

"To sum up, it looks like the young people have gotten engaged," James McKenzie remarked, getting up and uncorking a particularly good bottle of wine. "I'm eighty, Jack. I can't wait anymore for you to ask a simple question. Besides, the thing's long been decided. And at my age, I ought to eat my roast while it's warm or it'll get tough and chewing will be hard. So, let's have a quick toast to Jack and Charlotte. Any objections?"

George and Elizabeth Greenwood were delighted with the match, in spite of the surprise announcement. Naturally there would be whispering in town. Though Jack inspired respect from all sides, the sheep barons had not forgotten that he was the son of Gwyneira and a rustler. The biggest gossips would recall that fewer than nine months had elapsed between the McKenzies' wedding and Jack's birth, and everyone knew that Jack was not the heir to Kiward Station but could at best hope to fill a managerial position. The daughter of the immensely wealthy George Greenwood could undoubtedly have made a better match. That argument, however, left George cold. He knew Jack was hardworking and trustworthy, and he simply wanted to see his daughter happy—and married!

Jack and Charlotte married in the spring, right after the sheep had been herded into the highlands. Elizabeth had planned a romantic garden celebration on the banks of the Avon, but unfortunately it was rained out, and the guests rushed into the tents that had been set up just in case. Jack and Charlotte withdrew early from the party and drove to Kiward Station the very next day. They took over the rooms William and Kura Martyn had shared early in their marriage. William had furnished them with exceptional taste and at great cost, and Charlotte had nothing against living surrounded by such furniture. Jack only insisted on less opulent furnishing for the bedroom and asked the carpenter in Haldon for a simple bed and some wardrobes out of native wood.

"But no *kauri*," Charlotte insisted, smiling. "You know Tane Mahuta, the god of the forest, forced Papa and Rangi apart."

In Maori mythology, Papatuanuku, the earth, and Ranginui, the sky, had once been lovers, lying close in each other's arms in the cosmos. Their children decided to separate the two, thus creating light, air, and vegetation on the earth. But Rangi wept almost daily over the separation.

Jack laughed and embraced his wife. "Nothing will ever separate us again."

Although Jack and Charlotte were happy on Kiward Station, George Greenwood suggested a real honeymoon.

"It's time you saw the world, Jack," he insisted when Jack found a thousand reasons not to leave the farm. "The sheep are happy in the highlands, and your parents can take care of a few cattle on their own."

"A few *thousand* cattle," Jack noted.

George rolled his eyes. "You don't have to tuck them into bed yourself every day," he replied. "Your wife would love to see the Pancake Rocks."

Charlotte had suggested a trip to the West Coast. She was less interested in the rocks themselves than in talking to the most famous Maori researcher on the South Island: Caleb Biller. After she heard that Jack's niece Elaine and her husband not only lived in the area but knew Biller personally, she would not take no for an answer.

"As far as I know, the Lamberts and Billers aren't exactly friends," George said, but nothing would deter Charlotte.

"They don't have to sit there while I talk with Mr. Biller," she said. "They can just introduce us. Besides, it's an easy trip by train."

Jack could not object to that. George Greenwood had agreed to place his own salon car at their disposal. The luxury wagon was attached to the regular train, and the honeymooners could enjoy the trip in plush seats or even in bed, drinking champagne. Though Jack would have preferred riding a horse to a train and a shared camp under the starry sky to a rolling bed, Charlotte was enthusiastic, so he played along.

Tim Lambert had decided not to like Jack's young wife, Charlotte, too much—if only because she was forcing him to meet with Florence Biller. But the young woman took his heart by storm. Charlotte succeeded in not "overlooking" Tim's handicap but engaging with him candidly about it. She got along beautifully with Elaine and found in her an open-minded audience for her adventures as a suffragette, and the Lambert boys loved her.

"How is Lilian doing? Does she write?" Jack asked. The question had been weighing on him for some time. Although his marriage and the work on the farm fulfilled him, he still worried about Gloria. Her letters hardly put him at ease. Although she dutifully reported music lessons, reading circles in the garden, and summertime picnics on the banks of the Cam, he could detect none of Gloria's personality in her words. It was almost as if someone else were writing them.

Elaine nodded. "Of course she writes. The girls are made to every Friday afternoon. She always has something to say, you know. Though I ask myself how she gets her letters past the censor. The teachers must check the letters randomly, don't you think?"

She turned to Charlotte.

"Actually they respect the privacy of the letters. At least with the older forms and where I went to school," she informed Elaine.

"What sort of subversive writing is Lilian putting to paper?" Jack asked, unsettled. "Is she not happy?"

Elaine laughed. "She is. But I'm afraid Lily's idea of happiness and that of her teachers don't always match up. Here, see for yourself."

She took Lilian's last letter out of a pocket in her dress. Elaine liked to carry Lilian's letters with her and read them over and over until the next one arrived.

"'Dear Mummy, Daddy, and brothers,'" Jack read aloud. "'I got a bad grade on the English assignment where we were supposed to retell a story of Poe's. It was so sad that I gave it a different ending. But that was wrong. Edgar Allen Poe sometimes wrote some really sad stories and really weird ones too. But there is no such thing as ghosts, however. I know that because last weekend I was at Bloomingbridge Castle with Amanda Wolveridge. Her family has a real castle, and it is supposed to be haunted, but Amanda and I stayed up all night and did not see any ghosts. Just her stupid brother in a sheet. Other than that, we rode Amanda's ponies, and it was very fun. My pony was the fastest. Rube, can you send me a weta? Last week we stuck a spider in the map our teacher has to unroll. She was terribly frightened and leaped up on a chair. We could see her underwear. It would be much better with a weta since they sometimes jump after you.'"

Charlotte giggled as though she were still a little girl playing pranks on her teacher. Jack laughed, too, though he was disheartened. The letter was delightful; you could almost hear little Lilian prattling. Gloria's letters were almost eerie by comparison. He would have to dig deeper. Only he had no idea how to go about doing that.

6

Gloria hated every second at Oaks Garden.

Her spiteful roommate ripped her to pieces. Perhaps she envied Gloria's famous mother, but more likely she was just looking for a scapegoat on whom to take out all of her own frustrations. Either way, Gloria was incapable of paying the girl's scorn back in kind. Nor, however, could she ignore it. She was also well aware that she was far from adorable and looked awkward in her school uniform. And her lack of intelligence and talent was mercilessly brought to her attention every day.

Not that the school was such a treasure trove of creative talent. Despite the school's claim to be a bastion of the fine arts, most of the students smeared paint on their canvases with the same amateur strokes as Gloria and only managed to depict a house or garden from a halfway correct perspective with a good deal of help. Gabrielle Wentworth played the violin horrendously, and Melissa was not much better on the cello.

But choir was the worst. Everyone except Gloria enjoyed singing in the choir. Then again, none of the other students had to endure a torture comparable to that of the daughter of Kura-maro-tini Martyn.

"The daughter of the celebrated Mrs. Martyn!" Miss Wedgewood's eyes gleamed when she called Gloria up to the podium first thing. "I've looked forward to meeting you so. Our alto section is a little weak, and if you have even half your mother's voice, you should be able to hold it up. Could you sing an A for us?"

She struck the note on the piano, and Gloria attempted to repeat it. Gloria was already embarrassed at having to stand next to the piano in front of the class. The reference to her mother did the rest.

Gloria could not manage a single note. Although she had a strong and dulcet singing voice, the girl did not trust herself to sing even the simplest song properly and simply stood there self-consciously, unable to overcome her nerves.

"Hmm. You don't take after your mother at all," Miss Wedgewood finally said, clearly disappointed, and Gloria disappeared into the last row, next to Gabrielle, who took every opportunity to blame any mistakes on her.

Lilian wasn't any help. The girls were assigned to different courses and only saw one another in choir and during breaks. But Lilian was almost instantly surrounded by other girls. Though she did not exclude Gloria—quite the opposite, Lilian warmly welcomed her into her circle—the girl felt out of place. The lower-form girls looked at her with a mixture of bewilderment, envy, and caution, as a great rivalry reigned between the two wings at Oaks Garden; the girls did not visit each other except to play tricks. When Lilian invited her to a midnight party, Gloria snuck over and even almost enjoyed nibbling cake and drinking lemonade with the younger girls. But Gabrielle and her other roommates caught her on her return, speedily forced a confession from her, and immediately told on Lilian to the housemother. Miss Barnum caught the girls cleaning up after the party, and punishment ensued. They held Gloria responsible for the sad end of the festivities.

"Of course I believe you," Lilian said sympathetically. The girls met while doing their punishment exercises in the garden, which consisted of being forced to walk for hours, usually in the rain. They were not really allowed to talk, but Lily was unable to keep her mouth shut. "That Gabrielle is a monster. But the others don't want to have you around anymore. I'm so sorry!"

So Gloria remained alone. Lilian left almost every weekend to visit one or another friend's family. Many others did the same, so weekends at school consisted largely of outcasts. This left the girls very cross, and Gabrielle and Fiona took their low spirits out on Gloria.

Gloria saw Miss Bleachum every Sunday at church, her only ray of hope all week. However, the young governess did not look particularly happy either. Gloria was astonished to see her at the organ in Sawston that first Sunday.

"I had no idea you could play," she said when they spoke after service.

Sarah sighed. There had been some discussion with Christopher about her performance in the village church. Miss Taylor-Bennington had always played the organ—and much better than Sarah—but Christopher had insisted that Sarah "make her debut" in the parish, as he put it. Though he introduced her as his cousin, local gossip swirled about their impending marriage. Almost every woman with whom Sarah came into contact took it for granted—and already had ideas about how the future pastor's wife could make herself useful in the parish. Sarah demurely took over bible study and Sunday school, but despite her incontestable pedagogical talents, her efforts were not warmly received.

"Sarah, my dear, the women are complaining," Christopher explained after her second week. "You're turning bible lessons into a scientific lecture. All these stories from the Old Testament—do you have to do it that way?"

"I thought I'd read them bible passages featuring women," Sarah defended herself. "And the nicest are all in the Old Testament."

"The nicest? Like the one about Deborah, who goes with the commander into battle? Or the one about Jael, who kills her foe with a tent stake?" Christopher shook his head.

"Yes, well, the women in the Old Testament were a bit, well, more active than those in the New," Sarah admitted. "But they achieved a great deal. Esther, for example."

Christopher frowned. "Tell me, Sarah, do you sympathize with the suffragettes? That sounds rather inflammatory."

"It's in the Bible," Sarah remarked.

"But there are nicer passages too." Christopher laid his hands on the New Testament—and demonstrated to Sarah in the very next Sunday sermon what he thought of women in the Bible.

"The price of a virtuous woman is far above rubies," he began, only briefly touching on Eve's failings. "The grace of a wife delighteth her husband, and her discretion will fatten his bones."

The women of the parish reddened as if at a secret command but enjoyed the praise and were enthused by Mary's surrender to the will of the Lord and her motherly qualities. In the end Christopher reaped accolades from all sides.

"Read the 'Magnificat' with them in the next bible study and talk about the ways in which Mary was blessed," he directed Sarah. "That's not as long as all those bible stories, and the women do want to chat about other things too, you know."

Indeed there was more gossiping than praying in bible study, and the reverend was a favorite subject. All the women raved about him, endlessly praising his many good deeds for the parish.

Serious differences between Sarah and the parish only emerged when Christopher entrusted the Sunday school to her. Sarah loved the natural sciences, and answering students' questions truthfully was among her deepest pedagogical convictions.

"What could you possibly have been thinking?" Christopher asked when Sarah's first lesson with the children resulted in a deluge of angry protests from parents. "You're telling the children that we descend from apes?"

Sarah shrugged. "Billy Grant wanted to know if God really made all the animals in six days. And Charles Darwin has since disproved that theory. So I explained to him that the Bible tells us a very beautiful story that helps us to better comprehend the wonder of creation. But then I explained to the children what actually happened."

Christopher tore his hair out. "That has in no way been proven," he said indignantly. "And regardless, it doesn't belong in a Christian Sunday school. Be more careful what you tell the children in the future. We're not at the ends of the earth where such nihilistic ideas are perhaps tolerated."

Sarah did not want to admit it, but the longer she sampled the life of the future wife of a pastor, the more she longed to return to those ends of the earth. Until then she had always believed herself a good

Christian, but she began to fear that that would not be enough here. She had felt more gratified working with children. And little Gloria seemed to be struggling too.

Despite Christopher's visible impatience—he and Sarah were often invited to luncheon at a parishioner's after service, and he did not want to be late—she always withdrew, however briefly, with the girl and let Gloria talk.

"I'm getting bad grades, Miss Bleachum," Gloria complained, certain that this would interest the teacher more than Gabrielle's daily tortures. "I can't sing or read music or draw. But a few days ago I did see a frog, one as green as grass, Miss Bleachum, with tiny suction cups on its feet, and I sketched it. First a big picture of the frog and then a little one of its feet. Have a look, Miss Bleachum." Gloria proudly proffered a slightly smeared charcoal sketch, and Sarah was impressed.

"But Miss Blake-Sutherland thinks it's disgusting. I'm not supposed to be drawing disgusting things. Art is supposed to depict pretty things. Gabrielle got a B because she drew a flower. It didn't even look like a real flower. Geography is dull, they don't teach any science, and we don't have Latin, only French."

"But we did French too," Sarah said, feeling suddenly guilty that she had not better prepared the girl. They had only begun the year before, and she knew that the other girls had probably been studying it for ages.

Gloria confirmed that she was hopelessly behind. That gave Sarah Bleachum an idea.

"Perhaps I could tutor you," she suggested. "On Saturday or Sunday afternoon. Would you like that?"

Gloria beamed. "That would be wonderful. You can write to Grandmum Gwyn about payment."

Sarah shook her head. "I *want* to do it, Glory. I'll speak to Miss Arrowstone. We'll find a way to convince her."

Although Christopher advised against it, Sarah took up the matter with Miss Arrowstone the very next day. The headmistress was initially not enthusiastic.

"Miss Bleachum, we agreed that the girl must cut the apron strings. Gloria comes across as strange here; she doesn't get along with her classmates, and she rejects the subject matter. The bible history teacher recently brought her to me because she put forward Darwinian ideas in an essay. Instead of writing about original sin, she wrote something about the origin of species. I had to rebuke her sharply."

Sarah turned red.

"The girl has grown up a total stranger to the world," Miss Arrowstone declared with outrage. "And you are undoubtedly not entirely without fault. But so be it, the girl ran wild on that sheep farm. A little bit of homeschooling probably stood no chance against that. What's more, is it true what Lilian says? That her grandfather was really a livestock thief?"

Sarah Bleachum had to smile. "Lilian's great-grandfather," she corrected her. "Gloria is not related to James McKenzie."

"But she did grow up in the household of this dubious folk hero, did she not? It's all very opaque. And who is this Jack?" While she spoke, Miss Arrowstone drew a piece of paper out of her desk drawer.

Sarah recognized Gloria's large sloping handwriting.

"Do you read the girls' letters?" she asked, outraged.

"Not usually, Miss Bleachum. But this one . . ."

The students at Oaks Garden were forced to write home on Friday afternoons. Few of them had much to say, but they had learned to inflate small events—a good grade for a drawing, for example, or a new étude in their violin lessons—into the highlights of the week.

Gloria invariably sat mutely in front of her piece of paper. She simply couldn't bring herself to describe her misery. It was just a chance to revisit all the indignities she'd suffered that week: the Monday morning when she had once again found the school blouse she had assiduously ironed the night before wrinkled under all the clothes Gabrielle had taken out on Sunday evening.

"A shame for our house," Miss Coleridge declared, giving Gloria a few disciplinary marks. Gabrielle sneered.

Or Tuesday, when the headmistress had come to choir practice and insisted that the new arrivals sing for her. Miss Arrowstone wanted to know if the daughter of the celebrated Mrs. Martyn was really as hopeless as Miss Wedgewood maintained. Gloria had failed miserably. After being chastised for her poor posture at the podium, she broke off in the middle of the song and ran in tears from the podium to hide in the garden. She received more disciplinary marks when she only returned in time for dinner.

On Wednesday there had been the fuss about original sin.

On Thursday, Gabrielle had exchanged her sheet music for Gloria's at her piano lesson. She did not even know where to start in the workbook for advanced students, and as punishment, Miss Taylor-Bennington made her play from memory. All her arduous hours of practice that week had been for naught.

She could not possibly report all of that back home. She could not even write it down without bursting into tears. When she finally reached for her pen, she dipped the nib so forcefully into the ink that the drops fell like tears onto her writing paper. And then she wrote the only words that came to mind: "Jack, please, please, come take me home!"

"So you see, Miss Bleachum," Miss Arrowstone said. "Should we have sent this letter?"

Sarah gazed, stunned, at Gloria's cry for help. She bit her lip.

"I understand the need to be strict," she replied. "But I'm simply proposing a few additional French lessons. It will help Gloria integrate if she can follow along better in class."

The headmistress softened her stance.

"Very well, Miss Bleachum. If the reverend has nothing against it."

Sarah was piqued anew. What did Christopher have to do with her teaching Gloria? Since when did she need his permission to take on a pupil? But she maintained her composure. Nothing would be gained by further antagonizing Miss Arrowstone.

"Please tell him that was a lovely sermon on the place of women in the Bible," the headmistress remarked as she showed her visitor out. "We were all deeply touched."

Gloria arrived late to her first lesson that Saturday, shaken and in tears.

"I'm sorry, Miss Bleachum, but I had to write a letter first," she apologized. "I have to give it to Miss Coleridge this evening. But I . . ."

Sarah sighed.

"Then we should go over it together first. Do you have the letter paper with you?"

Dear Grandmum Gwyn, Grandpa James, and Jack,

Greetings from England. I should already have written you, but I have a lot of studying to do. I have piano lessons and sing in the choir. In English class we are reading poems by Edgar Allan Poe. We are also memorizing poems. I am making progress in drawing class. On the weekends I see Miss Bleachum. On Sunday we go to church.

I love you all,

Your Gloria

7

The tutoring on Saturday afternoons soon became the highlight of Gloria's week. Miss Bleachum did not confine herself to French lessons. They always dedicated their first hour to it with great concentration—Miss Arrowstone and Madame Laverne, the French teacher, were expecting to see progress, after all. But then Gloria would talk about her daily martyrdom at Gabrielle's hand, and Sarah would give her useful tips for dealing with it.

"You don't have to put up with everything, Gloria. There's nothing improper about asking the housemother for help sometimes. Especially when it comes to pranks like ruining your blouses with ink. And if you don't want to tell on her directly, ask the housemother to hold your things for you. Or stay up at night to see if the girl is up to anything, and swap your clothes for hers. Gabrielle will make quite a face when she finds the spots on her own blouse after you've already dressed and left. Or foist the dirty or wrinkled clothes on another roommate. Then Gabrielle will hear it from her. You'll be playing a prank on the girl yourself for once."

Gloria nodded despondently. When it came to antagonizing others, she lacked all imagination. Eventually, it occurred to her to let Lilian in on what was happening. Lilian and her friends were constantly playing pranks on teachers and classmates.

Lilian listened patiently to Gloria's woes and smiled softly. "That's the cow that told on us after the party, right? Well, of course I'll come up with something."

At her next violin lesson Gabrielle confronted an instrument that was completely out of tune. She usually plied a highly talented little violinist in Lilian's class with sweets to ensure her violin was in tune before her lessons. This time, however, she was forced to do it on her own before the eyes and ears of Miss Taylor-Bennington. The disgrace was complete, and Lilian giggled.

The successful prank filled Gloria with a sort of triumph, but no actual joy. Gwyneira would have attributed her need for harmony to her Maori ancestors; her grandmother Marama had a similar nature. But at Oaks Garden Gloria's peaceful demeanor was viewed as a weakness.

Only during her afternoons with Miss Bleachum did the happy Gloria who was interested in the world reawaken. In order not to be overheard, the two went on long walks after French lessons. Gloria fished for tadpoles in a pond, and Sarah found a hidden place in Mrs. Buster's garden where they could mature in a glass. Gloria observed the pollywogs' development with fascination, and Mrs. Buster almost died of fright when she discovered twenty spirited little frogs hopping through her flower beds. It took Sarah hours to gather them up and take them back to their pond, and she received another mild chiding from the reverend.

"That wasn't very ladylike, my love. You should spend more time thinking about how to be a role model for the parish women."

"So will you be marrying the reverend soon?" Gloria asked one day during the summer holidays. The girls who remained at Oaks Garden were not closely supervised, so Gloria stole into town almost every day to visit Miss Bleachum.

She had no easy answer to Gloria's question.

"I don't know," she said finally. "Everyone assumes so, but . . ."

"Do you love him, Miss Bleachum?" This impertinent question came from—who else?—Lilian. She, too, was spending part of her vacation at school, though she would be traveling to Somerset with a friend's family the following week.

Sarah blushed again, though less violently than a few months before. She had gotten used to the constant talk of her impending marriage.

"I think so," she said quietly, but she was not sure. The honest answer would have been that Sarah did not know because she still could not properly define the term "love." She used to believe she had a deep affinity with Christopher, but since she had come to England, her doubt had grown appreciably. It was becoming increasingly clear to her that she had little in common with the reverend. Sarah was striving for truth and definite knowledge. Faith was less important to her than truth.

Although the reverend was educated and intelligent, he cared more about being loved, admired, and respected than about knowledge and truth. He flattered the female members of the parish and refrained from critiquing the sins of the males. Sarah grew angry when Christopher merely placated yet another woman who came to lament that her husband had spent all their money in the pub and beat her when she protested.

Still—she had to admit that she was attracted to him. Given that everyone around her considered her to be practically engaged, she allowed him to pick her up and take her to picnics and on rides—if only to escape the crushing boredom of the village. When she was alone with him, she felt the charm with which he likewise captivated the parish women. He looked her in the eye, nodded intently at her observations, and sometimes, sometimes he touched her. It began with a gentle, almost accidental brushing of her hand when they reached for a chicken leg on the picnic blanket at the same time. It then became a conscious touching of the back of her hand with his fingers as if to emphasize a remark he had just made.

Sarah shivered at these intimacies. One day he reached for her hand to help her over a muddy spot on a walk, and she felt the safety and strength in it. He let go when the difficult spot had been overcome, but as Sarah gradually relaxed, he kept her hand in his, playing delicately with her fingers, and telling her how pretty she was. That unsettled Sarah, but she wanted to believe it, and how could anyone lie who held her hand like that? She began to look forward to his overtures. She no longer trembled with nervous excitement but instead with anticipation at the thought of Christopher wrapping his arms around her and speaking tender words.

Then one day he kissed her, in the reeds by the pond where she had gathered tadpoles with Gloria. His lips on hers robbed her first of her breath and then of her reason. As Christopher held her in his arms, she could no longer think; she was all feeling and pleasure. This had to be love, this disappearing and flowing into the arms of another. A spiritual affinity was friendship, but this . . . this was something else altogether. Of course Sarah Bleachum knew the word "lust" too. But that was unthinkable in the context of Christopher, or herself. What she was feeling here had to be something good, something holy. Yes, it had to be love.

From Christopher Bleachum's perspective, his cautious approach to Sarah had been more hardship than delight. Of course he had known that she would be prudish. Teaching schools were hardly better than abbeys. Abstinence was expected of female educators, and the young women were closely supervised. But he had still hoped to draw her out of her shell more quickly. He was used to women leaping into his arms, and he knew how to read their slightest signal. A batting of the eye, a smile, a nod. It did not take much to set Christopher alight, particularly when the woman was pretty and presented inviting curves. Then he would begin a forbidden game of which he was a master. The reverend would launch into innuendo and little flatteries. He would smile when the women blushed, seemingly ashamed, before offering their hand and shivering languorously as he caressed them first with his fingers, then with his lips. In the end it was always the women who wanted more and who generally chose the discreet locations for their rendezvous. The secrecy of their interludes further aroused Christopher, and the women let him get quickly to the point. For that reason, too, he preferred experienced women. The slow induction of a virgin into the joys of love offered him no pleasure.

That, however, seemed to be exactly what Sarah demanded. It appeared that she knew just enough about physical love to fear it and, conversely, that enjoyment was connected to it. Despite their differences, he remained convinced that she was suited to the role of a pastor's wife. Although she had yet to give him an emphatic yes, it seemed unlikely that she would change her mind now that he had introduced her to the whole parish as his future bride.

Sarah was smart and highly educated; if he just molded her a little, she could take on many of his responsibilities in the community. Although she could be stubborn—Christopher did not like it when she went about with that Martyn girl instead of interacting with the community—she was capable of compromise. Since their debate about Darwinism, she had been happy to withdraw from leading the religious upbringing of the Sunday school pupils. Instead she took them on nature walks to show them God's beautiful world. The students were learning more about plants and animals than about loving one's neighbor and penitence, but no one had complained.

Christopher was thoroughly optimistic that he could mold his somewhat bluestocking cousin into a well-mannered pastor's wife. When it came to the bishop's desire that she serve as a bulwark against assaults on the virtue of the handsome pastor, Christopher had less hope. Naturally he would try to be faithful, but Sarah and her laborious courtship were already boring him. Although Christopher felt neither love nor spiritual affinity for his cousin, marrying her was a practical choice based on reason.

"I don't think the reverend is in love with Miss Bleachum," Lilian said as she strolled back to school with Gloria.

"Why do you say that?" Gloria inquired. "Of course he loves her." Gloria could not imagine anyone in the world not loving Sarah Bleachum.

"He doesn't look at her like he does. Not like, well, not like, I don't know. But he looks at Mrs. Walker like it. And Brigit Pierce-Barrister."

"Brigit?" Gloria asked. "You're crazy."

A fellow student at Oaks Garden, Brigit Pierce-Barrister was older than most of them and completely filled out. The girls giggled about Brigit's "swollen breasts" under the regulation school uniform.

"There's no way the reverend could be in love with Brigit."

"Why not? Brigit is in love with him. And Mary Stellington too. I heard them swooning over him. Mary made him a bookmark from pressed flowers and gave it to him for Saint John's Eve. Now she's always staring at his Bible, hoping he'll use it and think of her. And Brigit says she'll be allowed to sing in service next week. She's afraid she won't be able to make a sound with him there. Even the girls in my class rave about him."

Gloria sighed. That anyone could swoon over Reverend Bleachum defied comprehension. First of all, he was much too old for all these girls. And besides, she still did not like him. Something about him seemed dishonest. Though he flattered her whenever they crossed paths, he never looked her in the eye. "He stands too close when he's talking and always lays his hand on the person's hand or shoulder . . ."

"Personally, I wouldn't marry him," Lilian prattled on. "You're right. Just the way he touches everyone. If I ever marry, my husband should only touch me and only say nice things to me, not to every woman he comes across. And he'll only be allowed to dance with me. What do you bet Reverend Bleachum dances with Brigit at the summer festival?"

Gloria was too preoccupied to answer. If the reverend did not love Miss Bleachum, he probably would not marry her. She would go back to New Zealand and look for a new job. Then what would become of Gloria?

Sarah Bleachum was not enjoying the parish's summer festival. Mrs. Buster had assigned her to the local matrons' table, where she was making dull conversation after having overseen the charity bazaar and the bake sale. Obliged to buy something herself, she was now in joyless possession of an egg cozy knit by Mrs. Buster and a crocheted cover for her teapot. She saw the reverend from afar, chatting with a few men, and then with Miss Arrowstone, who had come with nine students and two teachers.

Then Brigit Pierce-Barrister, looking like a plump nymph, came over and started fawning over the reverend. Her dress seemed much too childlike for her already fully developed figure, and Sarah wondered why Miss Arrowstone did not make the girl put her hair up.

Brigit said something to Christopher, and he answered with a smile. Sarah felt a prick of jealousy. Which was nonsense, of course. The girl might swoon over him, but the reverend would never encourage a seventeen-year-old girl.

Sarah considered whether she should stand up and stroll over to the Oaks Garden table. But Christopher would chide her again for that—and Sarah hated to arouse his displeasure. At first she had not made much of occasionally chafing him, but ever since they had admitted their love to one another, Christopher "punished" her more subtly instead. If Sarah angered him with some word or deed, he would not look at her for days, or refrained from holding her hand in that gentle, heartwarming way—and he certainly would not take her in his arms and kiss her.

Sarah had never thought about caresses before. She had not dreamed of men as some of the other girls at her teaching school had admitted to doing, and she rarely stroked her own body secretly under the covers. She had only experienced burning desire for the first time with Christopher, and she suffered when he kept her at a distance. In her imagination she experienced his kisses again and again, heard his deep voice uttering tender words.

Sometimes the word "obsessed" passed through her mind, but she shied away from thinking of her love for Christopher that way. "Enthralled" was better. Sarah dreamed of finding total fulfillment in Christopher's arms, and wished she could better express her desire to him. Though she had frozen when Christopher first touched her, she now seemed to melt. In such moments she could not wait to fix a wedding date. Christopher seemed to have no doubt that she would say yes, and he evidently did not think a romantic proposal necessary. There were times when that enraged Sarah, but as soon as he touched her, she calmed down. She thought perhaps she should just talk to him honestly. But then her pride would triumph over her weakness.

Her thoughts were interrupted as the band gathered and called for a dance. Sarah expected Christopher to come over to her, but instead he asked Miss Wedgewood to dance. After leading the music teacher in a waltz, it was Mrs. Buster's turn. And so it went.

"There, now you see. He's not dancing with Miss Bleachum," Lilian whispered triumphantly to Gloria. "He doesn't think much of her."

"Well, it's not like he's in love with Mrs. Buster," Gloria remarked.

"Of course not. But he can't just dance with the ones he's in love with. That would attract attention," Lilian explained precociously. "Just watch, he'll dance with a few more old ladies and then with Brigit."

Indeed, after leading several more "pillars of the community" across the dance floor, Christopher returned to the Oaks Garden table, where Brigit enthusiastically handed him a glass of iced tea.

"You're a good dancer, Reverend," she said, smiling coyly. "Is that proper for a man of God?"

Christopher laughed. "Even King David danced, Brigit," he replied. "God gave his children music and dance that they might enjoy them. Why shouldn't his servants take part in that?"

"Will you dance with me then?" Brigit inquired.

When Christopher nodded, even Gloria saw the spark in his eyes.

"Why not?" he said. "But do you know how? I didn't know Oaks Garden offered dance lessons."

Brigit laughed and winked. "A cousin back in Norfolk showed me how."

She laid her hand lightly on the reverend's arm as he led her onto the dance floor.

Gloria glanced at Sarah, who was also watching the scene unfold. Although she appeared relaxed, Gloria knew her well enough to recognize that she was angry.

Brigit leaned into Christopher's arms as if it were the most natural thing in the world and skillfully followed his lead. Although there was nothing improper in the way he held her, it was clear that he was not merely fulfilling an obligation.

"A lovely couple," Mrs. Buster remarked. "Although the girl is much too young for him. Don't you dance, Miss Bleachum?"

Sarah wanted to reply that she would love to dance if she were asked, but she refrained. For one, that would have been unbecoming, and for another it was not even true. Sarah was no great dancer. It was embarrassing to put herself on show with her glasses on, but without them she was almost blind. If only she were not feeling a burning desire to be wrapped in Christopher's arms on the dance floor like the impertinent little Brigit.

The reverend didn't believe it would be proper to dance more than two dances with one partner, especially one so young. So Christopher withdrew from Brigit after the waltz and led her back to her table. As he pulled her chair out for her, he heard the two girls whispering at the next table.

"You see, he's in love with her," Lilian declared triumphantly. "I told you so. He hasn't even looked at Miss Bleachum."

Christopher froze. That redheaded imp! Damn it! Was the attention he had paid to Brigit really so obvious, or did this girl simply have a sense for entanglements? Regardless, she was chatty. If he did not want to fall into disrepute, he would have to come up with a solution. Christopher thought of the bishop's latest reprimand. If one more story made it back to his superior, it could cost him his post. And Christopher liked Sawston so much. He took his leave of the Oaks Garden group and sauntered over to Sarah.

"Would you like to dance, my love?" he asked.

Sarah nodded, smiling radiantly, though she had looked hesitant before. Did she suspect something too? Christopher took her hand. He had to follow through now. Had he not long since decided that

Sarah was the wife God had chosen for him? It was time to accelerate matters.

Sarah removed her glasses and, half-blind, followed her cousin onto the dance floor. Sarah completely surrendered to his lead, but Christopher felt like he was holding a flour sack in his arms. Either he had to drag her or she stepped on his feet. He nonetheless forced himself to smile.

"Quite a festival, my love," he remarked. "And you had a big part in that. What would we have done without your help?"

Sarah looked up at him, but his face appeared blurred. "But I hardly get to spend time with you," she complained gently. "Do you have to dance with all these women? Mrs. Buster has already commented on it."

Hot and cold flashes passed through Christopher. So the old witch had noticed something too. There was no helping it. He would have to take the plunge. "Sarah, my love, Mrs. Buster will use any opportunity to spread nasty gossip. But if it's all right with you, we'll give her some good news to take with her too. I'd like to marry you, Sarah. Would you have anything against announcing it to the whole world?"

Sarah blushed and stopped dancing. He had finally asked! A tiny stirring within her still protested—Sarah considered a marriage proposal to be a rather intimate affair. She would also have expected that Christopher would want to hear her accept before he broadcast it. But these stirrings belonged to the old Sarah, the woman she had been before she knew true love. Sarah tried to smile.

"Please, I'd like, well, I have nothing against it."

"Miss Bleachum looks like she ran into a door," Lilian remarked.

The reverend had just asked the band to pause and from the dais announced that he had just officially engaged himself to Miss Sarah Bleachum. Sarah looked like she wanted to disappear, and her face was flushed.

Gloria felt for her. It had to be terrible to stand up there and be stared at by everyone. Several women in the crowd—Brigit among them—looked decidedly unenthusiastic at the news, but Gloria was happy that Miss Bleachum would remain nearby—to comfort her and dictate the letters she sent home so no one would notice how unhappy she was.

"I don't think she looks happy," Lilian persisted.

Gloria decided not to listen to her cousin.

8

Charlotte thought Jack was overreacting with regard to his concerns about Gloria.

"Yes, she writes a little stiffly," she acknowledged. "Especially compared to Lilian—she sounds like a little whirlwind. But Gloria is thirteen. She has other things to do besides put profound thoughts to paper. She probably just wants get it over with quickly and doesn't even think about what she's writing."

Jack frowned. They were in the train from Greymouth to Christchurch and had just been discussing the highlights of their honeymoon. Caleb Biller had proved to be an exceedingly stimulating conversation partner for Charlotte and had suggested several excursions. Once or twice he even accompanied the young couple to meet Maori tribes he knew.

"You'll go far as a researcher," Caleb said. "Hardly anyone has bothered with the sagas and myths. Kura and I were more interested in the music, and I was intrigued by their wood crafts. But it would be well worth your while to save the old stories before they become interwoven with more recent events. Obviously it's in the nature of oral culture that it adapts to the changing times, but they'll eventually regret it. It will be good to have the old tales preserved."

Charlotte was proud of the praise and dedicated herself to her studies with greater zeal. In the meantime, Jack had resumed his old friendship with Elaine. Their talk returned again and again to the two girls in England—and Jack's concern for Gloria grew as Elaine told him more about Lilian.

"Gloria isn't just being superficial," he told his wife. "On the contrary, she tends to reflect too much when she's busy with something.

And she was always full of life on Kiward Station. But there are no questions about the sheep or the dogs. She loved her pony, but hasn't even mentioned her. I can't believe that she's given all that up for the piano and painting instead."

Charlotte smiled. "Children change, Jack. You'll see that yourself when we have our own. The sooner the better, I think, or did you want to wait? I'd like a girl first and then a boy. What do you think? Or would you prefer a son first?" She was playing with her hair and preparing to undo her braid. As she did she cast a meaningful glance at the wide bed that dominated George Greenwood's parlor car.

Jack kissed her.

"I'll take whatever you give me," he said tenderly, picking her up and carrying her over to the bed.

"If you're so concerned, why don't you just write her?" Charlotte asked. "Write her a personal letter, not one of those long inventories Gwyneira sets down every few days: 'According to the last counts, Kiward Station has a stock of 11,361 sheep.' Who cares about that?"

Jack immediately felt better at the thought of writing to her. But just then, he had other things to do.

The whole village seemed caught up in the preparations for the wedding of its beloved reverend, which was scheduled for early September. Sarah maintained her composure when Mrs. Buster insisted on measuring her for a stylish wedding dress and listened patiently as the mothers of her Sunday school students proposed that their offspring carry her train and scatter flowers. As diplomatically as possible, she informed them that Gloria and Lilian would do those things. Gloria, however, would have been more than willing to give up her claim.

"I'm just not pretty, Miss Bleachum," she murmured. "People will only laugh if I were to be your maid of honor."

Sarah shook her head. "They'll laugh when I wear my glasses," she explained. "Though I haven't decided about them. Maybe I will leave them off."

"But then you'd get lost on the way to the altar. And the reverend must like you with your glasses too, *right*?"

Gloria laid the stress on the "right." She had long since given up hope to be loved for who she was. Though she believed the McKenzies when they said in their letters that they missed their great-granddaughter, she wondered whether they truly loved her. Or did it all have to do with the inheritance of Kiward Station? Gloria often brooded over why her great-grandmother had so easily kowtowed to the will of her parents. Jack had been against it, she thought, but then Jack had never answered her letter. He had probably forgotten her too.

"The reverend loves me with and without my glasses, Glory, just as I love you regardless of whether you look good in these ugly floral dresses."

Lilian, on the other hand, was excited about her wedding responsibilities and spoke of nothing else. She would have liked to play the organ, but Miss Wedgewood took that on, though she always looked a little put out at the rehearsals.

Christopher Bleachum was content with the way things were progressing, though he always felt wistful when he saw Brigit at service. He had not revived his budding relationship with the girl. Now that he was officially engaged, he wanted to stay faithful. No matter how hard it would be, he was determined to be a good and caring husband—even if he thought Emily Winter had begun eyeing him with interest again. She had to know that Sarah was not the woman he had dreamed of all his life, but neither Emily Winter nor Brigit Pierce-Barrister was destined to be the wife of a pastor. Christopher thought it very Christian and exceedingly heroic not to look at the two women anymore and instead turned his full attention on Sarah. She had long since become putty in his hands; things were going far too smoothly to arouse him even a little.

As the big day approached, the parish bubbled with excitement. Sarah tried on her dress and wept when it would not fit. The overly sumptuous frills covering the dress made her look childish, and her few curves were lost in a sea of satin and tulle that stretched and bulged in all the wrong places.

"I'm not vain, but I can't appear in front of the bishop like this," she lamented to Christopher. "All due respect to the good will of Mrs. Buster and Mrs. Holleer—but they can't really sew."

Christopher saw the necessity of Sarah walking down the aisle in something appropriate.

"Emily Winter is a skilled seamstress," he said. "She should be able to straighten it out. I'll talk to her tomorrow."

"Don't you find it ironic," Emily Winter remarked when Christopher knocked on her door with his request, "that I—of all people—should tailor the white dress for your virgin bride. She is still a virgin, is she not?"

Emily stood at the door to her house in a pose that had an instantly arousing effect on him. Petite but well-formed, she had gentle curves and a doll-like face with a soft, cream-colored complexion. Her eyelids hung heavily over her green-brown eyes, and her brown hair fell in thick tresses down her back when it was not tied in a low bun as it was now.

"Of course I haven't touched her," Christopher said. "And please, Emily, don't look at me like that. I'm almost a married man, and our time together caused enough trouble."

Emily emitted a raspy laugh. "Don't you want me anymore?"

"It's not about wanting, Emily. It's about my reputation. And yours, you shouldn't forget that. So, will you help Sarah?" Christopher tried desperately to hide his arousal.

"I'll do the best I can with the little mouse. We should shroud her with a thick veil, right?" She laughed again. "Send her over. I know Mrs. Buster. The dress will have to be completely redone."

Sarah appeared that same afternoon and wept all over again when she tried on her dress in front of Emily Winter. Emily raised her eyes to heaven. Another crybaby! But she would keep her promise. She quickly removed all the tulle and frills and prescribed a tight corset for Sarah.

"I won't be able to breathe in that," Sarah moaned, but Emily shook her head.

"A little breathlessness does a bride good. And the corset will boost your bosom and emphasize your hips. You could use it. You'll have a completely different figure, believe me."

Sarah watched with fascination in the mirror as Emily Winter pulled the dress in, tightened the skirt, and increased the décolleté.

"That's too much cleavage," Sarah protested, but Emily created a tulle inset that made the dress look high-necked while still drawing attention to Sarah's finally recognizable bosom. Sarah felt much better when she left Emily's house.

Sarah hardly recognized herself when she stood in front of the mirror on her wedding day. The dress fit like a glove. Although Sarah could hardly move in the corset, her figure was unbelievable.

Lilian and Gloria could hardly contain their excitement.

The girls' bridesmaids' dresses were not flattering. Mrs. Buster had insisted on pink dresses that clashed with Lilian's red locks and made Gloria look plump.

Emily Winter had done her best in any case. And she would demand her pay from Christopher for her services.

Christopher Bleachum awaited his bride alone in the sacristy. The bishop was outside, and Sarah was still being preened by the women. Christopher paced nervously.

He heard a side door to the anteroom open, and Emily Winter appeared in a formal apple-green dress with a dark-green shawl over it. Her luxuriant hair was held back with a wide barrette and her heavy locks fell gracefully over her shoulders. A pert little green hat emphasized the deep brown of her hair.

"Emily! What are you doing here?" The reverend looked both astounded and perturbed by her sudden appearance.

Emily Winter studied his slender but powerful physique in the elegant black frock coat he had borrowed for the wedding.

"Well, what else? I'm presenting you the fruits of my labor. Here." She turned to the little window of the sacristy and pointed outside, where the young bride was talking with Gloria and Lilian. Sarah was completely transformed.

"Do you like it?" Emily asked, pressing closer to Christopher.

He took a deep breath.

"You, ma'am, have worked a miracle."

Emily laughed. "Just a few parlor tricks. Tonight the princess will turn back into Cinderella. But by then there won't be any going back."

"There's no going back already." Christopher tried to withdraw from Emily's approach, but he felt arousal spreading through him, the allure of the forbidden. What if he were to take Emily one more time? Here, next to his church, just steps from the bishop and Sarah?

"But it's not too late for a few nice memories," Emily said temptingly. "Come, Reverend," she spoke the last word slowly and lasciviously, "my husband is already drinking to the health of the happy couple. The bishop is blessing all the village brats, and your Sarah is comforting that ugly little Gloria because she looks like a fat flamingo in that bridesmaid's dress. No one will bother us." She let her shawl fall.

"Come, Christopher, one last time."

Sarah could not make up her mind. She looked so pretty—for the first time in her life. She could picture the light in Christopher's eyes already as she walked down the aisle to him. He would hardly believe her transformation. He *had* to love her, now more than ever.

"Behold, thou art fair, my beloved." The Song of Songs would take on a whole new meaning for him and for Sarah too. Because she was fair. Love made her glow.

If only it weren't for her glasses. Sarah did not want to stumble blindly through her own wedding ceremony. But maybe there was a solution. Christopher should see her at least once without them, even if it brought bad luck. She would pop into the sacristy for a moment, tell him what a fabulous job Emily had done—and maybe he would even kiss her. Of course he would kiss her. Sarah gathered her dress and veil.

"I'll be right back, girls. Tell the bishop we can start in five minutes. But for now I need to . . ." She hurried around the church to the entrance to the sacristy.

Breathless from her corset but also from excitement, Sarah took her glasses off and felt around the anteroom. The door to the sacristy stood open. Something was moving, a strangely compact body lying halfway over an armchair, something green and black, and pinkish. Naked skin?

"Christopher?" Sarah felt in the folds of her dress for her glasses.

"Sarah, no!" Christopher Bleachum tried to prevent the worst, but Sarah had already put on her glasses.

The sight was not only disgraceful but disgusting.

And suddenly the lovestruck Sarah Bleachum transformed back into the smart young woman unafraid of questioning the world.

After staring, dazed, for a few seconds at the half-naked bodies in the room next to God's house, her eyes flashed with rage.

Pale, her mouth closed tight, she ripped the veil from her hair and flung it to the floor. Then she ran out.

"You need to get dressed, the bishop . . ." Emily said, coming to her senses first. But it was too late.

Christopher did not believe that Sarah would tell the bishop, but he must have seen her storming out of the sacristy.

The reverend ducked his head instinctively and prepared himself. The wrath of God would soon break over him.

"I'm sorry, Glory, I'm really sorry."

Sarah Bleachum cradled the sobbing girl in her arms. "But you have to understand that I can't remain under these circumstances. How would people look at me?"

"I don't care. But if you go back to New Zealand now . . . is my great-grandmum really sending you the money?"

As soon as Sarah had run past the confused wedding guests, her thoughts began to flow again. She had to leave—as soon as possible. Otherwise she would go mad. When Sarah reached her room she ripped off her dress, undid that fatal corset, and pulled on the first clothes she found. Then she packed up her things and set off for Cambridge.

She had seven miles to cover. At first she set off at nearly a run, but as her burning anger and shame dissipated, they gave way to exhaustion. She found a modest bed-and-breakfast and knocked at the door. And for the first time that awful day, she was in luck. The proprietress, a widow named Margaret Simpson, asked her no questions.

"You can tell me what happened later if you want," she said softly, placing a cup of tea in front of Sarah. "First you need to relax."

"I need to find a post office," Sarah said. She had begun to tremble. "I need to send a telegram, to New Zealand. Could I do that from here?"

Mrs. Simpson refilled her teacup and laid a wool jacket around the shoulders of her strange guest. "Of course. But it can wait until tomorrow."

Sarah would never have thought she would sleep that night, but to her surprise, she slept soundly—and when she awoke the next morning, she felt newly liberated. Deep down she was happy to be able to return home. If only it weren't for Gloria.

"She promised to pay for my trip should I, well, not have my hopes fulfilled here. And she'll keep that promise; she's already confirmed that," Sarah informed Gloria. She was scheduled to leave in just a few days. But she had to speak to Gloria before leaving. With a heavy heart she had ordered a cab to Oaks Garden and walked past the teachers and housemothers looking on sourly with her head held high. As expected, Gloria was inconsolable.

"Can't you at least stay in England?" she asked desperately. "Maybe Miss Arrowstone would hire you."

"After what happened, Glory? No, that's impossible. Just imagine my having to see Christopher at service every Sunday. I wish I could take you with me but that won't work right now. And your parents are coming to visit soon, Glory. You'll feel better then."

Gloria had her doubts about that. She was both excited and nervous about her reunion with her parents.

"I'll tell your great-grandmother how unhappy you are here," Sarah said halfheartedly. "Perhaps she can do something."

"Don't bother."

Gloria no longer believed in miracles.

She played with the letter in her pocket that had come that morning. Her great-grandmother had written to tell her that Jack was now married to Charlotte Greenwood. Surely they would soon have children. And he would forget all about Gloria.

"We are delighted to have you here," Miss Arrowstone said, greeting William Martyn euphorically. With few exceptions, William had always charmed women. The rotund headmistress was now purring like a cat as she gazed up at him adoringly. Though now middle-aged, he remained slender and stately; his hair was still blond and curly, and the light of his clear blue eyes, exaggerated by his slightly tanned face, made him irresistible. He and his beautiful wife, Kura, made an exceptionally attractive couple. Miss Arrowstone wondered how two such handsome, charismatic people could have brought such a mediocre child as Gloria into the world.

"We received a letter for Gloria that caused us some concern, to put it mildly." Miss Arrowstone fished an envelope from her desk drawer.

"How is Gloria doing anyway? I hope she's settled into life here."

Miss Arrowstone forced a smile. "Well, your daughter is still struggling with the transition. She is a little wild, you know, from her time Down Under."

William nodded and waved it away. "Horses, cows, and sheep, Miss Arrowstone," he said dramatically. "That's all people have in their heads there. We should have brought Gloria into a more stimulating setting sooner. But that's how it is, Miss Arrowstone. Great success only comes with great effort."

Miss Arrowstone smiled understandingly. "That's why your wife isn't with you to retrieve Gloria. We would have enjoyed seeing her again."

And hearing another free concert, thought William, although he answered amiably: "Kura was somewhat indisposed after the last tour. And you understand of course that even the smallest cold is cause for concern for a singer. So we thought it would be better for her to stay in London. We have a suite at the Ritz."

"I would have thought you would have your own town house, Mr. Martyn," Miss Arrowstone said, astonished.

William shook his head with slight regret. "Nor a country house, Miss Arrowstone. Though I've often broached the subject of a residence, my wife doesn't want to settle down. Her Maori heritage, I suspect." He smiled winningly. "But now, what about that letter you mentioned, Miss Arrowstone? Is someone harassing our daughter? Perhaps something else our Gloria will have to get used to. Successful artists always generate envy."

Miss Arrowstone handed the letter over. "I would not call it 'harassment.' And I'm a little uncomfortable with the fact that we opened the letter. But as the father of a daughter you will undoubtedly understand that we must mind the virtue of our charges. To be on the safe side, we open letters by male senders whose relationship to the girls we're not familiar with. If it proves harmless, as is almost always the case, we hand over the letter. But this time, well, read for yourself."

My dearest Gloria,

I'm not quite sure how I should begin this letter, but I'm too troubled to wait any longer. My beloved wife, Charlotte, encouraged me simply to write you and impart my concerns.

How are you, Gloria? Perhaps you think that a bothersome question. From your letters we take it that you are always busy. You write about playing the piano, drawing, and many activities with your new friends. But to me your letters seem strangely curt and stiff. Can it really be that you have forgotten all of us on Kiward Station? Do you really not want to know how your dog and horse are? I never read laughter between the lines and never hear a personal word. Quite the opposite, in fact; sometimes the few short sentences seem to radiate sadness. When I think of you, I always hear the last words you said to me before you left: 'If it's really bad, you'll come get me, right?' At the time I did not know how to answer. But the answer is: yes. If you're truly desperate, Gloria, if you're all alone and see no hope that things will get better, then write me, and I'll come. I don't know how I'll arrange it, but I'm here for you.

Your half granduncle who loves you more than anything,

Jack

William scanned the lines with furrowed brow.

"You were right to seize this letter, Miss Arrowstone," he remarked. "The relationship between my daughter and this man was always somewhat unhealthy. Throw the letter away."

Gloria was alone. Completely alone.

Paradise Lost

Canterbury Plains, Cambridge, Auckland, Cape Reinga,

America, Australia, and Greymouth

1914–1915

1

"At the risk of sounding like old Gerald Warden, something's not right."

James McKenzie shuffled through the former rose garden of Kiward Station heavily supported by his cane and leaning lightly on his wife's arm. Recently every movement had become a torment, his joints were stiffer than ever, and his rheum reminded him of countless nights spent under an open sky. He only left the house when he felt it was necessary, such as the return of the flocks and their shepherds out of the mountains. Though the management of the farm had long been in Jack's hands, the old foreman would not be denied a look at the well-fed ewes and lambs.

James McKenzie glanced at Charlotte's still slender form.

"Five years of marriage and the girl is still as thin as a blade of grass. Something isn't right there."

Gwyneira nodded. Though the subject came up often between them, neither of them wanted to bring it up directly with Jack or Charlotte.

"It's not for lack of effort," Gwyneira joked. "They still can hardly keep their hands off each other. It's unlikely that stops in the bedroom. But don't you think she's too thin, James? She's pretty as a picture, of course, but a little lean. Or am I imagining things? And those constant headaches."

Charlotte had suffered migraines for as long as she could remember. Even in the first few years of marriage, she had spent a week in her apartments with the windows shaded only to reemerge pale and haggard. Neither the Haldon doctor's powders nor the Maori midwife's herbs had helped. Gwyneira had noticed that they'd begun to occur more frequently.

"She's probably worried. She's always wanted children," James said. "What does Rongo say? Didn't you send her there again?"

Gwyneira shrugged. "I can only tell you what Dr. Barlow says. Charlotte told me that in his opinion everything was fine. I could hardly ask Rongo about Charlotte's health. But they're together a great deal for her research on Maori myths. If something were seriously wrong, Rongo would notice."

James nodded. "If I'm not mistaken," he then said, "it's time for me to go see Rongo Rongo myself. This rheumatism's killing me. But I can't ride to O'Keefe Station. Do you think Rongo would condescend to a house visit?" he smiled.

"During which you can carefully and inconspicuously sound her out about Charlotte's most intimate secrets?" Gwyneira teased him. "But do, I'm equally curious. Just make sure she won't tell Charlotte. And afterward I'll insist you take every bitter drop she prescribes."

Rongo Rongo paid a house call. The last few rains had worsened James's rheumatism to the point where he could hardly pull himself out of bed even just to reach his easy chair at the bay window.

"That is time, Mr. McKenzie, she rots our bones," sighed Rongo. In the tradition of her family's women, she practiced and taught healing. "I can ease the pain a bit, but the rheumatism can no longer be cured. More than anything, keep yourself warm and do not resist your weakness. It does not help to force your bones. That only makes it worse. Here," she said, handing him a packet of herbs. "Have them steep this in the kitchen tonight. Tomorrow Kiri will strain it, and you'll drink everything in one gulp. No matter how bitter it is. Ask Kiri. She takes the same thing, and she's much more active than you."

Kiri had been the cook at Kiward Station for decades and staunchly refused to leave her position to someone younger.

"Kiri is a child compared to me!" James insisted. "At her age I didn't even know what joint pain was."

Rongo smiled. "The gods touch this one now, that one later," she said with a touch of sadness. "Be happy you have been granted a long life, and many descendants."

"While we're on the subject," James began, switching to Maori. "How do things look for Charlotte? Will she have many descendants?"

James smiled almost a little conspiratorially, but Rongo Rongo remained serious.

"Mr. McKenzie, *wahine* Charlotte's curse is not childlessness," she said softly. "My grandmother advised me in cases like hers to carry out an exorcism, and I did."

"With Charlotte's consent?" James asked astonished.

Rongo nodded. "Yes, although she didn't take it seriously. She just wanted to know what such a session was like."

"It didn't do much good, did it?" James said. He had heard of many successful conjuring rituals, but they were only helpful if the person in question believed in their effect.

"Mr. McKenzie, it's not important whether Charlotte believes in the spirits. It's the spirits that must fear the power of the *tohunga*."

"And?" James asked. "Were these spirits sufficiently scared?"

Rongo frowned unhappily. "I'm not very powerful," she admitted. "And they are powerful spirits. I advised Charlotte to seek the advice of a *pakeha-tohunga* in Christchurch. Dr. Barlow in Haldon doesn't have any more power than I."

James was unsettled. Rongo Rongo had never before sent a patient to a Western doctor. She carried on a friendly rivalry with Dr. Barlow—sometimes one affected a speedy recovery, sometimes the other. Both had failed in Charlotte's case. And the diagnoses "Childlessness is not her curse" and "You must simply keep trying as medically there's no reason you can't conceive" resembled each other in a disconcerting way.

"I've counted the days," Charlotte said to her husband.

She had just brushed her hair, and Jack bent over her and breathed in the honey-blonde luxuriance, still surprised that so much beauty belonged to him.

"If we try today, I could conceive a baby."

Jack kissed her hair and the back of her neck. "I'm open to any attempt," he said and smiled. "But don't fret about children. I only want, only need you."

She knew he meant it. Jack had never left any doubt about how happy she made him.

"How do you even know how to count the days?" he asked.

"From Elaine," she explained. "And a—" She giggled a little and blushed. "A prostitute explained it to her. Granted, that was more about how to avoid getting pregnant. But the principle is the same, you know, only reversed."

"You talked to Elaine about our difficulties?" Jack asked, taken aback. "I thought what we do here only involved us?"

"You know Lainie. She's rather forward. When she was here last time she asked me about it directly. Oh Jack, I want a baby so badly. Lainie's boys are so sweet. And she had another letter from little Lilian."

"She's not so little anymore," grumbled Jack. "Gloria is eighteen, so Lilian must be fourteen or fifteen."

"She's charming in any case. I can't wait to meet her. In two years she'll finish her schooling. And Gloria in just a year. How quickly children grow up."

Jack nodded grimly. Even all these years later, he had not ceased to worry about Gloria—her short, vapid letters, her avoidance of his difficult questions, the limited information he could gather from the family about how she was really doing. Something was not right, but he could not get through to her. Though she was set to graduate the following summer, there was no talk of her return.

"After graduation I'll be traveling through Northern Europe with my parents," she had written in her last letter. She didn't mention whether she was excited about that or would rather come home straightaway, whether she would miss school or was considering continuing her education. When she spent her vacations with her parents instead of at school—which had happened three times in the last five years—she did not write at all.

"You'll be happy to see her come back, won't you?" Charlotte asked. She had finished tending to her hair, and was sliding her silken morning dress off her shoulders. Underneath she wore a finely sewn chemise. Jack realized that she had gotten thinner.

"If you want to have children, you need to eat more first," he said, changing the subject and wrapping his arms gently around his wife.

She laughed softly when he picked her up and laid her on the bed.

"You're too tiny to carry a baby."

Charlotte trembled lightly under his kisses, but then came back to Gloria. She did not like talking about her own figure; the Maori women teased her often enough that her husband soon would not like her anymore. Maori men preferred full-bodied women.

"But you may be disappointed," she warned Jack. "The Gloria who comes back probably bears no resemblance to the little girl from back then. She's no longer interested in dogs and horses. She'll love books and music. You should already be practicing your most cultivated conversation."

Jack's reason told him the same thing whenever he read one of Gloria's letters. But his heart would not believe it.

"She should tell Nimue that," he replied with a glance at Gloria's dog, which slept in the hall in front of their door. "And she's the heiress of Kiward Station. She'll have to take an interest in the farm, boarding school or no boarding school."

"Will the dog even still recognize her?"

"Oh, Nimue will remember. As for Gloria, she can't have become a different person. That just can't be."

Gloria tied her hair at the nape of her neck. It was still too thick to be tamed, but it was long now, and the other girls no longer teased her about her boyish hairstyle. It had been a long time since she cared what

Gabrielle, Fiona, and the others said about her. Gloria had developed a sort of buffer around her and simply no longer allowed their taunts to hurt her. That went for the remarks of most of the teachers too, particularly the new music teacher, Miss Beaver. Miss Wedgewood had married Reverend Bleachum three years before and left the school. Miss Beaver was an ardent admirer of Kura-maro-tini Martyn and was eager to meet Gloria, expecting greatness—when that wasn't forthcoming, she settled for details from each concert tour the girl had taken part in over the last few years. Gloria could not report much. She hated the vacations with her parents and the ensemble's members treated her with nothing but contempt.

Kura's interpretations of the *haka* had departed further and further from their traditional presentation; she suited them to Western standards and expected the Maori artists to do the same. The best among them, however, were unwilling to do that. Kura and William had therefore begun using half-*pakeha* performers. They were also closer to Western ideas of beauty, and that became the main criterion for their selection. Dance teachers and impresarios hired the novices and taught them what to do. Kura and William traveled with a sprawling cohort that filled five sleeping and salon cars. The private cars were simply hitched to the trains traveling throughout Europe.

When Gloria traveled with the show, she had to share her car with five other girls, in even closer proximity than at school. Sometimes she was lucky and the young dancers were too self-absorbed to notice anyone other than themselves. But others, jealous of Gloria and her rich and famous parents, liked to pick fights with her. She simply did her best to block out everyone around her.

"Hey, Glory, wake up! Are you still not ready?" Lilian burst into her room, ripping Gloria from her gloomy thoughts.

"What are you wearing?" she asked impatiently. "You don't need to wear your school uniform; this is a picnic! We're going to go watch the Cambridge boys train for the regatta. It'll be fun, Gloria. And we'll meet some boys. We get to leave this convent once a year, and what do you do?"

"I'd rather stay here," Gloria said glumly. "Or row in the boat myself. That must be fun."

Lilian rolled her eyes. "Get up; put on that blue dress your mother bought you in Antwerp. It's pretty and looks good on you."

Gloria sighed and cast a glance at Lilian's hourglass form. She was no doubt wearing a fashionable corset, not that she needed it. Lilian took after her mother and grandmother: short and slender, with curves in all the right places. The reform dress from Antwerp was indeed flattering, but it was hardly the latest thing in fashion, being considered rather an accessory for bluestockings and feminists.

Once Gloria had changed, Lilian plucked Gloria's eyebrows and touched them up with a burnt-out match she blackened with soot from the fireplace.

"There, much better. Trace a thin line around your eyes. Something thicker would suit you better, but Miss Arrowstone would notice and have a fit."

2

"Come on, the coach is about to leave," Lilian urged. Gloria often wondered what made Lilian so loyal to her.

Oaks Garden had an arrangement with the boys' college in Cambridge that allowed for occasional meetings with the girls. The events were closely supervised, but when certain couples nevertheless managed to fall in love, the match was nearly always a suitable one. The girls had to be prepared to come out in society, and that included some interaction with the opposite sex. So it was that fifteen excited girls were going to Cambridge, where the last few elimination races for the legendary rowing regatta were taking place.

The cook at Oaks Garden had prepared a picnic, and the two chaperoning teachers watched over the baskets as if they contained no less than the treasury's gold. The selection of an ideal picnic spot on the banks of the river seemed a huge production as well. As Lilian and her friends endlessly deliberated over the possibilities, Gloria wished herself far away. She would have liked to go for a stroll along the banks of the River Cam alone, observing birds and chasing frogs and lizards. She was still interested in nature, and was always drawing the wildlife she came upon in the fields, but she hadn't shown her pictures to her teachers in ages. Occasionally, she sent them off to Miss Bleachum, who had taken a position in a girls' school in Dunedin and wrote to Gloria regularly. Gloria was making tentative plans with her for after graduation. Dunedin had a university that took a limited number of girls, and she hoped to finally be able to pursue her interest in the natural sciences. Gloria had long since ceased to dream of a return to Kiward Station. It hurt her to remember that lost world, but she would hardly feel secure there now. Her parents had ripped her from there once. There was no guarantee they would not do it again.

Lilian and the others finally chose a spot on the riverbank close to the finish line. That way, the boys would already have their race behind them. They might be worn out, but they would at least have time to dedicate to the young ladies. A few of the girls, Lilian among them, wished to serve as lady luck before the start of the race and strolled over to the starting line before the race. Gloria stayed back and helped the teachers unpack the picnic baskets.

The jetty where the boats were moored was packed with boys. All of them wore collegiate sweaters or shirts, and all were muscular from their daily rowing practice. Lilian peered out coyly from under her parasol, daring an occasional shy smile when her gaze met that of one of the boys, and otherwise chatting with her friends as if she had no interest whatsoever in the opposite sex. Yet she had dedicated hours to her appearance that day. She was wearing a green dress whose neckline and hem were trimmed with brown lace. She wore her red hair down, with a wide sun hat. Though she did not need her parasol—it was March, after all, and a jacket would have been handier than protection from the sun—it was a more flirtatious accessory than a jacket, which would have covered her attractive décolleté.

The boys looked the girls over, knowing that a picnic was awaiting them at the end of the race. This was not the boys' first regatta, so they knew that only the boldest girls turned up at the starting line. The few boys who had sisters or cousins among the boarding-school students had a natural advantage. A friend of Lilian's saw her brother—and was immediately introduced to several young men. She pulled Lily and the other girls into the circle, and the ice was quickly broken. They chatted about the weather—"lovely, a real stroke of luck"—and about the composition of the team. The nomination of one or two of the boys was controversial, and the rowers discussed it volubly.

"Ben? That greenhorn? He can perform, of course, but he still has three years ahead of him to earn some fame. This is Rupert's last chance, and for my money, he's the better of the two."

"Ben trains harder."

"Ben is trying too hard."

Lilian listened, bored, and wondered who these boys were. Ben sounded interesting. It sounded as though he was younger than the others, which suited Lilian.

When one of the boys pointed out Rupert, a tall, broad-shouldered young man flirting with some other girls, Lily realized at once that he was out of the question for her. She did not like his boastful manner, which was recognizable even from a distance; besides, he was really too old for her. Then her gaze fell on a blond boy doing stretching exercises in a nearby inlet. Lilian thought he looked young and trustworthy. She casually separated from the group and strolled over to him, her heart beating a little faster as she did. Surely the chaperones would not want her wandering off on her own. But it was pleasant in the inlet, quieter than on the jetty. She could hear the boy's heavy breathing and make out his muscles straining beneath his thin shirt. Though clearly strong, he was slender, even wiry.

"Do you really believe that will help now?" Lilian asked.

The boy turned around, startled. He seemed to have been completely focused on his exercises. Lilian found herself looking into a clear, narrow face dominated by alert, light-green eyes. Though his face was perhaps a little colorless, his features were finely carved. His full lips were pursed in concentration.

"What?"

"Your exercises," Lilian continued. "I mean, if you can't do it by now, you won't be able to learn it before the race."

The boy laughed.

"They're not those kind of exercises; they're warm-ups. That way you get into the swing of things quicker when the time comes. Real athletes do them."

"I don't know much about sports," she admitted. "But if they're so helpful, why aren't the others doing them too?"

"Because they'd rather chat with the girls. They don't really take it seriously."

"Are you Ben?"

The boy laughed. "What did they tell you about me? Let me guess: 'Ben tries too hard.'"

It was Lilian's turn to laugh—a little conspiratorially. The boy looked her over, not without interest.

"It's not true, though," she remarked. "The way I see it, Ben is also chatting with a girl. Your boat's still going to lose the race." She winked at him while playing coyly with her parasol. Ben did not seem to notice, however; the reminder about the race caused him to drift off into his own world again.

"It doesn't matter anyway. They're going to nominate this Rupert Landon fellow for the final regatta. Because he's rowed in an eight every year of college. Even though we've lost every time he was stroke. The bloke puts on a good show. And so he's to get another chance for his last year."

"And you can't both row? I mean, there are eight places."

"But only one stroke. Hence Rupert or myself." Ben went back to his stretches.

"The stroke sets the pace, right?" Lilian asked.

Ben nodded. "Simply put, he makes sure the oars go in at even intervals. That's why he needs a good sense of rhythm. Which Rupert hasn't got."

"More's the pity for Cambridge. But you're still in your first year, aren't you? You can win next year." She sat down in the grass and watched him stretch. He moved lithely, a bit like a dancer. Lilian liked what she saw.

Ben made a face. "If there is a next time. Mr. Hallows, our history teacher, thinks there will be war."

Lilian looked at him, shocked. She hadn't heard anything about a war. The history imparted at Oaks Garden ended with the death of Queen Victoria. War had to do with Florence Nightingale. Kipling wrote something about it. But otherwise it was a heroic tale with horses and knight's armor.

"With whom?" she asked.

"I'm not entirely clear on that myself. Mr. Hallows isn't sure either, but there's no rowing in a war."

"That would be a real shame. Could you win today at least?"

Ben nodded, and his eyes flashed. "Today my eight is going up against his."

Lilian smiled. "Then I wish you luck. I'm Lily, by the way. From Oaks Garden. We're having a picnic at the finish line. Join us if you like. Even if you don't win."

"I'll win," said Ben, dedicating himself to his warm-ups again.

Lily remained a few more minutes, but then had the feeling she was in the way.

"Well, until then!" she said.

Ben did not hear her.

Lilian followed the race sitting on a blanket with Gloria. Lilian explained how her new friend Ben was commanding one of the eights, and was already talking about the steering of the boats as if she had spent the last three years on one.

When the race began, the girls cheered for their favorites. Though Ben initially kept his eight even with his opponent, he pulled ahead for the last third of the race and won by a good distance.

Lilian leaped up with excitement.

"He won! Now they have to let him start in London. They have to. Otherwise it wouldn't be fair!"

Ben, however, looked crestfallen as he strolled over to the girls.

"I told you they would choose Rupert," he declared, and Lilian thought she saw something like tears in his eyes. "Regardless if I won. And that's just what happened."

Lilian looked at him sympathetically. "But the race was fantastic. And if Cambridge loses in London now, everyone will know why. Come, eat something. These chicken legs are really good, and you can eat them with your hands. And this is gooseberry wine from the kitchen's garden. Well, not really wine, more like juice. But it's good."

Lilian served the boy quite naturally, laughing as she did so. Gloria wondered how she could chat with him so easily. Not that Ben intimidated her particularly, but she would not have known what to talk to him about.

"What's it like in college?" Lilian asked, her mouth full. "Is it terribly hard? Everyone says you have to be very smart to go to Cambridge."

"Sometimes it's merely a question of the right family connections," he explained. "If your father and grandfather went to Cambridge, everything is much simpler."

"And? Did yours? What do you study, anyway?"

"You don't look like a college student," Lilian's friend Hazel interjected. She had been unable to lure any boy into taking a place on her blanket and now wanted to take part in Lilian's conquest. She did not go about it very skillfully, however, and Ben reddened at once.

"I skipped a few years," he admitted, giving Lilian a wry smile. "I try too hard, as they say. And then Cambridge offered me a scholarship. Literature, languages, and English history. My parents are not exactly enthusiastic."

"That's silly of your parents," Lilian said, which caused Miss Beaver to rebuke her.

Ben, who found himself unintentionally at the center of all the female attention, coughed.

"I, er, must be going. I mean, I need to join my friends. But perhaps, would you care to accompany me a few steps, Lily? Just as far as the docks, of course."

Lily beamed. "Gladly," she said, about to stand up. But then she thought better of it at the last moment. Instead, she held her hand out to Ben for him to help her up and gracefully rose from her blanket.

"I'll be right back," she said to the group, shouldering her lacy parasol and floating off next to Ben.

Ben sighed with relief. But what was he to do now with the girl? He couldn't take her over to join the raucous boys whose eight he had just led to victory. One of them would probably steal her from him. Fortunately Lilian steered them straight to the copse of trees as soon as they were out of sight of the teachers.

"Let's go this way. It's shady over here. Such a warm day, don't you think?"

This last remark was not entirely true, but Ben nodded energetically. As they took a path that led through the woods, both of them felt freer than they had in a long time. He felt remarkably good with this lovely, smiling, chatty girl beside him. In her jingling, bright voice, she told him about Oaks Garden and how she, too, had been one of the youngest students when she first came.

"I was sent to boarding school with my cousin Gloria. Her parents insisted on sending her, but she's shy, and we come from very far away. I was sent with her so that she did not feel so alone. But she does anyway. Some people always feel alone."

Ben nodded with understanding. Lilian seemed to sense instinctively how he felt. Alone. He had had little in common with his classmates, even less with the much older boys in college. Ben was lucky that the work was easy for him and that he enjoyed it. Geology did not fascinate him like it did his father, nor did he favor economics like his mother. Ben saw himself more as a poet. As he found himself saying that aloud to someone for the first time, Lilian listened, rapt.

"Do you know any of your poems by heart? Please recite one!"

Ben reddened. "I don't know. I've never. No, I can't manage it. The words would get away from me."

Lilian frowned. "Oh, nonsense. If you really want to be a poet, you'll have to give readings someday. Come now."

The blood shot more intensely to Ben's face as he recited, turning his head from Lilian.

If you were a rose, I would swim to you through the dew.
If you were a leaf in a storm, with the wind I'd sing to you,
And I would know what you might be or who
Thinking songs for you until in dreams you might kiss me too.

"Oh, how lovely," Lilian sighed. "So deeply felt."

The boy looked at her sheepishly but did not detect any ridicule in her dreamy face.

"It even rhymes properly."

Ben nodded, his eyes shining.

"How old are you anyway?"

Ben reddened again. "Almost fifteen."

"Me too! That's a sign."

"That *is* a sign. Miss, I mean, Lilian, do you want to see me again?"

Lilian lowered her eyes demurely. "We could only meet in secret," she said tentatively. "You might be able to leave the college, but I . . ."

"Is there no way?" Ben asked. "I mean, I could come on Saturday, you know, and say I was your cousin or something."

Lilian laughed. "No one would believe that." She considered whether she should tell Ben about her New Zealand heritage, but refrained for the moment. She did not want to talk with the boy about coal and gold mines, whaling, and sheep husbandry.

"But I know a way, don't worry. If you walk a quarter mile south from the school gate along the fence, you'll come to a huge oak. Its branches reach over the fence, and it's easy to climb over. Wait for me there. You can help me climb over." To which she added coquettishly, "But you aren't to look up my skirt."

Ben reddened again, but was now unequivocally enthralled. "I'll come," he said breathlessly. "But it will be awhile. I have to go to London first. As a reserve oarsman I'll no doubt be assigned to a boat."

"I can wait," she said seriously—deep down finding it romantic. "But I fear we must return to the others. Hazel will be wondering what happened to me, and jealous as she is, she'll point out to Miss Beaver if I'm gone too long." She began to turn around, but Ben stopped her.

"Wait a moment. I know it's not proper, but I have to look into your eyes just now. I've been trying all afternoon, but I didn't want to stare. And so I couldn't tell exactly. Are they green or brown?"

Ben awkwardly laid his hands on Lilian's shoulders and drew her closer to him. He would never have admitted to her that he usually wore glasses.

Lily smiled and pushed back her wide hat. “Sometimes they’re green, sometimes brown, sprinkled a bit like cave pearl. When I’m happy they’re green; when I’m sad, brown.”

“And when you’re in love?” Ben asked.

He was not to find out that afternoon, as Lilian closed her eyes when he kissed her.

3

"It can't go on like this, Charlotte. Even Rongo Rongo thinks you should see a doctor in Christchurch."

Jack had long hesitated to speak to Charlotte about her headaches, but when he came home after a long day and found her once again racked with pain in a darkened room, he felt he had to say something. She had tied a wool shawl around her head, and her face looked pale, haggard, and contorted with pain.

"It's just a migraine, dearest," she said, trying to diminish it. "You know I've always gotten them."

"But this is the third time this month. That's far too many."

"It's the weather, my love, but I can get up and come down to dinner. It's just, I get dizzy so easily." Charlotte attempted to sit up.

"Don't get up, for heaven's sake!" Jack kissed her and pushed her gently back on her pillows. "I'll bring you dinner in bed. But do me a favor and don't blame it on the weather. We'll visit your parents, have a few nice days to ourselves, and go see a specialist who knows more about headaches than our village doctor. OK?"

Charlotte nodded. She just wanted to be left alone. She loved Jack, and his presence comforted her and eased her pain. But every conversation was a struggle. She felt sick at the thought of food, but she would pull herself together and manage a few bites. Jack ought not to worry. It was enough that she worried herself.

Lilian yearned after Ben but realized the day after the boat race that they had not set a specific date for their rendezvous. She had no idea when Ben would be waiting for her at the garden fence—or whether he had completely forgotten her. When the summer began without any sign of him, Lilian assumed the latter. But then her friend Meredith Rodhurst went home for the weekend and she saw her brother Julius, the Cambridge student Lily had met briefly at the boat race. When she came back to Oaks Garden, she was almost bursting with excitement.

"Lily, do you still think of the boy you invited to the picnic? Ben?"

Lilian's heart beat faster, but before she said anything, she pulled Meredith into the furthest corner of the corridor leading to the classrooms. This conversation was not for everyone.

"Of course I still think of Ben. Ever since destiny parted us, there hasn't been a minute in which I have not dreamed of him."

Meredith snorted with laughter. "'Ever since destiny parted us!' You're crazy."

"I'm in love," Lilian declared grandly.

"He is too," she declared. "My brother says he's always coming here and slinking around our garden like a lovestruck tomcat. But that won't do any good, of course. He needs more than luck."

Lilian's brain worked feverishly. "Couldn't we write each other? Your brother knows his last name, and . . ."

Meredith beamed at her. "You don't need to write him. I told Julius you'd meet Ben at the 'escape oak' on Friday at five."

Lilian leaped into her friend's arms.

"Oh, Meredith, I'll never forget this. What should I wear? I have so much to do."

Lilian floated away. She would spend the rest of the week making her plans. And counting the hours.

The question of which of her friends to let in on her big secret occupied Lilian for two full days. The chances of getting caught increased with each confidante. In the end, she only told Hazel and Gloria. Although the latter did not seem to care, Hazel trembled with excitement and helped with the careful selection of clothing and accessories. By Friday at four they had ruled out five different outfits, and the sixth dress, the one Lilian had finally thought suitable, proved to have a spot on it. Lilian was close to tears.

"But you can just brush it out," Hazel said. "Let me do it. Have you thought about what you're going to tell Miss Beaver? She'll be furious if you skip choir."

"I'll tell her I had a headache. Or, better yet, you tell her I've been having migraines lately. It runs in the family."

"Really?" Hazel asked.

Lilian shrugged. "Not that I know of. Although Uncle Jack's wife gets them, so it's not a total lie. In any case, choir is the best time to sneak out. Everyone's busy, even Mary Jane."

Mary Jane was Lilian and Hazel's sworn enemy. The girls could be sure that she would reveal any secret plans to the teacher. At ten minutes past four, just after Lilian had finished putting on her dress, there was a knock on the door. Lilian had a bad feeling when she saw that it was Alison, Mary Jane's best friend.

"You're to go to Miss Arrowstone, Lily," Alison reported. "Immediately."

Lilian spun around. "You didn't say anything, did you, Hazel? And Gloria . . ." Lilian could not imagine Gloria betraying her. But Miss Arrowstone had to know something.

"No one told me anything. I just happened to be walking down the hall, and Miss Arrowstone saw me and charged me with fetching you. Maybe you have a visitor."

Lilian blushed. A visitor? Ben? Had he not been able to restrain himself and was now trying to pass himself off as her cousin? Or had someone seen him at the fence and figured out why he was there? She would not put it past Mary Jane.

"And if you don't get going, there will be trouble," Alison remarked. "Why are you so dressed up anyway?"

Lilian hesitated. Should she change or not? If her meeting with Miss Arrowstone was brief, she would still be able to make the rendezvous. On the other hand, Miss Arrowstone would suspect something if she showed up in her Sunday best.

"Well, get going," Alison prodded her.

Lilian made her decision. If there was any chance of seeing Ben, she would have to accept a bit of trouble from Miss Arrowstone.

Miss Arrowstone was not alone in her office. Nor was she in a particularly good mood. She was conversing with an older man.

He turned around when Lilian entered.

"Lily! My lands, how pretty you are! As lovely as your mother at that age. You look much more grown up than in your photos."

"Which might be because our pupils wear their school uniforms to their photograph appointments," Miss Arrowstone remarked drily. "What gives us the dubious pleasure of seeing you dressed up as if for a ball?"

Lilian ignored her.

"Uncle George!" she exclaimed and flew into the arms of George Greenwood. The primary shareholder in the Lambert Mine had been a frequent guest of her parents in Greymouth, and Lilian's mother had been calling him uncle ever since *she* was a child. For Lilian and her brothers he was likewise almost family.

"How nice of you to come," Lilian said warmly. She even had some charm left over for Miss Arrowstone. "Alison told me I had a special visitor, so I changed quickly," she explained.

Miss Arrowstone snorted, disbelieving.

"In any event, you look enchanting, child," George declared. "But have a seat first before we get to the reason for my visit, which unfortunately is not a happy one."

Lilian turned pale. She did not know if she was permitted to sit in Miss Arrowstone's office. But if so, it was because exceptionally bad news awaited her.

"Is something wrong with Mummy, with Daddy?"

George shook his head. "They're well. Forgive me, Lily, if I scared you. Your brothers are also well. It's just that I'm concerned. I think that I'm not making myself very clear just now."

He smiled apologetically.

"But what is it then?" Lilian asked, still standing, and shifting her weight from one foot to the other.

"You may sit," Miss Arrowstone said graciously.

Lilian sat down on the edge of a visitor's chair.

"Maybe you'll be pleased about what I'm here to tell you," he remarked. "Though your parents told me that you're very happy here. That speaks well for your motivation and this school." Another nod, this time in the direction of Miss Arrowstone. "But nevertheless, I've been charged with taking you home on the next ship."

"What? Home? To Greymouth? Now? But why? I, I mean, I just have one year left." But she was thinking only of Ben. The room seemed to spin.

"Haven't you heard of the assassination in Sarajevo, Lilian?" her uncle asked. He looked at Miss Arrowstone, this time punitively, when Lilian shook her head.

"On the twenty-eighth of June. The heir to the Austro-Hungarian throne was murdered."

Lilian shrugged. "I'm very sorry for Austria-Hungary," she said politely, but completely disinterested. "And naturally for the family of his imperial highness."

"His wife was also shot. Well-informed circles in Europe are afraid it will lead to an outbreak of war. The government of Austria-Hungary has already made an ultimatum to Serbia to put the assassin on trial. If that doesn't happen, they'll declare war on Serbia."

"And?" Lilian asked. She only had a vague idea of where Serbia and Austria were on the map, but as far as she knew, both countries were far from Cambridge.

"Several alliances will come into play then, Lilian," George informed her. "I can't explain the details here, but war's been smoldering in several parts of the world. Once the fuse is lit, Europe will go up in flames, perhaps the whole world. It's unlikely there will be fighting in Australia and New Zealand, but your parents and I don't think England will be safe, and certainly not the sea. That's why we want you home before anything happens. Maybe it's overly cautious, as your teacher here believes"—George indicated Miss Arrowstone with his chin—"but we don't want to take any chances."

"But I want to stay here!" Lilian screamed. "My friends are here and . . ." She blushed.

George Greenwood smiled conspiratorially. "And perhaps a boyfriend? Perhaps all the more reason to hurry you home?"

Lilian said nothing.

"Well, it doesn't really matter how you feel about it," Miss Arrowstone remarked with drawn lips. "Just as this gentleman and your parents seem rather indifferent to my opinion on your completing your education in New Zealand. If I have understood Mr. Greenwood correctly, a ship is leaving London on July twenty-eighth for Lyttelton. A ticket has been booked for you. You'll be traveling to London with Mr. Greenwood tonight. You may skip choir. Your friends can help you pack."

Lilian wanted to throw a fit, but saw that there would be no sense in it. Then something struck her hard.

"What about Gloria?"

"So the war has begun?" Elizabeth Greenwood asked, balancing her teacup delicately between two fingers.

Charlotte did not hold hers quite so properly. Looking pale and nervous, she wrapped her hands around the fine porcelain as if to warm herself. The war in Europe was of no interest to her. She was much too preoccupied by her upcoming appointment with Dr. Alistar Barrington, a young internist with a reputation that extended far beyond Christchurch. Charlotte and Jack had had spent the night at her parents' house, wrapped in each other's arms and in a shared fear they did not want to voice aloud. Each had pretended to be more relaxed than the other. But now Jack showed his anxiety by talking more than usual.

"Austria-Hungary has declared war on Serbia," he explained. "That means the German Empire will get involved. Apparently they're already mobilizing. And Russia is allied with Serbia, France with Russia."

"Well, at least England has nothing to do with it," she said, relieved. "It's bad enough that the others will be knocking their heads together."

Jack shook his head. "George sees it differently. Great Britain has alliances with France and Russia. Maybe it will hold off at first. But over time . . ."

"Do you think it will it be a long war?" Charlotte asked.

Jack shrugged, but stroked her hand soothingly. "I don't know. I don't know anything about war, love. But it will hardly reach us here. Don't worry."

Jack glanced at his pocket watch.

"It's time, dear. Are you ready?"

Charlotte nodded. Jack looked just as anxious and miserable as she felt.

"Of course," she said with a forced smile. "I only hope the doctor won't keep us long. You don't mind if we visit the lady's tailor afterward, do you?" Her voice sounded pinched.

Jack shook his head, likewise striving for a casual smile. "I promised my father I'd pick up some scotch too. He claims nothing helps more with joint pain than rubbing them with good scotch. Not to mention the internal application."

Everyone laughed, but only Elizabeth actually seemed untroubled. Charlotte had experienced migraines her whole life. And she remained firmly convinced that these headaches, too, would prove to be nothing.

"Gloria!" George Greenwood was surprised. He had naturally expected Lilian when the proprietress of the pub where he'd just finished his supper announced that he had a visitor.

A perspiring, somewhat big-boned brunette now stood in front of him in an ill-fitting, pale-blue school uniform. George had known her as a happy child who had had been proud of "being one of the boys," as Gwyneira had laughingly described her. She was a bold rider, and he had watched, fascinated, as she had worked side by side with Jack during the shearing. She was so lively and skilled in the execution of her duties on the farm that George had easily overlooked her shyness toward strangers and her occasional awkwardness at social events.

The girl now standing before him had nothing in common with that self-assured little rider and dog trainer. Although she was close to tears, Gloria tried hard to maintain the anger that had moved her to this spontaneous action. Lily's report of Greenwood's appearance, her outrage at her parents' decision, and the trouble over this "stupid war" that was ruining her rendezvous with Ben had caused Gloria to boil over. For the first time since her days with Miss Bleachum, Gloria had left school without permission and run through the park, leaping up into the escape tree. On the other side she came upon the blond boy Lilian was so crazy about. He must have been frantic with worry, as five o'clock had long since passed.

"Do you have any news about Lily?" he asked as Gloria slid down to the ground in front of him. "Why hasn't she come?"

Gloria had no desire to bother with him.

"Lilian is going home," she explained curtly. "There's a war."

Ben began bombarding her with questions, but she rushed off to the village. She had not asked Lilian where she would find George Greenwood, but there were not many possibilities. Gloria found him straightaway in the first pub.

"It's not right!" she blurted out. "You have to take me, Uncle George. Maybe Jack doesn't care about me anymore now that he's married, but I have a right to be at Kiward Station. You can't take Lilian and leave me. That just won't do."

Gloria's eyes filled with tears.

George was taken off guard. He knew how to conduct tough negotiations with merchant houses all over the world. But nothing had prepared him for crying girls.

"Now, now, have a seat, Gloria. I'll have them bring you some tea. Or would you prefer lemonade? You look thirsty."

Gloria shook her head, causing her wild locks to free themselves from the careless knot she had tied at the nape of her neck.

"I don't want tea or lemonade. I want Kiward Station."

"You'll have that, too, eventually, Gloria," he said, trying to calm her. "But first things first. What's this nonsense about Jack, Gloria? Of course he still cares about you. Gwyn told me expressly to intervene with your parents when she heard that the Lamberts were bringing Lilian home. I can show you the telegrams."

Gloria's already tense features tightened further. She bit her lip.

"My parents don't want me to go? They don't care what will happen to me if there's a war?"

Until that moment Gloria had not wasted a thought on the actual outbreak of war. But now it dawned on her that perhaps Lilian's parents were not acting on a whim but out of serious concern.

"Certainly not, Gloria. On the contrary, your father may see the political situation more clearly than I. He's been living in Europe a long time, after all. As far as I know, you're likewise to leave school. At least for a while. William hopes the war will end soon and that you can properly finish your education. But this summer you'll be accompanying your parents to America. The tour has been planned for a long time, and for the moment there's no expectation that the United States will enter the war. The trip is supposed to last six months since the distance between venues is so vast. There won't be a performance every day. Kura will have more time to herself than usual, and she's looking forward to getting to know you better."

George smiled at Gloria as if he had just given her good news. But Gloria still seemed to be fighting back tears.

"To America? Even further away?" What could her mother possibly want from her? Gloria had hardly exchanged more than a few words with her during the last three summers they had spent together. And those words had rarely been edifying. "Don't stand in the way, Gloria"; "Pay a little more attention to what you wear, Gloria"; "Why don't you play the piano more often?" Gloria could not imagine that spending more time with her mother would bring them closer together.

"And after that, I'm to return to school?" Gloria was already almost nineteen, older than most of the other pupils at Oaks Garden. She had had enough of boarding school.

"I suppose we'll see when the time comes. Just let things take their course, Gloria. I can only tell you that it has nothing to do with your relatives in New Zealand. As Gwyn sees it, you could come back tomorrow."

George wanted to offer to have Gloria driven back to the school in his carriage, but when she walked out, exhausted and defeated, he did not dare follow. She might break down crying—a scene he would not have known how to handle.

He determined to speak once more with Gwyneira, James, and Jack when he arrived home. There had to be some way of changing William's and Kura's minds. This girl was as unhappy as could be. And traveling across America clearly wasn't going to raise her spirits.

"I can't really make a diagnosis, Mrs. McKenzie," Dr. Barrington said after thoroughly examining Charlotte. "But I am deeply concerned. It's still possible you merely suffer from migraines. It often happens that they become more frequent. But combined with the vertigo, the weight loss, your, hmm, irregular cycle . . ." Charlotte had blushingly admitted that, despite their best efforts, her desire for a child remained unfulfilled.

"Is it something serious?" Jack asked. The young doctor had just called him in; he had spent the last hour quaking and praying on a hard chair in the waiting room.

"Unfortunately, it might be," he said.

Jack's nerves were strained to the breaking point. "Maybe you shouldn't keep us on tenterhooks and just tell us what it might be."

Charlotte gave the impression she did not want to know. But Jack was a man who liked to look danger in the eye.

"Like I said, I can't make a diagnosis. But a few of your symptoms—though I can't be at all sure—could indicate a brain tumor."

"And what would that mean?" Jack pressed.

"I can't say for certain, Mr. McKenzie. It would depend on where the tumor is located, if it's even possible to locate it, and how quickly it's growing. All of that has to be examined. But I can't do it."

At least the man was honest. Charlotte put her hand into her husband's.

"Does that mean I'm going to die?" she asked hoarsely.

"For the moment none of it necessarily means anything. I think you should see Dr. Friedman in Auckland as quickly as possible. He's a brain specialist who studied with Professor von Bergmann in Berlin. If there's a brain expert and surgeon in this part of the world, then it's him."

"You mean, he'll cut the tumor out of me?" Charlotte asked.

"If it's possible," Barrington said. "But you shouldn't brood on it for the time being. Make the journey to Auckland and consult Dr. Friedman. But approach it calmly. Make a vacation of it. Take in the sights on the North Island. And try to forget what I've said. You may come back in a month, and your wife will be pregnant. With migraines, as with problems conceiving, I recommend a change of air."

Charlotte held Jack's hand in a vise grip when they stepped back onto the street.

"Do you still want to go to the lady's tailor?" he asked quietly.

Charlotte wanted to nod bravely, but then she saw his face and shook her head. "And you? Do you want to buy the whiskey?"

Jack pulled her closer to him. "I'll buy tickets to Blenheim. And then for the ferry to the North Island. For our vacation." His voice sounded gravelly.

Charlotte leaned in to him. "I've always wanted to see Waitangi," she said quietly.

"And the rain forests," Jack added.

"Tane Mahuta." Charlotte smiled. The Maori considered the massive kauri tree in the Waipoua Forest to be the god of the forest.

"Maybe not that," Jack whispered. "I don't want anything to do with gods who separate lovers."

4

Although Great Britain had been mobilized since the beginning of August, no one at Oaks Garden initially paid any notice to the war. Everyone assumed it would be a short war and volunteers flocked to the banners.

Gloria was fixated on her departure, which was set for August 20. The Martyns would be traveling with a small troupe and would recruit more dancers in America; Maori ancestry was no longer considered so important. Most of the singers and dancers coming along had been with the troupe for years and knew how to train new performers. One of them, Tamatea, appeared on August 19 to fetch Gloria.

Miss Arrowstone was decidedly ungracious when she called the girl into her office. Tamatea spread her arms out when Gloria entered.

"Gloria! *Haere mai!* I'm happy to see you."

Tamatea's whole face shone, and Gloria willingly fell into her arms.

"I'm happy too, *taua*," Gloria said. Her Maori was rusty, but she still remembered the greetings. Tamatea was clearly delighted at having been greeted as her grandmother. She belonged to the same generation as Kura's mother, Marama, and came from the same tribe. Thus, even though they were not related, she was considered to be among Gloria's "grandparents." And Tamatea had been the next best thing to a relative for Gloria when she was touring with her parents.

"It seems your parents could not find the time to pick you up," Miss Arrowstone said pointedly.

Tamatea nodded. "Yes. There's a great deal to do to prepare. That's why they sent me. Are you ready, Gloria? Then let's go!"

Gloria delighted in the appalled expression on Miss Arrowstone's face. A short while later, they were on their way. The journey with

Tamatea was much more pleasant than it would have been with William or Kura. The last few times, when her father had picked her up, conversation had been limited to an examination of the subject matter of the previous school year and a thorough description of Kura's successes, interspersed with complaints about the cost of dancers and transportation.

"Are you excited about America, *taua*?" Gloria inquired once she was sitting with Tamatea in the carriage to Cambridge. As Oaks Garden disappeared into the horizon, Gloria did not look back.

Tamatea shrugged. "For me, one country is like another," she said. "None is like that of the Ngai Tahu."

Gloria nodded sadly. "Will you go back someday?"

The older woman nodded. "Certainly. Maybe even soon. I grow too old for the stage. At least that's what your parents think. At home it is not unusual for grandmothers to dance and sing. But here only young people do that. I hardly perform anymore. Mostly I apply makeup to the girls—and I train them. The makeup is important. I paint the old tattoos on the faces. Then people can't see that the dancers aren't real Maori."

Gloria smiled. "Will you paint me sometime too, *taua*?"

Tamatea looked at her searchingly. "On you it would look real. You have the blood of the Ngai Tahu."

Gloria did not know why those words filled her with such pride. But after her conversation with Tamatea, she began to feel better than she had in a long time. It gave her the courage to approach her mother with her head held high.

William Martyn was overseeing the unloading of some crates of props as Tamatea and Gloria pulled up in front of the Ritz. A final good-bye concert was planned here before Kura and her troupe departed for the States.

"There you are, Tamatea. And Gloria! Wonderful to see you, my girl." William kissed her fleetingly on the cheek. "Take her straight up to her mother, Tamatea. Kura will be happy to see you, Glory. You can give her a hand." With that, he returned to his task.

Gloria's heart beat heavily. What could she possibly help her mother with?

The suite was located on the top floor. Gloria entered the elevator with a slight shiver as always. So did Tamatea. "If the gods had wanted man to betake himself to Rangi's arms, they would have given him wings," she whispered to Gloria as the elevator boy told her about the wonderful view from that floor.

"Come in." Kura seemed to sing even those simple words in her melodious voice.

"Gloria! Come in. I've been waiting for hours." Kura Martyn had been sitting at the grand piano looking through some notes. Now she got up eagerly and went to Gloria. She still looked young and lithe; no one would have believed she had a nineteen-year-old daughter. Kura herself was only in her midthirties.

Gloria greeted her shyly and waited for the usual remarks: how big she'd grown and how adult she looked—her mother always seemed surprised that Gloria was growing up. Kura Martyn had only grown more beautiful in recent years. Her hip-length hair was still a deep black—though now artfully put up. Her clear skin was the color of creamy coffee, and her eyes shone an azure blue. Her heavy eyelids gave her a dreamy expression and her full lips were a delicate red. She had her clothing custom made without regard for current fashion, and the designs unfailingly emphasized her figure, flirting with and flattering her curves.

"You must help me a bit, dear. Marisa, my pianist, has gotten sick—and right before the farewell concert in England. A rather nasty flu. She can hardly stay on her feet."

Gloria had a bad feeling.

"Don't worry, you don't have to accompany us onstage. We know that you have stage fright." Gloria could almost hear what Kura didn't say: *Aside from the fact that you're not very easy on the eyes.* Kura continued, "But I've just received a new arrangement. And it's gorgeous, a sort of ballad. The *haka* takes place in the background, a simple dance. Tamatea taught it to the dancers in five minutes. And in the foreground the spirits tell the story at the heart of the ballad. First a piece of music for the piano and *putorino*—just the spirit voice, very ethereal—and then piano and singing. I would just love to take it onstage tomorrow. It would be a worthy finale but also make people hungry for new material. But Marisa can't do it. If you play the piano part a few times, I'll be able to practice the flute. Here's the music. Sit down. It's quite simple."

Kura adjusted the piano stool for Gloria and took up the little flute she had laid on the piano. Gloria thumbed through the handwritten sheet music helplessly.

She had taken piano lessons for the last five years, and she did not lack dexterity. If she practiced long enough, she could even manage difficult pieces, but it was always an effort. Gloria had never sight-read music before. Her music teacher had always liked to first play the pieces they would be working on, pointing out trouble spots, and then going over them bar by bar.

Yet Gloria did not dare refuse now. With a will born of desperation, she struggled through the piece to please her mother. Kura listened, rather stunned, but did not interrupt her until she messed up for the third time on the same bar.

"An F-sharp, Gloria. Don't you see the sign in front of the F? Surely you've played it before. My God, are you just playing dumb, or are you really so untalented? Try it again."

Gloria, her nerves now completely shattered, tried but soon got stuck again.

"Maybe if you play it for me first?" she asked.

"Why should I play it for you? Can't you read?" Kura pointed to the sheet music with frustration. "Heavens, girl, what are we to do with you? I thought I could use you, but it is clear I cannot. Go to your room. I'll call the concierge. This is London, after all. We should be able to find a pianist who can assist me temporarily. And you'll listen to her play, Gloria. Your teachers at school have clearly let your education slide."

While her mother was on the phone, Gloria slunk around the suite until she finally found a room with a single bed. She threw herself on it and cried. She was ugly, useless, and dumb. She had no idea how she was supposed to survive the next six months.

Charlotte McKenzie needed two days to recover from the passage from Blenheim to Wellington. Jack was doing his best to make the trip pleasant, and Charlotte made every effort to enjoy it. She ate lobster in Kaikoura and pretended to care about the whales and dolphins they saw from a little boat. But the passage to the North Island had been too much for her. The sea was rough, and Charlotte never did have sea legs. She succumbed to vomiting again and again and was so dizzy by the end she could hardly walk. Jack practically carried her from the pier to the carriage and finally to the hotel room.

"We should leave for Auckland as soon as you feel better," he said when she once again covered the windows and got out the wool wrap. However, warmth and darkness had long ceased to offer much relief. Only the opium tincture that Dr. Barrington had prescribed helped anymore, but that muted not only her headaches but also her feelings and perception.

"But there was so much you wanted to see," Charlotte objected. "The rain forest. And Rotorua, the hot springs, the geysers."

Jack shook his head furiously. "To hell with all the geysers and trees on the whole North Island. We came here to see Dr. Friedman. I only said it because . . ."

"Because this is supposed to be a vacation," she said gently. "And because you didn't want me to worry."

"But you wanted to go to Waitangi. We can drive past there," Jack said, trying to calm himself.

Charlotte shook her head. "I only said that for the same reason."

Jack looked at her helplessly. But then something came to him. "We can do it on the return trip. We'll visit the doctor first. And once he's said that everything's all right, we'll travel the island. Sound good?"

"Yes, we'll do that," she said quietly.

"By the way, it's called Te Ika-a-Maui—Maui's fish. The North Island, I mean." Jack knew he was talking too much, but he could not bear to be silent. "The demigod Maui pulled it as a fish out of the sea."

"And his brothers hacked at it to partition it out, creating the mountains, cliffs, and valleys," Charlotte completed the story.

Jack admonished himself for his foolishness. Charlotte probably knew the Maori legend better than he did.

"He was a clever fellow anyway, that Maui," she continued, lost in thought. "He could slow down the sun. When the days passed too quickly for him, he caught it and forced it to move more slowly. I'd like to do that too."

Jack took her in his arms. "We'll leave for Auckland tomorrow."

Although a railroad connection had been in place for several years, the journey to Auckland could not be done in one day. The North Island Main Trunk Railway led up and down mountains, often through breathtakingly beautiful landscapes, but for Charlotte the journey was no less arduous than the sea passage.

"On the way back we'll take a slower route," Jack promised on the final day of their three-day journey.

Charlotte nodded indifferently. She yearned for a bed that did not move beneath her. It was hard to believe she had ever enjoyed their honeymoon in George Greenwood's private car. Back then she had drunk sparkling wine and laughed at the shaky bed. Now she could hardly keep a sip of tea down.

Both were relieved when they reached Auckland, but neither had a taste for the beauty of the city.

"We have to climb Mount Hobson or Mount Eden; the view is supposed to be fantastic," Jack remarked listlessly. The terrace-covered mountains cast a lush green glow over the city. The sea, its tide calmed by dozens of volcanic islands, looked an inviting azure blue, and Grafton

Bridge, the longest arched bridge in the world, completed only a few years earlier, stylishly spanned the Grafton Gully.

"Later," Charlotte said. She had stretched out on their hotel bed and wanted nothing more than to feel Jack's arms around her and imagine that this was nothing more than a bad dream. She was asleep in minutes.

First thing the next morning Jack set out in search of Dr. Friedman's practice. The brain specialist resided on the upscale Queen Street, which was lined with stately Victorian houses.

Jack rode the tram, a mode of transport that had always given him a childlike pleasure in Christchurch. On that sunny summer day in Auckland, however, he was only filled with fear and foreboding. But the doctor's manorial stone house inspired confidence—he had to be successful if he could afford such an elegant building. Dr. Barrington had already written Dr. Friedman. So when a secretary announced Jack, he didn't have to wait long before being ushered into the doctor's office.

Dr. Friedman was a short, rather delicate man with a bushy beard. He was no longer young—Jack placed him at over sixty—but his light-blue eyes looked as alert and curious as a much younger man's. The surgeon listened attentively as Jack described Charlotte's symptoms to him.

"So it's gotten worse since you consulted with Dr. Barrington?" he asked calmly.

Jack nodded. "My wife attributes it to traveling. She's always gotten seasick and the neck-breaking train route didn't help. She's suffering from increased dizziness and nausea."

Dr. Friedman smiled paternally. "Maybe she's pregnant," he suggested.

Jack did not manage to return the smile. "If only God would show us that mercy," he whispered.

Dr. Friedman sighed. "At the moment God is not exactly distributing his mercy with both hands," he murmured. "This senseless war alone into which Europe has blundered. How many lives will be destroyed there, how much money will be wasted that research needs so desperately? Medicine has begun to make rapid strides, young man. But for the next few years it will come to a standstill, and the only skills doctors will develop will be the amputation of limbs and the treating of bullet wounds. Bring your wife to me just as soon as she feels strong enough. I don't like to make house calls since all of my diagnostic instruments are here. And I hope with all my heart that everything proves benign."

Charlotte still needed a day to steel herself for the consultation, but the following morning she sat next to Jack in Dr. Friedman's waiting room. Jack had put his arm around her, and she curled against him like a scared child. She seemed smaller these days, he thought. Her face had always been narrow, but now it seemed to consist entirely of giant brown eyes, and her abundant hair was duller than it had once been. Jack did not want to leave her side when Dr. Friedman finally called her in for an examination.

He spent a fearful hour too tense to pray or even to think. It was pleasantly warm in the waiting room, but Jack felt an inner chill that not even the hot sunshine could ease.

Finally Dr. Friedman's secretary called him in. The doctor was sitting at his desk again. Across from him Charlotte was clinging to a cup of tea. At a sign from the doctor, the secretary filled a cup for Jack, and then tactfully left the room.

Dr. Friedman did not delay with a long preamble.

"Mr. and Mrs. McKenzie, Charlotte, I'm afraid I don't have good news. But you've already spoken with my very competent young colleague in Christchurch, and he did not conceal his fears from you. My examination has unfortunately confirmed his suspected diagnosis. My professional opinion is that you suffer from a growth in your brain. It's causing your headaches, vertigo, nausea, and all the other symptoms with which you are afflicted. And by the looks of it, it's growing, Mrs.

McKenzie. The symptoms today are already much more pronounced than they were when you saw Dr. Barrington."

Charlotte sipped her tea with resignation. Jack trembled with impatience.

"So what do we do now, Doctor? Can you cut the thing out?"

Dr. Friedman played with the expensive fountain pen that lay on the desk.

"No," he said quietly. "It's too deep in the skull. I've operated on a few tumors. Both here in New Zealand and back in the old country with Professor von Bergmann. But it's always risky. The brain is a sensitive organ, Mr. McKenzie. It's responsible for all of our senses, our thoughts, and feelings. You never know what you'll destroy when you cut around inside. While it's true that cutting the skull open and manipulating the brain have been practiced since antiquity, I don't know how many people survived it back then. Today, knowing the dangers of infection and working very cleanly, we can keep some people alive. But sometimes at a heavy price. Some people go blind or become lame. Or, they change."

"I don't care if Charlotte is lame. And I'd still have two eyes if she went blind. I just want her to stay with me." Jack felt for Charlotte's hand, but she pulled it away from him.

"But I care, dearest," she said quietly. "I don't know if I'd like to keep living if I won't be able to move or see and might still be in pain. And it would be even worse if I didn't love you anymore," she sobbed drily.

"How could that happen? Why would you stop loving me just because . . ." Jack turned to her, shocked.

"There can be personality changes," Dr. Friedman explained gravely. "Sometimes our scalpel seems to extinguish all feeling."

"And how big is the danger that something like that will happen?" Jack asked desperately. "There has to be something you can do."

Dr. Friedman shook his head. "I would not recommend operating in this case. The tumor is too deep down. Even if I could remove it, I would destroy too much brain mass. I might kill your wife in the process. Or dim her spirit. We shouldn't do that to her, Mr. McKenzie, Jack. We shouldn't rob her of the time that would otherwise remain."

Charlotte sat there with sunken head. The doctor had already given her his conclusions.

"You mean, she, she has to die? Even if you don't operate?" Jack grasped for any hope.

"Not right away," the doctor said vaguely.

"So you don't know?" Jack asked. "You mean she could still live a long time? She could . . ."

Dr. Friedman cast Charlotte a desperate gaze. She shook her head almost imperceptibly.

"How long your wife will still live, only God knows," the doctor said.

"She could also recover then?" Jack whispered. "The growth could cease to grow?"

Dr. Friedman raised his eyes to heaven. "It all lies in the hands of the Everlasting."

Jack inhaled deeply.

"What about other treatments, Dr. Friedman?" he asked. "Are there medicines that could help?"

The doctor shook his head. "I can give you something for the pain. Medicine that works reliably, at least for a while."

Charlotte stood up slowly. "Thank you very much, Doctor. It's better to know." She shook the doctor's hand.

Dr. Friedman nodded. "Consider at your own pace how you want to proceed," he said. "As I said, I don't recommend an operation, but if, in spite of that, you want to risk it anyway, I can try. Otherwise . . ."

"I don't want an operation," Charlotte said.

She had left the doctor's house holding on tightly to Jack. This time they did not take the tram. Jack stopped a horse carriage. Charlotte leaned back into the cushions, and Jack held her hand. They did not say another word until they reached their hotel room. But Charlotte did not lie down right away. She went to the window instead. The hotel offered a breathtaking view of Auckland's harbor, Waitemata—a fitting name for this natural bay that offered ships protection from the often hefty Pacific storms. Charlotte looked out over the shimmering green-blue water.

"If I could no longer see that," she said. "If I could no longer understand the meaning of words. Jack, I don't want to become a burden to you. It's not worth it. And everything about this operation. They would have to cut my hair. I'd be ugly."

"You'd never be ugly, Charlotte," Jack said, walking up behind her and kissing her hair while he, too, looked at the sea. Deep down he knew she was right. He would not want to live either if he could no longer perceive all the beauty around him. More than anything he would miss the sight of Charlotte. Her smile, her dimples, her clever brown eyes.

"But what should we do then?" he asked. "We can't just sit here and wait, or pray."

Charlotte smiled. "We won't do that either. There's no sense in it. The gods won't be moved so quickly. Like Maui we'd have to outsmart the sun, and the Goddess of Death."

"He wasn't very successful," Jack said, recalling the legend. The Maori demigod had tried to conquer the Goddess of Death as she slept. But the laughter of his companions betrayed him, and he died.

"He tried, at least," Charlotte insisted. "And we'll try too. Look, Jack, I have medicine from Dr. Friedman. I won't have to suffer any more pain. So we'll do all those things we decided to do. Tomorrow we'll drive to Waitangi. And we'll visit the local Maori tribes. And then I'd like to go to Cape Reinga. And to Rotorua, where there are still supposed to be Maori tribes that have hardly had contact with the *pakeha*. It would be interesting to hear if they tell their stories differently." Charlotte turned to face Jack. Her eyes shone.

Jack drew hope from them. "We'll do just that. That's the trick Maui would use: we won't pay attention to the tumor in your head. We'll forget it, and it'll disappear from being ignored."

Charlotte smiled dully.

"We just need to believe," she whispered.

5

Lilian Lambert's heartache only outlasted her departure from Oaks Garden by a few days. She was still taciturn in London, enjoying her role as the despondent lover. She imagined Ben trying desperately to find out something about her whereabouts, searching for years until he found her. She thought sadly of all the lovers in songs and stories who are driven to take their own lives after losing a loved one and are buried with a white dove on their breast. In reality, however, Lilian thought it unlikely that anyone would scare up a bird like that for her; plus, suicide made her skin crawl more than any other form of death. For that reason, she quite quickly gave herself over to her fate, and soon found her way back to her old, happy self. George Greenwood owed the most enjoyable sea passage of his life to her—in spite of all the war-related chatter among the other passengers. Lilian organized deck games that were otherwise rarely played because of the depressing wartime atmosphere, and was always in good spirits. George was happy to ignore the dispatches he received informing him of the latest hostilities and instead to ask to Lilian about her plans for the future. Naturally these plans did not involve the war. Lilian could not fathom that people really shot at each other. Such things happened in songs and stories, but not in twentieth-century Europe.

"I don't know if I'll ever marry," Lilian mused dramatically. Ben's loss might not have struck a fatal blow, but she still viewed her heart as broken. "Truly great love might be too much for one person's heart."

George Greenwood tried gallantly to keep a straight face. "Now who coined that phrase?" he asked with a smile.

Lilian blushed slightly. She could hardly admit that it was something Ben had whispered to her in the midst of their first kiss in that copse of trees on the Cam.

George ordered a coffee and thanked his server with a curt nod. Lilian gave the smart-looking waiter a smile that rather called into question her lack of desire to marry.

"And what will you do instead?" George inquired. "Do you want to become a bluestocking, perhaps studying as my Charlotte did?"

"Before she followed the sweet calling of the heart?"

George rolled his eyes. He did not know much about girls' schools with artistic-creative claims, but if such ghastly poetry was included in Oaks Garden's curriculum, then the quality of the teaching left a great deal to be desired.

"Before she met the man who would later become her husband," George corrected her. "And she remains very much interested in Maori culture. Is there any subject that is especially close to your heart?"

Lilian considered. "Not really," she said, biting into a pastry. Not even the Atlantic's strong swells could dim her appetite. "I could teach piano. Or painting. But I can't do either of those especially well."

George smiled. At least she was honest.

Lilian licked the crumbs from her pink lips. "Maybe I could help my father with his mine. Surely he'd like that."

George nodded. Tim Lambert had always spoiled his oldest daughter, and the prospect of finally seeing him again had helped Lilian get over the pain of leaving England more than anything else.

"In the tunnels?" George teased her.

Lilian looked at him punitively, but with a roguish gleam in her green-brown eyes. "Girls aren't allowed down there. The coal miners say a woman in the mine brings bad luck, which is nonsense, of course. But they really believe it. Not even Mrs. Biller goes down there.

"I'm very good at math," Lilian continued. "And I won't put up with anything—from other girls, I mean. Sometimes you have to be a bit snippy with the likes of Mary Jane Lawson. And Mrs. Biller is no different."

George was again struggling to hold back his mirth as he pictured little Lilian Lambert in a catfight with Florence Biller. By the look of it, Greymouth was in for some interesting times.

"Your father and Mrs. Biller will come to some agreement eventually. There's no room for rivalry during a war. All the mines will be pressed to the limits of their capacity. Europe needs coal for its steel production. They'll probably be working around the clock for years to come." He sighed. George Greenwood was a businessman, but he had always been fair. It went against his nature to profit from the war. And no one could accuse him of greed. He had not been thinking of war profits when he bought his shares in the Lambert Mine.

"In any event, you'll be quite a catch for some bachelor, Lily. Your father's few shares in the mine will make the Lamberts rich again."

Lilian shrugged. "If I ever marry, my husband should love me for who I am. Whether it's a beggar or a prince, all that matters is how our hearts speak to each other."

George burst out laughing. "At least the beggar would know how to appreciate your dowry," he then said. "But now my curiosity's piqued. I'm dying to know who'll win your heart."

Jack happily observed the energy with which Charlotte climbed the steep street to the lighthouse at Cape Reinga. Dr. Friedman's medicine had worked wonders. For three weeks Charlotte had been pain free and filled with renewed courage. Her visit to Waitangi had been a success. After visiting the place where Governor Hobson had received the Maori chieftains in 1840 in an improvised tent, they spent time with the tribes who lived nearby. She spoke for hours with older members of the tribes, who still remembered the stories their mothers and fathers had told them. Charlotte documented the Maori's feelings about the Treaty of Waitangi; she noted the second generation's interpretations of it and, importantly, the differing opinions of the men and women on the subject.

"The *pakeha* had a queen!" reported an old woman. "My mother really liked that. She was one of the tribal elders and would have liked to go to the meeting. But the men wanted to arrange things among themselves. They danced war-*haka* to raise their courage. Then their envoy arrived, and he spoke of his ruler, Victoria—her name means 'victory.' She was something like a goddess to him, and we were powerfully impressed. She promised us protection, and how was she supposed to do that from so far away if she wasn't a goddess? Later, though, there was conflict. Is it true that they are beginning to sing war songs over there where you come from?"

Charlotte confirmed the outbreak of war in Europe. "But we don't come from there," she said. "We've only traveled here from the South Island, from Te Waka a Maui."

The old woman smiled. "It's not important where you were born but where your ancestors come from. That's where you come from and thence will your spirits return when they free themselves."

"I wouldn't like it at all if my soul returned to England when I died," Jack joked when they left the settlement. "Or to Scotland or Wales. At least both of your parents come from London."

Charlotte smiled weakly. "But London is a bad place for ghosts," she said. "Too loud, too hectic. Hawaiki sounds nicer to me. An island in the blue sea."

"Coconuts that grow in your mouth if they don't fall on your head first," Jack teased her, but he was a little apprehensive. It was too early to speak so freely of death, even if only about the mythology of the Maori. New Zealand's natives had their origin on a Polynesian island they called Hawaiki. They had come from there in canoes to New Zealand, which they called Aotearoa, and to this day each family knew the name of the canoe that had brought their ancestors there. After a person died, according to the legends, his or her soul would return to Hawaiki.

Charlotte reached for Jack's hand. "I don't like coconuts," she said offhandedly. "But I'm done here in Waitangi. Should we head north tomorrow?"

The Ninety Mile Beach and Cape Reinga, one of the northernmost places in New Zealand, offered fantastic views of storm-tossed cliffs. The Pacific Ocean met the Tasmanian Sea here—for *pakeha,* it was simply a spectacular sight to behold; for the Maori a sacred destination.

"Won't that be too stressful for you, darling? The climb is steep, and you have to go the last few miles on foot. Are you sure you can manage? I know you haven't had any migraines for three weeks, but . . ."

He left unsaid what worried him: despite Charlotte's apparent energy, she seemed to have lost even more weight, which was no wonder since she hardly ate anything. Her hands in his felt like those of a fairy, and when he drew her close at night, her body felt feverishly hot. A mountain hike was the last thing he wanted her to do, but she had specifically expressed her desire to visit Cape Reinga multiple times.

Charlotte smiled. "Then you'll just have to carry me. Maybe we can rent horses or mules."

Jack drew his wife to him. "Very well, I'll carry you. Didn't I carry you over the threshold on our wedding night?"

The last *pakeha* settlement before Cape Reinga was Kaitaia, a small town that visitors only stumbled upon when they wanted to explore the northernmost part of the island. Jack took a room in a hostel and asked the proprietor about mounts, or better yet a carriage.

"It's still a few dozen miles to the cliffs," the proprietor said skeptically. "I wouldn't count on your wife lasting so long on a horse. You'd be better off taking a wagon, but it's challenging terrain, sir. You should consider whether that little view is worth it."

"It's more than a little view," Charlotte mused when Jack told her what he'd learned. "Jack, we'll never come so far north again. Don't worry about me; I'll make it."

So there they were, after a long ride through a desolate, rocky landscape interrupted at intervals by breathtaking views of sandy bays and long beaches.

"Ninety Mile Beach," Jack said. "Beautiful, isn't it? I've heard the sand is used in glassblowing. I'm not surprised as it shines like crystal."

Charlotte smiled. She had spoken little along the way, just letting the spectacular landscape, the sea, and the mountains sink in.

"There has to be a tree, a *pohutukawa*. It plays a role in the stories."

Jack frowned. "Are you sure? The area isn't exactly laden with trees."

The *pohutukawa* was an evergreen that bloomed red flowers, and it was ubiquitous on the North Island.

"At the cape," Charlotte said vaguely. Then she lapsed back into silence and remained so on the ascent to the cliffs as well. The hotel proprietor had been right: you could only reach the lighthouse by embarking on a strenuous hike on foot. But Charlotte did not seem to care. Though Jack saw perspiration on her face, she was smiling.

After several hours the lighthouse appeared in view. Jack hoped the keeper would like some company, and indeed he invited the visitors in for tea.

"I'd like to see the tree first," Charlotte said. The lighthouse keeper shook his head but pointed toward the cliffs.

"Over there. It's a rather stunted thing, though. I don't know why the natives make such a big fuss about it. It has to do with some spirits, and supposedly there's an entrance to the underworld there."

"And? Seen anything?" Jack joked.

The keeper, a bearded roughneck, shrugged. "I'm a good Christian, sir. Even if my ancestors brought their superstitions from Ireland, I keep the door closed on Samhain. But early in the year, the weather is usually so stormy that you wouldn't want to go chasing ghosts out of doors, if you know what I mean, sir."

Jack laughed. His mother had sometimes scared him as a child with Samhain, All Saints' Day. At that time the gates between the human and spirit world were supposedly not entirely closed, and sometimes you could see ghosts. Charlotte looked wistfully across the sea as Jack chatted with the lighthouse keeper.

"Are there any Maori settlements up here?" she asked.

"My wife researches native mythology," Jack added by way of explanation.

The keeper shook his head. "No permanent ones in the direct vicinity. Nothing grows here, after all. What would the people live on? But there are always tribes camped on the beach, fishing and making music. There are some there at the moment. The Maori don't take the overland route up here. They always take the path up from the beach, which, overall, is nicer. But it's a steep slope. It's not for you, madame." He smiled apologetically.

"But there must be some other way to reach the camp, right?" Jack asked.

"Yes, come in, have some tea, and I'll explain it to you."

Charlotte only followed reluctantly. She seemed unable to pull herself away from the sight of the frothing sea. Jack too found the meeting of the seas fascinating, but a strong wind had picked up, and it was getting cold.

"Unfortunately I can't offer you a place to stay," the man said regretfully. "Do you have a tent in your wagon? You won't be able to make it back to Kaitaia today."

"The Maori will take us in," Charlotte said. Though the lighthouse keeper seemed rather skeptical, Jack agreed.

"We've often stayed with them overnight. They're very hospitable. Especially when you speak their language. So how do we get to them?"

It was growing dark when they reached the tribe's camp, which consisted of a few rather primitive tents. At the center was a fire over which several large fish were roasting.

The tribe looked friendly, and when Jack greeted the children who approached them in Maori, the ice was broken immediately.

The children were permitted to care for the horses, which they clearly enjoyed, and the adults asked Jack and Charlotte to join them at the fire.

"Are you here for the spirits?" Jack inquired uncertainly after they had been offered roasted sweet potatoes and fresh fish. "I mean, that's the way it works for the *pakeha*. People go on pilgrimages to spiritual places."

Tipene, the chieftain, frowned. "We're here for the fish," he explained in the usual pragmatic style of the Maori. "A lot of them bite this time of year, and we like fishing. If you want, you can join us tomorrow."

Jack nodded. The Maori performed a sort of surf fishing that he'd never tried before.

"Then the women will have all day to talk," he said.

Tipene laughed. "They'll be conjuring the spirits," he explained. "Irihapeti is a *tohunga*. No one speaks more beautifully of Hawaiki than she."

He pointed to an old woman who had been deep in conversation with Charlotte for a long time. Jack was worried that it might be too much for her, but the women were already wrapped in blankets against the evening chill, and Irihapeti was placing another one around Charlotte's shoulders. Charlotte sipped at a steaming cup. Clearly she was content. Jack nonetheless detected a tension in her features that he did not like.

"Did you take your medicine, love?" he asked.

Charlotte nodded, but she looked like she was suffering. Jack recalled Dr. Friedman's words with unease: "Medicine that works reliably, at least for a while." But after such a stressful day, surely it was reasonable for Charlotte to look exhausted.

"Tell me about the spirits, Irihapeti," Charlotte said. "*Te rerenga wairua* means 'jumping-off place of the spirits,' does it not?"

Te rerenga wairua was the Maori name for Cape Reinga.

Irihapeti nodded and made room around the fire as a group of children pressed around her to hear the story.

"Whenever one of us dies," said the *tohunga* in a quiet, conjuring voice, "his spirit wanders to the north. Then he is pulled down to the sea, to this beach. If you close your eyes, you might feel a light breeze whenever one passes through our camp." A small girl shivered, and Irihapeti drew her close. "No, you needn't fear it, Pai. Merely welcome the soul." The moon was rising over the sea and bathing the beach in surreal light. "From here the spirits climb the cliffs, over exactly the path we took this morning.

"And then they weave rope of seaweed and descend to the *pohutukawa* tree up north. Have you seen it, Charlotte? It's many hundreds of years old. Perhaps its seed came with our ancestors from Hawaiki. The spirits leap from the tree, falling down to the roots, and then deeper still, down to Reinga."

"That's a sort of underworld, isn't it?" Charlotte asked. Jack noticed that she was not taking notes.

The old woman nodded. "The way then leads them to Ohaua, where the spirits once more enter the light to say good-bye to Aotearoa. And then . . ."

Ohaua was the highest point on the three small islands across from the coast.

"Then they never come back," Charlotte said quietly.

"Then they wander to Hawaiki, to the motherland." The old woman smiled. "You're very tired, aren't you, child?"

Charlotte nodded.

"Why don't you go to bed, dearest?" Jack asked. "You must be completely worn out. You can hear about the spirits tomorrow."

Charlotte nodded again. Her face looked almost empty. While she stared into the fire, Jack fetched their tent and Irihapeti showed him a place to set it up by the sea; the waves would sing the visitors to sleep.

Expecting to make contact with a Maori tribe, Charlotte and Jack had brought along a few gifts. Planting seeds for the women and a bottle of whiskey to contribute a bit to the mood around the campfire. Jack got them out now. Charlotte was ready to retire.

"I'll join you soon," Jack said tenderly and kissed her as they parted. Irihapeti gently laid her hand on Charlotte's cheek.

"*Haere mai*," she said quietly, "you're welcome here."

Jack started. He must have misunderstood something. Concerned, he took a big gulp of whiskey before passing the bottle. She smiled at him. Perhaps he was just a bit drunk.

While the men drank, Irihapeti and a few other women reached for their flutes, which surprised Jack anew. The Maori rarely accompanied conversation with music and hardly ever started in the middle of the night. But the women played quietly and reflectively, and more than once Jack caught the celebrated spirit voice of the *putorino* flute. Maybe the customs of the North Island were different, or perhaps this was part of some ritual that was celebrated here especially for departing spirits.

When Jack finally crept into his tent, he was tired from the whiskey, the monotonous flute music, and the men's long stories. It was a little eerie being lulled to sleep by the spirit voices, but it did not seem to trouble Charlotte. She appeared to be slumbering soundly next to him. Jack's heart was filled with tenderness as he looked at her in their primitive camp, her loose hair spread out on the blanket, her face not entirely relaxed, however. How long had it been since he had seen her sleep peacefully, unburdened by pain and fear? He pushed the thought aside. Charlotte was doing better; she would recover. He kissed her lightly on the forehead as he lay down beside her. Then he fell asleep.

Charlotte had been hearing the voices of the spirits all night. They had begun calling her as a gentle enticement, but now it was growing more insistent, more inviting. It was time.

Charlotte stood up and felt her way out of the tent. Jack was sleeping; it was better that way. She gave him a last look full of love. One day, in the sunshine of an island somewhere in the sea . . .

She followed the path Irihapeti had shown her, which rose steeply away from the beach. The moon provided just enough light, and Charlotte moved steadily but without haste. She did not feel alone. There were other souls sharing the climb with her. Charlotte thought she heard them whispering and laughing in excitement and anticipation but not fear. Now and again she stopped and looked down at the sea shining like crystal in the moonlight. Somewhere down there was Jack. When she passed the lighthouse, she tread cautiously among the shadows to avoid waking up the lighthouse keeper. The storm-tossed *pohutukawa* tree was not visible from the lighthouse. When she reached it, she was to weave a rope of seaweed. That had struck her as strange during Irihapeti's story. She would have to ask someone about it.

Charlotte smiled. No, she would not be writing down any more legends. She would instead become part of them. She stepped to the edge of the cliff near the tree. Far below, the waves broke on a small beach. The ocean rolled out beneath her, shimmering in the moonlight.

Hawaiki, Charlotte thought. Paradise.

Then she flew.

When Jack awoke, all was silent. That was unusual. After all, they had gone to sleep in the middle of an encampment full of Maori, and the beach should be filled with chatter and children's voices and the crackling of fires.

Jack felt next to him and discovered that Charlotte was gone. Strange, why had she not woken him? He rubbed his forehead and crawled out of the tent.

Sand and sea. Footprints but no tents. Only an old woman—Irihapeti, if his memory served—sat on the beach and watched the waves.

"Where did everyone go?" Fear was growing in Jack. It was as if he were waking into a strange nightmare.

"They're not far. But it's better for you to be alone today. Tipene thought you might be angry with us. Though you should not be. You should find peace." Irihapeti spoke slowly without looking at him.

"Why would I be angry with you?" Jack asked. "And where is Charlotte? Is she with the others? What's going on, *wahine*?"

"She wanted to show her spirit the way," Irihapeti said, turning to face to him. "She told me it was afraid of the separation from her body because there would be no Hawaiki for it. But here it needed only follow the others. You could not have helped her."

The old woman turned back to the sea.

Jack's head began to work. The spirits, the cliffs, the doctor's vague words. He had wanted to deny it, but Charlotte had known she would die.

But not like this! Not alone!

"She's not alone," Irihapeti said. Jack did not know if she was reading his mind or if he had spoken those last words aloud.

"I have to look for her."

Jack felt an overpowering surge of guilt as he ran toward the rocky path. How could he have slept? Why had he not noticed anything?

"You can wait for her here too," said Irihapeti.

Jack did not listen. He rushed up the steep path as if the furies were at his heels, stopping only occasionally to catch his breath. He had no eye for the beauty of the rocks or the sea. But he couldn't help but notice that the sky was cloudy, and everything seemed sunk in a strange blue twilight. Haunted light? Jack forced himself to move faster. Maybe he could still catch her. He should have asked the old woman when Charlotte had gone. But she probably did not know. For Maori *tohunga,* time passed differently.

When Jack finally reached the light tower, it was midday, but the sun still had not completely emerged. The lighthouse keeper greeted him cheerfully—until he saw the state Jack was in. There was no sign of Charlotte.

"There are dozens of places she might be," the lighthouse keeper said after Jack had explained his fears. "Maybe you're getting all worked up for nothing. These Maori grandmothers talk a lot when the days are long. Your wife may very well be with her friends, safe and sound. Frail as she looked, it's hard to believe she managed that ascent on her own."

Jack went to the cliffs above the *pohutukawa* tree. That's where she must have done it. He thought he could still feel Charlotte's presence. But no, that could not be. Her soul should long since have reached Ohaua.

Jack sent a silent greeting to the islands. He did not know why he felt no despair, but there was only emptiness in him, an ice-cold emptiness.

As though in a trance, he clambered back down the path. What if he were to stumble now? But Jack did not stumble. He was not ready for Hawaiki, not yet. Though filled with cold and darkness, he noticed the sun come out from behind the clouds, and his feet felt the path surely.

Irihapeti was still there when he returned to the beach.

"Come, *tane*," she said calmly and waded into the water.

Jack soon caught up to her, and then he saw it too. A blue dress tossed by the waves. Long blonde hair swaying in the tide.

"Charlotte!" Jack began to swim.

"You can simply wait," Irihapeti said. She remained standing far out in the water.

Jack embraced his wife's body and fought with the sea to bring it back to land. He was out of breath and at the end of his strength when he reached Irihapeti. She helped him carry Charlotte to land without a word. They laid her down on a blanket Irihapeti had spread out.

Jack pushed the hair out of his wife's face—and saw for the first time in a long time an expression of perfect peace. Charlotte was free of pain. And her soul was following the path of the spirits.

Jack shivered.

"I'm freezing," he said.

Irihapeti nodded.

"It will be a long time before the cold passes."

6

"So is that a *haka*?"

Gloria was standing next to Tamatea behind the improvised stage in the Ritz and listening to Kura's farewell concert. Marisa was feeling better and had just accompanied through the ballad that Gloria had tried unsuccessfully the day before. The girl would not have recognized the piece—Marisa brought the piano to whisper alongside the spirit voice of the *putorino* and acted as a bridge between the stomping rhythm of the war dance in the background and the ballad Kura was performing. Gloria had never heard anything like it in the Maori villages. Normally, those were simple rhythms accessible to people without much musical talent. These were much more complex, with diverging melodies and instruments. Hoping that Tamatea would not laugh at her, she asked about the difference.

"It's . . . art," Tamatea explained, reaching for the English word.

Tamatea chose her words carefully, but nevertheless managed to imply that she did not entirely approve of Kura's interpretation of Maori music.

William Martyn, who had overheard Gloria's question, cast a disapproving glance at Tamatea. He only spoke a little Maori, but knew from the two English words the meaning behind her reply.

"We're not purists on that point, Gloria," he said. "Who cares whether it's original Maori music or not? What matters is that people can follow it. We're even considering translating Kura's lyrics into English."

"But it says in the program that they're authentic." Gloria did not know exactly what bothered her, but she felt that something important to her was being betrayed. Maybe she was just too thin-skinned.

Earlier she had caught herself affectionately striking the *tumutumu*, comforted by the reminder that her country on the other side of the globe really did exist.

William rolled his eyes. "The program says lots of things," he said. "We saw a performance of this Mata Hari in Paris. Very pretty, very artistic—but she's certainly never seen the inside of an Indian temple. She's not even Indian. But the people don't care. They want exoticism and bare skin. We'll need to work on that if we want to keep people's attention."

"Even more bare skin?" Gloria asked. The dancers' costumes already displayed plenty of cleavage, and their *piupiu*—flax-leaf skirts—ended well above the knee, showing off the girls' naked legs.

"Don't be such a prude, dear," William laughed. "We're just thinking of shorter skirts, and doing away with this face-painting business," he said, casting an almost sullen look at Tamatea. "At least for the girls. The men should look fearsome. Particularly in America."

But Gloria had stopped listening. She was indifferent to her mother's work. What little of New Zealand she had once been able to find in the shows had disappeared. She was beginning to dread America.

The following day, she boarded the steamship listlessly. It had taken forever for all of Kura's stage props to be loaded onto the ship, but the singer insisted on overseeing it all herself. It was pouring down rain, and Gloria looked like a wet cat when she finally entered her first-class cabin, which she was thankfully sharing with Tamatea.

The passage from London to New York passed calmly. Gloria's parents mostly left her in peace. Kura reveled in her celebrity among the passengers, while William drank with the lords and danced with the ladies. The captain bombarded Kura with requests to sing for his passengers and officers, and she finally gave in. Naturally the concert was a total success—and Gloria suffered through the usual onslaught of shame: "Are you as musical as your mother? No? How unfortunate. But you must be very proud of your mother, Miss Martyn."

"How can people live here?" Tamatea asked as the ship passed Ellis Island and New York came into view. "The buildings are too tall to see the sky. The ground is sealed, the light artificial. And the city is filled with noise. I can hear it from here. That drives the spirits away. These people must be restless, uprooted."

It was true. New York was even bigger, louder, and darker than London; and if Gloria had been a spirit, she would have fled.

Kura, however, could hardly wait to venture out into this new, peculiar city. Her concert manager had sent her telegrams on the ship. There was enormous interest in her performances, and the first shows were already sold out. A few things still needed to be done beforehand, and Kura burned with desire for action. After disembarking, the Martyns took one of the new automobiles to the Waldorf Astoria. Gloria liked neither the rattling vehicle nor the intimidating elegance of the hotel lobby.

Gloria was largely left to her own devices during her first days in New York. William and Kura suggested she visit the Metropolitan Museum of Art, where she indifferently perused the many paintings her teachers had tried to make her excited about for years. She found the weapons and musical instruments somewhat more interesting, but in the end, she fled to Central Park and got lost in the expansive gardens. At least one could see the earth and sky there. But Manhattan's skyscrapers cut off the horizon and a haze lay over New York. On Kiward Station it was now spring. When Gloria shut her eyes, she saw newly shorn sheep in pastures green from rain, ready to be driven into the highlands toward the mountains. Jack would be riding with the animals, perhaps accompanied by his wife, Charlotte. Gwyneira had written that their marriage was a happy one. But who could be unhappy on Kiward Station?

George Greenwood could not accompany Lilian as far as Greymouth. Urgent business was waiting for him in Christchurch—as was the news of Charlotte's death. Gwyneira, who had come to pick up her great-granddaughter from Lyttelton, informed him that Elizabeth was expecting him at the hotel. Gwyneira, too, was in mourning but did not want to spoil Lilian's homecoming.

Lilian did not notice Gwyneira's subdued mood. The girl was delighted to be almost home, and she beamed when Gwyneira told her that she would see her mother that day. Unable to wait, Elaine had taken the night train from Greymouth, and Lilian and Gwyneira were on their way to retrieve her. After that mother and daughter were going to spend a few days on Kiward Station.

"What about Daddy?" Lilian asked. "He's not coming?"

"It seems he can't get away. The war and all. But, come. Let's head to the station."

"I'm not going to say you've grown," Elaine teased her daughter after finally releasing her. "That was to be expected, after all."

"I'm not that big," Lilian protested. "I'm not even as tall as you."

"I'm expecting you've grown mentally," Elaine joked. "After so many years at an English boarding school, you should be a walking dictionary."

"At least she can still ride," Gwyneira said, feigning mirth.

Gwyneira appeared strained and seemed to have aged greatly since Elaine's last visit. Elaine squeezed her grandmother's hand silently. She had learned of Jack and Charlotte's tragedy just before her departure.

"Is Jack still in the north?" she asked.

Gwyneira nodded. "Elizabeth would like to have Charlotte brought over, but how they're supposed to arrange that, nobody knows. They've been waiting for George—what a homecoming for him!"

"No telegram on the ship?"

"Would that have changed anything? Elizabeth wanted to tell him herself." Gwyneira broke off with a sidelong glance at Lilian.

"Is something the matter?" the girl asked.

Elaine sighed. "Your uncle Jack is in mourning, Lily, and bad news is likewise awaiting Uncle George. His daughter Charlotte, Jack's wife, died."

Gwyneira prayed Lilian would not ask for the details, but the girl did not seem much affected by the news. Lily hardly knew Jack, and she had never met Charlotte. After briefly expressing her regret, she began chattering away again. After telling Gwyneira about her friends' horses in England and Elaine about the sea journey, she began describing her plans to help her father run the mine.

Elaine smiled. "He'll need you. The mines are working at full capacity. Tim predicted it when the war broke out, but it's all happened so quickly. They're saying that the war will be over soon, so the industry has to hurry and make as much profit as possible. Florence Biller is carrying out massive upgrades on the Biller Mine, and the others have to see that they keep up. Are we really going to be able to fit all our baggage in this little chaise, Grandmum?"

The women had left the train station and walked to Gwyneira's buggy in front of which waited an elegant cob mare.

"No, we have a delivery wagon here that will take our things. But I thought you two might prefer a quick ride. And I don't want to leave James alone for too long. Charlotte's death struck him hard. We all liked her very much. And James, well, I'm very worried."

James McKenzie was restless. He should have been sad, but what he felt was closer to anger. Charlotte had been so young, so full of joie de vivre. And Jack had loved her immensely. James knew how it felt to love so dearly—he felt the same way about Gwyneira. Where had she gone again? James's memory had begun to fail recently, and he sometimes found himself waiting for the young girl who had raced her brown pony like a whirlwind over the Canterbury Plains. Then he would be surprised when Gwyneira's face was suddenly covered in wrinkles and her hair almost white.

He decided to go downstairs and welcome Gwyneira in front of the stables. Though his heart beat heavily, his limbs did not hurt that day. He could almost have gone riding. Yes, a ride would be nice.

James supported himself only lightly on his cane as he went down the steps. The horses whinnied as he entered the stables. Maaka, Jack's best friend and Kiward Station's foreman in Jack's absence, was puttering about. He laughed when James appeared.

"A good day to you, Mr. McKenzie. Couldn't wait to see Miss Lambert? But Mrs. McKenzie won't be back quite so soon."

"I think I'll ride out to meet them. Would you saddle me a horse?"

Maaka hesitated. "A horse, Mr. McKenzie? But it's been months since you rode."

"Then it's about time, isn't it?" James walked over to his brown gelding and patted his neck. "Did you miss me?" he asked. "Back in the day, when Gwyn arrived, I was riding a gray horse." He smiled at the memory.

"If you want a gray horse, one of the new shepherds has a roan. He'd certainly let you borrow him. It's a handsome horse."

He laughed. "Why not? Another gray horse."

He waited until Maaka had saddled the roan, and then bridled the horse himself.

"Many thanks, Maaka. Gwyn will be amazed."

James felt himself seized by youthful enthusiasm as he led the horse out. For once his bones were not betraying him. If only his heart were not dancing so strangely. Something wasn't right. He felt a twinge that spread through his arm. Maybe, James thought, I shouldn't ride. But, what the hell? What does Gwyn always say? "When you can't ride anymore, you're dead."

James mounted the horse and trotted down the road to Christchurch.

"Really? I can hold the reins?"

Although Lilian knew how to ride, she had never driven a carriage, and the mare pulling Gwyneira's chaise was no tired nag.

"It's quite similar to riding. Only you mustn't fall into tugging at the reins. They'll seem to get longer and longer, but it doesn't make much of an impression on the horse," Gwyneira explained, happy about Lilian's interest.

"A lot of people are buying automobiles now," she said to Elaine while Lily concentrated on managing the reins. "But I can't get used to the idea. I tried, of course. They're not hard to drive."

"You drove a car?" Elaine laughed. "Yourself?"

Gwyneira looked at her reproachfully. "And why not? I've always driven my own carriages. And believe me, compared to a cob stallion, an automobile is a lame duck."

"We have one ourselves now. After Florence Biller drove past so proudly in hers, Tim could not resist. Total nonsense. He can't even drive it himself in his splints, even getting in is difficult, and it's hell on his hips. But he'd never admit it. Roly is thrilled by the contraption, as are the boys. It's a toy for men."

Lilian had brought the horse under her control and had it moving at a brisk trot.

James saw the mare trotting along up ahead. It looked like Gwyneira was holding the reins, always going at top speed, and Igraine loved to accommodate. Wait, was that Igraine? He thought hazily that this horse must have a different name. Igraine had come from Wales with Gwyn when she was young. She could not still be alive.

But there she was, that distinctive head, those high movements, that long mane blowing in the wind. And Gwyn on the box, such a beautiful girl, how young she was, and that red hair, the alert expression, the shining face radiating the pure joy of the speedy ride and the responsive horse.

In a moment she would see him and her eyes would light up as they always did. James raised his hand to wave. At least that's what he wanted to do. But his hand did not respond. Then his head began to spin.

When Gwyneira saw the roan trotting up ahead, she, too, first thought it was an illusion. James on his old horse. But he should not be riding, he . . .

Gwyneira saw James sway. She called to Lilian to stop the carriage, but he was already falling off by the time the girl succeeded in stopping the mare. The roan came to a stop obediently beside him.

Elaine wanted to help her grandmother, but Gwyneira pushed her away as she leaped out of the chaise and ran to her husband.

"James! What's wrong, James?"

"Gwyn, my beautiful Gwyn."

James McKenzie died in the arms of an aging Gwyneira, but his eyes were filled with the image of the Welsh princess who had stolen his heart so many years before.

Gwyneira only whispered his name.

7

Gloria learned weeks later of the deaths in her family. The mail route from New Zealand to the United States was complicated, and, moreover, the letters arrived at Kura's concert agency in New York, which had to locate the troupe before forwarding the letters. The news reached them in New Orleans, a lively city that thoroughly electrified Gloria's mother. On the streets dark-skinned people played a jarringly different sort of music, and when Kura was not taking the stage herself, she was dragging William through the nightclubs of the French Quarter, listening to that strange music called jazz, and dancing.

The sad news from Kura's old homeland interested her little. Neither William nor Kura had known Charlotte, and James McKenzie had never been especially warm to them—a mutual feeling. Gwyneira had not felt up to spreading the news, so Elaine had written to their relatives on her behalf. She addressed the letter to the "Family Martyn." To write separately to Gloria seemed unnecessary, and therefore Gloria did not even learn the details. When Kura informed her almost casually that her great-grandfather had died, she was astounded at her sorrow.

"Are you crying, Gloria? He wasn't even your real grandfather. And he was over eighty. That's the way of the world. But I can sing that mourning-*haka* tonight. Yes, that suits New Orleans, it's a little morbid."

Gloria turned away. Even James's death would be misused to gain sympathy for Kura. Tamatea expressed her condolences to Gloria.

"He was a good man. The tribes always treasured him."

Gloria only gave in to her sadness when she was alone, which was rare. In the hotels, she shared the suites with her parents and spent the endless train rides quartered with the young dancers. Each prettier than the last, they were all "modern young women," proud of earning their own money and being free and untethered. Shy, plodding Gloria seemed to them a relic of past times, and they teased her about her English boarding-school education and her prudishness.

Her only friend was Tamatea, but even she was getting appreciably on Gloria's nerves. Tamatea was astounded by the endless cotton and sugarcane fields and tried to make Gloria excited about them. But Gloria had long since decided not to like anything about America. She preferred reading to looking out the train windows. Tamatea watched with concern as the girl sank ever deeper into a whirlpool of self-hatred and self-pity. Tamatea thought that Gloria would like the West. It wasn't green like the Canterbury Plains, but the red and blue mountains shimmered beyond the sunburnt grasses. There were horses and cattle, and the small, simple towns resembled Haldon.

But Gloria hardly dared stroll across a dusty street alone or look at the horses that had yet to be replaced here by cars. People recognized her at once as a member of the ensemble and so stared at her like an exotic animal. Gloria yearned for the end of the tour, but that was far off. Once they reached San Francisco, they were scheduled to return straight to New York by train, and Gloria was wishing for a direct passage back to New Zealand from there. She was no help at all to the troupe, and she desperately hoped that her parents would finally accept that she was expendable. Gloria belonged on Kiward Station.

San Francisco was a booming city. With its many Victorian-style buildings, it reminded Gloria of Christchurch, and she liked it more than New York or New Orleans. They had one last concert ahead of them before returning to New York, and William called the whole troupe together right before it began.

"I have some news to share with you. As you all know, we had originally planned to bring the tour to a close the day after tomorrow. My wife and I wanted to return to Europe. But with war still raging, our European tour plans have been cancelled. So Kura's concert agency offered to extend our stay in the States. How exactly we proceed will depend on all of you. If you would like to extend your engagements, we'll be moving on to Sacramento, Portland, and Seattle, then Chicago and Pittsburgh. The agency will work out the exact schedule. If you would like to terminate your contracts, then we'll have to return to New York, hire new dancers, and start again from there. So, what do you think? Care to keep going?"

The dancers cheered in agreement.

"What about me?"

William's revelation to the dancers had left Gloria frozen. Back at the hotel, where her parents were enjoying a post-concert drink, she managed to voice her anxiety.

William looked at her in amazement. "What about you? Why, you'll be coming with us; what else would you do?"

"But I'm of no use here." Gloria wanted to say more but couldn't bring herself to do so.

Kura laughed. "Of course you'll make yourself useful. And even if you don't, you can't return to Europe."

"There's no war at Kiward Station." Gloria wanted to scream, but it came out as little more than a whisper.

"Ah, so you want to go back to that sheep farm." William shook his head. "Gloria, sweetheart, New Zealand is halfway around the world. We couldn't possibly send you alone. And to what end? You're getting to know the world here, child. There'll be plenty of time for shearing sheep if that's what you really want to do. Just imagine, when we return to Europe after the war, you'll see France, Spain, Portugal, Poland, Russia. Perhaps we'll finally buy that town house in London. Yes, I know, Kura, you don't want to settle down. But just think of the little one. She has to have a debut suitable to her station. Someday you'll find a nice man and you'll marry. You were raised to be a lady, Gloria. Not some sheep farmer."

Gloria did not respond. Her face had drained of color, and she couldn't speak. A tour through Europe, a town house in London, debutante balls. When Kura and William had brought Gloria to England, they had never meant to send her back. She was to stay forever and ever, and though she might someday inherit Kiward Station, Kura would more than likely sell it as soon as Gwyneira died.

Gloria saw an endless sequence of humiliations before her: "Is that Mrs. Martyn's maid?"; "No, you won't believe it, but that's her daughter!"; "That oaf? She certainly doesn't take after her mother."

Gloria inhaled deeply. Though she wanted to speak her mind, there was nothing that would change her parents' minds. She would have to act, and alone.

The next morning Gloria wandered down to the bay. When she reached the docks, she headed for the passenger steamers. There were always luxurious first-class accommodations that required dozens of service workers. Though most of them were men, Gloria knew the stewards didn't make beds and peel potatoes. There had to be chamber and kitchen maids.

Gloria hoped to be able to hire herself onto such a ship and earn her passage. If only she knew which of the ships was bound for New Zealand. She paced uncertainly along the docks, which were busy with men working away, but Gloria could not bring herself to talk to anyone. Suddenly a gangly young man in sailor's clothing stopped in front of her and fixed his eyes on her curiously.

"Well, sweetheart? Gotten lost, have we? You won't make anything here, and if the coppers get a hold of you, there'll be trouble. Better try your luck at Fisherman's Wharf."

"I, which, er, ship here is bound for New Zealand?" Gloria asked.

"Off to the Kiwis, are we? That'll be tough, dearie."

Gloria bit her lip. Her father had said the same thing. Was there really no way to get from San Francisco to Polynesia?

"Look, girlie, we're here." The sailor squatted down and drew a map in the dust of the street. "And there, on the other side of the world, is Australia."

"But I want to go to New Zealand," Gloria repeated.

The man nodded. "New Zealand is real close to there."

"Two thousand six hundred miles."

The sailor made a dismissive hand gesture. "Hopscotch compared to the distance between here and Australia. For one, you have to get to China first. Which isn't hard. Practically every week there's a ship headed that way. But then: Indonesia, Australia, and from there, Kiwi land. But it's not worth it, sweetie. Believe me, I've been there. On what they call the South Island. On the one side, a few towns that look like good old England, a few pastures and sheep; on the other, coal mines and pubs. You could earn a little bit there. But—and no offense—girls like you are a dime a dozen there."

Gloria nodded, far from insulted. "I do come from there, after all."

The sailor roared with laughter. "Well, then you've traveled a long way, and hopefully you've learned something." He looked at her searchingly. "You're almost worth a try. You look clean, I suppose, and you're attractive. A little Polynesian, eh? I always liked the girls there, more than the scrawny birds that sell themselves here. So, how about it? What do you want for an hour around midday?"

Gloria looked at the man, taken aback. She did not need to look up to meet his gaze. He was about her size. Her heart warmed at the thought that he had called her "attractive." But he was also peculiar. Regardless, Gloria did not want to lose sight of this opportunity.

"I, I need to find a ship first. And work, because I, I don't have much money. You say I need to go to China first? Maybe you can help me. I was thinking of a passenger ship. Those need a service staff, after all."

The sailor rolled his eyes. "Sweetheart, nobody with all five senses takes a cruise to China. Only freight ships go there. Like me, I'm going with the Pacific Mail Steamship Company. Abalone to Canton, tea and silk back. But my captain doesn't hire girls."

"I'm strong. I could work on deck or unload freight."

The sailor shook his head. "The problem, dearie, is that half the crew think a woman would bring bad luck on board. And where would you sleep? Sure, the boys would fall over themselves for a cabin with you, but . . ."

The man stopped short. Then he let his gaze wander over her face and body. "Hmm, I just had an idea. You really don't have any money, sweetheart?"

Gloria shrugged. "A few dollars, but not much."

The sailor chewed his lip, giving his face a rodent-like appearance.

The man appeared to have reached a decision. "That's a shame. Because you'd have to make the risk worth my while if we really carry out what just went through my head. If it gets out, then I'd be sitting without a job in Canton. If the captain didn't just throw me overboard."

Gloria's gaze clouded. "Can he do that? I mean, you'd drown."

The sailor looked like he was trying to hold back his amusement, but he kept a straight face. "Of course he can, girlie. On his ship he has absolute authority. If he finds you out, he'll keelhaul you—and me too. So, how badly do you want to go to China?"

"I want to get home," Gloria said. "More than anything in the world. But how? Am I to hide?"

The man shook his head. "Nah, girlie, there aren't many hiding places on the ship. And with the limited provisions we take along, every hungry mouth stands out. I was thinking more of camouflage. Our cook is looking for a scullion."

Gloria's face brightened. "You mean, I'd disguise myself as a boy? I can do that, no problem. I used to always wear pants. When I was little, I mean. And I can do the work. No one will suspect a thing."

"We have to let the crew in on it. For compensation purposes too. You'll have to, well, if I arrange this for you, and everyone keeps their mouth shut, you'll have to be a little nice to us on the way."

"Of course I'll be nice," she promised. "I'm not catty like most girls."

"And I'll pocket the money, *capisce*? That's why I'm looking out for you. I'll make sure no one takes more than belongs to him."

"You're welcome to the money," she said generously. "But do you really make that much as a scullion?"

She did not understand why the sailor roared with laughter.

"You're a funny one. Well, come on, let's see if we can find a few rags that'll fit you. Over by Fisherman's Wharf there's a Jew who deals in old clothes. What's your name anyway?"

"Gloria. Gloria Mar . . ." She stopped short. She needed a new name. Suddenly the name of one of Lilian's ridiculous love songs shot through her head: "Jackaroe." It had to do with a girl who pretended to be a man to look for her love on the other side of the ocean.

"Call me Jack," Gloria said. Jack should bring her luck.

An hour later Gloria was standing in front of the cook, a fat, unctuous-looking man wearing what had once been a white apron over his sailor's outfit. Gloria was dressed in similar fashion. Harry, her new friend and protector, had selected for her a pair of worn woolen, loose-fitting blue pants, a white shirt, and an old black sweater. She had hidden her long hair in her collar since it would not fit under the peaked cap Harry had picked out.

"The hair's got to go," the cook declared after looking the girl over closely. "Even if it is a shame. With it down, she probably looks like a real doll. But otherwise you're right, Harry, she'll pass for a fella."

Though the cook had initially laughed at Harry's proposal, he'd subsequently proved willing to consider it. For whatever reason, this included pinching Gloria's butt and breasts. She found it unpleasant, but she had seen behavior like that among maids and servants before. If that was what it took to get the job, she could certainly endure it.

"Let's get one thing straight: I get three goes a week for free, and half the take. After all, I'm taking the biggest risk." The cook fixed Harry with a stern look.

"The ones sharing a cabin with her are taking the biggest risk," Harry countered. "She might have fooled you. Or do you follow your kitchen boys into the bathroom?"

The cook shook his arm threateningly.

Gloria looked around the galley while the men finalized the terms. The countertops, pots, and pans did not look very clean. The galley master really needed the help. Next to the greasy kitchen was an equally uninviting mess hall for the crew. Everything below deck was dark and constricted, and the crew's quarters were likely no nicer. But better to be bound for New Zealand in stifling quarters than trapped in her mother's luxury hotel suites or her father's town house.

"I can cut my hair off," she said calmly.

The two men appeared to have come to an agreement.

"All right, fine, I'll tell the paymaster the boy's coming tomorrow—or better the day after, just before we sail. Can you be here at five in the morning, Jack?" the cook asked with a leer.

The girl nodded. "I'll be right on time."

"Where can I change?" Gloria asked Harry as they left the freighter. It had just occurred to her that she would not be allowed to use the back room at Samuel's secondhand shop again.

Harry looked at her, astounded. "Can't you go home like that? Don't you have your own room?"

Gloria turned red. "Yes, no, well, I can't be seen in the hotel looking like this, I . . ."

"In the hotel!" Harry grinned. "Fancy word. Almost sounds like an upscale cathouse. But then again you have more class than other girls. Are you running from something, girlie? Damned if it don't look that way. But what's that to me? Just don't get caught."

Gloria said nothing.

"This," he laughed, "calls out for a colleague's help. Let's have a look where Jenny's roaming about."

Gloria followed him through the alleys around the docks. She sensed they were drifting into the red-light district, and she swallowed when she saw several girls on the street. A haggard blonde with a rodent-like countenance similar to Harry's was on display with a half-open bodice in front of a seafood restaurant from which issued the rank smell of fat.

"Harry, old boy! Back in the country again? Tired of them Chinks in Canton?" The girl laughed and embraced Harry in an almost sisterly fashion. Then she cast an eye over Gloria. "And what do you have there? Fresh meat, how nice. Where'd you pick up this baby face? He some country boy?"

"Jenny, sweetheart, if I were to push him into your bed, you'd be in for the shock of your life. But the illusion is working perfectly if even you don't notice anything, and you probably see more men in a week than our old paymaster does in a year."

"As God made them no less, my friend," Jenny snickered. "Well, what's wrong with the boy? Hmm. One second."

She turned serious as she examined Gloria more closely.

"This boy's a girl! Are you sleeping with the competition?"

Harry raised his hand appeasingly. "Jenny, no one compares to you. This girl here is more in the way of traveling wares. At any rate she'll be pleasing us on the ship. She wants to make it to the other end of the world more than anything."

"Why are you dressing her as a boy? Does that turn you on these days?"

"Jenny, darling, I'll explain everything later. But right now the girl needs a roof over her head while she turns back into a girl. Come on, have a little heart and let us into your room for a minute." Harry stroked Jenny's hair tenderly. She purred like a cat.

"So you can fuck someone else in there?"

"Now, Jenny, even if I lay her flat for a minute, just to test things out, tonight belongs to you. I'll take you out like a queen, Jenny dear. Lobster, shrimp. Whatever you want. Just fifteen minutes, Jenny, please!"

Gloria, who had barely followed the conversation, smiled gratefully when Jenny finally nodded and dropped a key into Harry's open hand.

"Is Jenny your girlfriend?" Gloria asked as she followed him into a run-down building that stank of urine and rotten cabbage. "She looks like a . . ."

"You really do come from another planet, don't you, girl? For someone in your line you're awfully naïve. Of course Jenny sells herself. But she has a heart of gold. But be quick. If she finds a john, she'll need the room."

The room was really a tiny shelter in an apartment that was divided up into several partitions. It contained a primitive stove, a table, a chair, and, most importantly, a bed. The sheets were far from clean. Gloria wrinkled her nose.

"Aren't you going to leave?" she asked as Harry let himself gingerly down onto the bed, eyeing her expectantly.

The sailor frowned. And for the first time an indignant expression crept onto his face.

"Sweetheart, prudery is sweet, sure, but you need to hurry a bit. So forget the theater, strip, and be good to me. Think of it as a down payment. Thanks to yours truly, you're halfway to China already."

Gloria looked at him, confused. Then she finally understood. "You mean, you want me to, to, give myself to you?" That was the only expression that came to her. Lilian liked to use it when the characters in her wild stories fell together into bed or, more often, into a haystack or the tall grass.

"You got it, sweetie. You have to pay for a ship passage. Or don't you still want to go to China?"

"New Zealand," Gloria said. She hesitated for a moment, but then she considered the alternative. What difference did it make if she slept with Harry now or with a man her parents picked out for her later? Besides, it sort of flattered her that Harry wanted her. In all the stories she had ever heard, people gave themselves to each other out of love. And Harry was prepared to undertake considerable risks for her. Gloria undressed—and was relieved to see him smiling again.

"Aren't you pretty," he said admiringly when Gloria was standing in front of him in her brassiere and hose. "Some flowers in your hair and a little grass skirt and you'd look like a Hawaiian girl."

In spite of her embarrassment, Gloria managed a little smile.

"Hawaiki is paradise," Gloria said.

"Then take me there, sweetheart."

Gloria screamed with shock when Harry lunged for her and pulled her onto the bed. But then she was quiet. She held still, utterly terrified, as he stripped the last articles of clothing from her body. Not bothering to undress himself, he yanked down his pants. Gloria froze when she saw his member looming in front of her. She closed her eyes and bit her lip when he penetrated her without ado and began thrusting forcefully. Something in her tore. Gloria gasped in pain and felt fluid run down her thigh. Was that blood? Harry moaned, and then collapsed on top of her. A moment later he righted himself, sobered and surprised.

"You were still a virgin? Tell me it isn't true. My God, girl, I thought . . . Man, a virgin, I would have gone about it differently. Exchange a few kisses first and all that." Sounding contrite, he awkwardly caressed Gloria's defiled body. "Sorry, girlie, but you should have told me. I'd also like to know what you're running from. I thought you had a mean pimp or something. But you . . ." He brushed the hair from her face with the same, almost tender gesture he had used on Jenny before.

Gloria glared at him.

"I paid, didn't I?" she said. "You wanted me to be good to you. So don't ask any questions."

Harry made a defensive motion with his hand. "All right, sweetheart, I don't even want to know. You come to the *Mary Lou* the day after tomorrow, and the rest is between us. I won't tell anyone, and well, I'll make sure you learn slowly. No hard feelings, right, sweetheart?"

Gloria nodded with clenched teeth.

"If you'd care to leave now," she said, "I'd like to dress."

Harry nodded. "Of course, princess. I'll be seeing you." He blew a kiss at her as he left.

When Gloria walked downstairs, Harry was standing in front of the building.

"I have to give the key back to Jenny," he said.

Gloria nodded. "I'll be seeing you."

8

Gloria slunk back to the hotel. Her stomach churned with disgust, and her body hurt, and she hoped her parents were not back yet. The last thing she wanted was to account for herself to Kura or William or even come up with a good story for Tamatea about where she had spent half the day. Thankfully, the suite was empty when she walked in. Breathing a sigh of relief, Gloria stowed away the men's clothing in the furthest corner of her wardrobe and ran a bath.

She slid into the hot water and scrubbed off the awful experience. She did not want to think anymore about it, nor about possible reprises on the ship. If there was no other way, she would let herself be at Harry's disposal. It was a relatively small price to pay for her passage home. Though it had been loathsome and painful, it had been over quickly and Gloria thought she could endure it. She clung fast to Harry's friendly words: "Aren't you pretty?"

No one had ever said that to her before.

Gloria could hardly rein in her impatience the next day. She returned to the docks to acquire another pair of pants, two shirts, and a warm jacket from Samuel. On her way home, she got lost and ended up again in front of the seafood restaurant where Jenny plied her trade. The whore glared suspiciously at her.

"You again? I thought you were disappearing across the ocean?"

Gloria nodded. Then she thought she ought to thank Jenny. "I really don't plan to compete with you. I'll be working as a cabin boy on the *Mary Lou*."

Jenny laughed. "A cabin boy? Well, Harry said otherwise. Come on, girl, you can't be that naïve, no matter what nonsense Harry tells you. He even tells me you were still a virgin yesterday. You'll have to teach me that trick."

Gloria blushed. Harry should not have talked to this girl about her. "But it's true," she said. "I, I didn't know."

"Didn't know what? That fellas never do anything for free? Did you think that Harry had plucked you off the street out of pure chivalry?"

Gloria did not answer.

"Do you at least have a shadow of a notion where little babies come from?" she inquired.

Gloria blushed again. "Yes, no, well, I know about sheep and horses."

Jenny laughed. "Sure, and yesterday Harry showed you how people go about it. Now, now, don't go pale, sweetheart. Not every shot's a hit. There's a bit you can do to prevent it. Beforehand and after. But afterward it's expensive and risky, and there aren't any abortionists at sea. I'll tell you what, sweetheart: I won't be able to whore myself up another meal here today, not before dark. How about you buy me, let's say, some good crab soup and sourdough bread, and in exchange I'll tell you what a girl needs to know."

Gloria hesitated. She didn't want to share in Jenny's disgusting secrets. On the other hand, the girl in front of her was clearly hungry. Gloria felt a twinge of sympathy. She nodded. Jenny smiled broadly at her, exposing two missing teeth.

"Good, then come along. No, not this shack. There are better places."

A short while later the girls were sitting in a dark and cramped but relatively clean cookshop. The food was surprisingly good, and Gloria even began to enjoy Jenny's company. Jenny didn't tease her, but simply explained the peculiarities of her profession.

"Don't let them kiss you on the mouth. That's disgusting, and if they want you from behind, or French-style, then charge them more. Do you know what French-style is?"

Gloria turned crimson when Jenny explained, but the girl didn't mock her. "I looked the same when I learned, dear. I didn't grow up in a cathouse, after all. I'm from the country, wanted to marry properly. But my father liked me too much, if you understand what I mean. In the end my sweetheart found out." Gloria expected to see tears in Jenny's eyes, but she seemed to have long since forgotten how to cry.

The girl gulped down three servings of crab soup, and, as she did, she casually enlightened Gloria on the feminine cycle and, most importantly, how to prevent conception. "Get a hold of some condoms. That's still the best. The fellas don't like to put one on, so you have to insist, and the whore who taught me swore by vinegar douches. It's not a sure thing, though."

Gloria eventually ceased blushing and even managed to ask a question. "What can you do so that it doesn't hurt so much?"

Jenny laughed. "Vegetable oil, child. It's like with machines: oil makes things go."

That evening Gloria stole the oil and vinegar from the table at the St. Francis hotel; she also set out some scissors, and with a wildly beating heart, she removed her passport from the drawer where her father kept their documents. It was a long time before she fell asleep. Her parents returned home around three, both happily drunk after a late-night reception.

When Gloria slipped out the door at four in the morning, they were sleeping soundly. The night porter, too, was not exactly alert. Gloria escaped the lobby just as he was fetching himself some tea. She was already wearing her men's clothing and had a bag with her change of clothes. As a girl Gloria had been fearful of walking the city streets at night, but as a boy no curious sidelong glances followed her. She ducked into a quiet residential street and cut her hair—without any regret—and tossed her locks into a garbage can. Gloria was gone. Here came Jack.

The harbor was already bustling, and no one noticed the cabin boy headed toward "China Dock." Harry was waiting for Gloria on deck and seemed relieved when she appeared.

"There you are. I was starting to fear that, after the business the day before yesterday . . . but forget it. Help us with the sails; the galley master won't need you till we're at sea. I did your job yesterday and stocked the larder for you. After all, you couldn't exactly come by. You'll . . ."

"I'll be good to you later," Gloria said. "What do you want me to do?"

The engines were running; the coal men had already been working for hours shoveling coal into the ovens to heat the water that produced the steam that powered the ship. The noise of the awakening ship filled her with anticipation. As the sun came up, the fully laden steamship lurched into motion. Gloria cast a relieved last look at San Francisco. Whatever awaited her, she must never come back here. From now on she would only look out over the sea—toward home.

After shoving off, however, Gloria had little opportunity to stare at the waves. If she came on deck at all, it was only at night, but often whole days passed without so much as a breath of fresh air. The work in the galley was hard; she carried the water and stirred the daily stew of salt meat and cabbage in gigantic pots; she scrubbed the stove, washed the utensils, and served the crew at table. She occasionally carried in food for the captain and his mates to the officers' mess hall, always fearful that her cover might be blown. Yet the men were very nice to the shy cabin boy. The captain noted his name, and the paymaster asked a few well-intentioned questions about his origins and family. He did not pry, however, when Gloria hemmed and hawed. Once the first mate praised her for the properly set table in the mess, and Gloria blushed, causing the men to laugh. They did not seem as if they would summarily throw stowaways overboard, but Gloria was inclined to believe Harry. She tried to believe much of what Harry said, above all the sweet nothings he sometimes whispered to her. She needed something to hold fast to in order not to go mad.

Because when the last meal of the day was over and the dishes were clean, Gloria's true work began.

Gloria could accept that she owed Harry and that the cook also wanted to be paid for his silence. But why she had to service all the other members of the crew remained a mystery. Not even the six men with whom she and Harry shared a cabin would have noticed that Jack was a girl since they did not undress for bed. But Harry insisted she make herself available every evening.

Gloria hated the cook's visits the most. She held her breath every time he threw his fat, stinking, unwashed body over her. He took considerably longer than Harry and occasionally forced her to take his member in her hand and knead it because it would not get hard on its own.

Afterward Gloria used up half of her valuable drinking water just to scrub her hands. Though there was no water for washing and no soap, Gloria tried to scrub herself every morning with some water; she hated to smell like all the men and have that peculiar scent—of love?—about her. No matter how hard she tried, she couldn't understand what the men got out of possessing her dirty, stinking body. Some even whispered to her about how good she smelled, and a few liked to lick her breasts, her stomach, or even the unspeakable parts of her body where they otherwise stuck their members. Harry limited himself to these activities on the days when Gloria was most likely to conceive. Other men would put on a condom, and a few insisted they would pull out before it got dangerous. However, Jenny had expressly warned against this method; thus Gloria would resort to the vinegar, with which she had begun to douche herself almost every day since there was plenty of it in the kitchen.

She tried to think as little as possible. Gloria did not hate the men who lay with her every night; she simply felt nothing for them. It had ceased to hurt if they rubbed themselves with oil first, and if it were not for the stench, the bodily fluids, and the shame, Gloria might have gotten bored. So she just counted the days and hours. The voyage to Canton would last roughly two weeks. She could survive that.

If only she knew what would come next. She would have to find a ship to Australia, but they did not sail as regularly as the cargo ships between China and San Francisco. It was a question of luck whether one would be at anchor when they arrived.

"If not, we'll take you on a barge down to Indonesia," Harry said nonchalantly. "You'll just have to transfer again."

Gloria was relieved but apprehensive when land finally came into view.

"Just stay here," Harry directed her when the ship had weighed anchor and the cargo was being unloaded. "I'll be back. We'll figure something out."

When Gloria was finally allowed to go on deck that evening, she ladled up some sea water and washed herself thoroughly. She hoped that she had finished with her services to the men once and for all. On the new ship no one would have to know that she was a girl.

Harry and the cook were in high spirits when they came back to the ship late that night.

"The, the very last time," the cook slurred. "Tomorrow the wares'll be unloaded, wares sold well!" He laughed.

"What wares?" Gloria asked. The goods the *Mary Lou* had carried had long since been unloaded.

"You, my sweet. Who else? Your boy sold you well, sweetheart, and I got my cut."

"Sold? Me?" Gloria turned, confused, to Harry.

"He means I've found a place for you on a ship," he explained reluctantly. "You're in luck, the ship goes all the way to Australia. Immigrant ship sailing under a British flag but full of Chinese. The steward who oversees steerage will cover for you."

"So does he need a cabinmate?" Gloria asked anxiously. "Will they hire me?"

The cook rolled his eyes. Harry glared at him and made him hold his tongue.

"Sweetheart, you don't need to hire on there. Like I said, it's swarming with people in steerage. One more mouth to feed won't draw any attention."

"And you'll have plenty of customers," the galley master chortled.

Gloria looked fearfully at Harry. "I have to be good to the steward, is that it?" she asked.

Harry nodded.

"But otherwise, in steerage there are a lot of women too, right? Immigrants usually travel with their whole family, don't they?" At least that's what Gloria had heard.

The cook laughed, but Harry frowned. "That's right, sweetheart, crowds of all sorts of Chinese. And now be especially good to me. Tomorrow we'll go into town and you'll meet the steward."

Gloria nodded. He would probably want to "test" her like Harry had in San Francisco. She steeled herself for a shelter as sleazy as Jenny's.

Canton was a confusing mix of narrow alleys and crowded markets. Some of the women scurried about strangely; they seemed to have very small feet. The men and women alike were tiny, and all of them seemed to talk without pause. Harry guided them through a market where spices, strange pickled vegetables, and animals—alive and dead—were for sale. Gloria winced when she saw desperately whining dogs.

"The cook on the ship is an Englishman, though, right?" she asked nervously.

Harry laughed. "I assume so. Don't worry, they're not going to feed you dog. Come on, we're almost there."

The steward of the *Niobe* was waiting in a sort of tearoom. There was no real furniture, however. Instead they kneeled around small lacquered tables. The man stood up respectfully to greet Gloria, but directed his speech toward Harry.

"Not exactly a beauty, is she?" he noted after looking Gloria over thoroughly.

"Hey, what do you want? An English rose? This one's more of a Polynesian type. Much better without clothing. And it's not like you have much to choose from."

The steward grumbled. He was no beauty either. Gloria did not even want to imagine what it would be like when he was on top of her. She forced herself to think of Australia. Australia, that was almost home.

"And she isn't used up? Still somewhat clean?"

Gloria looked to Harry for help.

"Gloria is very clean," he explained. "And she hasn't been in the trade long, a good girl, who just wants to get to the other end of the world for some reason. So take her or leave her. I can also give her to that Russian who's headed to Indonesia."

"Fifty dollars," the steward said.

"Do we have to go through all this again? And in front of the girl? Didn't we already reach an agreement yesterday?"

"She should know just what she's worth." The steward tried once more to assess Gloria's figure. "Then she won't cause me any trouble. What did we say again? Sixty?"

"Seventy-five. And not a cent less." Harry glared at the man and then gave Gloria an apologetic look. "I'll give you ten," he whispered.

Gloria could not even bring herself to nod.

Reluctantly the man pulled out his wallet and slowly counted out seventy-five dollars.

Gloria tried to meet Harry's eyes. "Is . . . is it true? You're selling me?" She was stunned.

Harry turned away from her reproachful look. "Look, sweetheart, it's not like that."

"What is it then?"

Gloria's new owner raised his eyes, annoyed, to heaven.

"Of course he's selling you, girl. This can't be new for you. If the fellow wasn't lying to me, you've already whored yourself to him for fourteen days. And now you'll do it for me, simple as that. So don't play the innocent country girl. We need to buy some rags for you first. My customers don't like girls in men's clothing."

Uncomprehending, Gloria allowed Harry to embrace her in parting. As he did, he slid ten dollars into her pocket.

"No hard feelings, sweetheart," he said, winking. "Do a good job, and they'll treat you well. In a few weeks' time, you'll be counting sheep in Kiwi land again."

Harry turned away. Gloria thought she heard him whistle as he left the tearoom.

"Don't shed any tears for him," remarked the steward. "That man found a golden egg in you. Now let's go; we're in a hurry. We leave for Down Under tonight."

9

Night was already falling as the steward led Gloria to the "Australia Dock." Gloria asked herself how he meant to smuggle a foreign boy—let alone a white girl—on the ship, but that proved simple. The decks were swarming with Chinese who wanted to emigrate. They seemed to have hardly any baggage; indeed, most of them carried their possessions aboard in a small bundle. The shipping company must have counted on this and sold many more tickets than usual. Since there were no suitcases or portmanteaus, they squeezed ten or twelve into the tiny quarters, instead of the normal six. To Gloria's amazement—and later horror—the passengers were almost exclusively men.

The steward steered Gloria through the throng and onto the deck—nobody bothered about the cabin boy with no papers—and then into the belly of the ship. He shoved Gloria into one of the cabins. There were six small berths on the walls. None of them were occupied. The steward pointed to a few folded blankets.

"You'd best make your bed on the floor so the fellows don't bump their heads while you service them."

Gloria looked doubtfully at her new master. "Am I going to live alone here? No one else is coming?"

She hardly dared hope, having assumed she'd have to share the steward's bed after finishing her work.

"Who are you expecting?" he asked. Then he smirked. "But don't worry. We won't let you get lonely. Listen, I'm going to see to that chaos out there. Make yourself scarce for now in case one of the crew gets lost down here. Once the ship gets going, and the men have their first hangover, you'll have plenty of company. Now make yourself pretty for me."

He pinched Gloria's cheek in parting and disappeared down the hall. Gloria could hardly believe her luck. Her own cabin! No more stinking male bodies at night, no snoring. Maybe she could undress unobserved for once and at least wash herself.

She spread the blankets on the floor, curled up under one of them, and slept, relieved and happy. When she woke up, she was headed for Australia, almost home.

The steward took no joy in possessing a woman in the normal fashion. The first night on board he forced Gloria to endure what Jenny had referred to as "other varieties of lovemaking."

She attempted to ignore the pain and think about something else while the man wore himself out on her. She eventually succeeded in transporting herself to a shearing shed on Kiward Station. The bleating of the sheep drowned out the murmur of the men outside. The pervasive lanolin scent of the wool covered up the stench of the steward's sweat, and Gloria counted the newly shorn sheep in her mind.

"Good girl," the steward said when he was done. "That fellow in Canton was right. You don't know much but you're willing. Now sleep tight. Tonight everyone has their own business to see to. Early tomorrow you start work."

"What am I supposed to do?" Gloria asked, confused. After all, she had heard she would not have to work in the kitchen.

The steward laughed. "What you do best, girl. At eight, when the night shift ends, the coal men like to wear themselves out before hitting the sack. Things go in three shifts here, sweetheart, which means you'll be working around the clock."

This seemed an exaggeration for the first few days as the crew was still sated from the whores in Canton, and the passengers were not so desperate that they would waste their small travel budget on a whore. But after the first week, Gloria rarely got any rest, and by the end of the second, her life had become an unending nightmare. The steward—his name was Richard Seaton, but Gloria could not think of him as a man with a name like any other—sold her without compunction to anyone who offered him a few cents, and he left her to the men without any ground rules. Though most of them did not have any special requests, no one hindered those who took their sadism out on her. Nor did anyone step in when two or three men shared the "ticket." Gloria tried to handle everything as passively as she had on the *Mary Lou*, but there had only been two or three men at most per night then. Now the torture began in the morning when the machinists and firemen finished with the night shift, and only ended late at night after the kitchen crew had wrapped up.

After fifteen clients or more each day, the protective effect of the oil began to fail. Gloria was sore, and not only in her private places. Her naked skin chafed on the rough blankets, and the wounds became inflamed since she did not have an opportunity to wash. After a few days her improvised bed became clotted and crusty from grime and the bodily fluids of countless men, and what was more, someone must have brought bugs. Early on, she clambered into a berth when she was alone and found time to sleep, but as time wore on, she had neither the solitude nor the energy to leave her improvised bed on the floor. Though her body was wasted, Gloria clung to her mental health. Desperately she dreamed herself far away from her dark dungeon, picturing herself herding sheep in the sunshine on Kiward Station, losing herself in the vastness of the Canterbury Plains, only to find herself again in the choir room at Oaks Garden standing in front of the piano and failing miserably at singing. Her daydreams increasingly turned to nightmares. Gloria noticed she had a fever, which made it increasingly difficult for her to conjure pleasant images or even to imagine pleasant feelings. Instead, feelings meant pain, disgust, and self-loathing—and the loathing hurt the least.

Gloria concentrated more and more on hatred. At first she directed her feelings toward the steward. She began to imagine killing him. Again and again. One way or another, the grislier the better. Then she transferred her hatred onto the johns. She envisioned the ship sinking and them all drowning. Or a fire that devoured their stinking bodies. When a man moaned on top of her, she dreamed it was from pain instead of pleasure. Only imagining their suffering gave her the strength to survive the indignities she endured.

She lost all sense of time, and she felt as though she had been on the ship for an eternity. But one day she smiled at one of the few men who still had a face to her.

"Today's the last time," the young fireman said. "Tomorrow we'll be in Darwin."

"In Australia?" Gloria asked. His voice plucked a long silent string in her. All but unbelievably, she felt a stirring of hope.

"Unless we've gotten lost." The man grinned. "We'll just have to see how you get off the ship. The immigration officials are really strict; everyone gets registered."

"The, the steward will smuggle me out," Gloria said, still dazed.

The fireman laughed. "I wouldn't count on that bloke. My God, girl, there's no reason for him to let you go."

"You, you mean . . ." Gloria sat up with effort.

"I mean the moment we reach Darwin, a key'll turn in that door," the man explained, pointing to the cabin door. "And not open up for you, if you catch my meaning. We're only staying here a few days; then we head back to Canton. That bastard could just put a bucket of water and a little food in here for a few days, and quick as you like he'll be making a profit on the return."

"But I, the agreement . . ." Gloria's head was spinning.

"You don't mean to tell me that this here was part of an 'agreement,' do you? Seaton bought you, and he'll get the most he can for his money. A dead whore can be easily thrown overboard, but if they catch you in Darwin and you tell them how you got here . . . Well, like I said: try and get out of here as quick as you can. Even at the risk of running into the harbormaster."

Gloria did not even manage to thank the man for his warning. Her thoughts tripped over each other as he left and two Chinese immigrants entered. Gloria ignored their pleasure and attempted to formulate a plan. It looked unlikely that the steward would let her go willingly. But she had not endured what she had only to be caught by the authorities and sent back to her parents in disgrace. Though they might send her to her relatives in New Zealand—it was closer and would perhaps be easier for the Australians to organize—they might not. And even in the best case, Gwyneira would learn what she had done on the ship. And that could not happen. No one could know. She would rather die.

She suddenly detected the sound of crates being moved and crew members hollering at each other on deck. It seemed that they were preparing to drop anchor. Gloria chided herself for not having noticed sooner. She had almost let the trap spring. She had to make her escape right away.

When the two Asians were done, she forced herself to stand up, and tied her few possessions into a bundle. She swapped her lousy, torn dress for her cabin-boy clothes. The pants and the shirt felt heavy to her, and she hoped she would be able to swim in them. But she had no choice. She would make it to land or drown.

On deck she met cool air. It was winter in this part of the world. She moved across the deck in the shadows of the lifeboats. She briefly considered taking one of them, but knew she would never manage to heave a tub like that overboard alone. Besides, it would be noisy and attract attention. Gloria glanced over the railing. Though the sea lay far below, it was calm. And the lights of the city were visible; it could not be far. The ship appeared hardly to be moving. Were they perhaps waiting on a pilot to lead the *Niobe* into harbor? In that case there was no great danger of being caught in the ship's propeller. However, the pilot could seize her while she swam. But first she would have to jump. Gloria shuddered at the height. She had not swum in years. Nor had she ever leaped into the water before.

But then she heard voices. Someone came on deck, and she knew that if they found her, her fate was sealed. Gloria inhaled deeply. Then she threw her bundle out to sea and jumped.

From the ship the beaches of Darwin had appeared close enough to reach out and touch, but Gloria did not seem to be getting any closer to land. She felt as though she had been swimming for hours. Despite the cold water and heavy clothes, she was free of fear. Gloria had tied her things to her back—holding them in her hand had hindered her swimming—and it was pleasant after that wretched cabin to be enveloped in water. Gloria felt the ocean was washing away not only the filth but also the shame. She occasionally dipped her face in the water and then, growing bolder, her head and hair as well in an effort to drown the lice. And she never stopped swimming.

It took Gloria all night and half a day before she dragged herself onto a lonely beach below Darwin. Later she would learn that it was called Casuarina, and that there were saltwater crocodiles there. But none appeared, and Gloria was so tired that she could hardly have helped herself from sinking to sleep in the sand even if she'd known.

She had been so cold and exhausted by the end that she could hardly swim. She held herself just above water, and let the swelling tide carry her in.

When she awoke it was evening. She sat up, a little dazed. She had done it. She had escaped the steward and the harbor police. Gloria wanted to laugh hysterically. She had reached the other end of the world and was only two thousand six hundred miles from New Zealand—not counting the land that stretched from Darwin to Sydney. Gloria did not know whether ships sailed between the Northern Territory and New Zealand's South Island, but from Sydney, she knew one could travel to Lyttelton.

Suddenly Gloria felt a gnawing hunger. She had to solve that before anything else, even if it meant stealing something edible. But that meant she would have to go into town, and her clothing was still damp; she would stand out if she slunk through the streets. Gloria pulled off her wool pullover and spread it on the sand. She did not dare take off her shirt and pants, however desolate the beach might seem. But as she turned out her pockets to dry them faster, she felt damp paper. When she drew it out, she looked in bewilderment at the ten-dollar bill, Harry's "good-bye present." Her share in her sale to the steward.

Gloria smiled. She was rich.

10

When Lilian finally made it back to Greymouth after an extended stay on Kiward Station, during which she helped her mother bury both James McKenzie and Charlotte, she was determined to be put to work.

"What do you want to do in the mine, birdie?" Tim asked, smiling. Though he would be delighted to have his darling daughter around him every day, he could not come up with any tasks for her off the top of his head.

"Whatever a person does in an office. Writing receipts, calling people." Lily had no fear of the new telephone that now had a place in every office. "I can do anything your secretary can do."

"And what will we do with my secretary?" he teased her.

"Maybe we need more, you know," she said vaguely. "Besides, there's plenty to do down in the mines."

Lilian began by taking over all the telephone operations, and, in no time, she had twisted her callers around her little finger one after another. She refused to take no for an answer from suppliers or shippers. The businesses in Greymouth were already used to being bossed around by a woman, though what Florence Biller approached with hardness, Lily managed with charm. For that reason alone, young business partners in particular expedited deliveries in order to get to know the girl with the bright telephone voice. And Lilian did not disappoint, taking the time to entertain them when they had to wait for her father or the foreman. Even interacting with the miners came easily to Lilian, though she, too, had to endure the superstitious stories about women in the mine.

Lilian tore through the office, taking on any task she could think of. Though she scalded herself constantly when brewing coffee, she quickly figured out how to keep books. Unlike the older office workers, she was excited by novelties like typewriters and learned to type in record time.

"It goes a lot faster than writing by hand," she said blithely. "You could write good stories with one of these."

Lilian's good spirits never failed to cheer her father up. Winter was always hard on him, and his hips and legs hurt unbearably in the cold, but the offices could hardly be shut against every draft. Chronically overworked during that first year of the war, he occasionally took out his bad mood on his secretaries, but with Lilian's presence that got better. Not only because he loved her, but also because she made fewer mistakes. The girl was clever and showed interest in running the enterprise. She asked her father dozens of questions on the way to work and often had the relevant documents ready for him before Tim had even explained to the office workers what he needed.

"We should have had her study mine engineering," Tim said to his wife as Lilian explained the concept of a hoisting tower to her little brother. "Or business management. I'm starting to believe that she could put some fear into Florence Biller."

Lilian had no real ambitions when it came to mine management, however. Working for her father was nothing more than a game for her. She wanted to do everything as well as possible and did so, but she did not dream of reviewing balance sheets the way Florence had at her age. Lilian still dreamed of love, though there were few suitable young men among Greymouth society.

"You're still too young anyway," Elaine told her when she complained about it. "First grow up, and then you'll find a husband."

Spring came and went without any possibility of romance for Lilian. To distract herself, she combed her parents' bookshelves. Fortunately she shared her mother's taste for romantic literature. Elaine did not complain when she ordered the latest novels from England—on the contrary, mother and daughter yearned with the heroines for their beloveds.

"Not that they have anything to do with reality," Elaine felt compelled to clarify, but Lilian dreamed on undeterred.

"You'll have the chance to dance on Sunday," her father said one day while Lilian was once again swooning over the debutante balls and dramatic entanglements in one of her novels. "If only at the church picnic. We also have to make an appearance at the charity bazaar. The Billers will be there too. As it happens, their oldest is back from Cambridge."

"Seriously? He's still so young. Did he graduate already?" Elaine was surprised.

"He's rather a high achiever. Like his father."

"Like his . . . ? Oh, Lily, run to the pantry and fetch some more cookies. Check the jar on the second shelf to the left."

Lilian left in a huff. She knew when she was being sent out.

"You won't believe it, but the boy looks like Caleb," Tim remarked. He knew Lainie loved gossip. "The same narrow face, the lanky frame."

"But didn't we all think it was her secretary?"

"I'm telling you what I saw at the hardware store. Matt told me I ought to look at the new crossbeams myself. And, well, Florence was there with the boy. All he has from his mother are his eyes; he seems very athletic. But supposedly he's a bookworm. Florence had just scolded him—in public, no less—because he couldn't differentiate screws from nails. She's trying to bring him in line now. He's supposed to help with the mine."

"But he can't have finished his studies." Elaine did the math. "He's Lily's age, a little younger even."

"They probably brought him back because of the war. His brother isn't even going to England. They're sending him to Dunedin, I heard. Europe isn't safe."

"This godforsaken war; does it seem unreal to you too?"

"Not when I look at our balance sheets. All that coal means steel. And steel means weapons, and weapons death. Cannons, machine guns, what an infernal invention. The poor fellows drop like flies in front of them. I could hardly tell you why." Tim frowned. "I'm just relieved our boys are too little to get into any trouble." The British army had recently begun recruiting in New Zealand and Australia, and the first contingent would be leaving for Europe soon.

By Sunday the constant rain had finally ceased, and Greymouth looked like it had been freshly washed. Yes, the mining sites marred the beautiful landscape a bit, but nature won the upper hand. Fern forests flourished up to the city limits, and the banks of the Grey River were full of romantic little spots. The church lay a little outside of town, and they passed by lush, green meadows on the way there.

"A little like England," Lilian said, remembering the day of the boat race in Cambridge. Ben had proved to be right. The famous regatta between Cambridge and Oxford had been cancelled for the first time on account of the war. Even after Rupert's graduation, Ben would not have had a chance to distinguish himself as a stroke.

The scene in front of the church looked exactly like what Lilian remembered from her childhood. Men were setting up tables; women were carrying picnic baskets and looking for shady places to deposit them during the church service. Since the weather was cooperating, the reverend had relocated the service outdoors. Excited children spread out blankets all around the improvised altar as their mothers and grandmothers decorated the tables for the bazaar that would take place later. Mrs. Tanner, who considered herself to be the most important pillar of the community, whispered with her friends about Madame Clarisse, the owner of the pub and brothel, who led her flock of easy women to church as she did every Sunday and apparently had no intention of skipping out on the picnic.

Elaine and her kitchen maid, Mary Flaherty, unpacked their basket while Roly and Tim discussed vehicles with the parish's other car owners.

"You ought rather to help me with the basket," Mary called to her boyfriend, Roly, who had just been boasting that the Lamberts' Cadillac easily had more horsepower than the other cars. Roly acquiesced with a sigh.

Elaine greeted her mother-in-law, Nellie Lambert, with a forced smile and pressed her brood to curtsy and bow. Then the little boys disappeared into the crowd. Lilian joined a few girls who were picking flowers for the altar.

Shortly before the church service began, the Billers' car pulled up. It was even bigger and more modern than the Lamberts'. While the men cast covetous looks at the vehicle, Elaine and her friend Charlene concentrated on the passengers. Matt Gawain had told his wife about the remarkable similarity between Caleb Biller and Florence's oldest son, and both of them held their breath when Caleb and the boy alighted from the vehicle. They were not disappointed. Even the somewhat grumpy expression on the boy's face reminded them of a young Caleb. Elaine could still vividly recall her first encounter with Caleb at a horse race. Caleb's father had forced him to take part, and the young man had hardly been able to contain his fear and revulsion.

The younger Biller also seemed not to have come entirely of his own free will. As his mother cast indignant glances at him, his shoulders sagged in resignation. Though more muscular than his father, Ben was just as tall and thin. Florence assembled her family around her. She was a compact woman, with a slightly doughy face that was sprinkled with freckles, and she wore her thick brown hair tied back in an austere bun. Florence forced a smile as she pushed her three boys toward the pastor. While the younger boys performed a quick bow, the eldest proved reticent. But then he saw the girl winding flowers around the altar, and his eyes flashed.

The short, red-haired girl.

Lilian was arranging the last few garlands and eyeing the altar with a furrowed brow. Yes, that would do. When she turned to the reverend, expecting praise, she instead found herself looking at clear, light-green eyes, a longish face, blond hair. The boy had the thoroughly trained body of a rower, which grew taut as he recognized her.

"Ben."

The boy's expression reflected disbelief as well. But then an almost otherworldly smile spread across his face.

"Lily! What are you doing here?"

War

Canterbury Plains, Greymouth, Gallipoli, and Wellington

1914–1916

1

When her clothes had dried, Gloria dragged herself into town. She was half-dead from hunger by then. It was getting cool, and she needed something to eat and a place to sleep. Finding food was not difficult. There were plenty of restaurants, tearooms, and cookshops in the harbor town. Gloria was careful not to come too close to either the harbor or the adjacent red-light district. She likewise avoided places where mostly men were sitting, regardless of how appetizing the odors coming from the kitchen were, or that she was dressed as a boy.

She came upon a small tearoom operated by a woman. It was almost empty, with only a few elderly customers. Gloria relaxed. It looked like several of them had been served a thick stew. Gloria shyly asked for a meal by pointing at the others' food, and the owner brought Gloria a large bowl of stew. She observed with pleasure how the apparent young man wolfed down the food.

With an almost conspiratorial smile, she fetched him seconds.

"Here, boy, it looks like you haven't eaten in days. What did you do, swim here from Indonesia?"

Gloria turned crimson and focused on lowering her voice. "How did you know that I . . ."

"That you came off a ship? That's not hard to figure. First off, I'd have noticed a boy as cute as you if you came from here. And what's more, you look like a seaman who's just disembarked. Your hair's just screaming for the barber, boy. You've still not much of a beard, though." The woman laughed. "But you've taken a bath. That's a good sign. And you haven't taken to whiskey. All very praiseworthy. First time aboard?"

Gloria nodded. "But it was awful," she blurted out. "I, I'd like to stay on land now."

The woman nodded understandingly. "So, what do you want to do now?"

Gloria shrugged. Then she gathered up all her courage.

"Would you know where I could find a place to sleep? I don't have much money, I . . ."

"I might have thought so. They hired you on for a few cents, the crooks. And then didn't feed you properly. Now you're just skin and bones. You can come again tomorrow, on my word, and I'll give you a good breakfast. As for places to sleep, the pastor at the Methodist church has a few habitations for men. Anyone who can makes a small donation, but if you don't have the money, no one will say anything."

She headed nervously over to the church on Knuckey Street. The pastor, a tall, blond man, was holding a scarcely attended service. Gloria glanced uneasily at three ragged-looking men in the second pew. Were they the guests at the men's lodging?

Gloria prayed politely but declined to sing along to the closing hymn. "Jack" was still young, but his voice should already have broken. As service ended, she sought the reverend and stuttered through the story she had told the woman at the tearoom: "Jack," a native New Yorker, had hired on to a ship to Darwin looking for adventure. The captain had exploited him, and the other men had been unfriendly.

"The way you look, they might just as well have been too friendly," the pastor remarked grimly. "You ought to thank God for having come out of that with your body and soul intact."

Gloria did not understand what he meant but reddened nevertheless.

"You're clearly a good boy. But you get your hair cut. Tonight you'll sleep here. We'll see about the rest tomorrow."

Gloria had almost hoped for a room to herself, but the men's lodgings proved to consist of five bunk beds crammed in a small, bare room; a crucifix on the wall provided the only decoration. Gloria sought out a bed in the furthest corner, hoping to be left alone, but as evening progressed, the room filled with "guests" of various ages. Once more Gloria found herself enduring the stench of unwashed bodies and men's sweat. At least it did not reek of whiskey; the reverend made sure of that. A few of the men played cards, while others chatted. An older man who had taken the bunk across from Gloria's attempted to draw her into conversation too. He introduced himself as Henry and asked for her name. Gloria answered monosyllabically, on her guard. This proved wise. Henry, apparently a seaman, did not swallow her story as readily as the undiscerning man of God.

"A ship from New York to Darwin? There's no such thing, lad. It'd have to sail half the world."

Gloria blushed. "I, they, they went to Indonesia first," she stammered, "to take on some cargo."

Henry frowned, but then began telling stories about his own trips, all of which had to do with his seemingly unending loneliness on board. Gloria hardly listened. She regretted her decision to stay the night, but at least it seemed safe enough.

Or was it? Once the oil lamps had been put out and Gloria had curled up to sleep, she felt a hand stroking her cheek. It was all she could do to keep herself from screaming.

"Did I wake you, Jacky?" Henry's voice, rather high-pitched for a man's, was near her face. "I was thinking, such a sweet lad, maybe you'd keep me warm tonight."

Gloria panicked.

"Leave me alone," she whispered sharply, not daring to scream. In her overheated imagination, she feared that they all might pile onto her. "Go away! I want to sleep alone."

"I won't tell the reverend about your ship to Darwin. You see, he don't like to be lied to."

Gloria trembled. She did not care what the geezer told the reverend. She only wanted to get away. But if he forced her "to be good to him," he'd find out she was a girl. With the courage born of desperation, she pulled back her knee and struck the man between the legs.

"Get gone," she growled.

Too loud. The men all around were stirring. But to her amazement, they took "Jack's" side.

"Henry, you pig, leave the boy in peace. You heard him; he doesn't want anything to do with you."

Henry groaned, and Gloria succeeded in pushing him away, evidently pushing him into somebody else.

"'Aven't 'ad enough yet, you queer bastard? You can get a beating 'ere too if you want."

Gloria did not understand but sighed with relief. Not wanting to take any more risks, she retreated to the water closet with her bed linens and engaged the bar lock. Then she huddled in her sheets as far from the urinals as possible. In the morning, she left the church before anyone awoke. She did not leave an offering. Instead she sought the nearest store and invested three of her valuable dollars in a knife and sheath she could affix to her waistband.

Next came the lice. The brief submersion in the sea had not taken care of them. With some reluctance, she entered a pharmacy and asked for the cheapest possible cure.

The pharmacist laughed. "The cheapest thing would be to shave your head, son. You need a haircut anyway. You look like a girl. Quick as you like, no hair, no lice. And follow it up by powdering your head with this." He handed some medicine over the counter.

Gloria bought the powder for a few cents, found a barber, and had her head completely shorn. She did not even recognize herself when she looked in the mirror.

"It'll grow back, lad," the barber laughed. "That'll be fifty cents."

Gloria felt strangely free as she headed toward the tearoom. She desperately needed a good breakfast and was prepared to pay for it. Her new friend kept her word, however, and piled baked beans, eggs, and ham on a plate at no charge.

"A little shorter would have been proper, but shaved bald! The girls won't like that, young man."

Gloria shrugged. As long as it didn't bother possible employers, she didn't care.

Finding a job proved difficult, however. All the more so because Gloria would not brave the harbor. Plenty of work could be found on the docks—people were always looking for help loading and unloading—but Gloria stuck to the town, to no avail. Ragged boys like Jack whom no one could vouch for were regarded with distrust. After half a day of looking in vain, Gloria almost wished she had not left the Methodist church so heedlessly. The pastor could surely have helped her. But her fear of Henry and the other men was stronger. She invested a few more precious cents in a room in a small inn. For the first time in months, she slept peacefully, alone and entirely securely between clean sheets. The next day, she was able to take the place of a messenger boy who had not shown up to work. She carried a few letters and packets from one office to another, earning just enough to keep her room another night. Though she managed to get a few more odd jobs in the following days, her financial situation was growing dire. Of her ten dollars, only four remained. A journey to Sydney was unthinkable unless she walked there.

So that is what she did. There was nothing for "Jack" to earn in Darwin. Hence Gloria set out along the coast, trying to find short-term work in smaller settlements. There were sure to be farms, she hoped, that needed a stableboy. Or fishermen who needed help with the catch.

Alas, all her hopes proved illusory. After two weeks, "Jack" had covered only a hundred miles, and all her money was gone. Crestfallen, she wandered the alleys of a tiny harbor town. Once again she had no place to sleep, and hunger gnawed at her. But she only had five cents left. She couldn't even get a meal in the dive she was just passing by.

"Hey, kid, wanna earn a few cents?"

Gloria started. It was a man on his way into a dubious-looking pub. She couldn't make out his face in the dark, but his hand was reaching into his pants.

"I'm a boy," Gloria whispered, feeling for her knife. "I . . ."

The man laughed. "Well, that's what I was hoping. I don't want anything with girls. I'm looking for a strapping lad to keep me company tonight. Come this way. I pay well, you know."

Gloria turned on her heels and ran until she was out of breath; then she collapsed on a bridge that spanned a river that flowed into the sea. Two skimpily dressed girls were strolling between the bridge and the harbor wall.

"Well, handsome? Looking for company tonight?"

Gloria fled anew, running until she stumbled onto a beach, sobbing. There were probably crocodiles nearby, but she didn't care. She lay trembling in the sand for a while, but then she began to think. She needed to get out of Australia. But it seemed hopeless to try and raise the money for the journey by honorable means. "Jack" might have scraped by working temporary jobs, but she could forget about a ticket to New Zealand.

The cynical voice of the steward came to her: "Just do what you're best at."

Gloria whimpered. But she could not deny it: she had never been paid much for anything except being "good" to men. Without Harry's ten dollars, she would not have survived. And if she worked for herself, there was clearly money to be made.

Gloria sat up. She had no choice. She had to try. It was undoubtedly dangerous—the other girls would not be happy about the competition—but there were many things normal whores would not do. Gloria likewise felt shame, pain, and fear from performing these acts, but there was nothing the men on the *Niobe* had not demanded of her. She had survived that, and she would weather this too.

Gloria felt sick, but she rummaged through "Jack's" bundle for the only dress she had and was relieved to find a hat as well. Reluctantly she put them on and strolled toward the bridge.

2

Not now, later," Lilian said between clenched teeth.

Though her unforeseen reunion with Ben had made her heart skip a beat, she knew that no exhibitions of joy would be appropriate just then. With Ben standing beside Florence and Caleb Biller, she knew he must be the son who had just returned from Cambridge. She knew also that neither the Billers nor Lilian's own father would be particularly pleased to know that their children had scratched their names into a tree in England with a heart around them.

Ben did not catch on so quickly. No wonder, since he still did not know Lilian's last name. But fortunately the reverend remedied that.

"Ben! How nice to see you again," he said. "And how you've grown. The young ladies of Greymouth will be falling over themselves to get you to ask them to dance. Allow me to introduce the first of them to you." He indicated Lilian and the two other girls who had been decorating the altar. "Erica Bensworth, Margaret O'Brien, and Lilian Lambert."

Erica and Margaret giggled as they curtsied; Lilian only managed an anxious smile. After all, she had just met Florence Biller's cool gaze. Lilian had dealt with her a few times in the context of her work for her father and had probably not left the best impression. Not only did she refuse to be intimidated by Florence, but she'd lured away clients and suppliers so that the Lambert Mine was attended to before the Biller Mine during busy times. In the Biller family circle, "little Lambert" was already labeled an "impertinent brat." Even Ben had heard his mother go on about her. And now he was standing across from the "little beast" in the flesh—and she had revealed herself to be Lily, the girl he had not been able to get out of his head since she had turned it, back in England.

Lilian gave him a quick wink. Ben understood.

The two families sat on opposite sides of the lawn during the service, but Lilian and Ben could not concentrate on the pastor. Both sighed with relief when the last song had died out and everyone made for the refreshments. Lilian managed to land a spot next to Ben in line for the punch bowl.

"Soon. When everyone's eaten and is tired, let's meet behind the church," she whispered to him.

"In the cemetery?" Ben asked.

Lilian sighed. She had not wanted to express herself so prosaically—and she had wondered whether the graveyard was suited to the first secret rendezvous between two lovers—but she had come to the conclusion that it was thoroughly romantic. A bit morbid perhaps but bittersweet too. Like a poem by Edgar Allan Poe.

Besides, there was no other spot guaranteed to be as parent-free as the cemetery.

She nodded. "Just keep your eyes on me. You'll see when I get up."

Ben nodded and poured himself some punch. Then he winked furtively at her and went on his way. Lilian watched him go, rapt. Finally something was happening. And it was just like in her novels—her long-lost sweetheart had returned. Lily sighed. But he was an enemy of her family. Like in Shakespeare! Much to her frustration, she had never been chosen to play Juliet in the Christmas performance at Oaks Garden. But now she was part of the story.

In the end it was Ben who left his family first and surreptitiously sauntered over to the church. Lily separated herself almost unwillingly from the table, where Elaine, Tim, Matt, and Charlene were chatting about the Billers' eldest son. Lilian's mother and Charlene simply could not get over how much the boy resembled his father. Lilian found their reaction a little strange. Her brothers resembled

Tim, and Charlene's eldest was the spitting image of Matt Gawain. But no one had ever wasted more than a word or two about that. In any case, the families kept each other well entertained, and no one paid attention when Lilian decamped. When she arrived at the churchyard, Ben was in the process of carving their initials into the old beech by the fence. Lilian thought it romantic, if perhaps not wise tactically. There could not be that many L. L.s and B. B.s in Greymouth, after all. But what could she do? She decided to feel flattered that Ben was taking risks for her.

He beamed at her as she came toward him between the gravestones.

"Lily, I thought I'd never see you again. This odd girl at Oaks Garden told me you were going home. I thought that meant London or Cornwall or somewhere in England. You didn't tell me you were from Greymouth."

"I thought you were from around Cambridge too. And I thought you were poor on account of the scholarship."

Ben laughed. "No, just young. Hence the preferential treatment. I skipped a few grades, and the universities were fighting for me. With the scholarship I could study what I wanted—not what my parents envisioned. Until now anyway. This stupid war gave them an excuse to bring me home. And now I sit in this dreadful office and am supposed to care about how to extract coal from underground. For all I care it could stay there."

Lilian frowned. The idea of leaving coal in the ground had never occurred to her and did not seem all that smart. After all, a person could sell it for a lot of money. But Ben was a poet and he saw things differently. So she smiled indulgently.

"You have two brothers. Couldn't one of them take over the mine? Then you could continue your studies."

"They're chomping at the bit for it. Sam is only twelve, but he knows more about the business than I do. It's a shame I'm the eldest. But let's talk about you, Lily. You haven't forgotten me?"

"Never. Things were so lovely in Cambridge. I really wanted to meet you that day. I would have done anything, but my uncle came for me that very afternoon. And I couldn't get away. But now here we are."

Ben smiled. "Here we are. Maybe we could, well, I mean . . ."

"You can look to see what color my eyes are again," Lilian said mischievously, stepping closer and looking up at him.

Ben caressed her cheek shyly, and then wrapped his arms around her. Lilian could have embraced the whole world when he kissed her.

"Who was the boy in the cemetery?"

Tim Lambert was rarely strict with his daughter, but now he loomed over her as threateningly as his crutches and leg splints would allow. Lilian was sitting at her desk in his office and had just hung up the phone. She looked more cheerful and radiant than usual—a more skillful observer than Tim might have seen she was in love. Tim, however, had more of a sense for business. He had just completed a transaction with Bud Winston, a lumber dealer, who was delivering the support beams for the planned mining expansion. Tim had snatched a whole wagonload of lumber out from under Florence Biller's nose. If Tim were honest, he primarily had Lilian to thank for that, as his daughter had led the negotiations. But that day he was less concerned with fairness than the rumors circulating in Greymouth. They must already have spread far if Bud Winston's men had heard them. After all, the lumber trade was hardly a bastion of gossips. And it was only eleven on Monday morning—by afternoon the whole city was guaranteed to know that Lilian Lambert was seeing a boy in secret.

"Don't deny it. Old Mrs. Tanner saw everything. She's nearsighted, though, so she couldn't make out the boy."

Lilian felt a twinge of uneasiness.

"What does she think she saw then?" she asked, as lightheartedly as she could manage. If Mrs. Tanner had observed the kiss, she was in trouble.

"You were talking with a boy. Secretly, in the cemetery. It seems the whole town is talking about it."

"Then it couldn't have been all that secret," Lily remarked, thumbing casually through a document. She breathed a silent sigh of relief.

Tim sank into his desk chair. That robbed him of his strategically advantageous position, but he was exhausted after his ride into town, and his hips hurt.

"Lilian, was it Ben Biller?" he asked. "Someone mentioned that name. And otherwise I can't think of anyone here who's a match for you in terms of age."

Lilian smiled at him divinely. Normally, assessing her conversation partners was among her strengths, but now she was in love.

"You think we're a match too? Oh, Daddy!" She leaped up and made as if to hug her father. "Ben is so wonderful. So gentle, so dear."

Tim frowned and pushed her away. "He's what? Lilian, you can't mean that. After strolling around between a few headstones for three minutes, you decided he's the man of your dreams?" He alternated between horror and amusement.

"That's right." Lilian beamed. "But we already knew each other from Cambridge." And she laid out the story of the boat race to her father, leaving out the bit about the kiss and the heart on the tree trunk.

"He writes poems, Daddy. For me!"

Tim rolled his eyes. "Lilian, that may all appear very romantic to you. But I would prefer that he write his poems for someone else. You're too young for a boyfriend, and he's too young for a girlfriend."

"Ben is very mature for his age," Lily said. "He skipped who knows how many grades."

"No doubt the boy is intelligent; his parents aren't dumb, after all. But he should use his brain and not go about flirting with the only girl in town with whom problems are guaranteed. You simply can't fall in love with the son of Florence Biller, Lily."

Tim waved a crutch to emphasize his words, appearing ridiculous even to himself.

Lilian threw her flaming red hair back and raised her head proudly. "Watch me."

"Tim, they're nothing but games. How can you take it seriously?" Elaine was sitting in the garden, watching her husband, who was snorting with rage, with a mixture of concern and amusement. Whenever Tim became excited about something, he couldn't sit still. Even years after the accident, he still took his limitations hard, and now he was limping back and forth, lamenting the obvious catastrophe Lilian and Ben were in the process of unleashing.

From Elaine's perspective, he shared in the guilt for the latest dramatic developments. That morning he could think of nothing better than to send his stubborn daughter home. Lilian had obediently mounted her small mare, but instead of heading straight home, she had decided that the horse desperately needed to stretch her legs that day. The well-paved road to the Biller Mine was the perfect place to gallop her, and halfway along the stretch she had come upon the Billers' car, which caused the horse to shy. The chauffeur stopped the car, and Ben hopped out.

What followed was hard to reconstruct without subjecting the two main participants to a highly embarrassing inquiry. The chauffeur—who had been ordered by a fuming Florence Biller to take her recalcitrant son home by the most direct route—reported that the young master had stepped out with the excuse that the young lady might need help subduing her horse. After which Ben, in truth just looking for Lily, disappeared into the fern forest near the river, where the chauffeur could not pursue him.

"Why had Florence sent Ben away?" Elaine inquired. Lilian still had not come home, but Elaine was not concerned. The girl often went for long rides, and Elaine still knew nothing about the confrontation between father and daughter that morning.

But now Tim had appeared at his usual time—apparently ready to give his daughter a piece of his mind. Elaine hadn't told him that Lily wasn't home yet since she knew he would only grow more agitated when he learned that she was off on a ride instead of reporting for the house arrest he had imposed that morning. That was why Elaine had steered him toward the garden. She wanted to gain some clarity on what had happened before he discovered Lily was gone.

"Well, why do you think?" Tim asked. "The good Mrs. Biller naturally got wind of the rumors too. Rumors like that spread like wildfire. It's a mystery to me how you haven't heard it yet."

Elaine shrugged. She preferred not to tell her husband that she and Charlene had met Madame Clarisse, the brothel owner, for tea that afternoon. The three women had maintained their old friendship over the years, but it was better if Matt and Tim did not learn of the relationship between their wives and the prostitutes. Though Madame Clarisse was a great source of gossip, her information arrived at night; during the day, while the honorable women chatted, the beauties of the night tended to be asleep.

"I have no doubt Florence is even more worked up about it than I am," Tim continued.

"Even more?" Elaine asked mockingly.

"She just called me. And if one could pour fire and brimstone down the telephone line, my office would have been reduced to ash. According to her chauffeur's testimony, our Lily dragged their Ben by the hair into a glade where she . . ." He stopped.

Elaine giggled. "The poor boy!"

"Lainie, please, take this seriously. Our relationship with the Billers is already strained enough. Lily mustn't make it worse." Tim finally sat down in one of the garden chairs.

"But Tim, what exactly is she going to do? If I've understood you correctly, she met the boy in Cambridge. They flirted a bit, and now Lily is beside herself because chance has brought them together again. You know how she is; she has a weakness for romance. Making a production of it is silly. On the contrary, you're only going to encourage her."

"They met secretly," Tim insisted.

"In broad daylight behind the church. So secretly they didn't even notice Mrs. Tanner was there."

"That makes it all the more worrisome," Tim grumbled. "They must have been awfully wrapped up with each other."

Elaine laughed. "Which is completely normal for young love. Believe me, Tim, the best thing would be to ignore it. And still better would be to condone their friendship openly. If the two of them meet secretly, they'll feel like Romeo and Juliet. But if the Capulets had invited young Montague to dinner, Juliet would soon have figured out that the boy only thought about sword fights and was too dimwitted to carry out simple instructions without stabbing himself right away."

Tim had to laugh despite himself. "The Capulets would have caused the dinner to end in a bloodbath, though. At least if they had Florence Biller's sensibilities. That's why it doesn't really matter how we feel about it. She won't tolerate their friendship under any circumstances. Besides, I already promised her I'd forbid Lilian from having any contact with her son." He stood up with great effort, in an effort to demonstrate his authority.

Elaine rolled her eyes.

"Well, we'll see how far you get with that."

"Florence, please, what awful thing did he do?" Caleb Biller tended to avoid confrontations with his wife, but he couldn't ignore this. He was sipping his second whiskey of the evening—the first had been to give him courage, the second so he could hold on to it when things got rough. But when Florence had stormed into the salon and started in on her accusations against Ben, he had almost dropped the costly crystal glass.

Florence Biller generally looked immaculate in her office "uniform"—never even betraying sweat marks in the height of summer—but this evening, her face was mottled, locks of hair had come loose from her bun, and her proper little blue hat sat crooked in her hair.

"He met with a girl," she declared in outrage, pacing the room. "Against my express instructions."

Caleb smiled. "Is this about girls writ large, about a very specific girl, or about the instructions?"

Florence glared at him. "It's about all of it. He is to obey my instructions. And as for the girl, of all the girls in the world, it just had to be Lilian Lambert. That impertinent little beast of more than questionable pedigree."

Caleb frowned. "Little Lilian is undoubtedly a bit unusual," he responded vaguely. In truth, he only knew the girl by sight, as well as from Florence's outbursts about her impertinence on the telephone. "But what's questionable about Timothy Lambert's pedigree?"

"You know as well as I do that Elaine O'Keefe used to be one of Madame Clarisse's girls. And Lilian was born only a few months after she married Tim Lambert. Need I go on?"

Caleb sighed. "Lainie was never a prostitute. She played the piano in the pub, nothing more. Tim's paternity is absolutely uncontested."

"Elaine O'Keefe shot her first husband dead." Florence played her trump.

"In self-defense, as I recall." Caleb hated to dig up old stories. "In any event, Tim is doing well. She didn't make a habit of it, and that's hardly something that can be passed on. Besides, Ben's only met Miss Lambert once. It's hardly like there's talk of marriage." Caleb poured his third whiskey.

"One thing leads to another. At any rate, she'll put ideas in his head. I found this on his desk earlier." She pulled a piece of paper from her pocket. "He's writing poems."

Caleb took the sheet and skimmed it quickly. "'Lily of Cambridge, my boat is your breath, and I will wait for it to my very death.' That's disconcerting," Caleb remarked and emptied his whiskey in one gulp. "He might be a good linguist, but I don't see any literary talent."

"Caleb, don't make light of this. The boy is stubborn, and I will drive that out of him. The poetry too. He will learn to think like a businessman."

Caleb reached for the whiskey bottle. "Never," he said bravely. "He's not born for that, Florence. No more so than I. He's my son too."

Florence turned to him. She smiled with ugly, curled lips, and Caleb shuddered when he recognized in her gaze the same contempt that he had so often seen in the eyes of his father.

"Clearly the root of the problem," she remarked venomously. "Do you hear the door? I think he's come home."

Florence listened attentively. Caleb did not hear anything, but his wife threw herself into position. "It's him. I'm going to go beat Miss Lambert out of him. And that poetry while I'm at it."

She rushed out.

Caleb knocked back another glass of whiskey.

"Well, we'll see how far you get with that," he mumbled, recalling that night years ago when he had "proved his manhood" to Florence. For the first and last time.

Caleb Biller's self-confidence had reached a low point when he asked Florence Biller for her hand. Caleb had desperately resisted the idea of getting married since he did not feel anything for women. Whenever he thought about love, male forms appeared before him, and he had only known excitement once. His roommate at boarding school in England had been his friend. More than his friend.

As the son of a mine owner in Greymouth, however, Caleb had no hope of living out his preference. Hoping for an heir for the Biller Mine, Caleb's parents went ahead and arranged for him to marry Florence Weber. Florence and Caleb came to their own agreement. Since such a marriage would give her the opportunity to achieve her dream of becoming a businesswoman and managing the Biller Mine, she settled for a platonic marriage. For Caleb, it meant that his parents would leave him in peace.

What had been left unsaid was that Florence intended to pass the mine on to her own flesh and blood. Caleb was horrified when he noticed the appraising looks she cast at office employees and even miners. The apparent elect back then was her secretary, a man by the name of Terrence Bloom. In his darker hours Caleb would have undoubtedly held his peace and ignored it. But in the first few months after their wedding, his confidence began to return. Relieved of the pressure of having to bumble along managing the mine, he began writing articles for academic journals, which garnered great enthusiasm. Maori art being a largely unexplored field, the journals fell over each other to publish Caleb's articles, and he soon found himself in a lively exchange of letters with various universities in the Old and New World. For the first time in his life, his crest was on the rise. He held his head up—he was not about to let some mining secretary make him grow horns.

Florence Biller lacked the sensitivity to recognize Caleb's feelings. Moreover, she had allowed herself to fall mildly in love with this man, her first lover. One night, when Caleb returned home earlier than expected from a Maori celebration, he came upon Florence and Terrence entwined in each other's arms. Although he was furious, he remained every inch the gentleman.

"Mr. Bloom, you will leave my house and my employ at once," Caleb said. "I'd rather not see you in Greymouth again. If anyone else thinks of hiring you, I'll bring my influence to bear. That would be very compromising for you because I must suppose you had hoped to enrich yourself, let's say, financially, off my family. However, if you were to disappear post haste, my wife would no doubt write you a good referral."

Terrence Bloom looked as taken aback by this speech as Florence did, but then he quickly got out of bed. Caleb did not grace him with a look as he hurried out, his clothes bundled in his arms.

"As for you, Florence." Caleb inhaled deeply. "Did you love this fellow or was it about breeding?" He spat the last word at her.

Florence would not be intimidated. "You don't really mean to deny me an heir? Your father would be very disappointed if it were revealed that you . . ." She cast a meaningful look at Caleb's lower body.

Caleb took a deep breath. The evening with the Maori had not only satisfied him artistically but also awakened other longings. As always when he saw the men dance their war-*haka*, he felt his sex harden. He now attempted to thrust the image of those muscular dancers before Florence's stocky, undressed body.

"I won't disappoint either him or you," Caleb said, opening his pants. He threw himself on top of her and worked up to thrusting by concentrating on the stomping rhythm of the *haka*, envisioning the play of muscles on the dancers. He thought of the strong hands of the men shaking their spears, their gleaming, sweaty bodies redolent of earth. Caleb thrust to the rhythm of the *haka*. He was the spear in the hand of his favorite dancer; he was enfolded, pressed, and finally released to strike the target; he was in harmony with the body and spirit of the warrior. As his weapon unloaded itself, Caleb collapsed on top of Florence.

"I'm sorry," he said quietly.

Florence pushed him away, stood up, and staggered into the bathroom.

"I should apologize," she remarked. "What I did was unforgivable. What you did, well, let's call it our duty."

Caleb never fulfilled his duty again, but Florence now took pains not to cause him affront. She blushed deeply when she revealed she was pregnant a few weeks later.

"Naturally, I don't know if . . ."

Caleb nodded, long since sober and still ashamed. "You wanted an heir. Whether I have one matters little to me."

Though Caleb and Florence were initially unsure about little Ben's parentage, it soon became obvious. Ben not only resembled Caleb physically, but in personality as well. He had the same brooding character as his father, as well as his inquisitive spirit. Ben could read at the age of four and could hardly be pulled away from his father's books. Pursuing an early interest in languages, he buried himself in Caleb's dictionaries and soaked up the Maori his father spoke to him like a sponge.

By the age of seven, he was bored to death in Greymouth's primary school, and Florence agreed with her husband's wishes to send Ben to England. Caleb hoped for the highest possible intellectual advancement of his son, Florence for his normalization. The quiet, sensitive boy—who had mastered complicated arithmetic but could be easily swindled by his little brothers in a candy store—struck her as odd. Sam, her second born, who fortunately resembled her much more than the young foreman who had sired him, struck her as markedly more normal. He got in fights like a real boy, and instead of establishing comparisons between Maori and other Polynesian languages, he tried instead to rip the legs off wetas. The third born, Jake, also took more after Florence, although she recognized clear resemblances between herself and his father, a bookkeeper. The foreman was let go and the bookkeeper was promoted to a higher position at a different coal mine in the region as soon as the pregnancies were a sure thing. Only then would she admit to Caleb that she was once again in a family way. He had recognized every child as his own without comment.

Caleb smiled at the thought of his only flesh-and-blood son. He could not fault him for a relationship with Lilian Lambert. On the contrary, he had never felt so relieved. Yes, perhaps the wrong girl had won Ben's heart. But Caleb had not passed on his own unfortunate preference. His son would not have to struggle against desires for which the world would condemn him.

While their parents fought and grumbled, Lilian and Ben wandered hand in hand through the fern forest by the river. Wanting to be reminded of their walk along the riverbank in England, they fought their way up embankments and through half-rotted underwood. Lilian's eyes lit up when Ben chivalrously helped her over uneven terrain. When there were no obstacles to overcome, they enthusiastically made plans for the future. Ben was not unhappy about his return to New Zealand, as the universities in Dunedin, Wellington, and Auckland offered considerably better research possibilities in the field of linguistics that interested him.

"In principle every Polynesian island had its own language, even if they were related. But that's the opportunity—if one compares

Maori to the other languages, the region of origin of New Zealand's first settlers could be located."

Though she hardly spoke a word of Maori, Lilian hung off his every word. Until then, she had couldn't have cared less where the fabled land of Hawaiki lay. But when Ben spoke of it, that was a different story.

Lilian told him of her stay at Kiward Station where, despite the recent tragedies, she had once again been very happy. She wanted to live on a farm someday, have many animals around her, and plenty of children.

Ben too hung off her every word, though he did not care much for cats or dogs and rode horses only reluctantly. He liked cars considerably more. As for babies, he found their noise rather aggravating. But when Lilian raved about family life, that, too, was a different story.

Later, Lilian wrote a long letter to a friend in England describing how much she and Ben had in common, and Ben raved in a new poem about the meeting of soul mates.

3

Gwyneira McKenzie changed for dinner, glad to accept the help of one of her Maori maids. Until recently she had hardly felt her age, but after the events of the previous weeks, she often felt too exhausted to put on her corset or exchange her day dress for a proper evening gown. She continued with the ritual, though she did not really know why since she had found it a burdensome and impractical tradition even as a young woman. She would only be sharing the table with her miserable, monosyllabic son whose despair cut her to the heart. She too was mourning; she missed James with every fiber of her being. They had hardly been separated for even a day. But she had seen the loss of James coming. Charlotte was different. Jack had expected a long life with her. They had wanted children, made plans. Gwyneira could very well understand why Jack was inconsolable.

With a sigh she allowed Wai to wrap a black shawl around her shoulders. Since James's death Gwyneira had dressed in mourning—another custom she held up despite thinking it was nonsense. She did not need to demonstrate her sorrow. Jack did not care; he had been dressing normally since the end of the burials himself.

"May I go now, Mrs. McKenzie? Kiri wants me to help in the kitchen." Wai did not have to ask, but she was new in the house and a bit shy.

Gwyneira nodded and pulled herself together to give her an encouraging smile.

"Of course, Wai. Thank you. And when you go home tonight, take a few potatoes to plant for Rongo. Her sleeping tea helped me greatly."

The girl nodded and left.

Gwyneira thought warmly of the Maori who made their home on Kiward Station. She was even grateful to Tonga, the chieftain and her former enemy, for he had helped her solve the seemingly impossible dilemma of where to bury James.

In the property's family cemetery, Gerald Warden, the founder of Kiward Station, his wife, Barbara, and his son, Paul, lay buried side by side. Gwyneira had raised a memorial for Lucas Warden, her first husband. James, however, had not been a Warden, and everything in Gwyneira bristled against burying him next to them. Gerald Warden had pursued his former foreman as a rustler, and he would have been beside himself if he'd ever found out that James had fathered his first grandchild, Fleurette. To lay the two men next to each other in death was wrong, but she couldn't summon the energy to designate a second burial ground.

Too numb to think, she reluctantly agreed to receive Tonga, who had come to pay his respects on behalf of the tribe. After expressing his condolences politely in impeccable English, he told her there was something important to discuss.

Probably another territorial claim, she had thought, or trouble with sheep trespassing on land the Maori considered *tapu*, holy and untouchable. But then the chief surprised her. "You know, Mrs. McKenzie," he remarked, "that it is very important to my people to keep the spirits of family members close together and happy. An appropriate gravesite is important to us, and Mr. McKenzie knew that. Thus he met with our understanding when he came to our tribal elders with a special request. It concerned a *urupa*, a burial place for him, and later for you and your son."

Gwyneira swallowed.

"If you agree, Mrs. McKenzie, we permit you the placement of a graveyard on the holy site you and Mr. McKenzie called the circle of stone warriors. Mr. McKenzie claimed it has a special meaning for you."

Gwyneira had blushed deeply at that and came close to bursting into tears in the presence of the chieftain. The circle of stone warriors, a collection of rocks in the grassland that appeared to form a circle, had been their meeting place and love nest many years ago. Gwyneira was convinced that their daughter, Fleurette, had been conceived there.

Nevertheless she managed to thank Tonga in a dignified manner, and a few days later James was lain between the stones, in the presence of close family and the Maori tribe. Gwyneira thought that appropriate. James would have much preferred the Maori's mourning-*haka* to the chamber music group that played at Charlotte's burial in Christchurch, where her parents had asked that she be buried.

Charlotte probably would have seen things the same way, but Jack was in no condition to organize anything. He left the funeral to the Greenwoods and was hardly responsive at the reception. He returned to Kiward Station immediately afterward and gave himself fully to his sorrow. Gwyneira and Jack's friends among the shepherds tried to cheer him up or at least distract him, but even when he did what was asked of him, he was hardly there. If there were decisions to be made, Gwyneira made them together with the foreman. Jack only spoke when necessary; he hardly ate and spent most of his time brooding in the apartments he had shared with Charlotte. He declined to look through her things and give them away. Once Gwyneira found him on the bed, one of Charlotte's dresses in his arms.

"It still smells like her," he said, embarrassed.

Gwyneira withdrew without a word.

That evening Jack appeared at the dinner table in a clean, light summer suit, instead of his usual work pants and shirt.

"Mother." Jack positioned a chair for her. "I have something to discuss with you."

"Can't it wait until after dinner? I see you've dressed up tonight, and I'd enjoy spending some time with you. Have you sent the men with the last sheep on their way?"

It was November, and the sheep should already have been herded into the mountains. But Gwyneira had wanted to keep an eye on a few stragglers. Now a few shepherds were moving them into the foothills.

"Yes," he said finally. "And in all honesty, Mother, I was seriously thinking of going with the sheep. I can't take it. I tried, but I can't. Everything here, every corner, every piece of furniture, every face, reminds me of Charlotte. And I can't bear it. You said it yourself, I'm letting myself go." Jack ran a hand nervously through his auburn hair. It was clearly difficult for him to continue speaking.

"I understand. But what do you want to do? I don't think a hermit's life in the mountains is the answer. Perhaps you could spend a few weeks with Fleurette and Ruben."

"And help in their hardware store?" Jack asked with a crooked grin. "I don't know if that's where my strengths lie. And please don't say Greymouth next. I like Lainie and Tim, but I'd be no better as a miner. And I don't want to be a burden to anyone. I want to be helpful." Jack bit his lip, then squared himself. "To get to the point, Mother, there's no sense dragging it out. I've joined the ANZAC."

"The what?"

Jack rubbed his forehead. This would be harder than he had expected.

"The ANZAC. The Australian and New Zealand Army Corps."

"The army? You can't be serious, Jack. There's a war on!"

"Precisely, Mother. They'll send us to Europe. That'll help me clear my head."

Gwyneira glared at her son. "I should think so. When bullets are buzzing around your ears, it'll be hard to think about Charlotte. Are you in your right mind, Jack? Do you want to get yourself killed? Do you even know why they're fighting?"

"The colonies have promised the motherland their unconditional support," Jack said, playing with his napkin.

"Politicians always talk nonsense."

Her son had ripped Gwyneira out of her sorrowful lethargy. She sat upright and argued with flashing eyes. "You have no idea what this war is about, but you want to take off to shoot total strangers who never did anything to you. Why not just jump off a cliff like Charlotte?"

"It's not about suicide," Jack said in agony. "It's about, about . . ."

"It's about putting God to the test, isn't it?" Gwyneira stood up and went to the whiskey cabinet. She had lost her appetite and needed something stronger than table wine. "That's it, Jack, isn't it? You'll see how far you can go before the devil takes you. But that's nonsense, and you know it!"

"I'm sorry, but you won't change my mind. Besides, there's nothing I can do. I've already enlisted."

Gwyneira filled her glass and turned back to her son, her eyes filled with despair.

"And what about me? You're leaving me all alone, Jack."

Jack sighed. He had thought about his mother, pushing his decision off again and again to avoid causing her pain. Jack hoped that Gloria would be sent home soon, thus giving Gwyneira a new occupation and will to live. He did not feel capable of raising his mother's spirits. He wanted to go away; it did not matter where.

"I'm sorry, Mother." He wanted to hug her but could not bring himself to stand up and put his arms around her. "But it won't last long anyway. They say the war will be over in a few weeks, and then I can maybe look around Europe for a bit. We're off to Australia first anyway. The fleet is casting off from Sydney. Thirty-six ships, Mother. The largest convoy that has ever crossed the Indian Ocean."

Gwyneira drained her whiskey. She did not care about this great convoy, or about this war in Europe. She only felt her world falling apart.

Roly O'Brien helped Tim dress for a formal dinner that was to take place that evening with the local mine operators and representatives of the New Zealand Railway Corporation. After dinner, the men would withdraw to discuss the changes demanded by the war—above all, the increase in the quotas and possible mutual transportation arrangements. The mines all had been expanded, and more train cars and special trains were needed to transport the coal to the international ports on the East Coast. Tim smiled at the thought of the railroad representatives' confused reaction when Florence Biller not only joined the men but did all the talking.

Since the incident with Lilian and Ben, the Lamberts' and Billers' relationship had markedly worsened. Florence seemed to hold Tim personally accountable for the fact that Ben continued to write poems instead of taking a serious interest in the mine. Tim wondered if Florence would bring her son with her—perhaps in place of her husband. The Lamberts had decided to leave Lilian at home, and she had been fuming all day.

Roly O'Brien was unusually quiet, and his reticence finally caught Tim's attention.

"What's wrong, Roly?"

"Well, Mr. Lambert, I wonder, do you think you could do without me for a few weeks?"

Now that he'd come out with it, Roly looked at Tim hopefully. He had just helped Tim into his vest and was holding the jacket ready. Tim put it on before answering.

"Are you planning a vacation, Roly? Not a bad idea; you haven't had more than a day off since you started working for me. But why so suddenly? And where are you going? A honeymoon perhaps?"

Roly turned beet red. "No, no, I still haven't asked Mary, I mean, I, well, the other boys say before you marry, you ought to have seen something of the world."

Tim frowned. "What boys? Bobby and Greg in the mine? What grand bit of the world do they plan on seeing before they meet Birdie or Carrie at the altar?"

"Bobby and Greg are joining the army," Roly replied, brushing some lint from Tim's jacket. "Shall I shave you first, Mr. Lambert? You've sprouted a little stubble since this morning."

Tim looked at Roly in alarm. "The boys signed up for the ANZAC? Don't tell me you plan to do the same, Roly."

Roly nodded. "I did. Mom says it was too rushed, but the boys wouldn't leave me alone. In any case, I signed." He lowered his eyes.

Tim fell back on his chair. "Roly, for heaven's sake. But we can delay that. If I go to the recruitment office and make it crystal clear to them that I can't run the mine without your help . . ."

"You'd do that for me?" Roly looked touched.

Tim sighed. He hated the thought of confronting soldiers and admitting weakness. "Of course. And for your mother. The Lambert Mine took her husband. So I owe it to her to take the best possible care of her son."

"And if I, if I don't want you to? To take it back, I mean?"

Tim sighed again. "Now have a seat, Roly, we need to discuss this."

"But Mr. Lambert, your dinner. Mrs. Lambert will be waiting."

Tim shook his head and pointed to the other chair in the room. "My wife won't starve, and dinner can start without us. But shipping off to war, how did you even come up with such a stupid idea? Did any German or Austrian or Hungarian or whomever else you're supposed to go shoot ever do anything to you?"

Roly chewed his lower lip. "Of course not, Mr. Lambert, but the motherland . . . Bobby and Greg. . ."

"Bobby and Greg seem to have more to do with it than the motherland," Tim remarked. "My God, Roly, I know you grew up with those boys and call them your friends. But Matt Gawain doesn't care for them; they drink more than they work. We only hold on to them because there's a shortage of workers. No wonder they were seized by the desire for adventure—the army is more honorable by far than being let go. But you don't have to go with them, Roly. You have a secure position, everyone appreciates you, and a girl as good as Mary Flaherty is waiting for you to propose."

"They say I don't have any backbone. Nurse boy or queer boy, what's the difference?"

Roly had always borne the nickname "nurse boy"—which he earned caring for Tim—with dignity. But the ridicule nagged at him. The work of a caretaker didn't count for much among the rough boys on the West Coast.

"And now you're going to risk your life for this nonsense?" Tim asked. "Roly, this is no harmless adventure; this is war. There'll be bullets flying. Have you ever even held a gun? What does your mother have to say about it?"

"She's angry. She says she doesn't understand why we're fighting since no one attacked us. So she thinks I ought to stay where I am. But she doesn't see. She's just a woman, after all."

"Your mother will have to bury you if you fall, Roly. Assuming England makes the effort to ship dead New Zealanders home. They'll probably bury you all right there in France."

"I've never been to France. Sure, you can talk when it comes to adventure. You've already been all over Europe. But what about us? We'll never get out of here. In the army we'll see foreign countries."

"Is that what they told you at the recruitment office? War is not a vacation."

"But it won't last long. Just a few weeks, they say. And we're going to a training camp first, in Australia. The war may be over by the time we're done."

"Oh, Roly. I wish you'd told me sooner. Look, I don't know what will happen, but I know mining and business; we're preparing for years of war. So, please, listen to your mother and Mary. She'll give you something to think about when you tell her about it. I'll work on getting you out of your contract tomorrow."

Roly shook his head. He looked determined.

"I can't, Mr. Lambert. If I chicken out now, no one in town will ever look me in the eye again. You can't do that to me."

"All right, fine, Roly, I'll get by without you. But not forever, you understand? You'll be so good as to survive, come back, and marry your girl. Do I make myself clear?"

Roly grinned. "Crystal."

4

People packed the streets, waving and cheering at the soldiers as they made their way to the Dunedin harbor in unruly six-man columns. Roly O'Brien, Greg McNamara, and Bobby O'Mally marched cheerfully in the third row, prouder than they had ever been in their lives. Laughing, they pinned the flowers the girls of Dunedin tossed them onto their new brown uniform jackets.

"Didn't I tell you it would be grand?" Greg asked, jostling Roly a bit drunkenly. Bobby had brought some whiskey to the assembly yard. Though alcohol was forbidden, that didn't bother the freshly minted soldiers, most of whom were used to running wild. Except for a few who had tried to make it as gold miners, hardly any of them had ever held a steady job.

"Then at least you boys have practice digging trenches," the lieutenant said when he asked the new recruits about their areas of expertise. Though Roly could have mentioned his experience as a caretaker, he kept it to himself.

The harbor was full of people who'd come to see their heroes off. Only a few—mostly tearful mothers and wives—were related to the men. The rest were cheering the soldiers heading off on their grand adventure. They admired the gleaming insignia of the ANZAC on the recruits' wide-brimmed hats and alternated between calls of huzzah for Great Britain and taunts directed at Germany, which the recruits responded to with good humor. The embarkment was a peculiar festival. Since not everyone was able to find a place on deck to wave good-bye to their admirers, some sat with their legs dangling over the side. Roly was only just able to save Bobby—drunk with excitement and cheap whiskey—from falling in the water.

Jack McKenzie held himself above the fray. He had marched silently in the last row with no eye for the cheering crowd. All the commotion had already almost made him regret his decision. He had wanted to go off to war but seemed to have landed at the fair. While the others celebrated as the ship set sail, he stashed his few possessions in his tiny locker. Perhaps it had been a mistake to sign on to an infantry division.

Jack flopped down on his berth. He had secured one of the lower beds for himself. The primitive lodgings had been quickly outfitted with three-level berths meant to house nine men. They did not seem very secure, and Jack hoped no big fellow would be bedding down above him.

But he was to get no peace. Shortly after the ship had weighed anchor, just as Jack was hoping the waves would rock him to sleep, someone or something stumbled down the stairs. Two young boys, a blond, stocky fellow and a stick of a boy with curly red-brown hair, were supporting a third, who was slurring something to himself.

"He can't be seasick already, can he, Roly?" the blond boy asked.

The curly-haired fellow rolled his eyes. "He's just three sheets to the wind. Help me heave him into the second bunk. Let's hope he doesn't spew."

Jack hoped the same. The men did not billet their friend directly above him, but next to him instead.

"He already did, and he looks like he's at death's door." The blond looked nervous.

Curly felt expertly for his friend's pulse. "Nah, nothing's wrong with him. He just needs to sleep it off. Is there any water here? He's going to have a hell of a thirst when he wakes up."

"The tap's in the hall," Jack said.

The blond reached for a bucket and staggered out.

Curly thanked Jack, taking a look at him for the first time.

"Do we know each other?" he asked.

Jack eyed him more closely and had a vague recollection of him. He had seen the young man somewhere before, but not on the farm.

"You're from Greymouth, right?" he asked.

Roly nodded. "You're Jack McKenzie! Mrs. Lambert's cousin. You paid us a visit a few years ago. With your wife." Roly beamed as Jack painfully recalled his honeymoon with Charlotte to Greymouth.

Then he remembered: the boy had been the one looking after Tim Lambert.

"Were you able to just leave Tim like that?" he asked.

Roly nodded. "He'll be able to get by for a few weeks without me. Probably better than your wife without you," he grinned. But his smile disappeared as soon as he saw Jack's anguished face.

"Did I, did I say something wrong, sir?"

Jack swallowed and shook his head. "My wife died not long ago. But you couldn't have known that. What was your name again?"

"Roly, Mr. McKenzie, sir. Roland O'Brien, but everyone calls me Roly. And I'm very sorry, Mr. McKenzie, truly. Forgive me."

Jack waved it away. "Just call me Jack. You can forget the 'mister' and 'sir.' I'm just Private Jack McKenzie now."

"And I'm Private O'Brien. Isn't it exciting, sir? Private O'Brien." His blond friend had returned and placed the bucket next to the bed.

"This is Private Greg McNamara. And that fellow is Bobby O'Mally. Normally he's not so quiet. He celebrated a little too much is all. Just think, Greg, this is Jack McKenzie from the plains. Mrs. Lambert's cousin." While Roly chattered cheerfully, he retrieved a canteen from his belongings, filled it up for Bobby, held it to the boy's lips, and wet a handkerchief, which he laid on Bobby's forehead.

Jack wondered why Roly had not signed up as a medic. Roly's treatment of his afflicted friend was extremely professional, and he did not even bat an eye when Bobby threw up again, fortunately in a bucket.

Jack, however, had had enough of the stench of vomit, as well as the young men's unclouded cheer. He muttered something about "getting fresh air" and made his way on deck, where celebrations were still under way. Jack headed aft and cast a last glance at the quickly receding New Zealand coast. Jack tried not to think of Charlotte, but as always it was useless. He knew that he would eventually have to stop pining for her every second of the day. But so far he had seen no way out.

Jack found the first night on board the improvised troop transport a living hell. None of his cabinmates were sober, which some of them made clear by getting up every few minutes, stumbling on deck, and throwing up into the sea. Others slept soundly, snoring and sniffling in every register. Jack fled on deck early the next morning and ran directly into the frustrated lieutenant.

"It looks like a pigsty here!" the man roared at him, and Jack could not exactly deny it. The farewell orgies of the day before had left in their wake a stench of urine and vomit, and piles of empty bottles and leftover food. "They call themselves recruits! I've never seen such an undisciplined bunch of . . ."

Lieutenant Keeler spoke with an English accent. Apparently they had sent him from the motherland to supervise the training of the Kiwis. Jack almost felt sorry for him. No doubt the man knew how to train soldiers, but he looked fresh out of the military academy. Most of his subordinates were older and more hard-bitten than he.

"These boys aren't exactly the flower of New Zealand's youth," Jack said with a lopsided grin. "But they'll prove themselves on the front. They're used to a tough slog."

"Is that so?" the officer asked with biting sarcasm. "Lovely of you to share your extensive knowledge with regards to your countrymen. Naturally you consider yourself to be a cut above, do you not, Private . . .?"

"McKenzie, sir." Jack sighed. He realized he had forgotten the "sir" in his first reply and knew that the man would take all his frustration out on him. "And no, sir, I don't think myself a cut above."

"Then prove it to me, Private McKenzie. Make this spic and span. In an hour this deck had better gleam."

As the young officer marched away, Jack went in search of a mop and bucket. He struggled against a burgeoning anger. After all, he had sought something to keep him occupied, and there was water enough. As he was hauling his third bucket out of the sea, Roly O'Brien joined him.

"I'll help you, Mr. McKenzie. I can't sleep anyway. Bobby and that fellow from Otago—what was his name again?—John, are snoring up a storm."

Jack smiled at him. "Just Jack, Roly. And by the looks of it, we'll have to get used to the noise. The boys aren't likely to stop anytime soon."

"They don't have any more whiskey."

Jack laughed. "They'll find fresh supplies in Australia. And in France. What do they drink there? Calvados?"

Roly frowned. He had clearly never heard of Calvados, but then he laughed. "Wine. Mr. and Mrs. Lambert drink French wine. Mrs. Lambert's father sends it to them from Queenstown. But I don't care much for the stuff. I prefer a good whiskey. Don't you, Mr. McKenzie?"

Jack had come upon two more early birds and made no bones about recruiting them to swab the deck. Three more appeared shortly thereafter, and when the lieutenant returned an hour later, the deck was indeed gleaming. Still damp, but clean.

"Very good, Private McKenzie." Fortunately the officer did not hold a grudge. "You may go to breakfast with your men. The galley is manned."

Jack nodded while Roly attempted to salute the officer. He still didn't quite have the hang of it, but he managed to wring a smile from the lieutenant.

"You'll get it yet," he mumbled, strolling away.

A dozen ships were already anchored when the *Great Britain* pulled into the bay at Albany, and many more joined them in the coming days until thirty-six troop transports had assembled, flanked by various battleships. Roly marveled at the gleaming cannons of the *Sydney* and the *Melbourne*, massive warships meant to protect the grand convoy.

"As if anyone would even dare to attack us," he said. Like most of the other soldiers, he felt an irrepressible pride at the mighty fleet. The sight of the ships, the flags, and the many thousands of men in uniform assembled on deck for the departure even affected Jack. The sun shone, the sea lay gleaming blue and flat as a mirror, and the beautiful coast of Albany spread out behind them. Roly, Greg, and Bobby waved, beaming as the convoy set off. Jack felt an uncertain sense of relief. He had wanted to leave everything behind him, and now he finally had. He turned away from the land and looked toward the unknown.

After a few days at sea, the young Lieutenant Keeler called his men on deck. He had an important announcement to make. Since not all of the eight hundred people would fit on deck, and the lieutenant's voice could hardly be heard by those further back, it took several hours for everyone to hear the news: Turkey had declared war on England, so instead of heading to France, the ANZAC would be deployed in the theater of the Dardanelles strait.

"Straight where?" Roly asked, confused.

Jack shrugged. He knew nothing of southeastern European geography.

"Training for combat operations will take place in Egypt," the lieutenant declared. "After a short stop in Colombo, we'll be heading for Alexandria."

Two weeks later, the fleet reached Suez. Here, for the first time, the recruits heard about combat operations on land. Apparently the Turks had made several assaults on the Suez Canal. Lieutenant Keeler established watches and ordered his men to be on the alert as they passed through. Roly spent a stressful night staring at the dark border of the canal and nervously eyeing every campfire and settlement whose lights reached the ship, but nothing of note actually came to pass.

In Alexandria the ships were unloaded, but the ANZACs did not see much of the famous trading city. The British officers steered the excited troops straight to a train depot.

"To Cairo," Greg said, almost disbelieving. All the foreign city names, the narrow, sun-heated streets, the short men in their Arab caftans, the clamor of foreign language, and the unusual sounds and scents of the city fascinated the boys but confused them as well. Despite the proximity of his friends, Roly felt lost in a strange world, even a little homesick.

Jack breathed in the foreignness, finding salvation in the new impressions and occasionally managing to stop brooding about Charlotte—if only he could quit drafting letters to her in his head. Jack considered to whom he could write instead, and finally decided on Gloria. Though he had hardly heard from her, he still felt connected to her.

He described his journey by ship with the proud fleet and later riding to Cairo in a train crammed full of recruits. Not much could be seen of the landscape since the troops were transported at night and reached the city in the first hours of morning. It was still pitch black, and to the men's surprise sharply cold, as they marched the several miles to the training camp—an unexpectedly nerve-racking trek after the weeks of forced indolence onboard the ship.

Jack was frozen solid and tired when they reached the tent city called Zeitoun. Sixteen men shared each shelter; Roly and his friends remained with Jack. With sighs of relief, they took possession of a three-level bunk bed.

Several of the boys—city boys, by the looks of it—were even more exhausted than the boys from Greymouth. Their new uniform boots pinched, and two of their tentmates seemed unable to take another step. They groaned as they removed their boots.

Jack pulled himself together. Someone had to restore order. He pulled Bobby back to his feet and ordered him to go in search of food. Then he told Greg to go for blankets.

"We could just sleep in our clothes," Greg said.

Jack shook his head. "Then we'll get reprimanded tomorrow for our wrinkled uniforms. This is a training camp, boy. Vacation's over; now you're a soldier."

Roly was already rummaging in the first-aid kit included in the recruits' basic equipment and produced some bandages. "No ointment," he remarked critically, "but what's this here?"

He held up a small bottle.

"*Manuka*, tea-tree oil," said one of their comrades whose features suggested Maori ancestry. "An ancient home remedy among the tribes. If you rub it on those fellows' feet, they'll heal faster."

Jack nodded. *Manuka* was used for first aid on Kiward Station as well—though on the sheep and horses.

"But wash your feet first," Jack said. It already stank in the tent. "Who'll volunteer to fetch water?"

The next morning their tent did exceptionally well in the inspection carried out by a sleep-deprived Lieutenant Keeler, and Jack received his first promotion, to lance corporal. Though the position involved little more than what Jack had already been doing—taking responsibility for his men and ensuring their accommodations, uniforms, and, most importantly, weapons were kept clean—Roly admired Jack's new rank without reserve.

"I wonder if I'll ever manage that, Corporal McKenzie? Being promoted must be amazing. Or receiving a medal. There are medals for bravery in the face of the enemy, you know."

"But first you need enemies," Greg grumbled. He had not enjoyed their first exercises that morning. He did not see how marching in rank and file and falling prone on command would be of any use in roughing up the Turks. Jack sighed. Greg seemed to imagine war as a large-scale pub brawl.

Still there was no alternative for him other than to learn how to seek cover, crawl over the ground, dig trenches, and handle rifles and bayonets. Most of the soldiers had fun with the bayonets—and the New Zealanders developed considerable skill as riflemen. After all, many of them had been shooting small wild animals from an early age; thanks to the plague of rabbits, every boy in the Canterbury Plains knew how to handle a rifle.

The Kiwi troops showed less of a gift when it came to following orders quickly. They were not good at marching in step, and to the horror of their British drill masters, they often inquired about the sense of an exercise before they threw themselves in the desert sand as ordered. And they proved distinctly unenthusiastic about trench-digging exercises.

"Man, I've been doing that since I was thirteen," Greg complained. "No one needs to show me how to use a spade."

Jack studied the techniques even as he bristled at the thought of spending weeks at a time in a foxhole. In reality the placement of trenches demanded considerable strategic and architectural skill—for example, they should never be arranged in a straight line but rather in a sort of zigzag pattern. No soldier should be able to see farther than five yards ahead, making it difficult for the enemy to orient themselves when they broke into a trench. Fire bays and traverses needed to be added, and expanding the trench network without fear of bombardment necessitated knowledge of tunnel construction. The experienced miners routinely dug tunnels in the ground that simply collapsed in the desert. Bobby and Greg laughed about it, but Roly surprised Jack one time by rushing out, pale with fear, after the men had just had another load of sand dumped on them.

"I can't, Corporal McKenzie," he whispered, feeling for his back-pack. Each first-aid kit now contained not only bandages but a flask. "Here, want any?"

Roly held the flask out to Jack. His hands were shaking.

Jack gave the contents a quick sniff. High-proof liquor.

"Roly, I ought to report you for this. Drinking on duty. You're not normally like this."

Unlike his buddies, Roly only rarely visited the improvised bars and bordellos that had sprung up quick as lightning around the camp. More often he attended the film showings organized by the YMCA. And on weekends he usually joined Jack and the other better-educated soldiers on their excursions to the pyramids and the Sphinx. Roly had not even gotten drunk after his recent promotion to lance corporal.

"It's medicine, Corporal McKenzie. If I take a gulp now and then, I can deal with the trenches." Roly corked the bottle again but was still pale.

"Poor Roly's been buried once before," Greg said, laughing as if it were the greatest joke in the history of Greymouth, "and he's been scared ever since." The men hooted and slapped the sheepish Roly on the shoulder. Jack, however, was unsettled. Though it had only been a drill, Roly O'Brien was clearly shaken. It would be a problem if Roly could not tolerate confined spaces and darkness when they went into battle.

Jack, who had since been decorated with the rank of full corporal and who was now responsible for three dozen men, took his concern to the training officer in charge.

"Corporal O'Brien was buried for three days in a mine, Major, sir. It still bothers him. I would recommend his transfer to a supply company or another division not based in the trenches."

"And how exactly do you know that we'll be based in trenches, Corporal?" Major Hollander asked with a grin.

"I would imagine so, sir. It seems to be the most effective way of securing positions in this war."

"You're a gifted strategist, Corporal. But better save that for when you've made it to general. For the time being, you shouldn't be thinking, only following orders. I'll keep an eye on that little sissy O'Brien. Cave-in! He'll get over that, Corporal, I guarantee it. And oh yes, inform your men that we're breaking camp. At midnight on April eleventh, we're taking the train to Cairo and then shipping off for the Dardanelles."

Jack walked off, frustrated but with his heart beating heavily. For better or worse, they were entering the war.

5

The ship assignments were different this time. What had originally been a colorful haphazard mass had been grouped into divisions and battalions with a variety of ranks and specialist teams. Jack had been assigned former coal and gold miners who could dig trenches with breathtaking alacrity. Jack figured they wouldn't put these men in the front line. If there were an attack, they would first secure positions. It therefore was logical that his group shared the same transport as the medics and doctors of the field hospital. Ironically the first person to save a life as they hauled equipment on board was Jack McKenzie.

The troop transports lay at anchor just outside the harbor, and the men and material were brought on board in boats. Operating from a rowboat, Jack and some of his men secured a ramp, which they used to pass tents and stretchers up to the ship; the sea was choppy, and a strong wind was blowing. Anything not secured on deck was being blown overboard. Hats were flying through the air, as was the occasional carelessly stowed empty backpack. But what suddenly splashed in the water next to Jack was considerably heavier than a backpack—and moreover let out a heartrending howl after impact. Jack was astonished when a small brown mutt surfaced and began paddling for its life.

"Take over for me," he called to Roly, pressing the rope he had been holding into his hand. Then he pulled his shirt over his head, slipped out of his boots, and leaped into the water. Within a few strokes, he had reached the dog and pulled the shivering animal to him. Jack knew that swimming against the tide back to the boat would be difficult, but then the rowboat appeared beside him. Roly had not hesitated a moment. Let the ramp sway—they would rescue their corporal first.

Jack handed the dog to Roly, then pulled himself on board.

"So who or what are you?" Roly asked the little dog, who sprayed all the rowers as it shook itself dry. It was small, bowlegged, and stocky, and its giant button eyes looked as if someone had circled them with kohl.

"A dachshund, I'd guess," Jack said. The dog wagged its tail. On the deck of the ship, a hectic scene was unfolding.

"Paddy! Paddy, come here. Damn it, where is that mutt?" An enervated adjutant stormed out of the officers' quarters. "Help me, boys, I need to find the beast before Beeston goes mad."

Jack and the others grinned at each other. "Clearly he belongs to the unit, maybe even the officer corps. Let's head back to the ship. You boys heard him, they miss their pup." Jack held on tight to the dog until they reached the ramp.

A thickset middle-aged man in a staff doctor's uniform had just appeared on deck. Joseph Beeston, Commander of the Fourth Field Ambulance.

"Paddy! Oh God, I hope he hasn't fallen in the water again with this swell."

When the rowboat had returned to its position, Jack climbed up the ramp, keeping an iron grip on the trembling Paddy all the way up the rocking planks.

"Are you looking for this fellow, sir?" he asked smiling.

Commander Beeston looked greatly relieved as he took the dog from Jack.

"Overboard?" he asked.

Jack nodded. "But was quickly rescued in a heroic action by the Fourth New Zealand Infantry Division, Commander, sir." He saluted.

"Victoria Cross, Victoria Cross," Roly and the others in the boat chanted. The Victoria Cross was the highest honor the British Empire offered to those who fought on the front line.

Commander Beeston smiled. "I can't offer you that, Corporal, but a towel and a glass of whiskey to warm you up, I can. Please follow me."

The staff doctor headed toward his quarters, trailed by his dog. Jack followed him curiously. He had yet to see an officer's cabin with his own eyes and was quite impressed by the mahogany furniture and general luxury of their rooms. Commander Beeston's adjutant handed him a fluffy bath towel while the staff doctor uncorked a bottle of single-malt whiskey. Jack sipped indulgently at the drink.

"Oh, and do bring us some hot tea, Walters. This young man needs to warm back up."

Jack assured the commander that it was not all that cold outside, but Beeston shook his head. "No arguments. Can't have you getting a lung infection and this mischief-maker here having the first death of Gallipoli on his conscience. Can we, Paddy?"

Paddy wagged his tail again when he heard his name. The staff doctor rubbed the dog dry.

"Gallipoli, sir?" Jack asked.

Beeston laughed. "Oh, I hope I'm not giving away military secrets. But we've just been informed that's our first deployment point. A rocky backwater at the entrance to the Dardanelles. Not of any actual importance, but it will secure the advance on Constantinople. If we drive the Turks back that far, then they're practically conquered."

"And so we're headed straight there?"

"Almost. First we're headed to the staging post for this operation, Lemnos. An island that belongs to . . ."

"Greece, sir."

Beeston nodded. "We'll carry out a few more maneuvers there, since my battalion has been training for conditions in France rather than here. But we'll head out shortly after that. Is this your first engagement with the enemy?"

Jack nodded. "New Zealand is not a very warlike nation. Even our natives are peaceful."

"And the most dangerous native beast is the mosquito, I know. Australia is somewhat rougher."

"We won't fall behind the Aussies in a fight," Jack said proudly and almost a little insulted.

"I'm sure that's true. But now I'm afraid I must send you back to your men, Corporal . . ."

"Jack McKenzie, sir."

"Corporal McKenzie. I'll make note of your name. You've done well by me. Now, shake, Paddy, shake." The staff doctor bent down to his dog and tried to wring a "sit" out of him, but Paddy was not receptive to commands.

Jack smiled and crouched down in front of the dog. He pulled lightly on the dog's collar, straightening up himself a bit—and Paddy plopped down on his rear. At a prompting motion of Jack's hand, the dog offered his paw to shake.

Commander Beeston was thunderstruck. "How did you do that?"

"A very simple dog-training technique," Jack replied. "I learned it when I was a child. And this little guy is rascally but smart. If you gave me a few weeks with him, sir, I could teach him to herd sheep."

Beeston smiled. "Now you've saved the dog and impressed his master."

Jack grinned. "That's New Zealand, sir. In Australia they shoot predators; we teach them to shake."

"Then I'm excited to see how the Turks react," Beeston said. Jack McKenzie—he certainly would not forget that name.

Lemnos was a small, picturesque island with a craggy coastline, narrow beaches, and towering cliffs. The ANZAC soldiers looked on with fascination, moved to pity by the poverty of the simple stone houses and the Stone Age wooden plows pulled by oxen. Some of the natives still wrapped themselves in lambskin, and either went barefoot over the stony landscape or protected their feet with rawhide sheep's leather sandals. The island's harbor was now filled with modern military technology, including twenty battleships. The men hardly had any time to let the sight affect them, as they started practicing disembarking maneuvers in full combat gear right away. Over and over again all week, they shimmied down rope ladders and rowed to land, sometimes at night and always as silently as possible.

"It's not hard to do by itself," Roly observed on the fourth day as their unit steered toward a narrow beach, "but what about when they're shooting at you from land?"

"Oh, they won't dare," Greg said, "with all the warships behind us. They'll be providing us with cover, you see."

But Jack shared Roly's concerns. The Turks were not going to give up their beach, let alone their town, without a fight. And had Beeston not said something about a "rocky backwater"? The defenders would likely be sitting in secure positions and firing down at them from some cliff.

"Oh, if the Turks are anything like these poor villagers on Lemnos, then they shouldn't put up much of a fight," said Bobby. "Maybe we should have brought a few of the Maori's war clubs with us. Then it'd be a fairer fight."

Jack raised his eyebrows. Judging from what he had seen, the Greeks on Lemnos were perfectly capable of using a rifle. He dreaded the prospect of having to shoot at people soon.

On April 24, 1915, it was time. As the fleet weighed anchor, led by the *Queen Elizabeth*—lovingly called "Lizzie" by the men—the men once again assembled on deck. Full of pride, they left Lemnos behind them.

"Isn't this wonderful, Corporal McKenzie?" Roly hardly knew where he should look first, at the majestic ships all around or the sun-drenched coast of Lemnos.

"Just Jack," Jack corrected him mechanically. His enthusiasm was more tempered than that of his comrades. The fleet was indeed a glorious sight, but he could not shake the feeling that it was carrying its human freight into death. The evening before—after a rousing address by General Bridges to the assembled troops—Lieutenant Keeler had called his unit leaders to a briefing. Jack now knew the plan of attack and had seen maps of the coast of Gallipoli. Landing on that beach would be hellish, and Jack was not the only one who thought so.

He'd seen his fears reflected in the faces of the British officers, some of whom were battle tested.

The ship carrying Jack's unit was one of the last to arrive at Gallipoli. As morning dawned, they found themselves in a gathering of ships in front of Kabatepe. The boats carrying the first landing troops were fully manned. On the decks of the troop transports, men were waiting to transfer to destroyers. These small, fast warships displaced little water and could bring the troops closer to the beach. Each of them pulled twelve rescue boats in two rows containing six soldiers and five sailors. The latter were to row the boat back to the ship once they had unloaded their human cargo on shore.

The first landing troops consisted entirely of Australians. Jack realized they were sending the youngest soldiers into battle.

With a shudder Jack remembered his mother's words from his childhood: "At that age people still believe in their own invincibility." He must have been around thirteen years old when a bolt of lightning struck the cow barn on Kiward Station. Jack and his friend Maaka had rushed into the fire, braving death to save the enraged breeding bulls. It had seemed heroic to the boys, but Gwyneira had been furious.

The men Jack put in the landing boats were no more than eighteen. Though the army only accepted volunteers over the age of twenty-one, no one looked closely. The landing troops laughed and waved with their rifles. Heavy backpacks hung from their shoulders. Oars glided silently through the water.

Jack let his gaze wander over the dark beach and the cliffs. It was 4:29 a.m. At 4:30 the attack would begin. A yellow light flared up on one of the hills for a few seconds. A deathly stillness reigned over the water for a moment, and then the silhouette of a man appeared on one of the plateaus above. Somebody screamed something, and a bullet was fired, striking the sea.

The British warships began firing with all guns blazing as the Turks stormed the beach. Some shot from the beach itself, others from the three-hundred-foot cliffs. Jack saw the men on the beach fall, mowed down by the warships' firestorm. It was more difficult to target the slopes, where soldiers with nests of machine guns fired on the rowboats headed toward the beach.

"My God, they're, they're shooting," Roly whispered.

"What did you think would happen?" Greg yelled at him.

Roly did not answer. His childlike eyes, already large, grew larger. Even as the soldiers in the boats were being mowed down, more and more reached the shore, leaped onto the beach, and sought cover behind the rocks. The Turks then fired on the sailors rowing back.

"I can't go out into that, damn it." Bobby O'Mally shivered. "Do we have to?"

"No," Jack said. "Our turn comes later. With the medics, maybe even later. Thank God we're better at digging than shooting."

To Jack's amazement, most of his men were still burning to throw themselves into the fight on the shore. They waited impatiently for the attackers to fight their way through to an inland plateau about a mile from shore, where it would be their job to provide the newly landed troops with cover, or try to anyway. When their turn came to move on land, the beach was still under fire, and the New Zealanders received their baptism by fire. Jack and his men secured the unloading of the field hospitals, which were already desperately needed. The wounded filled the beach, and Commander Beeston gave orders to set up the tents right there.

"And see to it that the shooting here stops," he roared at the New Zealanders. "I can't work with bullets buzzing past my head."

Lieutenant Keeler gathered up his men for the push inland. Jack and the others had been shouldering the stretchers. A battalion of Australians prepared to give them covering fire.

"We'll begin digging trenches right behind the front lines," Keeler ordered. "You know how the three-trench system goes: one for the reserves, a large trench in the middle, and one at the front. I'd say sixty-five yards between each."

Jack nodded. That was the typical British defense system. The forward trench was generally only occupied in the morning and evening when the battles raged most heavily. The middle trench—also called the support or "travel" trench—was where the soldiers spent most of the time, and reserve troops could gather in the third trench when an offensive was taking place.

Jack and his men dug the last one first, which was relatively safe since the front lay far enough in front of them that they received cover. Bit by bit, however, the trench diggers inched toward the front line, where they implemented the elaborate trench construction techniques they'd learned. Those techniques were similar to the procedure for extending mining shafts except that only the floor and walls were reinforced. Once the tunnels were a few yards deep, they would collapse the roofs, which often tumbled down on the workers' shoulders. The sound alone was enough to send Roly into a panic, so Jack assigned him to the rear where he could dig and remove rubble under an open sky, and he gave it his all.

Roly was strong as a bear, and the other coal and gold miners no less so. Nevertheless, even with hundreds of men on the job, it took many hours to raise the first trench system. Jack and his men dug straight through the first night in Gallipoli. It had turned bitterly cold and begun to rain, and the soldiers in the forward positions lay wet and anxious in the mud with their weapons. The Turks fired incessantly, and food and water support was not yet operational.

"See to it that you install a few bunkers," instructed Major Hollander, who already had experience with trench warfare in France. "The men need to be somewhere dry as soon as relief comes."

Jack nodded and directed his men to reinforce parts of the trench with boarding. In one of these reinforced sections, his men finally fell asleep as the sun rose over Gallipoli. Even Roly followed his friends beneath the earth, but he could not rest and eventually slipped out and sought shelter beneath his waxed jacket. Although the shooting continued, he felt much safer than in the bunker.

Already that morning it was clear that the Turks would not let themselves be driven inland as quickly as the troops had hoped. The attackers prepared for a longer siege and separated the soldiers into two divisions. The Australians would hold the right side of the front, the New Zealanders the left. The men finally had some time to orient themselves a bit.

"A beautiful area if you're a hermit," Greg remarked sarcastically. The shores of Gallipoli were not very populated.

Jack attempted not to think about the cliffs at Cape Reinga.

"What's behind those?" Roly asked, pointing at the mountains.

"More mountains," answered Jack. "With pretty steep valleys in between. There's no flat ground anywhere. And everything's covered with scrub, ideal for the Turks to camouflage themselves."

"Did they tell you lot that beforehand?" Bobby asked. "I mean, did they know? Why'd they send us here then?"

"Didn't you hear what the general said? This is one of the hardest tasks that can be asked of a soldier, but we of the ANZAC will conquer it." Roly struck his chest proudly.

"It won't be easy," said Jack, "and if you even want a chance at being a hero, you should get back to digging. Otherwise they'll pick you off like rabbits."

The Turks had begun laying out their own trench system by then, which was probably no less complicated than that of the British. Though the British artillery had managed to knock out several machine-gun nests, Jack and the others were relieved when the first trenches were finished and offered them protection. Only Roly seemed to fear the earthworks more than the enemy fire. He continued to sleep outside instead of ensconcing himself in a bunker. A few rocks between the trenches and the beach gave him his only cover.

Jack continued to look on this with concern; it only became truly precarious, however, as the trench construction inched closer to the Turks and precipitated fierce resistance.

As Jack's unit continued to dig deeper into the earth, Roly, driven by the others' jeers, toiled with clenched teeth. Even with a face pale as death, he still managed to do more than Greg and Bobby. Jack McKenzie and Lieutenant Keeler took turns admonishing the two of them.

"I'm not a mole," Bobby grumbled, and Jack turned his eyes toward heaven. Greg, too, had announced that he would much rather go on patrols than scrabble about in the dirt. The terrain being so cramped, the opposing forces had dug in little more than a hundred yards from each other and had been providing the ANZAC troops with harassing fire all day, which motivated Jack to dig at top speed. He wanted to finish and clear the field for the artillery. After all, it was only a matter of time before the Turks would have their trenches fully manned and more heavily armed.

And then his worst fears came true all at once. Unlike the ANZACs, the Turks had hand grenades, and someone on the other side began using the New Zealanders for target practice.

Jack and his men were working below ground when the first grenade exploded in the trench behind them. It sent earth flying and tore up the men who had been laying joists there. Though they did not have a direct view of the spot—the angle protected them from the spewing shrapnel and flying debris—Jack and the others heard the screams.

Jack quickly recognized the danger.

"Get out of here! Quick, into the trenches."

The communication trenches behind them offered protection and the opportunity to withdraw, but Jack figured they would be crammed with soldiers pushing toward the front.

"Nonsense!" Lieutenant Keeler thundered. "To the defensive stations. Into the finished trenches and fire back. Fix bayonets in case anyone breaks through. Shut the bastards out."

Before the men could even work out the contradictory commands, more grenades started exploding all around, one of them directly over their heads. The earth shook, and the tunnels collapsed. The men instinctively held boards over their heads. Though they could hardly be buried since the tunnels were little more than a yard beneath the surface—and the collapsing soil actually provided them with cover—Roly O'Brien could no longer think. Instead of lying flat, he shook the earth off himself in a daze, sat up halfway, and started to run toward the back. When he saw the trench crammed with men, he began to climb out. Someone pulled him down by his belt. Roly fought back and suddenly found himself facing Major Hollander.

"Now what's all this, soldier?"

Roly stared back at him with a crazed look in his eyes. "I have to get out of here," he screamed and made another attempt to break free. "I need to get out. The mine is collapsing."

"You mean to desert, soldier?"

Roly did not understand him. "Out! We all need to get out."

"The man doesn't know what he's saying, sir." Lieutenant Keeler, having worked his way out of the rubble, now interceded. "First encounter with the enemy, sir. It's panic, sir."

"We'll beat that out of him," the major said, landing two powerful slaps on Roly's cheeks. Roly fell backward, but came halfway back to his senses and felt for his rifle.

"Excellent," Lieutenant Keeler said. "Ready your rifle, find an embrasure, return fire. The quicker you do, the quicker you'll get out of here."

"This will have consequences. For you as well, Lieutenant," said Major Hollander. "You nearly let the rat desert. When this is over, I want to see both of you in my tent." Then he threw himself into battle.

Roly allowed two of his comrades to lead him to a niche in the trench, where they forced him to aim his rifle. Though the air was filled with lead, he was no longer underground. Roly could breathe again.

The ANZACs were firing with full force, supported by their artillery. Though it grew gradually quieter in the Turkish trenches, it seemed to take an eternity for night to descend and the fire to ebb. The most dangerous times were the morning and evening hours since twilight offered more cover than daylight. During the day it was mostly quiet, and at night both sides limited themselves to the occasional harassing fire.

Jack and his men were ordered to the rear lines. Only a small force remained in the main battle trench. The rescue troops set to work gathering up the casualties. Bobby O'Mally threw up when he saw the shredded body parts of the men who had been working behind him. Lieutenant Keeler had been lightly wounded, and Roly treated the grazing wound with tea-tree oil and bandages.

"You do that well, Lance Corporal," said the lieutenant. "But about before."

"The major's not really going to put him in front of a tribunal, is he, sir?" Jack asked, worried.

"Nah, I doubt it. A panic attack like that during the first encounter with the enemy happens. Besides, he fought very bravely afterward. The only bad piece of luck was that he ran right into the major. We'll think of something. Don't hang your head, O'Brien. The major is a bit overzealous, but he'll calm down. Now let's put it behind us."

Jack tried not to worry about Roly and Keeler, but he didn't relax until Roly was back safe and sound from his meeting with the major.

"The major chided both of us," Roly explained, "But otherwise it wasn't bad. Only, tomorrow we're to volunteer for a morning attack; they're sending a few regiments to Cape Helles, where the English made their landing."

"By ship?" Jack asked.

"Overland. We're supposed to fall on the Turks' rear and capture some mountain."

Greg grinned. "Sounds like an adventure. What do you say, Bobby, we'll sign up too."

Roly smiled hopefully. "What about you, Corporal McKenzie?" he asked.

"Just Jack. I don't know, Roly."

"Now don't be a stick-in-the-mud, Corporal," Bobby laughed. "You might be a sergeant by the time we come back."

"They degra . . . anyway, I'm just a private again," Roly said.

"If you capture this mountain, you'll be a general," Greg said. "And we'll all get the Victoria Cross. Come on, let's go see Keeler." He got up from his pallet, threw on his uniform jacket, and looked around for his hat. "Let's go, Bobby! And you don't really mean to chicken out, do you, Jack?"

Jack did not know what to say. He thought he could hear his mother's voice: "It's about putting God to the test." Perhaps his mother had been right. But having stood in the Turks' line of fire that day and fired blindly into the smoke and muzzle flashes of the other side, he was now certain he was not seeking death. So far he did not find anything heroic about this war, and he could not bring himself to hate the Turks. Driven by alliances with people they did not know, they were defending a country from soldiers fighting for a nation they did not actually know either. It all seemed nonsensical, almost unreal. Although he would fulfill his duty and prove himself wherever they ordered him to go, he did not feel compelled to go to Cape Helles.

"Do come along, Corporal McKenzie," Roly insisted. "A mountain isn't so bad."

Jack joined his men reluctantly. For reasons incomprehensible to him, he felt some need to protect Roly. So he followed them through the trenches to Lieutenant Keeler's bunker behind the lines. Keeler was packing his things.

"Him too?" Jack asked Roly.

Roly nodded. "He's commanding a platoon. The lieutenant of the Third Division fell today."

Greg saluted sharply. Keeler looked at him with a tired expression on his face.

"Is something the matter?" Keeler asked.

Bobby O'Mally explained. "We'd finally like to fight, sir. Stand face-to-face with the enemy."

As Jack understood it, they were to fall on the Turks' rear. But he did not say anything. Lieutenant Keeler looked almost disbelieving. He looked from one man to the next.

"You two," he said, pointing to Greg and Bobby, "I'll take. But not you, McKenzie."

Jack bristled. "Why not, sir? Do you not trust me to . . ."

Keeler held up his hand. "It has nothing to do with trust. But you're a corporal, McKenzie, and you have a good grip on your work here. You're indispensable."

Something in his face made Jack swallow any reply.

"But it's only two or three days, sir," Roly said.

Keeler looked like he wanted to say something, but held back. Jack felt he could read Keeler's thoughts. He recalled the maps they had been shown before the landing. Capturing the high ground, euphemistically called "Baby 700," was a suicide mission.

"A man can die anywhere," Jack said quietly.

Keeler inhaled deeply. "A man can also survive, and that's what we're going to do. We march at daybreak, boys. And you, Corporal McKenzie, work on reinforcing the trenches that were shot at today. Those trenches are the difference between life and death. So make your men sweat. Move out."

6

Roly and his friends set out at first light. Jack heard the noise, laughter, and cheerful farewells. The men left behind in the trenches seemed almost to envy the men ordered to the assault unit. Many of them repeated their complaints about being on "mole duty" while the others could look forward to adventure.

Jack didn't hear a thing about those fighting for Cape Helles for four days, but he hardly had time to worry in the interim. Major Hollander and other members of the English command were putting massive pressure on the trenching columns.

"Turkish troops are gathering; reinforcements are arriving. There could be a counteroffensive any day. The fortifications must hold."

On the fourth day Jack staggered into his quarters, exhausted and with sore fingers. They had spent the whole day securing the trenches with barbed wire, and Jack had undertaken the bulk of the work in his sector. Unlike the miners, he had worked with barbed wire on the farm—he hated it, but it was the most effective way to fence in cow pastures. However, he had never been shot at before while putting it up. He decided to partake in the alcohol rations he had saved up over the previous days. They were allotted a small glass of brandy each day, and Jack, who rarely drank alone, had not touched his booze since Roly's departure.

"Corporal McKenzie?"

Jack raised himself wearily from his billet. The young man standing in front of Jack's quarters was wearing a medic's uniform.

"We were told to bring this man to you," he explained and pushed a filthy Roly O'Brien, now clad only in rags, into the dugout. Roly resisted, but only weakly. Jack stepped outside.

"On whose orders?" he asked.

"His lieutenant's. Keeler. He's with us in the hospital, and the boy was just wandering around there. He dragged the lieutenant into camp earlier this evening. Probably saved his life. He would never have made it over the rocks alone. But afterward, this fellow was completely done, hardly knows his own name."

"Bobby," Roly said quietly.

"See there, you heard it, Corporal. His name is really Roland. Beeston looked it up. Bobby O'Mally was killed."

Roly sobbed. Jack put his arm around him.

"Thank you, Sergeant. I'll see to him. How is the lieutenant?"

"I'm not sure. I'm on rescue duty; others are caring for the wounded. But I think Beeston plans to remove Keeler's arm tonight."

"Bobby is dead," Roly whispered. "And Greg, they shot off his legs. One, one of those new guns that just shoot so incredibly fast. Ratatatat, one bullet after another, you know? Then everything was over. There was just blood, blood everywhere, but I, I pulled him into one of the trenches, and they came and got him. Maybe he'll get better."

Roly shook uncontrollably. Jack poured him some brandy.

"So how did it all turn out? Did you take the hill?" Jack asked.

"Yes, no. I'm so cold."

Jack helped him out of what was left of his uniform and threw his trench coat over Roly. It was a warm spring night, but he understood the chill that crippled him.

"They defended the hill like, like madmen, as if there were something special about that idiotic pile of dirt." Roly pulled the coat tighter around him.

Jack wondered if he should dare to light a fire. Roly needed something warm, and he gathered wood scraps.

"We were fish in a barrel. They shot hundreds of us; there were dead bodies everywhere. But we did it. Greg, Bobby, and I and a few others. Mostly Aussies. We took the blasted hill and dug in. But then no reinforcements came. We had nothing to eat, no water. It was cold at night, and our uniforms were damp and torn and bloody."

He pointed to the tattered remains of his pants. "And the Turks never stopped firing."

Roly started when he heard the shooting on the front. "And then a grenade struck, and there was nothing left of Bobby. It happened so fast. One moment he was there, the next there was just blood and a hand. Greg cried and couldn't stop. And then we were told to withdraw. But there were Turks everywhere you looked, so we crawled back, downhill this time. But then we saw the bushes and thought we'd run for cover because the Aussies' trenches were there. We ran, oh God, Corporal McKenzie, I thought my lungs would explode, I was so tired. And then it hit Greg." Roly sobbed. "I want to go home, Corporal McKenzie. I want to go home."

Jack put his arm around him and rocked him. When the water in the pot over the fire began to boil, Jack let go of Roly and forced him to wash up and drink some tea. With no small amount of guilt, Jack raided Greg McNamara's locker for his whiskey there. Though it could no longer do Greg any good, Roly needed something to bolster him.

"Everything will look different tomorrow," he said, although he did not believe it. He knew the Turks' counteroffensive might start at any moment.

Surprisingly, the ANZACs enjoyed a few days' reprieve. When the time finally came, their defenses held, and they had some luck besides. By pure chance, a British reconnaissance plane flew over Gallipoli and became aware of the Turkish advance. General Bridges did not hesitate long. He had all stations manned.

Jack and Roly found themselves once more on the front line.

"To your positions and fix bayonets," Major Hollander whispered. It sounded hollow as a ghost's voice, and Roly shivered. The predawn air was still sharply cold, and the men had already been waiting for hours.

Jack cast a glance at the two new men in his unit. While Roly had been fighting at Cape Helles, New Zealand had sent reinforcements.

Bobby and Greg had been replaced by two young soldiers from the North Island. Both men came from sheep farms like Jack. The second wave of Aussie and Kiwi volunteers no longer consisted primarily of adventurers, crooks, and poor wretches but, instead, of patriots. Many of them had lied about their age to join up. One of Jack's men had just turned nineteen. This confirmed Jack's suspicion from the assault on the coast: the youngest served as cannon fodder. Only their fearlessness enabled them to carry out these suicide missions without protest.

"This is the most dangerous position," Jack whispered to his men. "This is where they'll try to break through. The distance between the trenches is short, and their layout over there makes a sharp bend. They can provide excellent covering fire from the right and left as they attack from that niche. So I'll need the best marksmen to follow me. Yes, here under the roof."

Jack had ordered for the most sensitive section of the trench to be reinforced with a sort of wooden grating, and they hadn't been sparing with the barbed wire. "And don't fire blindly. Wait until they're near and you're sure to hit them. The major is anticipating an overwhelming force, so save your bullets."

"I'd like to remain outside, Corporal McKenzie," Roly said.

Jack nodded. "Go back to the reserve trench," he said, aware that he was countermanding the major's orders to hold their section of the front.

"I can't do that."

"Go," Jack said. But there was no time to say anything more. The Turks had begun pouring out of their trenches and were on the attack. Machine guns began firing from the hills, and the first attackers lobbed grenades into enemy positions.

Jack aimed and fired. Load, fire, load, fire.

Jack had used the word "inferno" carelessly in the past, but after that day he never would again. Slipping on the blood of their comrades and tumbling over their bodies, the attackers leaped into the trenches, where men stuck bayonets into their bodies. Fountains of blood rained down onto the shooting platforms. Jack heard cries of pain and a howl of horror. Roly? But he couldn't look back. Any mistake could cost him his life.

One of the young soldiers lunged halfway out of the trench to attack the oncoming enemy with his bayonet—and paid with his life. Shot through with bullets, he fell back into the trench next to Jack. Someone else replaced him. Jack saw an armed grenade in the hands of an oncoming Turk. He fired, but the shot was glancing, and the man still managed to throw it. Too short, however. The ground in front of Jack exploded, and debris and body parts rained down on the men in the trench.

"The mine is collapsing," Jack heard Roly call out. "We need to run, everybody out."

Roly dropped his gun and tried to climb out of the trench, but another soldier pulled him back. Jack saw out of the corner of his eye how he then attempted to push his way through the men to get behind the lines. Another grenade exploded in the trench—a rain of blood and earth.

Roly screamed, and Jack threw himself to the ground. A few Turks used the opportunity to push through, and Jack spun around and attacked. Desperate as an animal in a trap, he stabbed and struck all around him. It was hopeless to try shooting there. This was close-quarters combat. Jack stuck his bayonet into the men in front of him without thinking, eventually striking with his shovel because the bayonet was too cumbersome. He tore giant wounds in them—almost separating one soldier's head from his body when he struck the man in his throat.

"Get the dead out of here," he roared at Roly. Jack and the others were able to kill the Turks who made it into the line, and they returned to firing. The flood of Turks did not abate. More men broke through, but in their rush, they ran right into the barbed wire. Jack watched in horror as they got entangled and fell into the trench with the wire, bleeding from hundreds of scratches. Jack's men were snagged in it themselves, and all around them grenades continued exploding. Swirling dust and powder smoke darkened their vision. Jack heard Roly whimpering as rocks and limbs rained down on them. The boy must have crawled into a corner somewhere. Jack was just relieved that he was not in the way anymore.

Major Hollander saw things differently. When things died down for a few seconds, Jack heard him roaring.

"What is this, soldier? Take up your rifle and shoot. Damn it, Private, I'm talking to you. This is cowardice before the enemy."

Jack had a bad feeling.

"Can you manage here on your own?" he asked the youth who had been defending the trench next to him.

"Of course, Corporal. But maybe someone could do something about the bodies." The young man began firing again, but Jack knew what he meant. A jumble of leftover planking, body parts, and barbed wire had wreaked havoc with their section of the trench.

After orienting himself, Jack discovered Roly cowering in a niche—as far away from the embrasures as possible, half buried in filth and rubble, trembling and crying like a child.

"The mine, the mine, Mr. Lambert."

"Soldier, stand up, and take your weapon," Major Hollander ordered, kicking at the young man, but not even that brought Roly to his senses.

Jack threw himself between his friend and the major. "Sir, he cannot, sir. It's as I told you before, sir. Let them take him away when the rescue team comes. He's in a total panic."

"I call it cowardice before the enemy, McKenzie." The major moved to haul Roly to his feet.

Just then, another grenade exploded behind them, and more Turks leaped into the trench, howling as the barbed wire tore into them. Jack looked for the young man from the North Island before leaping back into the fray. He was lying on the ground screaming. The grenade had shredded his right arm, and his blood was mixing with that of the enemy.

"Medic!"

No one paid any more attention to Roly, and Jack eventually ceased to think at all. He merely struck and shot, losing all sense of time. Finally, around five o' clock, the firing stopped and the wave of assaults ebbed. The Turks must have recognized that the battle could not be won like this. Major Hollander, as bloody and filthy as his soldiers, drew out his pocket watch. "Teatime," he said.

Jack let his gun fall. He felt leaden with exhaustion and emptiness. It was over. The corpses of friend and foe were piled all around him, but he was alive. God did not seem to want Jack McKenzie.

"Get rid of these swine and then off with you to the rear." The major indicated the casualties lying in the trenches. "This trench will be manned by the reserve."

The major struck his foot against one of the corpses as if to reinforce his command. Suddenly the man moved.

"So dark, the mine, so dark, the gas, if it catches light."

"Roly," Jack called and bent down to him. "Roly, you're not in a mine."

"That cowardly son of a bitch is still lying around?" The major leaped on the whimpering Roly, ripping aside a board that the man had used for cover, and delivered a brutal hook to the chin.

"He holes himself up and shits his pants in fear."

This last sentiment was no lie. Roly stank of urine and excrement.

"Where's your rifle, Private?"

Roly seemed not to understand the words. His rifle could no longer be found. It was likely buried under dirt and blood.

"Stand up and come with me; you're under arrest. We'll have to see what to do about you. If it's up to me, there'll be a drumhead court-martial. Cowardice before the enemy."

The major pointed his gun at Roly, who reflexively put his hands up and stood at attention. He staggered off ahead of the officer. Jack would have liked to help the boy, but couldn't think of a way to do so. He was too tired to think, too exhausted to do anything. He stumbled through the trenches with the other soldiers.

"Forty-two thousand," someone said. "They say there were forty-two thousand. And ten thousand are dead."

Jack felt no horror, and no triumph. He fell onto his billet and sank into sleep. That night no nightmares tormented him. He did not even have the strength to feel the cold.

As the sun rose again over Gallipoli, the victorious defenders assembled around hundreds of fires, spooning their breakfast and exchanging heroic tales. A few of them were already bathing on the beach. Although it was still chilly, the men wanted to cleanse themselves of the stench of blood and powder. The Turks did not shoot at the swimmers with their usual energy. Normally they halfheartedly shot at bathers, who, for their part, made a game out of submerging just before the bullets struck. But that morning the enemy was burying its dead. Though there was no official armistice—this was merely an act of humanity—the Australians and New Zealanders tossed corpses over the edge of their trenches and did not shoot at the Turks' rescue units.

After seeing to it that the survivors of his company had gotten something to eat, Jack headed to the beach to look for Roly. He found the improvised brig in a tent on the beach, guarded by an older sergeant and two young soldiers.

"Who are you looking for? The coward? We've only just got him civilized today; yesterday he was completely off the rails, you know. I wanted to call a doctor, but they had their hands full. Now he's back to his senses. He's mortified and keeps trying to tell me something about a mine." The sergeant stirred his tea jovially. "Something really must have hit him in the head."

Jack was relieved, but it did not bode well that they were still holding Roly now that he was doing better.

"So what's going to happen to him?" he inquired. "Major Hollander . . ."

"He would have liked to shoot him right there and then. Cowardice before the enemy," the sergeant replied. "Do you want some tea?"

Jack declined. "Can he do that? I mean . . ."

The sergeant shrugged. "They'll probably send him to Lemnos for a court-martial. It would be a bit of a waste to shoot him, don't you think? I imagine he'll go with a penal unit. Which amounts to the same thing in the end, but before that they can still dig some trenches in France."

"In France?" Jack asked, horrified.

The man nodded. "They won't have enough for a penal unit of just Aussies. Do you want to see him?"

Jack shook his head. It would do no good to speak to Roly. There was nothing he could say to comfort him. He had to take action before they took him to Lemnos. Once the proceedings got under way, there would be no way to stop them.

Jack thanked the superintendent and made his way to the field hospital.

"Commander Joseph Beeston—where do I find him?" Jack asked the first nurse he saw.

"He's about to operate. The doctors have all been working round the clock. They're all in that tent over there. Just ask for him. But you might have to wait. It's chaos in there."

Jack entered the tents where the improvised operating rooms were housed. A nurse was carrying out bloody bags. He fought the urge to vomit as he caught the mawkish scent of blood mixed with Lysol vapor and ether. The floor of the tent was covered in blood; the men cleaning it could hardly keep up. Doctors were working at several tables, where groaning and screams could be heard.

"Commander Beeston?" Jack tried his luck with one of the doctors, who could hardly be differentiated from one another in their surgical masks and aprons.

"Last table on the right, next to the mutt." The doctor pointed with a bloody scalpel.

Jack recognized Paddy right away. The little dog lay in the tent's furthest corner looking very agitated. His panting and trembling almost reminded Jack of Roly.

"Commander Beeston? Can I speak with you briefly?"

The doctor turned halfway toward him, and Jack found himself looking into exhausted eyes behind thick glasses. Beeston's apron was smeared with blood, his arms bloody to the elbows. He seemed to be trying desperately to mend something in his patient's intestines.

"Do I know you? Ah yes, of course, Private McKenzie. No, Corporal. Congratulations." Commander Beeston managed a weak smile.

"I need to speak with you quickly," Jack said. Hospital ships would be leaving for Lemnos soon, and someone might have the idea of sending the prisoners with them.

"All right. But you'll have to wait. When I'm done with this fellow here, I'll take a break. Relief must be coming from Lemnos; we can't manage here any longer. Wait at the 'casino,' as they call that shack. And if you can, take Paddy with you. He's about to collapse." Beeston turned back to his patient.

Jack tried to draw the dog out from the corner, but it whined. Jack finally put a leash on Paddy and convinced the dog to follow him out of the tent. When Jack entered the primitive canvas shelter dubbed the casino, a young medical officer was lying asleep on a cot; another doctor took a long gulp from a whiskey bottle, splashed water from a washstand on his face, and then hurried out again.

Jack decided to wait in front of the tent and passed the time with a few obedience lessons for Paddy. The dog was soon following the commands with zeal. Jack briefly forgot about the trench combat the day before.

"Clever dog," Jack said and suddenly felt a searing pang of homesickness. What had possessed him to leave Kiward Station, the collies, and the sheep just to dig himself in at the end of the world and shoot at strangers?

"You have a knack with dogs," Commander Beeston said, when he appeared two hours later, looking even more exhausted than before. "I should have left Paddy on the ship. Yesterday, however."

"Yesterday we all reached our limits," Jack said, "some more than others."

"Come in, come in," Commander Beeston said, holding the entrance open for him and began searching for the whiskey bottle. He filled two glasses. "You'd like one, wouldn't you?"

Jack nodded.

"Now, what can I do for you?" Beeston asked.

Jack told him.

"I don't know. It's true I owe you something, but cowardice before the enemy? I have no use for a coward here either."

"Private O'Brien isn't cowardly. On the contrary, after the battle at Cape Helles he received a commendation for bringing two wounded men out from enemy lines. And he likewise fought at the head when they stormed that godforsaken hill. But the man's claustrophobic. He goes crazy in the trenches."

"Our rescue troops must also go into the trenches," Beeston said.

"And into no-man's-land. No one else is exactly eager to do that, is he?" Jack asked. "Besides, you probably won't want to employ him in rescue operations, an experienced nurse like that."

Beeston furrowed his brow. "The man has medical training?"

A half hour later Commander Beeston formally requested that Major Hollander transfer Private Roland O'Brien to medical service.

"It would be a real shame to send him to a penal unit, Major. According to his friend, he's a trained nurse. We can't just throw him to the wolves in France."

Another hour later, Jack McKenzie breathed easy. Roly was saved. Still, Jack wrote to Tim Lambert in Greymouth just in case. After that he wrote to Gloria. He did not want to burden her, and he did not know whether he should send the letter. But if he did not tell someone about the war, Jack knew he would go crazy.

7

By the time Gloria reached Sydney several months after leaving Darwin, she hated the whole world. She loathed the johns who used her without compunction—and then proved unwilling to pay extra for "special services." She had drawn her knife more than once to force the men to pay. Small-town men, harmless when it came down to it, they usually backed down when the steel gleamed.

Gloria likewise hated the other prostitutes who were not prepared to accept a new girl into their midst. Her knife had come into play then too. The girls were much too jaded to react to simple threats, and most of them were better fighters than Gloria. Twice she found herself in the gutter, badly beaten, and one opponent robbed her of that day's earnings to boot. Not that Gloria was real competition. The men only chose her when they wanted something unusual.

At first Gloria did not understand the connection, but then she realized that it was her shaved head that fascinated the men. Though she had feared initially that her radical hairstyle would hurt her business, the more deviant men found her smooth scalp irresistible. Thus Gloria shaved her head anew at the slightest growth of stubble.

Gloria also hated the honorable women and the shop owners from whom she bought her few groceries. She hated their smugness and their reluctance to help her. She had made it a habit to travel as a boy and transform into a woman only at night. She felt safer in men's clothing and could more easily hide from the other prostitutes who used the daylight hours to hunt for their "vagabond" competition.

More than anything, however, Gloria hated the country that had used her up. Although accustomed to long distances, she couldn't get over Australia. To reach Sydney from Darwin, she had been forced to work her way across thousands of miles, including the sparsely populated Northern Territory. Gloria had no eye for the beauty of the desert regions she traversed, often on foot or in the wagon of some sympathetic farmer or horny gold miner. She cared neither for the rock formations nor the strangely formed termite mounds and spectacular sunrises and sunsets.

By the time she finally arrived in Sydney, short, red-brown locks played about Gloria's lean face. She had let her hair grow out again—because her papers identified her as Gloria, not "Jack"—and she bought two modest but respectable traveling outfits. Although she had to work longer for it, Gloria was determined to book a second-class room.

The first boat bound for New Zealand was headed to Dunedin, which was a lucky break for Gloria. She had hoped to avoid having to go to the North Island. Less pleasant was the fact that the *Queen Ann* would not weigh anchor for a week. Gloria struggled with whether she should spend the week as "Jack" in a shelter, thus saving money, or take a room for herself, using up the last of her reserves. She quickly cast aside the most lucrative solution of "working" for a few more days. Better not to take any more risks.

As the time grew near, Gloria found herself shaken by panic attacks. Would her great-grandmother still be alive? Had Kura and William perhaps sold Kiward Station out of spite for Gloria's having run away? If they had, did she bear some responsibility for Jack and Grandmum Gwyn's home being lost? Gloria hardly dared think of Jack. Would she hate him as she hated all men?

Gloria spent the time until her ship's departure trembling and alone in a cheap hostel. She spent the last of her money on a carriage in order not to have to walk through the docklands, and then all but ran on board the *Queen Ann*. Gloria thought she might weep with relief when she was shown to her cabin, which she shared with an excited young girl traveling with her parents to New Zealand.

During the two-week crossing, Gloria took every opportunity to eat her fill, attempting to make up for the near constant hunger she had endured in Australia. Though she initially found it difficult to behave politely—having too often stuffed bread and cheese into her mouth before some stronger urchin could swipe it—the structured mealtimes and tidy dining room on the ship reawakened her memories of Oaks Garden and Gloria began to carry herself as she had then. She shuffled with sunken head to her place, wished those around her bon appétit without looking at them, and then ate as quickly as possible. If someone spoke to her, she answered monosyllabically. She succeeded masterfully at playing the role of the shy, well-bred girl. Only once, when she snuck through the ship's ballroom toward her cabin and a young man asked her to dance, did her "other self" surface. She glared at him with such hatred that he almost fell backward, and Gloria even frightened herself. If he had touched her, she would have reflexively drawn her knife, which she still always carried with her.

And then New Zealand—Aotearoa—finally appeared before them on the horizon. From the ship she recognized the silhouettes of the mountains. Home. She was finally home. She had heard that some of the immigrants in her great-grandmother's day had fallen on their knees and kissed the ground after reaching their new country alive, and she knew how they felt. She felt an overpowering sense of relief as the *Queen Ann* passed into Port Chalmers.

As Gloria stood on deck gazing out at her destination, she realized that she had no idea what exactly she would do when she arrived. New Zealand had always been her objective. But now what?

"Those traveling to Dunedin should take the train," the steward informed the passengers. "The trains run regularly."

"We're not arriving in Dunedin?" Gloria asked.

"No, Miss, Port Chalmers is a separate town. But it's easy to reach Dunedin."

As long as one had more than a few Australian cents in her pocket. Gloria was in a trance as she walked down the gangplank and stepped onto New Zealand soil again. She wandered aimlessly along the water's edge, eventually sitting down on a bench and staring out over the calm bay. She had so often imagined how she would rejoice when she finally reached New Zealand, but she felt nothing but emptiness. No more despair and no fear. But no joy either. It was as if everything in her were dead.

"Good evening, young lady. Can I help you with anything?"

Gloria started. Instinctively she wanted to feel for her knife, but she turned around first instead. It was a man, but in a constable's uniform.

"No, I'm, I'm relaxing," Gloria stammered.

The constable nodded, though he frowned as he did so. "You've been relaxing for two hours," he said with a look at his pocket watch. "And it's getting dark. So if you have someplace to be, you should hurry. And if you don't have one, then please think of one. Otherwise I would have to come up with something. You don't look like a port whore, but it's part of my job to keep young ladies from having dumb ideas. Do we understand each other?"

She nodded. He was right. She could not stay where she was.

"Where do you belong, young lady?" the officer asked amiably.

"On Kiward Station," Gloria said. "In Haldon, on the Canterbury Plains."

"Dear Lord," the constable said. "You won't be able to make it there tonight, child. Isn't there anything closer?"

"Queenstown, Otago?" she asked mechanically. Lilian's grandparents lived there, though Gloria hardly knew them.

The constable smiled. "That's closer, but not exactly around the corner. If you don't know anyone in Port Chalmers—what about Dunedin?"

Dunedin. Gloria had written the name on envelopes a thousand times. Of course she knew someone in Dunedin. If she had not moved away, taken a different position, or married, that is. It had been a long time since she had last written to Sarah Bleachum.

"The Princess Alice School for Girls?" she asked.

The constable nodded. "That would do. It's only a few miles down the road."

"Good, I can walk there. Which direction is it? Is there a paved road?"

Again she provoked a frown from the constable. "Tell me, child, where did you come from? The woods? Naturally there are paved streets all around Dunedin. We'll find you a carriage. How's that sound?"

"I don't have any money."

The officer sighed. "I thought that might be the case. You look like you've seen hard times. How did you think of the school? Do you know somebody there?"

"Sarah Bleachum. A teacher." She still felt numb and oddly unconcerned about where she would spend the night. Sarah Bleachum belonged to a different world.

"And what's your name?" the constable asked.

Gloria gave her name.

"Very well, Miss Martyn. Then I propose the following solution. Around the corner here is the police station—now don't look so scared, we don't bite. If you don't have anything against following me there, we could call up the Princess Alice School. If there really is a Miss Bleachum there who has a soft spot in her heart for you, she'll no doubt take on the costs of a carriage."

A short while later, Gloria was sitting with a cup of tea in the police station. After a few minutes on the phone, the constable turned to Gloria. "Yes, there is a Miss Sarah Bleachum there, but she's teaching at the moment. Astronomy. Strange subject. I never would have thought that girls took an interest in it. The headmistress says that I ought to put you in a taxi and send you along anyway. They'll cover the cost."

Gloria set off in a roomy automobile. As they pulled up to the main building, Gloria was reminded of Oaks Garden, though the Princess Alice School was smaller and prettier architecturally, with bay windows and turrets built in the light-colored sandstone typical of the region. Gloria's heart beat heavily as the car stopped in front of the steps. What if Miss Bleachum did not recognize her or wanted nothing to do with her? What would she have to do to pay for this taxi ride?

The driver accompanied her up the stairs and inside. She found herself in an entrance hall where an inviting fireplace kept out the autumn chill. An older woman appeared and smiled at Gloria.

"I'm Mrs. Lancaster, the headmistress," she explained after paying the driver. "I'm eager to see who's dropped in on us from Australia." She smiled at Gloria. "Our Miss Bleachum is too. She doesn't know anyone in Australia."

Gloria was searching for words to clarify when she saw Miss Bleachum coming down the stairs. Her tutor had aged a bit, but it suited her. Holding herself erect and moving with firm strides, she appeared more self-assured than before. Her dark hair was tied in a knot, and she did not play nervously with her glasses when she saw the strangers in the foyer.

"A visitor for me?" she asked. Miss Bleachum looked over at the taxi driver first.

"I'm the one," Gloria said quietly.

Miss Bleachum furrowed her brow and stepped closer. Even with her glasses she now had only mediocre vision.

"Gloria," she whispered. "Gloria Martyn."

Miss Bleachum looked confused for a moment, but then her eyes shone.

"I would never have recognized you, dear. You look so grown-up. And so thin—you look like you've been starved. But of course it's you. My Gloria."

Miss Bleachum embraced her.

"I've been so worried about you since you stopped writing," Miss Bleachum said, running her hand over Gloria's short, frizzy hair. "And your Mrs. McKenzie has been so distressed. I contacted her a few months ago to ask where you were, and she told me you'd run off. I always feared something like that might happen. But now here you are. My Gloria."

Gloria nodded numbly. "My Gloria." Miss Bleachum's Gloria, Grandmum Gwyn's Gloria. She felt something fall away within her. And then she leaned on Miss Bleachum's shoulder and began to weep. First in short, dry sobs, then tears. Sarah Bleachum led the girl to a sofa in the entrance hall, sat down, and pulled her close. She held Gloria tightly pressed against her while the girl wept and wept and wept.

Mrs. Lancaster stood there stunned.

"Poor girl," she murmured. "Doesn't she have a mother?"

Sarah looked up and shook her head almost imperceptibly. "That's a long story."

Gloria cried almost all night and half of the next day. In between she fell exhausted into a brief slumber, only to start sobbing again as soon as she awoke. Sarah and Mrs. Lancaster had managed to lead her up to Sarah's room, and Mrs. Lancaster had soup and bread sent up. Gloria inhaled the food, only to cling to Sarah again and begin crying anew.

Mrs. Lancaster gave Sarah the next day off. She sat beside Gloria until the girl finally stopped sobbing and sank into a deep sleep. Then she covered her up and knocked on the headmistress's door. Mrs. Lancaster was sitting at a scrupulously clean desk and drinking tea. She offered Sarah a place and fetched a cup for her.

"I should make a telephone call," Sarah said as she sipped her tea. "But I don't know."

"You're completely exhausted, Sarah," the headmistress said, pushing a slice of tea cake toward her. "Maybe you should lie down for a bit first. I can inform the family, you know. Just tell me where to reach the girl's relatives."

"She might not like that. Don't get me wrong, Gloria has relatives here who think the world of her. But so much has been decided over her head. I'd prefer to wait until she's calmed down."

"What do you think happened to her, Miss Bleachum? Who is she anyway? A former student of yours, I gather, but where is she from?"

Sarah Bleachum sighed. "Could I have another cup of tea?" And then she told the whole story of Kura and Gloria Martyn.

"It seems she couldn't take it anymore and ran away. As for what she encountered on her journey to and through Australia, I have no idea. Mrs. McKenzie told me Gloria fled her parents' hotel room with nothing more than her passport. Only she can tell us the rest. But so far she's done nothing but cry."

Mrs. Lancaster nodded thoughtfully. "It's best you don't ask. She'll talk when she feels ready. Or she won't say a word."

"But she has to talk sometime. It can't have been so terrible that she keeps it to herself forever."

Mrs. Lancaster blushed slightly, but she met Sarah's gaze. She was anything but naïve.

"Sarah, think about it. A girl, without money, without assistance, making her way halfway across the world. You probably don't even want to know what the poor thing has endured. There are some memories you can only live with if you don't share them with anyone."

Sarah turned a deep crimson. She seemed to want to ask a question, but she lowered her eyes.

"I won't ask," she whispered.

When Gloria awoke the next morning, she felt better but completely drained. She lacked the energy to do or decide anything, and she was thankful that Sarah gave her time. In those first few days she followed the teacher around like a puppy. Sarah allowed Gloria to listen in while she instructed the older students. The atmosphere was friendly, and the girls didn't tease her when she sat rigidly at a desk, staring absently at the board or out the window.

Gloria knew that she would have to leave the school eventually, and something in her longed to see Kiward Station again. She wouldn't have believed it if anyone had told her during her journey that she would remain only a short train ride away from Christchurch for days. It didn't matter how many times Sarah Bleachum told her that Gwyneira was worried about her and would receive her with open arms—Gloria was afraid of seeing her family. Her great-grandmother had always been able to tell when she was faking something. What if Gloria could not manage to deceive her now? What if she recognized what had become of her? Worse still was the thought of Jack. What would he think of her? Did he have that instinct her johns had possessed that instantly recognized the whore in her?

Sarah saw with concern that her ward was beginning to establish herself at the school. She sought out Gloria in the little room that Mrs. Lancaster had assigned her.

"Gloria, this can't continue," Sarah said softly. "We need to inform your grandmother. You've already been here two weeks. You're safe, but we can't let her go on worrying about you."

Gloria's eyes filled with tears. "You want me to leave?"

"Of course not. But you didn't travel halfway around the world to bury yourself away in a boarding school in Dunedin. You wanted to go home, Gloria. It's time."

"But I, I can't like this." Gloria played nervously with her hair.

Sarah smiled. "Mrs. McKenzie doesn't care about corkscrew curls. You don't need to dress up for her or your dog."

"My dog?" Gloria asked.

Sarah nodded. "Wasn't its name Nimue?"

Gloria's thoughts raced. Could Nimue still be alive eight years after she'd left?

"And you can't stay here anyway," Sarah continued. "The school is going to be closed indefinitely after summer vacation. Mrs. Lancaster has decided to turn the building into a hospital during the war."

Gloria looked at her confused. There was a war, of course. But not in New Zealand. Yes, they were recruiting volunteers, but since there were no battles here, why a hospital?

Sarah Bleachum read the question on Gloria's face.

"Gloria, dear, did you never hear of a place called Gallipoli?"

8

Feeling relieved—if also a little ashamed that he had ended up a "nurse boy" again—Roly O'Brien was transferred to Commander Beeston's medical brigade. He proved to be exceptionally well suited to the work.

"It seems I owe you another one," Commander Beeston told Jack when the two men met on the beach on a warm July evening. "Your Private O'Brien is worth two of my nurses." Paddy leaped about in the waves, and the men were in a festive mood. It had been quiet on the front for weeks; apparently the Turks were waiting them out.

Jack waved the compliment away. "I knew Roly would do good work. But you did me a huge favor." He looked at Paddy. "He's acclimated to the sound of gunfire, I see."

"There's hardly anything to hear these days. But that won't last. We're here to claim the road to Constantinople. Not to splash around." He pointed to a few young soldiers playing in the water.

"You mean we're going to attack soon?" Jack asked, alarmed. He and his men had been expanding the trench network on the northern flank. The ground was stony and uneven, and extremely difficult to dig through. Any assault would come at a heavy price. On the other hand, the Turks would never expect it.

"Sooner or later. Reinforcements are on the way. More medical brigades too—so they're expecting more blood." Commander Beeston petted his dog. "Sometimes I ask myself what I'm doing here."

Jack did not answer. At least the doctors reduced the suffering of the wounded. He regretted his decision, though he had certainly reached his goal: he no longer thought of Charlotte day and night. The nightmares in which he struck Turkish soldiers again and again and waded through blood in the trenches had supplanted the bittersweet dreams of his wife—and during the day, he thought first and foremost of survival. War had taught him perhaps not to forget the dead but to leave them in peace.

Like all the men he yearned for letters from home. Jack was as happy as a child when his mother wrote with news of Kiward Station. Even Elizabeth Greenwood occasionally managed a letter, as did Elaine Lambert. There was only no word from Gloria, which unsettled Jack more and more. It had been more than six months since he had sent Gloria his first letter from Egypt. She could have answered long ago.

Jack felt lonely since Roly had been transferred. He hadn't connected with the other men in his platoon. He was now their sergeant, having been promoted after the slaughter in the trenches, and friendships did not develop between soldiers and their superiors. He spent his evenings largely alone, mulling over the senselessness of his existence.

Over the following days, the signs of an approaching offensive multiplied. New troops arrived, and trenches were being dug and secured around the clock. Water tanks were installed and water carried up to them. The men grumbled that they had to do everything themselves. The few pack animals were not assigned to the front.

"Otherwise the enemy would realize that something was brewing over here," Jack explained. "That's why we dig at night. Now go, men, it's in our own interest to surprise the poor fellows. Fifty yards lie between their trenches and ours. We'll have to cross that."

On August 5, Jack and the other noncommissioned officers were ordered to a briefing on the beach. Major Hollander laid out the strategy for the planned assault.

"Men, we're launching an offensive tomorrow. Our goal is to drive the Turks back to Constantinople, and this time we'll do it."

"But, sir, if we jump out of the trenches, they'll shoot down on us like rabbits," one veteran said. Jack was thinking the same thing.

"Is that cowardice I hear, Corporal?" the major asked. "Afraid of death, soldier?"

"I have no intention of committing suicide," the man mumbled, though so quietly that only those standing next to him heard.

"Our goal is to break through their left flank. The distances between the trenches are short there, so we should be able to overrun them. To fool them, we'll begin with a feint attack tomorrow. Our group will then head for Lone Pine for the real attack the day after next."

Lone Pine referred to a very secure Turkish battle station. The opposing trench network was broad there, and there was plenty of space for enemy troops to gather.

"Our goal is to have our opponent's troops concentrate there, so we have an easier time on the northern flank. We'll attack with the second wave. I expect that you'll support our comrades at Lone Pine and keep the enemy busy from your positions. The actual assault will take place in the afternoon at seventeen hundred thirty. Three whistles, three waves of attack. Godspeed to one and all."

What did God care about the way to Constantinople?

On his way back to his quarters, Jack ran into Roly.

"Sergeant McKenzie, have you heard? We're attacking tomorrow." Roly glued himself to Jack's heels. Since Jack had more or less saved his life with the transfer, he had become touchingly devoted and now wanted nothing more than to tell Jack what he assumed would be new information. The medical troops had been made aware of the plan of attack in order to make the necessary preparations.

"Just Jack," Jack corrected him as usual. "Yes, we were just informed. Be glad you don't have to move out."

Roly made a face. "But I do have to go out; I'm with the rescue troops. So maybe we'll see each other tomorrow?"

"We're positioned on the north flank, Roly, so we have a day's reprieve. But why did they send you with the rescue troops? Did you do something?"

Roly laughed. "Nah. It's just that the medical reinforcements didn't arrive until today. The commander cursed up a storm. Right off the ships and straight into the fight. They don't even know the basics. So he's keeping them in the field hospital, and the rest of us have to go. But I don't mind. I don't need to go in the trenches."

"No-man's-land is dangerous. It gets gruesome, Roly. It'll be like before, only this time it's us running over the open field."

"But we've got our white armbands," Roly said as if they made him invulnerable. "I'll manage."

Jack could only wish him luck. The next day he hardly had time to think about his friend. The noise from Lone Pine was infernal. When Jack raised the periscope over the trench's ridge, he could see the soldiers falling. The Turks were firing across the entire front. Jack and his men grimly returned fire in hopes of wearing down their enemy.

"If we tire them out today, we'll have a better chance tomorrow," Jack explained to his men. The younger among them nodded enthusiastically; the older ones only frowned.

"But they change the men on duty," a lance corporal asserted.

Jack did not respond.

August 7 was a shining midsummer day on the Turkish coast. The sea shimmered in the sun. The scrub on the mountainsides was bleached—and the blood was drying in the no-man's-land between the fronts. While Jack was listlessly eating his porridge, considering whether to drink his alcohol ration before the battle or hope to survive and celebrate afterward, Roly came by.

"I've got your mail," he said and threw Jack a bundle of letters for his men. "It should raise the men's spirits to hear from their loved ones. Mary wrote me too."

Jack sorted through the mail and found a letter from Kiward Station. Still nothing from Gloria.

"How was it yesterday?" he asked.

Roly's face went pale. "Horrible. So many dead. Their bombs and shrapnel tear men apart, Sergeant McKenzie. They're doing almost nothing but amputations in the field hospital. If there's even enough left to cut off. And some of the Turkish trenches are roofed, so be careful. You have to jump over them and then come in through the communications trenches. I know I'm not very smart. But we can't do it, Sergeant McKenzie. Not with a hundred thousand men."

Jack nodded. "We'll do our best, Roly."

Roly looked at him as if he were not in his right mind and huffed, "And we'll die for nothing."

Jack opened his mother's letter as soon as Roly had gone. He savored hearing her voice in his mind. Though she was not a gifted writer, strong emotions had clearly guided her pen.

Dearest Jack,

You wrote that it's peaceful where you are on the front, and I can only pray that it stays that way. Every time I receive a letter of yours, I sigh with relief even though I know the letters often take weeks to arrive. You must stay alive. Jack, I miss you so much. All the more so since our hope that Gloria might finally come home won't be fulfilled soon, or at least not simply. Yesterday I received a call from Kura. She made the call herself and was absolutely furious.

It looks like Gloria disappeared from her hotel in San Francisco. They've ruled out kidnapping since she took her travel documents with her. No passage on any ship was booked with her name, so there's no proof she's left America, but Kura assumes that she'll turn up here. How she thinks that will happen is a mystery to me, but she's practically holding me responsible for Gloria's flight. Kura is completely beside herself. In the same breath though she said how ungrateful the girl was and cursed Gloria's inability to make herself useful. It's a mystery to me why she didn't simply send the girl home when she wanted to go. In any event Gloria is missing, and I'm very worried. If only I could hope that you would come back soon.

You needn't worry about the farm. Everything is running well with Maaka's oversight. The prices of wool and meat are high; everything seems to be making a profit from the war. But I think about you and all the others, for whom the fighting means only suffering.

Take care of yourself, Jack. I need you.
Your mother, Gwyneira McKenzie

Jack buried his face in his hands. So now Gloria too. He lost whatever he loved.

Jack was totally fearless when the first combat whistle finally sounded. Many of the first attackers who leaped out of the trenches were struck when they so much as raised their heads above cover. Only a few managed to run across no-man's-land, and none reached the opposing trenches.

Then came the second assault wave.

Jack no longer thought; he launched himself out of the trench, and he ran, ran, ran, and almost made it.

Something struck him in the chest. He reached to wipe it away and felt blood. It was strange; it didn't hurt, but he could not continue running and felt awfully heavy. Jack fell to the ground and tried to understand what had happened. He felt the heat of the sun, looked into the radiant blue sky. His hands no longer responded but simply scratched at the hard ground. The third attack wave raced over him. Now they were fighting over in the Turkish trenches. Jack blinked into the sun.

And then there was a face. A round, youthful face with hair damp from sweat.

"Sergeant McKenzie."

"Just Jack," he whispered. He tasted blood and felt like he had to cough. And then he felt nothing more.

A Long Road

Greymouth, Canterbury Plains, and Auckland

1915–1918

1

Timothy and Elaine Lambert had no talent as prison guards. Tim had initially insisted that Lilian's disappearance be punished with house arrest. After all, she had acted against his express orders by "seducing" Ben into that stroll through the fern forest. But after she had served her sentence, Tim forgave his daughter, and Lilian again enjoyed all the freedoms her parents usually allowed her.

Ben, however, was a different story. Florence Biller assembled all her forces to keep her son away from Lilian. His house arrest lasted for months, and she hardly let him out of her sight. In the morning he rode to the mine with her in the car and completed his office work under her watchful eye. At home he was under constant observation.

One day Ben tried to sneak a letter to Lilian out with the mine's mail, but it was immediately discovered by his mother.

"What rubbish. The girl must be an idiot to fall for this," Florence said after scanning the poem that Ben had written. "'My heart flows to you with the raindrops.' Raindrops don't flow, Ben, they fall. And hearts don't flow either. Now get to work on these receipts. Balance them with the delivery orders, please, and enter them into the purchase journal. Without any flourishes or rhymes." Florence crumpled up the poem and its envelope and tossed them out the window.

The young wife of an office messenger who had stopped in to bring her husband lunch heard Florence's outburst from the anteroom and was moved by the boy's art. When she left, she picked up the letter, smoothed it out, put it back in its envelope, and threw it in the next mailbox she passed—albeit without putting a stamp on it first. Thus it fell into Elaine's hands when the letter carrier asked for payment.

Elaine was torn about what to do. Tim would have undoubtedly destroyed the letter, but Elaine could not bring herself to do that. She finally decided to read the letter herself, and then, if it were harmless, she would pass it on to Lilian.

Lilian was outraged when she finally received the opened, crumpled missive.

"Haven't you ever heard of privacy?" she hissed at her mother. "You didn't remove anything?"

Elaine shook her head. "I swear," she replied, laughing. "Besides, it was already crumpled and not properly sealed when it arrived. By the way, reading that made my hair stand on end. If you're thinking of living off Ben's writing someday, I don't see a bright future."

"The poems are only for me, you know," Lilian said. "You couldn't understand them."

"And then she disappeared into her room for three hours with Ben's melting hearts," Elaine later informed her husband, who was just back from a business trip to Westport.

Tim frowned. He was exhausted after the journey over the largely unpaved roads.

"Lainie, this isn't funny. We had agreed not to support this nonsense. How could you give her the letter?"

Elaine guided Tim to an armchair, helped him to put up his legs, and began to gently massage his shoulders. "This isn't a prison, Tim. People have the right to read their own mail. I shouldn't even have opened the letter, but I was trying to be responsible. You know how I feel about this: puppy love is harmless. If we make a production out of it, it will only get worse."

Tim snorted. "I, for one, am going to watch her more closely in the future. She can be my chauffeur now that Roly's gone. It'll keep her busy, and I'll be able to keep an eye on her. Please just forbid her from writing back to the boy. If Florence finds out, she'll be on the telephone in a flash."

Lilian did not reply to Ben's letter right away, as she knew her answer would land on his mother's desk. Besides, she was busy for several days learning to drive a car, which she found enormously fun.

But Lilian continued to dream of Ben, whose poems she kept beneath her pillow. She came up with one idea after another to make contact with the boy and finally landed on a plan. She bribed her youngest brother, Billy, with three licorice rolls in exchange for inconspicuously bumping into Ben Biller on Sunday before church service. Pretending to play a game of tag, Billy ran into Ben, almost causing him to fall, and clung fast to him to keep his balance.

"Hollow of the beech tree, cemetery," Billy whispered importantly. "Where the branches cross to the right, head height." Billy then winked and peeled off.

Toward the end of the service, Ben stood up and left the church. Florence initially looked upset, but when she spied Lilian with her parents, she seemed reassured. Ben only had to find the paper now. Lilian prayed with genuine enthusiasm for the first time that morning.

She later saw a conspicuously happy Ben in front of the church. The boy was so radiant that Lilian feared his mother might ask questions. However, Florence was chatting with the reverend and did not even notice that Lilian winked at her son. The hollow in the beech tree was a turning point in their relationship.

The period that followed proved an exceptionally exciting one for the young lovers. True, they only saw each other in church, but they kept up a lively written correspondence. Lilian especially was always coming up with new hiding places where she would leave notes or small presents for Ben. Ben was less suited to conspiracy, but followed suit, exchanging her homemade cookies for bouquets of dried flowers, and her lavishly decorated letters—complete with hand-drawn vines in bloom, little hearts, and angels—for new odes to her beauty and intelligence.

Lilian occasionally included quotes from a poetry anthology, but she mostly reported on her daily life—her horse, the car she loved, and of course her burning desire to see Ben again face-to-face.

"Couldn't you sneak out at night? Do you have a tree outside your window or something like that?" she asked.

Ben had never considered slipping out of his house at night, but he was so enchanted by the idea that he immediately wrote a poem about how Lilian's hair must shine in the moonlight.

Lilian found that charming, but she was disappointed. In his poems Ben could go on for hours about the heroic deeds he would perform and the dangers he would face to earn a kiss from Lilian's lips. But in reality he did nothing. Finally the girl decided to act.

"Thursday night, 11:30 in the stables of the Lucky Horse," she wrote. That meeting place sent blood to Ben's face: the Lucky Horse was not only a pub but Madame Clarisse's brothel. He spent several sleepless nights brooding over how his beautiful, innocent Lily could fall into such a den of sin and whether his conscience could condone such a plan. Lilian had no such qualms about it. As always she was thinking practically. The Lucky Horse was a convenient spot because her father met his friends for drinks there every Thursday, and she chauffeured him there and back. Though she was supposed to park in the light of the streetlamp and stay in the car, Lilian knew the area around the Lucky Horse well. When Lilian was little, Elaine had often taken her when she visited Madame Clarisse, and she had played nearby. If Lilian parked in the back after dropping off her father, there was hardly any chance of attracting attention.

Lilian's heart thumped heavily as she slipped into the pub's stables under cover of darkness. Only one horse was munching hay, and Ben was already there. Lilian almost screamed when he pulled her to him like a character in some film and kissed her.

"You're crushing me," she said. "Is the coast clear? Did anyone suspect anything?"

Ben shook his head. "They don't think I'm capable of such a thing," he said proudly.

The pair spent the next half hour exchanging caresses, lovers' oaths, and complaints about the state of their lives.

"I'm simply no good at office work. And I don't care at all for mining. I even had to go down in the mines."

"And?" Lilian asked, riveted. "What was it like?"

"Dark," Ben responded before it dawned on him that this was a rather weak description for a poet. "Dark as the grave," he added.

Lilian frowned. "But don't you have those modern mine lamps? Uncle Matt says the mines are lit up like a dance hall."

"For me it was dark as hell."

Lilian resisted the urge to remark that hell was probably rather well lit too.

"And I'm no good at all that balance-sheet work either. Recently I was off by almost a thousand dollars. My mother was livid."

Lilian did not find that totally incomprehensible. Nevertheless she stroked her boyfriend's cheeks comfortingly. "But surely they're sending you back to university, aren't they? After all, mining engineering is something that requires study. Oh, Ben, but then you'll be even further away."

As Lilian curled up against him, he dared to pull her down onto a pile of hay. She held still as he kissed her face—and then her neck and her cleavage. Lilian pushed her hands under his shirt and gently caressed his muscular chest and back.

"Next Thursday then?" she asked breathlessly when they finally parted.

Ben nodded. He felt very heroic.

Since their first meeting in the pub's stables, Lilian's happiness knew no bounds. She savored their secret love as well as the work for her father. The war demanded constant expansions of the mine's production capacities, and Tim was always meeting with other mining engineers, railroad men, and businesspeople. Lilian even accompanied him to business meals and events from time to time, and Elaine observed with pleasure that Lilian flirted and danced at these. Though she suspected that her daughter still carried a torch for Ben Biller, she knew nothing about their secret meetings.

Florence Biller had even less of an idea, though she found plenty of other reasons to get upset about her eldest son. Ben's obvious lack of interest in the mine and his inability to complete even the simplest tasks drove her to distraction. As Ben's hopes of attending the University of Otago in Dunedin dwindled, his despair grew. Though his father pleaded that he be permitted to study a few semesters of mining engineering or economics, his pleas fell on Florence's deaf ears.

"Mining engineering? Don't make me laugh. Our Ben an engineer? He jumps for cover when the coffee machine boils," she said. "Besides, he can learn far more about business from me than he can in Dunedin."

Caleb could only hope that Florence's interest in Ben would wane once Sam was old enough to work with her, and that way Ben would someday be able to pursue an academic career. Unfortunately, Ben lacked his father's patience. Seeing no way out of his situation, he grew increasingly depressed.

"At least this way we'll stay together," Lilian comforted him. But not even that prospect could cheer him.

"What sort of way is this to be together?" he complained. "Perpetual secrecy, constant fear of being discovered. How long can this go on, Lily?"

"Until we turn twenty-one, of course," she explained. "Then they can't order us around anymore. We just have to hold out a little longer."

"A little?" Ben asked despairingly. "That's years from now."

"True love is put to difficult tests. It's always like that in books and songs."

Ben sighed. "I'm considering running away and joining the army."

Lilian was alarmed. "Anything but that, Ben. Then they'll shoot you. Besides, you have to be twenty-one to join the ANZAC."

"You can fool them, though. And I can prove that I was at Cambridge. Normally you have to be over eighteen for that."

"But not twenty-one," Lilian insisted, frightened. Roly O'Brien's letters about Gallipoli made her blood freeze. War was romantic in books and songs, but the reality appeared otherwise. And Ben holding a gun? He would undoubtedly write wonderful verse about the heroism of his comrades, but she did not think him capable of shooting. She would have to think of something.

It was almost a month before Lilian saw Ben again, as she had accompanied her father to Blenheim for a conference. Lambert Mine was expanding to include a coke furnace. Ben received this information without interest, not realizing that his mother probably would have killed to be the first to know about it, and Lilian was much too distracted by Ben's caresses to worry about the possible consequences of revealing any secrets.

After the long absence, Ben's kisses tasted even sweeter—and they strengthened her resolve about the decision she had come to in Blenheim. A secret visit to the civil registry office had also contributed considerably.

"I'm seventeen now, you know. So I can marry."

"Whom did you have in mind?" Ben asked, bravely opening the top buttons on her blouse.

"You, of course. It's quite simple, really. We'll take the train to Christchurch and then to Blenheim. From there, we'll catch the ferry to Wellington. We can marry there. Or Auckland. That's probably safer. They might look for us in Wellington."

"But I don't have any papers," Ben objected. "They won't believe I'm eighteen."

"Seventeen's old enough, for boys too. We can wait until your birthday. Besides, you only need to swear you're not married anywhere else or related to me by blood or anything."

Under twenty years of age, parental consent was also required, but Lilian did not burden Ben with that for now. She intended to forge her father's signature, and she had even less compunction about doing so for Florence Biller.

"Then you can just study in Auckland. That works too, doesn't it?"

Ben bit his lower lip.

"Perfectly," he replied. "They take research of Maori culture very seriously. They're even building a museum for artifacts. My father is very excited. He's thinking of going to visit soon. If he catches us, though . . ."

Lilian groaned. Sometimes Ben was a bit too tentative for her taste.

"Once we're married, Ben, we're married. It's not something you can easily undo. Besides, it would be easy to avoid your father in a city as big as Auckland."

Ben nodded.

It was an intriguing possibility, though he still could not really imagine it. His heart hammered at the mere thought of fleeing to the North Island. He would never dare go through with it.

2

Gwyneira McKenzie had always thought that Kiward Station's manor house was too big. Even when she had shared it with her family, many rooms had stood empty. Gwyneira had never felt lonely, though—that is, until James and Charlotte died, Jack joined the army, and Gloria disappeared. She fled the empty house to the stables and shearing sheds whenever she could, but now it was June of 1916, and winter had descended. While battles raged across the planet, a ghostly quiet hung over Kiward Station. Outside, the gentle rain so typical of the Canterbury Plains was falling. The animals withdrew into the shelters, and the farmworkers had probably retreated to play poker in the stables.

Gwyneira was worried about Jack—he had not written for an eternity, and yet he must long since have left that beach in Turkey. Gallipoli. Although Gwyneira still did not know how to pronounce it properly, it was no longer necessary to know. After a final, desperate offensive, the British had given up the beachhead and withdrawn the ANZAC troops. Apparently in fine shape and with hardly any reported casualties. Though the newspapers in Christchurch celebrated the news as a victory, it was nothing but a grandiose failure. And Jack probably did not want to admit it. Gwyneira thought that could be the only explanation for his silence.

But she worried about Gloria most of all. It had been more than a year since she had disappeared from the hotel in San Francisco, and no one had heard from her since. The private detectives that her parents had hired had turned up nothing. Gloria could be anywhere. George Greenwood, who knew San Francisco, had even gone so far as to suggest that she might not have made it out of that den of sin alive.

"Sorry, Mrs. McKenzie, but food ready." Kiri, her old housekeeper, opened the door to Gwyneira's small study.

Gwyneira sighed. "I'm not hungry, Kiri, and I wouldn't be able to eat a thing if you serve me in the dining room. I'll come to you in the kitchen, and we'll have a bite together, if that's all right with you?"

Kiri nodded. Both she and Moana, the cook, had been more like friends than servants to Gwyneira for many years. They had not prepared a large meal anyway, just roasted fish and cooked sweet potatoes.

"Rongo Rongo say Gloria not dead," Moana said soothingly when Gwyneira only put a few morsels on her plate. "She consulted spirits, *tikki* say her heart sings sad songs but is not far."

"Thank you, Moana," Gwyneira said, forcing a smile.

In the salon, the telephone rang, startling Kiri and Moana.

"Spirits call," Moana said, but made no motion to go answer the phone. Kiri was braver—and more curious. The strange little box from which voices emanated struck both Maori women as eerie. To be honest, Gwyneira felt similarly, though she appreciated its advantages. When Kiri returned, she turned to Gwyneira.

"Call from Dunedin, says operator. We take it?"

"Of course." Gwyneira stood up. She had been expecting a call back from the veterinarian in Christchurch who had a new worming medicine for sheep. But Dunedin?

She waited patiently while the operator patched her through.

"You can talk now," an enthusiastic voice finally said. Gwyneira sighed. The operator in Haldon was infamous for listening in on every conversation and discussing the contents with her friends.

"This is Kiward Station, Gwyneira McKenzie speaking."

It was quiet for a moment. Then came a sort of coughing and a choked voice.

"Grandmum? It's, it's Gloria."

Gwyneira would not hear of anyone else picking up her great-granddaughter from Dunedin.

"Will you manage all right, even with the long train ride?" Miss Bleachum fretted. Since Gloria had not managed more than a few words beyond her greeting, Gwyneira had spoken in considerably more detail with the teacher. Gwyneira could hardly make sense of it, but that might have had to do with her racing heart. All that mattered was that Gloria was alive, and she was in New Zealand.

"Of course I'll survive a train ride; I don't have to pull the car myself," she replied with her usual determination. "I'm not taking any more chances. I'm not leaving the girl alone again under any circumstances. Please have her stay with you, and I'll be there in no more than three days. Take good care of her!"

Ignoring her age, Gwyneira danced through the salon, then back to the kitchen with a glass of champagne in her hand.

"I'm going to Dunedin, girls, to pick up Gloria. Oh yes, and Rongo Rongo should come get a sack of seeds from you. She did well with her spirits."

Gwyneira knew something was amiss as soon as she spotted Gloria and Miss Bleachum on the train platform in Dunedin. In her high-necked, navy-blue traveling outfit, Gloria appeared to be nervously clinging to Miss Bleachum's hand. In fact, they both looked a bit spinsterish. Even Gwyneira's own outfit was more modern and colorful than Gloria's. Overjoyed at her great-granddaughter's return home, Gwyneira had finally laid aside her sad black dress and donned a deep marine-blue traveling dress with white trim on the collar and cuffs. A matching hat sat pertly on her now white hair.

"Gloria!" Gwyneira blinked through her lorgnette, which she found more elegant than the unflattering glasses she owned. Though her eyes were still quite sharp for her age, she wanted to be able to see her long-lost great-granddaughter. "You've grown up."

Gwyneira's smile and her words concealed the chill that ran through her upon closely examining Gloria. The girl did not merely look grown-up; she looked old. Her eyes were almost expressionless.

Her behavior, however, was almost childishly fearful. Miss Bleachum had to gently remove Gloria's hand from her own and push her toward her great-grandmother. When Gwyneira embraced her, she sensed that Gloria found the contact unpleasant.

"Gloria, dear, I'm so happy you're back. How did you even manage it? You must tell me everything."

Gwyneira held Gloria's hands firmly. They were ice cold.

A shadow flitted across Gloria's face. Though her face still showed the traces of a suntan, she seemed to turn pale.

"Naturally you don't have to, Gloria," Miss Bleachum said softly, giving Gwyneira a meaningful look. "Gloria prefers not to speak about her experiences. We only know that she traveled through China and Australia."

Gwyneira nodded in amazement. "To undertake such a journey alone! I'm proud of you, my dear."

At that, Gloria burst into tears.

Gwyneira accompanied Miss Bleachum and Gloria back to the school and endured a tense teatime with them. Mrs. Lancaster joined them, and the teachers did everything they could to bring about a conversation between Gloria and her great-grandmother, but to no avail. Unable to lift her gaze from her plate, Gloria answered Gwyneira's questions monosyllabically while picking apart her tea cake.

"Do you plan to take the night train, Mrs. McKenzie, or can I offer you lodging for the night?" Mrs. Lancaster asked solicitously.

Gwyneira shook her head. "Taking that trip twice in the same day would be a bit much for my old bones. I've booked a hotel room in Dunedin. But if you'd be so good as to call us a taxi."

At the words "us" and "hotel," Gloria turned white as chalk. Gwyneira saw that she was giving Miss Bleachum beseeching looks, but the teacher shook her head. Gwyneira could no longer follow along. Did Gloria not want to go? It looked as if she were scared to death of leaving the school. Gwyneira considered accepting Mrs.

Lancaster's offer to stay the night, but then she changed her mind. That would only push the problem off another day. Besides, then she would have to give up the plan to go shopping in Dunedin the next morning. And if she had correctly understood Miss Bleachum, Gloria desperately needed a few new things.

"Would you go fetch your things then, dear?" she asked, pretending not to notice Gloria's reluctance. "Or haven't you packed yet? Nothing wrong with that. Surely Miss Bleachum will help, and I can chat a bit with Mrs. Lancaster in the meantime."

Sarah Bleachum took the hint and withdrew with Gloria. Mrs. Lancaster confirmed Gwyneira's impressions. "It's undoubtedly right to take the girl today, and she does need new clothing. She only owns two outfits. I've suggested to Miss Bleachum more than once that they go shopping for her; we would have loaned her the money. But Gloria did not want to."

Gwyneira arched her brows. "Then she didn't select that, hmm, ensemble with the help of you ladies?"

Mrs. Lancaster laughed. "Mrs. McKenzie, this is a girls' school, not a convent. Our students wear normal school uniforms, but outside school hours we don't force them to dress like medieval schoolmarms. Personally I find that even Miss Bleachum . . . but let's forget that. She no doubt has reasons for, well, suppressing her femininity. And I fear Gloria does too. You'll have to have a great deal of patience with her."

Gwyneira smiled. "I have all the patience in the world. At least with dogs and horses. It sometimes fails me with people, but I'll do my best."

"You're a widow?"

A shadow fell across Gwyneira's face. "Yes, for almost two years now. I'll never really get used to it."

"I'm sorry; I didn't mean to stir up old sorrows. It's only that . . . do any men live in your household, Mrs. McKenzie?" Mrs. Lancaster bit her lip.

"Mrs. Lancaster, I run a sheep farm"—she smiled—"not a convent. We employ shepherds and managers, and a Maori tribe lives on our land. What do you mean by the question?"

Mrs. Lancaster was clearly struggling to answer. "Gloria has trouble around men, Mrs. McKenzie. What is, what is with this Jack? Gloria told us about him, and I think Jack is the main reason she's afraid of returning home."

Gwyneira glared at the headmistress, vacillating between astonishment and rage. "She's afraid of Jack? But my son would never make her uncomfortable. They always had a wonderful relationship. Besides, Jack doesn't live on Kiward Station at the moment. He's in the army."

"I'm sorry, Mrs. McKenzie—unless you're one of those women who can hardly wait to send their boys to war. But that should make Gloria's reacclimatization easier."

Gwyneira did not believe it, but before she could continue the thoroughly confusing conversation, Miss Bleachum pushed Gloria into the room. The girl looked pale but composed. In the taxi to the hotel, Gwyneira told her about Jack and attempted to interpret her reaction. Gloria's expression alternated between shock and relief.

"Everything will be different," she said quietly.

"Not that different, dear. Not much changes on a sheep farm. Lambs are born, we herd the sheep into the highlands, we herd them back down, they're sheared, we sell the wool—every year, Gloria. It's always the same."

Gloria tried to cling to that.

The shopping trip the next morning proved arduous. Gloria didn't even want to leave the hotel, and when Gwyneira finally succeeded in dragging her into a store, she turned to the ugliest, biggest, and darkest dresses.

"When you were young, you liked to wear pants," Gwyneira said. She didn't back down until Gloria agreed to try on one of the almost shockingly modern pant-skirts, which the suffragettes had made popular for women who rode bicycles or drove cars. In England the trend had almost run its course, but in New Zealand, the loose-fitting pant-skirts were the latest thing. They suited Gloria brilliantly; she looked into the mirror amazed. A completely different girl stared back at her.

Gwyneira insisted that Gloria buy the pant-skirt and that she keep it on for the train ride, being very practical for such an occasion. Gloria squirmed, however, under the appraising eyes of the other passengers. Even Gwyneira could hardly take her eyes off Gloria when she was finally sitting across from her in their compartment.

"Do I have something on my face?" Gloria finally asked, annoyed.

"Not at all. Sorry to stare, dear. But, the resemblance is uncanny."

"Resemblance to whom?" Gloria asked gruffly.

"To Marama," she replied. "Your grandmother. And your grandfather, Paul. Unfortunately there aren't any photographs of them; otherwise, I could show you. It's as if someone laid their images on top of each other. Sometimes I see Paul when I look at you from the right and Marama when I look from the left."

In fact, Gloria's features reminded her more of Marama than Paul. By Maori standards, her wide face with the high cheekbones was quite pretty, and her figure matched exactly with the ideal of the natives. Her grouchy, withdrawn gaze, perpetually slightly furrowed brow, and tensely parted mouth reminded Gwyneira of Paul. He, too, had been angry at the world. Gwyneira felt a pang of fear.

At Gwyneira's express instructions, a chaise with two cobs was awaiting them at the train station. Maaka had argued that the trip would go more quickly in the car, but Gwyneira had insisted that Gloria would be happy to see the horses.

Gloria's countenance did indeed brighten for the first time when she spotted the cobs. She stopped in alarm, however, when she saw that Maaka was driving.

"*Kia ora*, Glory," the foreman said, greeting her warmly. "*Haere mai*. We're very happy to have you home." He beamed, but Gloria seemed to find it difficult to thank him.

"Come on, Glory, take a look at the horses," Gwyneira said, calling the girl back to herself. "They're half sisters of Cuchulainn's. Ceredwen is Raven's too, the horse I used to ride, and Colleen is . . ." She rattled off a pedigree.

Gloria listened. She seemed to remember the horses, and her face displayed more interest than it had during all the family stories Gwyneira had tried to entertain her with on the train.

"And Princess?"

"She's still around. But she's a bit too light for this coach." She was going to continue, but then all conversation was drowned out by deafening barking. Suddenly the dog that Maaka had tied up beneath the box could smell them.

"I thought I'd bring her along, Glory," he said, untying the leash.

Nimue shot toward the women, and Gwyneira bent over to greet her as she always did. But the dog had no eyes for Gwyneira. Almost howling with joy, she leaped up on Gloria.

"My Nimue?" Gloria kneeled down onto the street, forgetting her new clothes. She hugged the dog to her heart, and Nimue covered her in wet kisses. "But she can't be. I was afraid."

"That she was dead?" Gwyneira asked. "So that's why you didn't ask about her. She was still very young when you left, and border collies live a long time. She might live another ten years."

Gloria's face lost all its reserve and stiffness. So there was someone she loved.

Gwyneira smiled at her. Then she took her place on the box.

"Will you let me drive, Maaka?" Gwyneira asked.

He laughed. "I figured I'd have to give up the reins, Mrs. McKenzie, but if it's all the same to you, I'd like to stay in Christchurch anyway. I thought I'd stop by Mr. Greenwood's office for the wool receipt, you know."

"And Reti's charming daughter," Gwyneira teased him. It was an open secret that Maaka was in love with the daughter of George Greenwood's business manager, Reti. "Feel free to stay here, Maaka, but don't do anything stupid. The girl was raised according to Western tradition. She's waiting for a proposal with flowers and chocolates. Maybe you could even write her a poem."

Maaka frowned. "I'd never propose to a girl that dumb. She doesn't want some *tohunga* who tells her stories, and she's no child you win over with candy. Flowers bloom over the whole island in spring; it's bad luck if you pluck them without reason." He smiled. "But I've got this." He pulled out a jade stone that he'd whittled into a small god. "I found the stone myself. My spirits have touched it."

Gwyneira smiled. "How lovely. She'll like that. Say hello to Reti for me, and to Elizabeth Greenwood if you see her."

Maaka nodded and walked off with a wave good-bye.

Gloria had listened to the conversation stone-faced, further tensing up when Gwyneira teased the young man about his flirting. Had she been unhappy in love?

"Did a man ever give you anything, Gloria?" she asked gently.

Gloria, her dog pressed against her, glared at Gwyneira hatefully. "More than I cared for."

She did not say another word for many miles.

Gwyneira likewise kept quiet while the mares trotted through the Canterbury Plains. Though it might have been wise for them to stay at the White Hart in town, it was a beautiful, clear night and the sky was full of stars; the Seven Sisters twinkled above them.

"*Matariki*," Gwyneira said. James had taught her the name a long time ago.

Gloria nodded. "And *ika-o-te-rangi*. The Milky Way. The Maori call it the 'heavenly fish.'"

"You still remember how to speak it." Gwyneira smiled. "Marama will be happy. She always feared you would forget your Maori. She thinks Kura's forgotten the language. Which I think is strange. She sings in Maori, so how could she have forgotten the words?"

"Not the words," Gloria said.

Gwyneira shrugged. Soon the sun would rise, and they were approaching Kiward Station. She was sure Gloria must recognize the pastures and the lake they were passing.

"Can I drive?" the girl asked hoarsely. Her desire to steer the cobs on the approach was so great that she even let go of Nimue.

Just as Gwyneira was about to hand over the reins, she recalled the day Lilian returned from England. With Lilian's laughing eyes and her hair blowing in the wind, Gwyneira had been wholly caught up in her great-granddaughter's joy in the horses and the fast ride. And then James had come galloping toward them on that gray horse. Suddenly, Gwyneira could not bring herself to hand over the reins. It had brought bad luck before.

"No, better not." Gwyneira's fingers clenched the reins.

Gloria's face hardened. She did not say another word until they reached the stables. When one of the shepherds greeted the women as they pulled up, she wanted to disappear.

"Let me unharness them for you, Mrs. McKenzie and Miss . . . Martyn?"

The man was still young, a white man. He had not known Gloria as a child. His eyes widened at the sight of the young woman in the chic pant-skirt—he had never seen a lady dressed like that before. While Gwyneira saw in his expression fascination and admiration, Gloria saw nothing but naked lust.

"Thank you, Frank," Gwyneira said, handing him the reins. "Where's Princess at the moment? Miss Martyn would like to see her straightaway. She was her pony as a child."

"In the paddock behind the stables, Miss," Frank Wilkenson said. "If you'd like, I'd be happy to take you. She'd cut a good figure pulling a light gig."

Gloria did not say anything.

"You do know how to drive a carriage, don't you, Miss Martyn?"

Gloria cast a sour look at Gwyneira.

"No," she said shortly.

"Well, you certainly made an impression on him," Gwyneira said, attempting a light gibe in an effort to lighten the girl's mood. "He's a nice young man and very skilled with horses. I'd think about his offer. Princess would make a good driving horse. I'm an idiot for not having thought of it myself."

Gloria seemed to want to respond, but she changed her mind and followed her great-grandmother in silence. Her face only brightened again when she saw the chestnut mare outside next to the other horses.

"Princess, my love."

Though the horse did not recognize her former mistress—after eight years that would have been too much to ask—Gloria knew not to expect her to and did not hold it against the animal. She stooped under the fence and went up to the mare to stroke her. Princess let her and even rubbed her head briefly against Gloria's shoulder.

"I'll clean you tomorrow," Gloria said, smiling.

Gloria returned to Gwyneira with a radiant look on her face.

"Where's the foal?" she asked.

"What foal?" But then Gwyneira suddenly recalled the horse Jack had promised Gloria she could ride when she came back.

Gwyneira bit her lip.

"Gloria, dear, I'm sorry, but . . ."

"Did it die?" Gloria asked quietly.

"Of course not, nothing like that. She's a handsome little mare. And she's doing well. But I gave her to Lilian. I'm so sorry, Gloria, but it didn't look like you'd be coming home so soon. And you never wrote that you still rode like you used to."

Gloria stared at Gwyneira with naked hatred in her eyes.

"When you can't ride anymore, you're dead. Didn't you always say that? Was I, am I?"

"Gloria, I didn't mean anything by it. It was just that the little mare had nothing to do, and Lilian got along well with her. Look, Gloria, all the horses in the stables belong to you. Frank can show you the young horses tomorrow. A few four-year-olds already run very nicely. Or maybe you'd prefer a nice three-year-old you can work with yourself."

"Don't they really belong to my mother?" Gloria asked coldly. "Like everything here? Including me? What if she wants me back? Will you just send me off again?"

Gwyneira wanted to embrace her, but the girl seemed enveloped by an icy wind.

"Oh, Glory," Gwyneira sighed. She did not know what to say. She had never been the greatest diplomat, and this situation was entirely too much for her. She wished her friend Helen were here. Or James. They would know how to make clear to Gloria how welcome she was.

"We can simply put the blankets back on Princess," she finally said. Gwyneira preferred to solve problems with actions not words.

"Can we go in?" Gloria asked, ignoring the offer. "Where am I to stay anyway? Is my room still there? Or did you give it to Lilian too?"

Gwyneira decided not to answer. Instead she walked slowly ahead of Gloria toward the Kiward Station kitchen. At the last moment it occurred to her that Gloria might misinterpret that too.

"You don't mind that we, I mean, we could of course go in through the main entrance, but at my age it's often too strenuous with all the steps."

Gloria rolled her eyes.

"Grandmum, I'd like to go to my room. I don't really care how I get there."

But they were not able to retire so quickly. Kiri, Moana, and Gloria's grandmother Marama were waiting in the kitchen.

"*Haere mai, mokopuna*. How nice to have you here again."

Gwyneira observed how the Maori women danced zealously around Gloria, all of them greeting her as a granddaughter and making as if to rub their faces on hers in the traditional *hongi*. If they were as dismayed by the sight of Gloria as Gwyneira had been the day before, at least they knew how to hide it.

Marama took Gloria's hands and said something in their language. Gwyneira did not understand it exactly, but she thought it was some kind of apology.

"Forgive your mother, my daughter, *mokopuna*. She never understood people."

Gloria let the heartfelt greetings wash over her. She smiled only when Nimue, driven to ecstasy by the raucous joy of the women, began to run around barking.

"For now, rest. But tonight, good food," Kiri declared. Perhaps she attributed Gloria's lack of enthusiasm to her exhaustion. "We'll make *kumera*, sweet potatoes. You surely not eaten since going away to England."

Gwyneira finally led Gloria up to her room—the same one she had occupied before she left. She noted happily that the tension in the girl's face relaxed when she entered the room. Gwyneira had changed nothing. Pictures of horses still decorated the wall, including the last photograph of Gloria with Princess, as did a few childishly awkward drawings.

"You see, we always expected you back," Gwyneira said stiffly, but Gloria only smiled when she saw Marama's present lying on the bed. As a child, she had often hastily thrown her breeches there in order "to turn into a girl," as Jack had always called it, for dinner. And now there were brand-new breeches lying there, from the same old pattern Marama had tailored.

Gwyneira tried to return the smile. "So maybe tomorrow you'll pick out a horse?" she asked tentatively.

The light in Gloria's eyes went out.

"Maybe," she said.

Gwyneira was relieved to close the door behind her.

Gloria walked around the room once, looking at all the pictures on the walls, the colorful rug, the pieces of jade and other colored stones she had collected with Jack. Then she threw herself down on the bed,

Nimue in her arms, and cried. When her tears finally ceased to flow, the sun already stood high in the sky.

She had made it. She was back on Kiward Station. She knew she should be happy. The hard times were past. But she did not feel any joy.

She felt only rage.

3

The idea of eloping was a wonderful dream, and Lilian and Ben embellished the fantasy a bit more every time they met. Everything—news of the war, Gloria's return—was eclipsed by Lilian's thoughts of their romantic flight. Completely consumed by her love for Ben, she was fearless about the prospect of going through with it. Ben shared her dreams, but without really believing them. Until a bitterly cold evening in spring when events took a turn.

George Greenwood was in town. He, Tim Lambert, and Matt Gawain had decided to announce the construction of the coke furnace. They had invited the Billers, the manager of the Blackburn Mine, and several other important businessmen to a celebratory dinner at one of the best hotels on the quay. There they planned to reveal that all the local mines would soon be able to have their coal worked into coke right in Greymouth. While the owners of the smaller mines would probably be delighted by the news, Florence Biller would likely be furious at not having summoned the courage and capital for the expansion herself. The investment would add huge profits for the Lambert Mine.

For Lilian and Ben, the occasion was also a milestone. For the first time in a year, their parents were bringing them together at a social event. George Greenwood had asked that his charming travel partner might be seated across from him.

"Well, how are things with that heart of yours?" he teased her good-naturedly when she sat down. She was wearing a new apple-green dress, her first real evening gown, and she looked enchanting. "Have you given it away or would you rather take over your father's mine?"

Lilian turned a deep red. "I, uh, there is someone," she said. Uncle George had always taken her seriously. Surely he would not behave as childishly as Ben's parents and her own when he learned about her sweetheart. "But it's still a secret."

George smiled. "Then we won't want to go into it," he said, silently determining to talk to Elaine about it later. She had told him about Lilian and Ben's puppy love, but she clearly thought it had passed. George, however, did not think that was the case. And unlike the others, he noticed that Lilian and Ben vanished at one point. Lilian had gone to fetch her mother's stole from the car, and Ben slipped away while Florence was arguing with the business manager of the Blackburn Mine.

George decided this was the perfect moment to make the big announcement. He tapped his glass.

Ben reached Lilian just as she was closing the car door. He beamed at her.

"I had to see you alone, Lily."

Lilian let him embrace her but looked concerned at how exposed they were. When an icy gust of wind blew down from the mountains, Lily suggested that they get in the car, and she slid into the backseat. Ben followed and began kissing her.

"Leave yourself something for the wedding night," she teased him. "It's almost your birthday. Do we want to wait here until then, or should we leave for Auckland before?"

Ben was startled but came up with a temporary loophole.

"We'd better wait. After all, where would we be able to stay before we were married?"

"We'll simply look for a landlord who doesn't ask for our marriage certificate," she explained practically.

Ben blushed. "You mean, we, uh, we're going to do it before?"

"I think so. Just to be on the safe side. In case things don't fit or something."

"What do you mean, 'don't fit?'" Ben asked.

It was Lilian's turn to blush. "Well, as I understand it, it has something to do with putting things together."

"But I think it always fits."

"How do you know? Have you done it before?" Her countenance alternated between one of hope that he had some experience and bitter thoughts of infidelity.

Ben shook his head, outraged. "Of course not. I would never do that with anyone but you. But, but . . . the other boys at college . . ."

Lilian understood. Ben's fellow students had all been older. Naturally they had known more than he did.

"All right, good," she said, "but it can't hurt to try it out. You do want to, don't you?"

"Here?" Ben asked. "Now?"

It was tempting. The car was pleasantly warm and much more comfortable than the stables. But Lilian didn't think the time was right.

"No, it's too early. But in Auckland."

Ben began to kiss her more urgently. The thought of trying it there and then was irresistible.

"But then it will be too late. We wouldn't be able to go back if it didn't fit."

Lilian thought for a moment. Then she let him pull up her dress and stroke her thighs. He had never done that before, but it surpassed all the joy she felt when he caressed her breast. She moaned languorously.

"It'll fit," she murmured.

Florence Biller seethed with rage. Again this Greenwood with his huge fortune. It had surely been Tim's idea. Though she had considered doing the same, she would never have been able to do it secretly the way Lambert had. She would have needed an engineering office and to pursue outside investors. As it was, she got no help from Caleb, and Ben was proving to be as hopeless as his father. As her frustration mounted, she looked around for her eldest son. When she didn't see him, she scanned the room for the Lambert girl.

Florence picked up her shawl to get some air. She knew she needed to calm down before anyone saw how angry she was. She thought she'd made her exit unobserved, but George Greenwood saw her out of the corner of his eye and tipped off Elaine.

"Lainie? I think our dear smoking-mad Mrs. Biller is missing her son."

"So? He can't have gone far."

"Aren't you missing someone?"

"Oh no. Did she say anything? Doesn't matter, I'd better track them down before Florence does. Just what is that girl thinking?"

More amused than unsettled, Elaine made her way outside—just in time to witness Florence Biller ripping open the back of the Cadillac and tearing her son out of the car.

"Get out. Our business is going belly-up, and you're amusing yourself with your little whore."

"It's not what you think," stammered Ben. He tried to make sure, as surreptitiously as possible, that his pants were buttoned.

"And you, Miss Lambert."

Elaine appeared behind Florence, and Ben attempted a sort of bow.

"I can explain, Mother, Mrs. Lambert. We want to get married."

Elaine stared at her daughter, speechless, as Lilian moved to get out of the car.

"Don't you have anything to say?" Florence raved. "Your little whore . . ."

"Don't take that tone with me, Florence," Elaine roared at her. "Even if our children have perhaps, well, overstepped the boundaries of proper behavior, my daughter is no whore. Come on out, Lily. And make yourself halfway presentable. Maybe you should send your son home, Florence. After all, it is in everyone's interest to avoid a scandal here. Lilian, go back inside and wash your face. Florence, we'll have to talk to the two of them later. And maybe with each other too," Elaine said, trying to maintain her composure.

"Talk? What's there to talk about? But it figures, the daughter of a bar wench." Florence snorted.

"Oh, and yet you had no compunctions about sleeping with the highest bidder," Elaine replied. "Am I mistaken or weren't you interested in my husband for a while? A cripple with a mine seemed ripe with opportunity, didn't it? It's just a shame for you that Tim's head was still working, but in the end a queer with a mine was the winning ticket anyway."

"Lainie, I think that's enough," Matt Gawain broke in. "And you calm down too, Mrs. Biller. Otherwise the whole town will be talking about you tomorrow. We're already going to have to pay that porter over there for his silence. Lilian, your father is waiting for you, and Mr. Greenwood would like to dance with you."

Elaine bit her lip. She rarely let herself be moved to such outbursts. But calling Lilian a "whore" crossed the line.

"Well, she's not entirely wrong, now is she?" Tim Lambert thundered. It was late, and it would undoubtedly have been better to discuss Lilian and Ben's interlude in the morning. But Tim had caught wind of something with George whispering to Elaine, and then to Matt, who had looked alarmed. Followed by the drained expression on Elaine's face when she returned, the traces of tears on Lilian's cheeks, and Florence and Ben's disappearance. Tim was no fool. Though they managed to retain their composure for the rest of the evening, Tim pounced on Lilian as soon as they got home.

"If I've understood correctly, that little bastard took off your dress and . . ."

"Nothing happened! We only cuddled a bit."

"With his hands up your dress?"

"We want to get married."

"Married! What utter nonsense. How old are you? Your mother might dismiss it as puppy love, but it's clearly gone too far if you're spreading your legs for him in my car."

Tim Lambert wanted to give his daughter a good beating for causing a scandal on his big day. Now Florence Biller would try even harder to put obstacles in his path. Worst of all, they had lost the Biller Mine as an important client for the coke furnace. Florence Biller was guaranteed to be brooding over plans for her own addition even if it ruined her.

"I . . ."

Elaine came to Lilian's aid. "Tim, unless it suddenly flared up again tonight—and Lilian assures me that isn't the case—the children have been together for almost two years. Maybe they really do make a good couple. Florence has to see . . ."

"Florence doesn't have to do anything. Nor do we. Except send Lilian away as soon as possible. What if she were to go to your parents, Lainie? She could help in the warehouse. She's got a knack for it. And your father will keep an eye on her."

"I love Ben," Lilian sobbed. "And I won't be sent away. We're going to marry and . . ."

"You shut your mouth," Tim ordered her.

"Lily, you should go to bed," Elaine said. "We'll talk about this tomorrow."

"There's nothing to talk about," Tim said.

Lilian fled to her room and cried herself to sleep while her parents fought bitterly. It rarely happened, but that night they came to an impasse, only reconciling in the early morning hours and sleeping through the hail of stones a desperate Ben Biller unskillfully aimed at Lilian's bedroom window.

Lilian's ears were more sensitive. When the first rock finally struck its target, she awoke, threw open her window, and ducked to avoid the next stone.

"Quiet," she whispered, amazed but charmed by the situation.

"I have to talk to you." Ben sounded choked, not the least bit romantic. "Can you come down?"

Lilian threw on a bathrobe and met Ben in the garden beneath her window.

"Did you get in trouble?" she asked. "My father almost exploded. Just imagine, he . . ."

"They want to send me away," Ben broke in. "My mother does, in any case; my father couldn't get a word in edgewise."

Lilian giggled. "They want to send me away too, to Queenstown. But naturally I'm not going."

"I'm supposed to go to the North Island. Relatives of ours have a coal mine there. And I'm to work there; my mother already spoke to my uncle on the phone. She was in such an awful rage she called him up in the middle of the night."

"She can't force you," she said soothingly. "Just tell her you won't go, that you don't want to work in an office."

"Lily, you don't understand." Ben seized her upper arms as if he wanted to shake her, but then he buried his face in her hair instead. "I'm not going to work in an office; they're sending me into a mine. My uncle says at his mine everyone has to work their way up from the pickax, meaning at least a few months as a miner underground. He says that drove the nonsense out of his boys' heads too."

"*You're* supposed to mine for coal?" Lilian asked.

"I tried . . . I wanted to tell her that I wouldn't do it, that she couldn't drag me by my hair onto the ferry, and all those things you're always saying. But I couldn't, Lily. When I'm in front of her, it's like I'm frozen. I can't get a word out."

"Well, we have been planning to run away."

"That's why I'm here. Let's go, Lily. Right now, on the early train."

Lilian frowned. "But the early train goes to Westport, Ben. The one to Christchurch doesn't run until eleven."

"There's a coal train that goes from our mine to Christchurch. At six o'clock in the morning. The cars are ready. The train workers just connect them when the locomotive comes. If we climb onto one now, no one will notice."

"But we'll be covered in coal when we arrive in Christchurch," Lilian objected.

"Then we'll just get out earlier and wash up somewhere." Ben's plan sprang from a courage born of desperation.

Lilian improved upon it at lightning speed.

"We need blankets, or better yet, a tarp to keep out the coal dust. It won't be perfect, but it will be better than nothing. Do you have anything like that at the mine? You must. And we should put on our oldest clothes. Then we can throw them away when get to Christchurch—we'll be arriving at the goods depot anyway, right? We'll be able to find a shed or something where we can change. I just have to pack. Where are your things, Ben?"

Ben looked at her, uncomprehending.

"Ben! Your bag. Did you want to go as you are? Without so much as a change of clothes? And do you have your passport? We'll need it to marry."

Ben had not thought that far ahead, so he would have to go back home. Lilian sighed.

Lilian only needed a few minutes to gather her things. She closed the door behind her without looking back. Elated by the prospect of the adventure ahead, she led Ben to the garage. She steered the car out of the garage.

"Close the door, Ben. Then they won't notice right away that the car's gone. No, the left bolt. My God, can't you shut a door without pinching your fingers?"

Ben sucked on his squashed thumb as Lilian drove. He shivered at his own courage.

"I'm supposed to go back in the house? What if my parents wake up?"

"They had a long day. Just don't drop anything in the stairwell. And don't forget your passport."

Lilian spent a nerve-racking half hour behind the wheel, a few streets down from the Billers' town house. She imagined a thousand complications, but Ben finally slid in next to her.

"My father," he murmured, "he caught me."

"What?" Lily asked. "How are you here then? You didn't knock him out or shoot him or anything, did you?" Though Lilian didn't think Ben capable of violence, that's what always happened in books and films.

Ben shook his head. "No, he gave this to me." The boy fished a hundred-dollar bill out of his pocket. "I had gathered my things, but I still needed my passport, which was in his study, so I went in, and there he was. In the dark. With a bottle of whiskey. And he just looked at me and said . . ."

"Yes?" Lilian asked, eager for his heroic words of farewell.

"He said, 'You're going?' And I said yes. And then he rummaged in his pocket for the money and said, 'Sorry. I don't have any more on me right now.'"

"And?" Lily asked, impatient.

"And nothing. I left. Oh, I did say thanks."

Lilian sighed with relief. Though it lacked drama, Ben had made his escape—and with the blessing of his father, no less.

"We'll drive the car into the forest next to the mine. They'll find it there tomorrow," Lilian said. "Do you have the key for the gate, or will we have to climb over it?"

Ben had the key, and the train cars were sitting there as he had described. With an hour until the locomotive was expected, there was no one there, and Ben and Lilian shoveled a shelter into the mountain of coal. By the time they were on their way, they looked like coal miners. Ben laughed and kissed a little of the dust from Lilian's nose.

"Where are we anyway?" she asked, glancing at the breathtaking panorama of the southern mountains. The train was crossing over a narrow bridge barely able to hold its weight. Lilian held her breath. Beneath them gaped a canyon at the bottom of which flowed a blue-white mountain stream.

"A long way from the West Coast, at least," Ben said, relieved. "Do you think they know we're gone yet?"

"Definitely," Lilian said. "The real question is whether they know that we left on this train. If they figure it out, they'll seize us in Christchurch."

"Couldn't we get off earlier?" Ben asked.

"This train doesn't make any stops before Christchurch. But let's see. We could hop off as the train slows through Arthur's Pass and then catch the passenger train, which will stop in Rolleston, the last stop before Christchurch."

When they passed through the Arthur's Pass station, the train didn't stop, but it slowed down. Lily boldly threw her bag from the car and jumped before it picked up speed again. Ben followed suit, and they set off in search of a body of water where they could clean themselves up. They soon found a stream and set up camp. Although the day was sunny, Arthur's Pass was considerably higher in altitude than Greymouth and hoarfrost still covered the ground. They shivered at the thought of getting wet or even changing clothes.

"Brave enough to jump in the water?" Lily teased, slipping reluctantly out of her blackened hose.

"If you are," Ben said, pulling his shirt off.

"I'd have to undress," Lilian said.

"You have to do that anyway."

"Not entirely." Feigning coyness, Lilian batted her eyes. "But I'll do it if you do." She began unbuttoning her dirty dress as she spoke. Ben hardly felt the cold anymore as she undid her corset and presented herself to him in nothing but her underwear.

"Now you," Lilian said with glinting eyes.

She watched with fascination as Ben took off his pants.

"So that's what that looks like," she remarked when he finally stood before her naked. "I had pictured it bigger."

Ben blushed deeply. "It depends on the weather," he murmured. "Now you. Everything."

Lilian undressed completely too, only to throw her coal-dusted coat immediately around her shivering body.

"You'll be all black in a moment," Ben said. "But you're beautiful."

Lily laughed, embarrassed. "And you're filthy," she said. "Come on, I'll wash you."

She dipped her slip in the stream and pounced on Ben. They played like children in the icy water, spraying each other, and trying to rub the coal dust off their bodies. Lilian had brought soap, but it was still not easy. The dust clung in a greasy film to their skin, and without warm water, there was no way to wash it off completely. At least Lilian had thought to cover her hair with a kerchief. Ben had to wash his and almost froze to death in the process. The result left something to be desired.

"Well, you look older anyway," Lilian said. "Your gray hair set in early."

Ben had to laugh. He had rarely had as much fun as this carefree tussling in a stream near Arthur's Pass. Lilian looked ecstatic.

Eventually, they were wearing clean clothes. Ben had not thought to bring a warm coat, and Lilian had decided against bringing a shawl because her bag was already too heavy. Ben tried to keep her warm by wrapping his arm around her as they strolled back to the train station to wait for the passenger train to Christchurch.

"You're sure it stops here?" Ben asked.

Lilian nodded with chattering teeth. "And I hope it's heated. We're close enough. We can wait here." She pointed to a group of bushes within view of the platform and moved to sit on her bag behind them.

"Here? I mean, we could go to the platform and buy a ticket, and they might have washrooms."

"Ben, if we stroll in there now and buy a ticket, the first thing the signalman is going to do is ask us where we came from. And what are we supposed to tell him? That we came on foot over the mountains? You're much too honest, Ben. I hope you never have to become a thief to feed us like Henry Martin in that old folk song. We'd starve."

"And how does Miss Brigand Queen see the situation?" Ben asked, insulted. "We have to board the train somehow."

"Simple! People often get off here to gawk at the pass and stretch their legs. We'll just mingle with them and then climb aboard. I doubt they'll check tickets. After all, who's going to stow away out here in the wilderness?"

Sneaking onto the train had proved easy enough. The biggest danger was of being seen by some acquaintance since the Lamberts and the Billers knew half of Greymouth. They finally found a compartment filled with travelers from Christchurch. An older couple even shared their provisions with the hungry young couple.

"My husband is a coal miner, you see," Lilian said to explain the gray streak in Ben's blond hair. "But there's no future in that. Well, there is a future, of course. The mines are all at capacity because of the war. We, er, the Lamberts are even building a coke furnace now, but well, we don't see a future for us in mining. We want to start anew in the Canterbury Plains with, well, maybe with a sewing-machine business."

While Lilian chattered away, Ben lost himself in the gorgeous landscape streaming by out the window. Beech forests, riverbanks, and wild mountainsides gave way to foothills and finally the grassland of the Canterbury Plains.

Lilian and Ben got off at Rolleston.

"Did you have to talk the whole time?" Ben asked indignantly. "Those people are going to remember us now."

"Yes, as a young couple from the mining settlement," Lily said, unconcerned. "Come on, Ben, there aren't any detectives waiting in Christchurch to question train passengers. At least not yet. And later they won't even be able to find those people."

"We won't really be safe until we're in Auckland," Ben said.

"Yes, a big city would be good. Come on, with a little luck we'll soon be on the train to Blenheim."

The rest of the journey to Christchurch proved more of an adventure. Although a few farmers took them part of the way on their wagons, they did not reach the city until evening when it was already dark. Ben pleaded for them to take a room somewhere, but Lilian hesitated.

"I've been here before, Ben. Someone might recognize me. Maybe not by name but as a relative of my grandmum. We look quite alike.

And this is George Greenwood's town. If he makes inquiries, he'll be on our trail."

"And what does the Brigand Queen suggest?" Ben asked sourly.

They ended up at the freight depot on a load of sheepskin. In the shed next to them a herd of cattle waiting to be transported provided additional warmth—as well as the penetrating stench of dung and urine.

"Yesterday we looked like coal miners; tomorrow we'll stink," Ben complained. "What's next?"

Lilian snuggled into his arms. "Ben, it's romantic. This is our love story. Think of Romeo and Juliet."

"They killed themselves," Ben remarked grumpily.

Lilian giggled. "See, we're doing better than they did," she said before yawning and closing her eyes.

4

People shied away a bit from Ben and Lilian when they sat down on the train to Blenheim the next morning. Although the stench of cattle dung had dissipated, the lanolin scent of the wool clung to their clothing. Lilian did not care, as it gave them more space at the window. Though not as lovely as the path through the mountains, the coastline was a mesmerizing mix of snow-white beaches and cliffs that fell steeply into the sea.

The journey took almost all day, and when the train pulled in, they were too tired to think of any maneuvers to cover their tracks. They agreed to take a room in an inn instead of looking for a new hiding place to sleep.

"We'll be on the ferry tomorrow anyway; after that it won't matter," Lilian said, leaning into Ben as they left the train station arm in arm. "Only you can't blush when you introduce me as Mrs. Biller. Otherwise people will think we're lying."

They decided on a small, clean hotel. Though it was a splurge, both of them tacitly assumed that this would be their wedding night. Ben paid with his father's money, which put quite a dent in their reserves. Add the ferry and maybe a night in Wellington and his money would be gone. Lilian was less concerned. As if it were the most natural thing in the world, she produced her own savings in the amount of three hundred dollars. Unlike Florence Biller—who viewed Ben's work as a contribution to the family fortune—Tim Lambert had always paid his daughter for her work in the office. And although Lilian had spent a small fortune every month on stationery, perfume, volumes of poetry, and romantic novels, she had managed to stash some away under her mattress.

"My dowry," she proudly declared. Ben kissed her and then together they inspected the room with its wide marriage bed and the bathroom, which was dominated by a giant claw-foot tub.

"We can both fit in there," Lilian laughed.

Ben blushed. "I don't know, if, is that proper?"

"Nothing we're doing here is proper. And we've already taken our clothes off once. There's no difference between here and Arthur's Pass—except that the water here is warm."

The last of their inhibitions fell away in the hot, perfumed water. They washed each other's hair, and rubbed soap on each other's bodies—and this time Lilian did not complain about the size of Ben's sex. Before they drowned while attempting to consummate their relationship, they climbed out of the tub and ran to the bed. Ben dried them off, and they began a second attempt.

Neither of them really knew how to proceed properly, but after some initial discomfort for Lilian, they finally succeeded in their act of love, and ecstasy carried her past the pain. Afterward, they laughed and cried with happiness, curled up in each other's arms.

"So that was right, wasn't it?" Lilian whispered. "A little blood is normal. At least that's what the girls in my boarding school said. It's just a good thing that we'll be gone tomorrow before the maid comes, otherwise we'd definitely have to pay for the sheets. I'm ravenous. Shall we order room service?"

Between the late dinner and an opulent breakfast the next morning, they squandered most of the rest of Ben's money but agreed to save on their real wedding in exchange. On the ferry that day they were so happy they were practically floating. While other passengers groaned with seasickness, Lilian and Ben tried to take a stroll about the deck, laughing hysterically over the boat's rocking.

When they reached Wellington, they boarded the night train to Auckland. Lilian dreamed of a sleeping car, but that would have demolished their entire budget. So she slept through the first night of their journey in her seat, curled up close against Ben's shoulder. Ben hardly dared stir. He still could not entirely believe that fate had sent him this girl. As the train crossed the North Island, he composed new poems in his mind.

After a day and another night on the rails, they reached Auckland in the first light of the rising sun. Lilian suggested they begin looking for an apartment right away and began asking at the train station.

"Look around the west side of town," the stationmaster advised them, "unless you're richer than you look."

"Where's the university?" Ben asked.

Following his instructions, they made their way toward campus, basking in the tepid breeze and warmth of the subtropical city.

"Palm trees," Lilian gaped, "and giant kauri pines. Everything's bigger than back home!"

After the ornamented buildings in Cambridge and Oxford, Ben found the university a bit disappointing. Tired and hungry, but also exhilarated from the initial success of their adventure, the pair roamed through the streets around the campus waiting for the registration office to open.

Lilian waited patiently while Ben laid out all the documentation of his previous studies. It looked like they would accept him with open arms. The university wanted to develop its Maori studies program, and a student who had graduated Cambridge would only enhance the department's status. The students who worked in the office provided Ben with the names and addresses of all the professors in the department, handed him a course catalog, and advised him to come back around midday.

Lilian then broke in and asked about lodgings. She was exhausted—though not opposed to repeating their wedding night before going to sleep. For both things, however, they could not do without a bed.

"We have a list of renters," one of the men said doubtfully, "but most of them are private rooms intended for young, single men. A few ladies take in girls too when their references check out. But a married couple? I don't know."

Lilian and Ben spent the next several hours walking the streets without success. None of the renters would open up their apartments to a couple.

"No, no, dearies, there's two of you now, but in a year there'll be little ones if one's not already on the way. And then I'll have my retirement filled with screaming babies."

"Will there be little ones in a year?" Lilian asked flirtatiously as they stepped back onto the street.

Ben looked at her, shocked. "It'd be a little early, don't you think?" That said, he had no idea how it might be avoided. "So what are we going to do now?"

They followed the stationmaster's suggestion and headed west of the university district to a neighborhood inhabited by artisans and laborers. The first two apartments with "For Rent" signs in the window were located above a carpenter's and a baker's. Lilian's mouth watered at the scent of fresh bread. Yet the renters were not enthused about renting to a young couple who had no work and only lofty dreams.

"How do you intend to pay the rent?"

Sobered, they continued on. As they approached the docks, the houses began to look dingier. They eventually came upon a sign in the window of a sleazy-looking pub. The apartment that was advertised was nothing more than a large room with a kitchenette and a bathroom down the hall.

"In the evening it can get a little loud," admitted the landlord. "And the furniture, well, I had to kick the last tenants out. No-good riffraff."

The furniture was filthy, smeared with sticky liquids, and the last residents' dirty dishes were still in the sink. Ben made a disgusted face when he saw maggots on them.

"Take your time looking around. Just don't take anything with you," said the landlord before returning to the pub. Not that there was anything worth stealing.

"It's a rat hole," Ben said.

"But it's cheap," Lilian said. They would be able to live there for months on her money. "Sure, it's a little run-down, but it'll do. You are, after all, a poet, an artist."

"You mean it's going to rain in here too?" Ben thought about Spitzweg's painting *The Poor Poet.*

Lilian laughed. "Come on, it has character. That has to inspire you."

"It's a rat hole," Ben repeated.

"If we clean it thoroughly and buy some more furniture, it won't be that bad. Besides, we're not going to find anything else. Let's take it. After all, we still need to buy a bed today." Not even Lilian could whitewash the stained mattress and decrepit bed frame.

A few hours later they had given the room a good scrub and at Ben's urging treated the floor and walls with a generous quantity of anti-pest powder. After acquiring a used bed that had seen better days, they finally repeated their wedding night in their own home. In the pub below, it began to get rowdy. "A little loud" proved to be quite an understatement. Raising a child there—the remark of the landlord on Princess Street had not left either of their heads—would be out of the question.

Lilian and Ben agreed not to let it come to that, albeit without taking any actual measures to prevent it.

"The question isn't whether we *can* find them. It's whether we *want* to find them," remarked George Greenwood.

Even without making rigorous inquiries of all the passengers, it would not have been difficult for him and the Lamberts to pick up Lilian and Ben's tracks and follow them to the ferry at Blenheim. The only difficulty was the first leg of their journey—it took almost two days before Florence Biller was willing to cooperate enough to investigate the transportation out of the Biller Mine. The ticket salesman in Christchurch remembered Ben right away. From Blenheim it became even simpler.

Tim Lambert was beside himself when he heard about their staying overnight in a hotel in Blenheim. Elaine bore it more calmly.

"Dearest, what did you expect? At least we know they took the ferry from Blenheim and they're on the North Island. We should inform the Billers."

"Florence probably already knows all this. She could have figured out everything we have."

Not as easily as George Greenwood, however, whose firm had branches in practically all of New Zealand's larger cities. And as it happened, the Billers had undertaken no measures to that effect. Florence appeared determined simply to forget her unfilial eldest son. Only Caleb accepted Tim's invitation to a meeting.

"I'm convinced that my son has no dishonorable intentions," he said with slight embarrassment to Elaine after they had all exchanged greetings.

Tim gave an angry snort.

"I'm sure he didn't need to use force to carry my daughter off," Elaine said, smiling, "but let's stick to the matter at hand, Caleb. Nobody's making accusations. The question is merely how to proceed from here."

George Greenwood nodded. "As I said, we know they're on the North Island, and we can assume that they've located to one of the bigger cities. Probably one of the university towns—after all, it's unlikely your son has hired himself out as a shepherd or signed up to work with a coal mine, wouldn't you agree, Mr. Biller?"

"That's precisely why he ran away," he said with clenched teeth. "In a way it's all our fault."

"So Wellington or Auckland?" Elaine asked.

"If you want to find them, I'd advise you to get a private detective," Greenwood suggested.

"What do you mean *if*?" Tim asked. "Naturally we're going to bring them back. They're just children."

"If we wait another few weeks, they'll probably already be married," Elaine said. "If they aren't already. I wouldn't be surprised if Lilian moved up Ben's date of birth."

"But this is madness," Tim cursed. "Something like this won't last a lifetime."

Elaine frowned. "I wasn't much older when I came to Greymouth. That didn't stop you."

"Please, Lainie, they're sixteen and seventeen."

"First loves can sometimes take a rather impetuous course," George Greenwood said.

"We could have the marriage voided," insisted Tim.

"Then what?" asked Elaine. "Are we going to send Lily to Queenstown where we can hope they find some way to wall her in while Ben ends up in the mines? That's completely unrealistic. Tim, as much as I would like to know where Lily is hiding and what she's doing, the best thing would be to leave her alone. They should try standing on their own two feet. It can't do any harm. When things go sour, they'll come back."

"Lilian could get pregnant," Tim remarked.

Caleb blushed.

"She might already be," said Elaine. "All the more reason to give them time to get married. Look at it this way, Tim: the baby would inherit the Biller Mine. Can you think of anything that would upset Florence more?"

That same day Lilian and Ben got married at the civil registry office in Auckland. Their parents' declaration of consent was forged, as was the birth date on Ben's passport. Tim Lambert's consent for Lilian to marry looked particularly authentic since it was written on his custom letterhead. It was a little wrinkled, but the registrar did not ask any questions.

5

Mrs. McKenzie, what's wrong with the young Miss Martyn?" Maaka had obviously been struggling with the question for a while, and Gwyneira had been expecting it for some time.

"We all try to be nice to her, but she's simply rude. Earlier I thought she was going to hit Frank, when all he did was try to help her onto her horse."

Gwyneira had gotten a bad feeling when she saw Gloria riding away as if hounded by the furies—much too quickly for the unexercised horse. Granted, the horse Gloria had chosen was vivacious and difficult, and Gwyneira had made clear that the mare wasn't a good choice after Gloria's long hiatus from riding, but she had ignored Gwyneira's advice. Frank Wilkenson even made an extra effort to be kind to the girl. Gwyneira thought he might be in love—and that Gloria couldn't handle that. Not that Wilkenson was in any way importunate. But Gloria was invariably rude, and according to Maaka had even raised her riding crop against him. If things continued this way, Frank would quit, and Gwyneira would lose a valuable worker.

The other shepherds, most of whom were Maori, had less trouble with the young mistress. But they, too, kept their distance after Gloria had spat at them the first few times.

"I don't know either, Maaka. Kiri and Moana would like nothing more than to spoil her, but she's no different in the house. Make it clear to Frank that she's serious. If she doesn't want to flirt with him, he'll have to accept that."

Maaka nodded.

"How does she do with the sheep?" Gwyneira asked. She didn't particularly want to discuss Gloria's problems with her foreman, but his opinion interested her greatly. After all, in Nimue Gloria had an exceptional sheepdog, and she had always enjoyed working with animals.

"Well, she doesn't have much experience, but that's not really the problem. Nimue can read every command just from her looks, and she has a talent for handling animals, always has had—just like Jack. Have you heard from him yet?"

Maaka was clearly trying to change the subject.

Gwyneira merely shook her head despondently.

"Still no word. Just that notice a few months ago that he was wounded in the battle at Gallipoli. And that's all after three requests to the high command. Gallipoli isn't something they want to talk about. They've scattered the ANZAC forces to the four corners. So we'll have to wait until Jack writes himself. Or until . . ." She kept the rest to herself. Gwyneira tried to think about the alternative as little about it as possible. "So what was it you want to say about Gloria?" she asked.

Maaka took a deep breath. "She's very good with the animals, Mrs. McKenzie. Just not with the people. She won't listen to anything and isolates herself. But she has to realize that we must work as a team, especially with the cattle. She's not dumb, after all. But she seems incapable of teamwork."

"So be it, Maaka. Talk to Frank; he needs to step back. And keep Gloria busy with the sheep and dogs. Nothing can go wrong there. And one more thing, please take the riding pony to the stallion. You know, Gloria's pony, Princess."

Gloria had Ceredwen gallop until both horse and rider were out of breath. Nimue ran with her tongue hanging out behind them. Normally Gloria made allowances for the dog, but that day, all she wanted was to get away, as fast as possible. She knew that she had overreacted; she should not have struck out at Frank Wilkenson. But when he had gripped Ceredwen's reins and reached for her stirrup, something in her had exploded. This was not the first time it had happened, but until then her lightning-fast reactions had always been useful for keeping men at bay. On Kiward Station, however, such behavior would get her into trouble—Maaka might already be talking to her great-grandmother.

She had intended to herd a few ewes to a winter pasture, but she had forgotten about the animals in her confrontation with Frank. Now it would be senseless to turn back. She would rather check on the outposts—or ride to the circle of stone warriors. She had only been there once since her return, to visit Grandpa James's grave. But Gwyneira had accompanied her then, and Gloria had felt watched and self-conscious. Did Gwyneira have to constantly correct her form sitting on a horse and holding the reins? Had she not watched Gloria too searchingly, displeased that Gloria did not cry at her husband's grave? Gloria always found herself fighting her insecurity when she was with Gwyneira. In fact, there was no one on Kiward Station in whose presence she felt secure. Maaka wanted to tell her how to herd the cattle; Frank Wilkenson thought he knew which horse suited her best. Everyone picked on her. It was just like at Oaks Garden. She could not do anything right.

Caught between rage and brooding, Gloria reached the rock formation. Mighty stone blocks formed a circle that was almost comparable to the menhir formations at Stonehenge. But here it had been nature at work, not the hand of man. The Maori saw in the ring a sign from the gods that this land was sacred. Except during specified days or times, they tended to avoid such places. So Gloria was surprised when she noticed smoke rising from the ring. As she approached she saw a small fire. A young Maori sat beside it.

"What are you doing here?" she yelled at him.

The young man seemed to awaken out of a deep meditation. When he turned toward her, Gloria was startled to see that the man's face was covered in *moko*, his people's traditional tattoos. Lines wound out from his nose, extending above his eyebrows, over his cheeks, and along his chin. Gloria knew this pattern, as Tamatea liked to paint it on Kura's dancers every evening. Unlike traditional Maori, he wore jeans, a flannel shirt, and a leather jacket.

"You're Wiremu," Gloria said.

The man nodded. The only young Maori in his tribe to still bear the tattoos of his ancestors, the chieftain's son wore his name like a badge. Most young Maori had dropped the tradition when the whites arrived, but as Tonga's son, he had been marked with the designs at a young age.

Wiremu threw another piece of wood into the fire.

"You can't light a fire here," Gloria informed him. "This place is *tapu*."

"I can't eat anything here," he corrected her. "If I were to stay here a long time, I'd have to go hungry. But no one's forcing me to freeze while communing with the spirits."

Gloria tried to hold fast to her anger, but she could not stop herself from smiling. She steered her horse into the circle and was thankful that Wiremu refrained from asking her what she was doing. She was not sure if the *tapu* allowed someone to ride there.

"Weren't you going to university?" she asked. She vaguely recalled a letter from her great-grandmother explaining that Wiremu had attended high school in Christchurch and was then planning to attend either Christ's College or the university in Dunedin.

Wiremu nodded. "I went to Dunedin."

"But?" Gloria asked.

"I gave it up." Wiremu's hand ran seemingly unconsciously over his tattoos.

Gloria did not ask him anything more about it. She knew how it felt when people stared at you. Surely it made no difference whether they did it because you did not look like your mother or because you too closely resembled the stereotypes of your people.

"What are you going to do now?" she inquired.

"This and that. Hunt. Fish. Work on my *mana*."

A Maori man's *mana* defined his influence within his tribe. If Wiremu distinguished himself as a warrior, dancer, storyteller, hunter, and gatherer, he had a good chance of becoming chief, despite the fact that he was the youngest son. Even a girl could lead a tribe, though that was rare. Most Maori women exercised their power behind the "throne."

"You're Gloria," Wiremu said. "We used to play together as children. And my father wanted us to marry."

"I'm not going to marry."

Wiremu laughed. "That will deeply upset my father. Good thing you're not his daughter. Otherwise he'd surely find some *tapu* that bound a chieftain's daughter to the hand of some chieftain's son. There are a great many *tapu* concerning a chieftain's daughter."

"Among the *pakeha* too, even if it's called something else. And you don't even need to be a princess."

"Heiress will do as well," Wiremu said perceptively. "How was America?"

"Big."

Wiremu seemed satisfied with that. Gloria was thankful that he did not ask about Australia.

"Is it true that everyone is equal there?"

"Are you joking?"

Wiremu smiled. "Don't you want to come down from that horse?"

"No," Gloria said.

"A *tapu*?" Wiremu asked.

She smiled.

The next day Wiremu was waiting at the fence that enclosed the winter pasture. After calling to Nimue to herd some ewes into a nearby corral, she rode Ceredwen over to Wiremu.

"What are you doing here?" she asked, her voice softer than when she'd asked him the same question the day before.

"I'm enforcing a *tapu*. In all seriousness. It's almost embarrassing. You're going to start to believe I'm the tribal witch doctor, but my father sent me to make sure you're keeping the sheep within the borders."

Gloria frowned. "Isn't the stream the border?"

"Yes, but my father discovered a sacred site behind that corner. Or something like that. A couple of people fought there ages ago. Blood flowed and that sanctified the ground. He wants you to respect that."

"If it were up to your father, all New Zealand would be *tapu*," Gloria said, becoming agitated.

Wiremu grinned. "Exactly."

"But then you would not be able to eat anywhere."

"Indeed." Wiremu laughed. "You should tell him that. Come down to the village, Gloria. Marama thinks you visit her too rarely as it is. I just caught a few fish in a completely *tapu*-free stream. We could roast them and, who knows, talk about *tapu* in England?"

Gloria found herself in a bind. Gwyneira, too, had suggested that she visit Marama since she was riding in that direction.

"If you don't want to get down, I can hand the food up to you."

Gloria almost had to laugh. Albeit a little reluctantly, she directed Ceredwen toward the Maori village.

Though Gloria had no talent for chitchat, she eventually made an attempt at conversation as she slowed her horse to an amble alongside him. "What did you want to be?" she asked. "At the university, I mean."

Wiremu frowned. "Doctor. A surgeon, actually."

"Oh." Gloria could almost hear the whispering. They had probably called him "medicine man" behind his back.

Wiremu lowered his eyes when he saw her looking down at his tattoos. He was embarrassed, even here on his land among his people. Not that the blue-black tendrils disfigured him in any way; on the contrary, they softened his somewhat square face. But to have Wiremu in a Western operating room? Impossible.

"My father wanted me to study law," he continued to break the silence.

"Would that have worked out better?"

Wiremu snorted. "I would have had to limit myself to Maori affairs. I would have made a living, though, since there are more and more legal disputes. 'A task fit for a warrior.'"

"Your father?"

Wiremu nodded. "I just don't like to fight with words."

"What if you studied herbal medicine?" Gloria suggested. "You could become a *tohunga*."

"And spend my days extracting tea-tree oil?" he asked bitterly. "Or becoming one with the universe? Listening to the voices of nature? *Te Reo?*"

"You tried it," Gloria said, venturing a guess. "That's why you were in the circle of stone warriors, right?"

The blood shot to Wiremu's face. "The spirits were not very open."

"They never are," Gloria whispered.

"Just let your breath flow. No, Heremini, try not to wrinkle your nose. That's better. Ani, you're not going to become one with the *koauau* by changing; it'll accept you as you are. The *nguru* wants to feel your breath, Heremini." Marama sat in front of the meeting hall teaching two girls how to play the flutes. Ani's and Heremini's efforts to produce the notes were making Marama and the other women around her laugh.

Gloria was horrified, but the girls giggled too. They did not seem to think it such a tragedy that they could only draw a few squeaky sounds from the flutes.

"Gloria," Marama said, standing up when she saw her granddaughter. "How nice to see you. You come here so rarely we ought to dance a greeting *haka* for you."

Normally only honored guests—and therefore mostly outsiders—were greeted with a dance. But Ani and Heremini leaped up, raised their flutes and began playing their instruments like *mere pounamu*—war axes. When they began to chant verses, Marama asked them to be quiet.

"Now, stop it. Gloria's no outsider. She belongs to the tribe. Besides, you ought to be ashamed of your croaking. Better try it again with the flutes. Gloria, *mokopuna*, don't you want to come down from your horse?"

Gloria blushed and slipped down from the saddle. Wiremu grinned and moved to take her mare away.

"May I take the throne of the chieftain's daughter to graze somewhere, or would I be trespassing on a *tapu*?" he whispered to her.

"Horses eat everywhere," Gloria said. She was surprised when Wiremu understood it as a joke and laughed.

"Horses live in gods' good graces," he added as he removed Ceredwen's saddle.

"*Taua*, here are fish for dinner. I've invited Gloria," Wiremu said, turning to Marama.

"We'll roast them later. But Gloria does not need an invitation; she is always welcome. Sit with us, Gloria. Can you still play the *koauau*?"

Gloria blushed. Marama had shown her how to make music with the flute as a child, and she had proved quite adroit at breath management. Though she had less of a talent for melody, she did not want to decline in front of the tribe. Nervously, she reached for the flute and blew into it with her nose as she had been taught, startling herself as she did so. The *koauau* let out a sort of moan that became a cry. Marama picked up the *nguru*, put it to her mouth, and began to provide a wild, stirring rhythm. Gloria winced when someone joined in with the *pahu pounamu*. The girls, Ani and Heremini, got up and began to dance again. They were still so small that their war-*haka* did not look particularly martial, but they nonetheless demonstrated the self-assured movements of the Maori warrior women of old.

"Does Kura perform this *haka*? How do you know it?" Marama asked her granddaughter. "It's a very old piece—from the time when Maori men and women still fought side by side. It's better known on the North Island."

Gloria reddened. She had not known the dance before, having struck the opening note by accident. But the *koauau* had screamed out her rage—and Marama had led her into battle. Gloria had the feeling not so much of having made music as of having lived it.

"*Kia ora*, daughters! Should I be afraid? Has war broken out?" A deep voice vibrated behind them as dusk began to fall, and Rongo Rongo stepped into the light of the fire that Wiremu had lit.

"I must warm myself, children; let me by the fire, unless you need it right now to temper your spear points." Rongo rubbed her short, powerful fingers over the fire. Behind Rongo, Gloria recognized Tonga, the chief. She had not seen Tonga since she'd been back, and his dark, tattooed face almost scared her.

But Tonga smiled. "Look, Gloria daughter of those who came to Aotearoa on the *Uruau* and on the *Dublin*."

Gloria blushed. She knew the introduction ritual of the Maori—on important occasions, a person would name the canoe on which his ancestors had come to New Zealand hundreds of years before. Gloria's *pakeha* matriarch had traveled to New Zealand only sixty years before aboard the *Dublin*.

"Have you come here to claim your inheritance? That of the Ngai Tahu or that of the Wardens?"

Gloria did not know how to respond.

"Leave her alone," Marama said. "She's here to eat and talk with us. Don't listen to him, Gloria. Why don't you help Wiremu and the girls prepare the fish?"

Gloria fled gratefully to the stream that flowed beside the village. She had not gutted fish since she was a little girl and had learned to fish from Jack. At first she was awkward, but to her amazement the other girls did not laugh at her. When Wiremu came over to show her how to do it, Gloria backed away from him.

"Would you rather dig up some sweet potatoes?" asked an older girl named Pau who had noticed Gloria's reaction. "Come with me then."

Pau linked arms with her in a friendly way as they walked to the field.

"Wiremu must like you," she laughed. "He never usually cooks with us, just plays the great warrior. And he took care of your horse too."

"I don't like him," Gloria said gruffly.

Pau raised her hands defensively. "Don't be mad. I only thought, well, he's a good fellow and the chief's son. Most girls would like him."

"He's a man," Gloria blurted out as if that justified her condemnation.

"Yes," Pau said calmly, handing Gloria a shovel. "Dig in that bed to the right. And pick the smaller ones; they have a stronger flavor. We'll wash them in the stream afterward."

"Don't pick on the girl, Tonga. It's best you just leave her alone. She has suffered much." Rongo Rongo watched Gloria as she left with the other girls to prepare the food.

"Is that what the spirits tell you?" Tonga asked, half-mockingly. He respected Rongo, but as much as he liked to appeal to tribal tradition, communing with the spirits of his ancestors did not work any better for him than for his son.

"My memory of the globe Mrs. O'Keefe had at school tells me that," she said. "Do you no longer remember where America is located, Tonga? Or how big Australia is? Ten times bigger than Aotearoa. Gloria walked, or rode, through that. No one knows how she managed it. A *pakeha* girl, Tonga."

"She's half-Maori," Tonga said.

"A quarter," Rongo corrected him. "And not one raised with the knowledge of how to survive in the wilderness. You have heard of Australia, haven't you? The heat, the snakes. She would not have been able to do that all alone."

"She could also hardly have swum across the ocean herself," Tonga said, laughing.

"Exactly," said Rongo, and her face reflected her sorrow.

Marama didn't press her granddaughter for details of her travels or Kura that evening. She simply allowed the girl to sit peacefully by the fire and listen to the conversation and stories unfolding around the fire. When Gloria was finally saddling her horse—after declining Wiremu's offer of help—Tonga approached her. She was startled and kept her distance.

"Daughter of the Ngai Tahu," he said at last. "Whatever was done to you, it was done by *pakeha*."

6

After the first few exciting weeks of marriage, Lilian Biller realized with a shock that their cash reserves had shrunk considerably. Although their rent was affordable, food and clothing, books for Ben's studies, and even basic used furnishings, silverware, and linens had cost a great deal more than she'd anticipated. Turning her attention to how to make money, Lilian spoke to her husband first.

"Can you take on some work at the university?"

Ben looked up from the book he was reading, irritated. "Dearest, I work every day in the university."

"I was referring to paid work. Does your professor need any help? Aren't there some courses you could teach or something?"

Ben shook his head apologetically. The linguistics department at the University of Auckland was still small. The number of students hardly justified a full professor's attention, let alone an assistant. And subjects like "the comparison of Polynesian dialects for the purpose of locating the Maori settlers' region of origin"—though of great interest to his professor—would hardly fill a lecture hall.

"Well, then you'll just have to look for something else," Lilian said, interrupting his long-winded explanation of the situation. "We need money, dearest, there's no way around it."

"But my studies! If I concentrate on them now, then later . . ."

"Later we'll be starving, Ben. Find something you can do alongside your studies. If I work too, we'll manage."

Lilian kissed him encouragingly.

Lilian was able to find a respectable number of piano students in no time. She concentrated her efforts on the artisans' quarter, steering clear of academic families, since the housewife might play better than Lilian could. Among the hardworking second-generation immigrants who had often achieved more than modest wealth with their flourishing workshops, there was a desire to imitate the rich, and this included a basic musical education for their children.

Lilian's notices, which she'd hung in grocery stores and pubs, garnered an unexpectedly large response, and Lilian quickly won over nervous parents as easily as her students. It was obviously impressive that she had studied music in England, but they were most reassured by the fact that they could speak comfortably with her. In addition, Lilian did not precisely follow the classic precepts. She reduced finger exercises and études to a minimum so that her students could often hammer out a simple song by the third or fourth lesson. And since her clientele preferred singing to attending piano concerts, she placed emphasis on simple accompaniments to popular songs and patriotic pieces. Her strategy paid off: nothing convinced her students' parents of their child's talent and their teacher's genius more than the fact that they could gather around the piano at the very next family gathering and wail "It's a Long Way to Tipperary."

Ben found it considerably more difficult to earn money and had to rely on his physical strength to make ends meet. Unskilled labor jobs could be found at practically any time of the day or night in the harbor. So Ben loaded and unloaded ships and freight wagons, mostly in the morning before his lectures began.

The couple got by without too much trouble for a few months. They even earned enough for a proper table and two chairs. Their apartment over the pub remained unsatisfactory, however. It was still loud, stank of beer and old grease, and Lily complained that she could not take on any piano students in the evening because she was afraid of walking through their neighborhood alone. The bathroom in the hall was a disaster—it never occurred to any of the other tenants to clean it. Lilian would not and could not stay for long—especially not once she began to struggle with morning sickness.

"So the time's finally come," giggled her thoroughly degenerate neighbor when Lilian, pale faced and still in her bathrobe, lurched out of the bathroom and back to her apartment. "I was wondering if you had a bun in the oven."

The woman had four children herself, so she knew of what she spoke. Lilian, nevertheless, managed a trip to the doctor, which devoured the remainder of her savings. Elated, she danced her way to the docks to pick up Ben.

"Isn't that grand, Ben? A baby!" Lilian said as she arrived on the quay. He was carrying a few sacks from one of the ships to a freight wagon and looked completely exhausted. Lilian took no notice. She was overjoyed and full of plans.

Ben could not share in her joy. He had begun work at five that morning, spent the day at the university, and now found himself back on the docks. After putting in two shifts, he had been hoping to be able to study undisturbed for the next few days. Lilian's pregnancy would now force him to push himself even harder. Their family had to be supported, after all, and he would have to take that on alone for the foreseeable future.

"It won't be that bad, Ben," Lilian comforted him. "I can teach for a few more months. And you can just hurry your dissertation along a bit. Once you've earned your doctorate, they're sure to give you a paid job. Your professor is awfully excited about your work."

That was indeed the case, but one couldn't live off academic accolades alone. Ben did not see much hope for a second linguistics chair at the University of Auckland. Especially not for such a young graduate.

"But you don't make enough working in the harbor," she noted, "especially not if we're going to look for a new apartment."

"I'll think of something," Ben promised vaguely, then smiled. "We'll manage. Lily, a baby! And we did it all on our own."

Lilian loved Ben with all her heart, but she had long since discovered that his sensational mental dexterity applied more to the syntax and word melody of Polynesian relative clauses than to solving the challenges of daily life. Not trusting him to "think of something" on his own, she tried to figure out herself which of his talents they might use to their profit. One day, on the way to meet a piano student, she passed the offices of the *Auckland Herald*. A newspaper. And Ben was a poet. Writing ought to come easily to him. And it had to pay better than unloading freighters.

Lilian entered the building and found herself in a medium-sized office space where several men were hammering away on typewriters, talking on the phone, and filing stories.

Lilian addressed the nearest person.

"Who's in charge here?" she asked with her sweetest smile.

"Thomas Wilson," the man answered without really looking at her. He appeared to be editing an article and alternated between chewing on his pencil and dragging urgently on a cigarette.

"There." The man pointed with his pencil to a door with a plaque that read "Editor in Chief."

Lilian knocked.

"Come in, Carter. And I hope this time you're ready," a voice thundered from inside.

Lilian pushed open the door. "I don't mean to disturb you," she said softly.

"You're not disturbing anything until the boys out there give me some text to review. But seems like that'll take a while. What can I do for you?" Though the man behind the desk made no motion to stand up, he offered Lilian a seat with a sweep of his hand. His wide, slightly flushed face was dominated by a hammer nose, and his dark hair was beginning to gray. Though his gray-blue eyes were small, he sized up Lilian with youthful energy.

Lilian sat down in the leather chair on the other side of his messy, paper-strewn desk.

"What does one have to be able to do to write for your newspaper?" she asked, not bothering with introductions.

Wilson grinned. "Write," he said simply. "And thinking would be a plus. But as that lot out there proves daily, it's not a necessity."

"My husband is a linguist. And he writes poetry."

Wilson observed with fascination the way her eyes brightened.

"That should cover the basics," he remarked.

Lilian beamed. "That's wonderful, that is, if you're hiring. He desperately needs a job."

"There's no fixed position vacant at the moment, though I might well throw someone out today. But I can always use freelance writers." Wilson took a drag off his cigarette.

"He's looking for a job that he can do alongside his university work," Lilian specified.

Wilson nodded. "One doesn't make much as a linguist, eh?"

"So far nothing at all. And yet Ben's brilliant, according to his professor. Everyone says it. He even had a scholarship to Cambridge, but with the war and all . . ."

"Your husband doesn't have anything in print he can point to yet?" Wilson asked.

"No. But like I said, he writes poetry." She smiled. "Wonderful poetry."

Wilson snorted. "We don't print poetry. But I'd be willing to read one of his poems. Maybe your husband has something to teach me."

"Here!" Lilian said and began rummaging in her handbag. Triumphantly she pulled out a tattered piece of letter paper. "I always keep the most beautiful one with me."

She looked at him, expecting approval as Wilson unfolded the page and perused the text. The corner of his mouth twitched almost imperceptibly as he read.

"At least he doesn't make any spelling errors," he concluded.

"Of course not. Besides that, he speaks French and Maori and a few Polynesian dialects that . . ."

"Fine, fine, young lady. I get it. He's nature's crowning achievement. Maori, you say? Then he should know a little something about the spirit world, eh?"

"I don't know what you're getting at."

"It was a joke. But if your husband's interested, we have here an invitation to a séance. A certain Mrs. Margery Crandon out of Boston and a few of Auckland's notables are planning to conjure a few spirits this evening. She's a medium and does this for a living. We'd like someone to cover the event—might be something for the culture pages. But all my boys have declined. Not a one of them wants to wake the dead with Mrs. Crandon. And I've sent my freelancers elsewhere. If your husband would like to step in, this would be an ideal test piece. After that, we'll see."

"What, uh, does it offer financially?" inquired Lilian.

Wilson laughed. "Summoning spirits or the article? Well, our workers are paid by the line. As for mediums, I have no idea—by the number of spirits summoned maybe?"

Before Lilian could ask any more questions, one of Wilson's workers whipped the door open.

"Here are the proofs, boss." He threw a stack of messy-looking pages onto the desk.

"Took you long enough," Wilson growled. "So young lady, what's your name anyway? Here's the invitation. I want the text on my desk by tomorrow at five, the earlier the better. Understood?"

"Ben Biller," she said. "That's my husband's name, I mean."

Wilson was already busy with other things. "I'll see him tomorrow."

"I've been to a séance before," Lily said while she laid out Ben's best and only suit. "In England. One of my mother's friends was a spiritualist. She was always having mediums over. Once when I was there too. It was rather eerie."

"It matters much less whether it's eerie than whether it stands up to scientific scrutiny," Ben said, a little irritated. Lilian's initiative had surprised him—particularly its immediate starting date—but writing articles would certainly suit him better than unloading barges. He was nevertheless a bit concerned that working for a daily newspaper would hurt his reputation as a linguist.

"You can use another name, you know," Lilian reminded him impatiently. "Now quit standing around and change. You could do this job blindfolded."

Lilian was already asleep when Ben returned, and she was still asleep when he left in the morning to go to work on the docks. She spent the better part of the day worrying about whether Ben had managed to finish his article by the deadline. He only came home at half past three, but to Lilian's relief he had drafted it between two of his seminars.

"Hurry and take it to Mr. Wilson," she said. "Then you'll have it there in plenty of time. He said five at the latest."

"Listen, Lily, I told a professor I'd go over some work with him. I have to leave now. Can't you take the article?"

"Of course I can. But shouldn't you meet Mr. Wilson in person?"

"Next time, dear, yes. This time, we'll let my work speak for itself. That's not a problem, is it?"

Ben was out the door before Lilian could object. Resigned, she threw on her shawl and headed out the door. When she arrived, Thomas Wilson was bent over a few articles and making corrections with a furrowed brow.

"Well? You again, young lady? Where's your husband hiding? Did Mrs. Crandon make him disappear?"

Lilian smiled. "She rather makes things appear, ectoplasm and the like. Unfortunately, my husband couldn't get away from the university today. But he asked me to bring you his story."

Wilson skimmed the article. Then he threw it on the desk and glared angrily at Lilian. His face had reddened again.

"Girl, what are you thinking? I'm supposed to print this utter drivel? To be frank, I'm sure your husband has his good qualities, but this . . ."

Alarmed, Lilian reached for the page.

Auckland, March 29, 1917

On March 28, Mrs. Margery Crandon of Boston provided fascinating insight into the variability of dimensions for a small circle of Auckland's intellectuals. Even those skeptical regarding the verification of spiritual phenomena had to grant that the amorphous white substance the twenty-nine-year-old American produces by purely spiritual means cannot be explained by the laws of nature. This fragile material, called "ectoplasm" in the nomenclature, projected the image of a spirit, with whom she communicates in a fascinating language. "Enochian" impresses by its syntax and diction that it does not conform to the glossolalia that arises in religious contexts. As for the verification of the identities of the spirits summoned by Mrs. Crandon, the outside observer is naturally left to his subjective interpretation. Here, however, Mrs. Crandon defers to well-known author and soldier Sir Arthur Conan Doyle, who has declared her pronouncements veracious and whose integrity, it goes without saying, is elevated above all doubt.

"Oh God," Lilian let slip.

Thomas Wilson grinned.

"I meant, of course, oh God, how could I forget. Mr. Wilson, I'm terribly sorry, but my husband asked me to make a few small changes to the text first before handing you the clean copy. This is just the first draft, but I, I just didn't think, and"—she felt for a piece of paper in her bag that Thomas Wilson recognized as the letter paper with the poem on it—"naturally I couldn't expect you to read his chicken scratch. Please let me have a little time to make the corrections my husband outlined here." A slight blush spread over Lilian's face.

Wilson nodded.

"Due at five o'clock," he said and took out his gold pocket watch. "So you still have fifteen minutes. Get to it." He tossed her a writing pad and turned back to his proofs. Out of the corner of his eye he saw the young woman hesitate for a few seconds before her pencil began racing across the page. Just under fifteen minutes later, completely out of breath, she pushed a new draft over to him.

Medium or charlatan? Spiritualist unsettles Auckland society.

Twenty-nine-year-old spiritualist Margery Crandon, whose passport identifies her as an American, made her appearance in front of a group of honorable representatives of Auckland society and this *Herald* reporter. Mrs. Crandon herself purports to have ancestry from a Romanian noble family. The connection this author sees to Strauss's *Gypsy Baron* is worth noting—because there are several things about Mrs. Crandon's performance that are reminiscent of an operetta, or rather, a variety show. Her entrance and backdrops created the desired effect of pleasant creepiness. In addition, Mrs. Crandon demonstrated a considerable talent for showmanship with the production of "ectoplasm," in which her "familiar spirit" supposedly manifested itself—though it must be said that it revealed a greater similarity to a piece of wet tulle than to an appearance from the Great Beyond—as well as detailed conversation in unknown languages such as "Enochian."

Mrs. Crandon manipulated that and other spirits with the skill of a trained puppet master, enabling her to convince several of those present of the authenticity of her conjured phantoms. She could not, however, stand up to the incorruptibly critical gaze of the *Auckland Herald*, nor did her reference to Sir Arthur Conan Doyle's evident admiration of her convince us. Sir Arthur Conan Doyle is a man who combines an excess of imagination with great personal integrity. No doubt he finds it easier to believe that a lady who appears to be above all doubt could summon spirits than knowingly deceive her noble and honorable patrons.

Thomas Wilson had to laugh.

"Your husband has a sharp pen," he declared, pleased. "And he seems to know a thing or two about spiritual communication to have dictated this directly into your hand—or had you memorized it before? No matter. How Mr. Biller produces his stories is no concern of mine. We'll have to cut the *Gypsy Baron* reference. Most of our readers aren't that educated. A few of the words also have too many syllables, and the sentences could be shorter. Otherwise, very good. Have them pay you twenty dollars at the front. Oh yes, and send your husband to the pier tomorrow. A ship is arriving from England—it's carrying invalids, soldiers who were at Gallipoli. We'd like a story on that. Just patriotic enough that no one feels his toes are being stepped on but critical enough that every last man asks himself why we let our boys bite the dirt on that Turkish beach. A good day to you, Mrs. Biller."

Lilian accompanied Ben to the harbor and spoke with a nurse and a few veterans, the sight of whom deeply shocked her. Then she replaced Ben's stiff report—which described, point by point, the geographic peculiarities of the Turkish coast, the importance of the Dardanelles to the course of the war, and the Turkish defensive positions—with a stirring description of the last battles and a highly emotional eulogy of the successful final evacuation of the troops: "Although the sight of all these young men results in feelings of great pride, the author could not help but feel saddened that so many lost their health on a distant beach in the Mediterranean. Gallipoli will always be synonymous not only with heroism but also with the senselessness and gruesomeness of war."

"Get rid of 'synonymous,'" Thomas Wilson remarked. "No one will understand that. Write 'a symbol for' and fix the sentence to follow that change. Now tell me what your name is. I can't keep calling you Ben."

7

Writing under the pen name BB, Lilian Biller spent the next few months writing articles about ships' christenings, the anniversary of the Treaty of Waitangi, conferences of the woodworking industry, and expansions to the university. To Mr. Wilson's delight, she was able to wring amusing details out of even the dullest subject matter. She enjoyed the work so much that she reduced the time she spent teaching piano lessons. Working for the paper did not, however, solve her underlying problem. She had to leave the house to attend events and talk with people, but she was growing increasingly unwieldy. With a baby, she wouldn't be able to do it at all—right when their young family would need more money.

Using Ben as her representative was hopeless. He had no knack for the easy, humorous writing style that was required, tending as he did toward ponderous formulations and grandiloquence. When she could no longer hide her pregnancy, Lilian expressed her concerns to Thomas Wilson.

"Not one of my dresses fits anymore. I couldn't possibly go to this duke's reception. And it's only going to get worse."

The editor thought for a moment. Then he rubbed the wrinkle that always appeared between his eyes during strenuous contemplation.

"Do you know what, Lilian? What we really need—more than articles about Duke Such-and-such's visit to dedicate the this-and-that building—is a few nice little stories. Something to give folks hope. We're in the third year of the war, and the pages are filled with reports of battles and losses. The streets are filled with the heroes of Gallipoli on their crutches, and the ANZAC boys are bleeding in France and Palestine. The economy has stagnated; people are worried. And not without reason. The world has become a battlefield, and no one knows why. In short, the general mood is depressed."

"Oh yes?" Lilian asked. Aside from their financial concerns, she was still happy with Ben and had not picked up on any of that.

"Must be love," grumbled Wilson. He had since come to know his little reporter better and knew a bit about the couple's story.

Lilian nodded.

Wilson laughed. "Anyway, I'd be happy to expand the culture section to include a few happy stories. Short stories, not research work, just pure imagination. What do you think? Could you write something like that?"

"I can try," Lilian declared. She had her first idea on the way home.

Two days later she brought Wilson the story of a children's nurse from Hamilton who took the cross-country train every Sunday to visit her elderly mother in Auckland. She had been doing it since the train line opened, and Lilian described the delight with which Graham Nelson, the conductor, encountered the young woman for the first time. He saw her in the train every week thereafter. Each fell in love with the other but never dared to exchange more than two words. Only after a few years, once the mother had died and the nurse stopped taking the train, did the conductor pluck up the courage to look for her. It ended with a wedding. Lilian enriched the story with descriptions of the landscape and evoked both New Zealand's pride in its railway companies and the nurse's sacrificing nature, as she could hardly tear herself away from her little charges in the hospital.

Wilson rolled his eyes but printed the text the very next Saturday. His readers, particularly the women, were moved to tears. Lilian followed it up with the story of a hero of Gallipoli whose girlfriend thought him dead but resisted courting anyone else until the man finally returned home wounded after several years.

From then on that column in the culture pages was hers. The female readers longed for new stories from BB.

"You should write a novel," Thomas Wilson remarked after flipping through Lilian's newest piece. "People are crazy about your stories. Seriously, Lilian, judging by readers' letters, I could print one of your sob stories every day."

"Does that pay well?" Lilian inquired.

Wilson smiled. "Simple mammon. What about artistic fulfillment?"

Lilian frowned. "How much?" she asked.

Wilson found her adorable.

"All right, listen, Lilian, we'll do it like this: you try writing one or two chapters, and then I'll accompany you to a publisher friend of mine. We'll have to travel to Wellington for that, though. Can you manage it?"

Lilian laughed. "Which? The train ride or the two chapters? The latter isn't a problem. And if I finish them quickly, the baby won't even have to join us in the compartment."

"I'd be very grateful for that," grumbled Wilson.

Three days later Lilian was back with two chapters and a brief synopsis. *The Mistress of Kenway Station* told the story of a young Scotswoman who allows herself to be drawn to New Zealand by a suitor—it was based on a mix of her great-grandmothers Gwyneira's and Helen's stories. She vividly depicted the sea passage and the young woman's first encounter with the thoroughly dour sheep baron Moran Kenway. The girl ends up surrounded by luxury but imprisoned, mistreated, and unhappy on a farm far from any human settlements—Lilian felt only slight pangs of guilt for using her mother's first marriage as material. But fortunately the heroine's childhood friend never forgot her. He follows her to New Zealand, makes a fortune in no time mining for gold, and rushes to free the girl.

Thomas Wilson skimmed the text and rubbed his eyes.

"Well?" Lilian asked, looking a bit sleep deprived. Neither love nor the racket from the pub were to blame this time—it was the ecstasy of writing that had kept her awake. She had hardly been able to set her story aside. "What do you think?"

"Terrible," Wilson remarked. "But people will rip it off the shelves. I'll send it straight to Wellington. Let's see what Joe Anderson has to say about it."

Ben Biller adamantly resisted the idea of letting Lilian travel to Wellington alone and Wilson ended up having to buy him a train ticket as well. While Wilson and Lilian negotiated with Joe Anderson, Ben met with representatives of the university there and talked with them about possible visiting professorships. In the end Lilian signed a contract not only for *The Mistress of Kenway Station* but also for an entire series. Wilson advised her to hold off on that since the advance would be a good deal higher if her first book sold well. But Lilian shook her head.

"We need the money now," she explained and immediately began developing another outline. *The Heiress of Wakanui* took shape as a sort of New Zealand version of Pocahontas, in which a *pakeha* fell in love with a Maori princess.

"I imagine it being incredibly romantic," Lily said over dinner with Wilson, Anderson, and Ben at a fancy restaurant that evening. "During times of war, Maori warriors had to crawl beneath the legs of the chieftain's daughter, which symbolized their transformation from peaceful men to merciless warriors. When she learns that her father is going to let these men loose on her sweetheart . . ."

"Chieftain's daughters who performed the duties of a priestess were under very strict *tapu*," Ben noted sourly. "It's unlikely that a girl like that would even lay eyes on a *pakeha*, let alone that he'd survive it."

"Now don't take it too far with your science, dearest," Lilian laughed. "I'm not writing a study of Maori culture, just a good story."

"When it comes to emotional overloading, this ritual in particular in its function of dehumanizing the warriors . . ." As Ben launched into a longer explanation, Lilian listened with a gentle smile, continuing to enjoy her oysters all the while.

"Pay no attention to him," Thomas Wilson remarked quietly to Joe Anderson. "The girl loves him like an exotic animal. His behavior and way of communicating might be completely foreign to her, but she willingly pays for food and the vet."

Then he turned back to Lilian. "What are we going to do about your name, Lilian? I'd suggest a *nom de plume.* But maybe we'll keep the initials? What do you think of Brenda Boleyn?"

Lilian spent the last few weeks of her pregnancy at her desk in her cozy new apartment near the university. Her book advance covered the rent as well as some nicer furniture and a hospital delivery, on which both Ben and Thomas Wilson placed great value. Her contractions started just as she wrote the last sentence of *The Mistress of Kenway Station.*

"I wanted to edit it first," Lilian said regretfully, but then she let Ben urge her into a cab.

The birth proved to be an awful experience: Ben was not permitted to be present, and the delivery room was cold and stank of Lysol. Lilian's feet were tied to a sort of gallows and a squarely built nurse snapped at her anytime she so much as whimpered. This woman had nothing in common with the angelic being from Lilian's first short story, and Lily decided that the reality of giving birth was considerably less pleasant than the way songs and novels depicted it.

Only the sight of her son soothed her.

"We'll name him Galahad," she said when they finally allowed a deathly pale and sleepless Ben to come to her.

"Galahad?" he asked, confused. "What kind of name is that? In my family . . ."

"It's a name for a hero," Lilian declared, not revealing to Ben that his son was to be christened for a Grail knight and for the rescuer in *The Mistress of Kenway Station.* "And when I look back at your family . . ."

Ben laughed. "You mean, one day he'll dare to contradict his grandmother?"

Lilian giggled. "He'll probably toss her right out of his mine."

While Lilian typed out *The Heiress of Wakanui* on the typewriter Thomas Wilson had given her at the birth of her son, little Galahad lay in his crib next to her, occasionally being rocked or sung to sleep with romantic songs. At night he lay between his parents, temporarily preventing the creation of another baby. Lilian was now taking precautions anyway. Ben had finally summoned the courage to ask his fellow students about safe contraceptive options and actually bought the recommended condoms. Though it was annoying to put on the thick rubber devices before making love, Lilian had no desire for further encounters with the sergeant-like nurse in the Auckland hospital. That was fine by Ben; he was just happy to have finally put working on the docks behind him. *The Mistress of Kenway Station* had been feeding the whole family for half a year. Ben graduated at the beginning of 1918 as the youngest PhD in the British Empire and received a visiting professorship in Wellington.

Lilian and Ben were happy.

8

What's Gloria doing with the Maori all the time?"

Although reluctant to discuss family problems with Maaka, Gwyneira had no one else to turn to with her concerns. Gloria said little, Marama equally little, and she still had not heard a word from Jack. However, Roly O'Brien, who occasionally wrote to Tim and Elaine, had accompanied the transport of wounded that had taken Jack from Gallipoli, and mentioned his friend often in his letters. At first his news had sounded foreboding—"Sergeant McKenzie is still hovering between life and death," but more recently, he'd written that "Sergeant McKenzie is doing a bit better," and, "Sergeant McKenzie can finally stand." The background of the story remained unclear.

Gwyneira comforted herself that Jack was alive at least, even if he had lost an arm or a leg. Why he did not write himself or dictate letters to anyone was a puzzle to her, but she knew her son. Jack did not like to communicate. When he was struck by a stroke of fate, he withdrew into himself. After Charlotte's death, he hadn't said a word for weeks.

Though Gwyneira was hurt, she tried to suppress it. Gloria was, for the moment, the more urgent problem. Though the girl no longer chafed against the shepherds or snubbed the help, she disappeared almost every day to the Maori village with her horse and dog. What that signified, Gwyneira did not know since Gloria said little to her and only rarely appeared at mealtimes. She mostly ate with the Maori, not seeming to grow tired of their cuisine, which consisted of little more than sweet potatoes and flat bread if the hunters were unsuccessful. But Gloria seemed to prefer that to any meal with her great-grandmother.

Little by little the drawings and toys from her childhood disappeared from her room, making way for decorative items of Maori art, some of which were so awkwardly made that Gwyneira concluded that Gloria was trying her own hand at carving ornaments.

Maaka confirmed this.

"Miss Martyn is doing what the women do this time of year—sit together, sew, carve, cultivate the fields. Gloria is often with Rongo."

That was not bad news. Gwyneira thoroughly cherished the Maori midwife.

"They speak with the spirits."

That made Gwyneira nervous. Gloria had been acting strangely since her return. If she were conjuring spirits now, was she on her way to going mad?

"Take hold of the tree calmly; feel its strength and its soul." Rongo then directed Gloria to speak to the tree while she prepared to harvest the *rongoa*, or medicine, from the *kohekohe* leaves. Only a *tohunga* was permitted to touch the hallowed plants used for *rongoa*. Gloria, however, had been permitted to help with the picking and drying of the *koromiko* leaves, which were effective against diarrhea and other digestive problems. Gloria obediently noted what Rongo told her, but talking to the tree was too much for her.

"What makes you think the tree has less of a soul than you?" Rongo asked. "Because it doesn't talk? Gwyneira says the same about you."

Gloria laughed awkwardly.

"Or because it does not defend itself when someone strikes it with an ax? Might it have its reasons?"

"What sort of reasons?" Gloria asked. "What sort of reasons are there for letting yourself be knocked down?"

Rongo shrugged. "Don't ask me. Ask the tree."

Gloria leaned against the southern beech's hard bark and tried to feel the strength of the wood. Rongo had her do this with every kind of plant, as well as with rocks and waterfalls, and Gloria did it because she enjoyed the peace that coursed through all these—these what? Beings? Things? She liked spending time with Rongo and all her spirits.

Having completed her harvesting ceremony, Rongo began lecturing on the distillation of extracts from the *kohekohe* leaves and bark.

"It's effective against sore throats," she explained, "and you can cook honey out of it."

"Why don't you write that down?" Gloria asked, leaving her tree and walking through the sparse woodland at Rongo's side. "Then everyone could read it."

"Only if they've learned to read. Otherwise, they'd have to ask me anyway." She smiled. "But when I was as old as you, I thought the same thing. I even asked my grandmother, Matahorua, to write it down."

"But she didn't want to?"

"She didn't see the sense in it. Whoever did not need the knowledge did not need to burden themselves with it. Whoever wants to learn must take the time to ask. And so becomes a *tohunga*."

"But if you write it down, you keep the knowledge for those who come later."

"That's how *pakeha* think. You always want to keep everything. Write it down and you end up forgetting it more quickly. We keep the knowledge inside us. In every individual. And we keep it alive. *I nga wa o mua*. Do you know what that means?"

Gloria nodded. Literally it meant "from the time that will come." In truth, though, everything in the past was denoted that way—to the endless confusion of all *pakeha* who ever attempted to learn Maori. Gloria had never really thought about it before. But now she felt angry.

"Live in the past?" she asked. "Stir up again and again what you'd most like to forget?"

Rongo drew Gloria next to her on a rock and tenderly stroked her hair. She knew they were no longer talking about preserving knowledge such as how one made *rongoa* from blossoms and bark.

"When you lose your memory, you lose yourself," she said softly. "Your history makes you what you are."

"And if I don't want to be that?" Gloria asked.

Rongo took her hand. "Your journey is still far from complete. You'll continue to gather memories. And change. That's another reason we don't write anything down, Gloria. Writing something down is writing it into dogma. And now, show me the tree you were speaking to earlier."

"How am I supposed to find it again? There are dozens of beech trees here. And they all look the same."

"Close your eyes, daughter. It will call to you."

Gloria was still angry, but she followed the wise woman's directions. A short while later, she ran, sure of her goal, straight to her tree.

Rongo Rongo smiled.

Although Gloria's memories remained difficult for her, life was easier with her Maori family. Though Gwyneira did not ask questions and was clearly trying to withhold criticism, Gloria thought she detected disapproval in her eyes and heard accusations in her voice.

Marama shook her head when Gloria confessed this to her. "Your eyes and Gwyn's eyes are the same. And your voices might be confused one for the other."

Gloria wanted to object that this was nonsense. She had porcelain blue eyes while Gwyneira's were azure. And Gwyneira's voice was considerably higher than Gloria's. But she had long since learned that Marama's words were not to be taken literally.

"You'll understand it soon enough," Rongo said calmly when Gloria complained about it to her. "Give it time."

"Why don't you want to let her go then? Nothing will happen to her with us," Marama said in her singsong voice. She sat across from Gwyneira in the village meeting hall. Normally, she would have received her mother-in-law outside without ceremony, but it was raining. Gwyneira knew the etiquette and had mastered the *karanga*, the greeting ritual, before entering a meeting hall. She had taken off her shoes without prompting and not complained about her arthritic joints when she lowered herself to the ground.

The tribe was planning a migration, and Gloria had insisted on joining it.

"I know that. But she's supposed to get used to living on Kiward Station again. And she can't do that if she wanders around with all of you for months at a time. Marama, if it's out of financial need . . ."

"We don't need alms!" Marama rarely raised her voice, but Gwyneira's last comment wounded her pride. The tribes of the South Island migrated because the crop yields were often meager. When their stores began to decline, they set out to live for a few months from hunting and fishing. Marama and her people would not have spoken of it in terms of "need." The land offered enough nourishment—just not when they were in the village. It was an adventure and a pleasure, at least for the younger members of the tribe. There was also a spiritual component to the migrations. They grew closer to the land, becoming one with the mountains and rivers that offered them food and shelter. The children got to know sacred grounds that lay further away and renewed their connection to Te Waka a Maui.

"I know, but, what's this about Wiremu, Marama? Maaka says she speaks with him."

"Yes. I've noticed that too. He is the only man with whom she even occasionally speaks. I find the latter point more disconcerting than the former."

Gwyneira took a deep breath. She was finding it difficult to remain calm. "Marama. You know Tonga. This is not an invitation to take a walk with the tribe. This is a marriage proposal. He wants to make a match between Gloria and Wiremu."

Marama shrugged.

"If Gloria loves Wiremu, you won't separate the two of them. If she doesn't love Wiremu, Tonga won't marry them. He can't force them to sleep together in the communal hall. So leave it to Gloria."

"I can't do that. She's the heiress. If she marries Wiremu . . ."

"Then the land still won't belong to Tonga and the tribe but to Gloria and Wiremu's children. Perhaps they'll be the first sheep barons with Maori blood. Perhaps they'll give the land back to the tribe. You won't be around for that, Gwyn, nor will Tonga. But the mountains will still stand, and the wind will play in the tops of the trees." Marama made a gesture of submission to the power of the gods.

Gwyneira sighed. She had never been particularly even-tempered. And now she felt a deep desire to smash something. Preferably Tonga's treasured chief's ax, the insignia of his power.

"Marama, I can't allow this. I have to . . ."

Marama bade her be quiet with a graceful gesture. Again she seemed sterner than usual.

"Gwyneira McKenzie," she said firmly. "I left both children to you. First Kura, then Gloria. You raised them in the manner of *pakeha*. And look what has become of them."

Gwyneira glared at her. "Kura is happy."

"Kura is a wanderer in a foreign land," whispered Marama. "Without rest. Without tribe."

Gwyneira was convinced that Kura saw it completely differently, but in the eyes of Marama, a full-blooded Maori, who lived with and off the land, her daughter was lost.

"And Gloria . . ." Gwyneira trailed off.

"Let Gloria go, Gwyn," Marama said softly. "Don't make any more mistakes."

Gwyneira nodded, resigned. She suddenly felt old. Very old.

Marama pressed her forehead and her nose affectionately to Gwyneira's in parting.

"You *pakeha*," she murmured, "all your streets must be straight and even. You tear them from the earth without hearing its groans. And yet the winding, rocky ways are the shorter ones if you take them in peace."

9

Gloria followed Marama through the wet knee-high grass. It had been raining unceasingly for hours, and even Nimue was no longer enjoying herself. The laughing and chatting that usually prevailed during the migration had long since ebbed, and each man and woman forged on stoically, lost in their own thoughts. Gloria wondered whether she was the only one yearning for a dry place to sleep or whether some feeling of camaraderie that she could not feel strengthened the others. After a three-day march through largely wet weather, she had almost had enough adventure. And yet she had been so excited about the migration, longing to set out ever since Gwyneira had finally given her approval. Gloria had wanted to consider her acquiescence a triumph, but her great-grandmother had looked so sad, old, and hurt that she had almost considered staying.

"I'm letting you go because I don't want to lose you," Gwyneira had said, which sounded like something Marama would say. "I hope you find what you're looking for."

Living together had only become more difficult after that. Gloria wanted to feed off Gwyneira's rejection but she was guilty instead, and it angered her that she felt like a child again.

She would not let herself be embraced by Gwyneira when she left but exchanged a heartfelt *hongi*, which was the more intimate gesture. She felt Gwyneira's dry but warm skin on her own and breathed in her scent of honey and roses. She had used the same soap when Gloria was small, and it reminded Gloria of her comforting hugs. Jack had smelled like leather and hoof grease. But why was she thinking of Jack?

Gloria had sighed with relief when they finally departed, and the first hours of the migration had been wonderful. She had felt herself free and open to new impressions—but also safe and secure with her tribe. The women and children traditionally walked in the middle of the group with the heavy tents and cooking equipment, while the men walked on the flanks with their spears and hunting gear. After a few hours Gloria began to wonder whether that was right.

"But they have to be able to move," Pau explained to her, "if someone attacks us."

Gloria sighed. They were still on the grounds of Kiward Station. And even in the McKenzie Highlands, there were no enemy tribes. No one threatened the Ngai Tahu. But maybe she needed to stop thinking like a *pakeha*.

Before setting out, Gloria had given no thought to the hardships of the journey. She believed herself tougher than everyone else; after all, she had crossed the deserts of Australia, often on her own two feet. But back then she had been driven by sheer desperation, possessed by nothing but her goal.

The Canterbury Plains, however, which were now slowly transitioning into the foothills of the southern mountains, were a different story. It had begun to rain a few hours into the migration, and Gloria was completely soaked through. When the tents were erected in the evening and everyone else began to curl up with each other for warmth, Gloria retreated nervously to a corner, wrapping herself in a clammy blanket. She had not considered what it would be like to sleep in the communal tent. She lay awake for hours listening to snoring and even to the occasional covert giggling and suppressed cries of lust from couples making love. Gloria wanted to flee, but it was still raining outside.

The bad weather continued for several days. Gloria wondered fleetingly how Gwyneira and her workers meant to bring in the hay, but she had her own more immediate problems. Her jodhpur boots—which were well-suited to riding and farmwork—were slowly coming apart in the constant moisture. The Maori went barefoot and recommended that Gloria do the same. Though she eventually shed her wet boots, she was unaccustomed to extended hikes in her bare feet.

By the fifth day, she could no longer comprehend how she could have given up her tranquil, dry room on Kiward Station for this and gratefully accepted the tarpaulin that Wiremu brought her. Though he would never admit it, he looked just as unhappy and cold as she did. But Wiremu also had enjoyed a *pakeha* upbringing. His years at boarding school in Christchurch had left their mark. Gloria sensed that perhaps he, too, regretted his choice. He had wanted to be a doctor, but instead found himself walking through the wilderness with his tribe. She cast an eye at Tonga, who walked ahead of his people, undeterred.

"Could we not rest earlier?" Gloria asked desperately. "I don't understand what drives all of you onward." She fell silent when she realized her faux pas. She should not have said "all of you." She had to learn to think of herself and the Ngai Tahu as "we" if she wanted to belong. And she did want to belong.

"Our supplies are running low, Glory," Wiremu explained. "We can't hunt. No rabbit will risk leaving its warren in this weather. And the river is too fast, so the fish won't swim into the traps. So we're moving toward Lake Tekapo."

They would camp for several weeks at the lake, where there were plenty of fish and nearby forests rich with game.

"We've made camp there since time immemorial," Wiremu said, smiling. "The lake is even named for that—*po* means 'night,' *taka* means 'sleeping mat.'"

In the evening the rain finally abated.

"It rarely rains at the lake," Rongo explained. "How could Rangi weep at the sight of such beauty?"

Lake Tekapo was indeed a breathtaking sight in the last light of day. The grassland of the plains waved in the wind on the northern shore while the southern mountains rose majestically beyond the lake. The water shimmered a dark turquoise in the sunlight. The tribe's women greeted the lake with song and laughter. Rongo festively ladled out the first of the water, and they managed to build a fire. The men left to hunt, and even if the game was scant, there was roasted fish and flat bread made from the last of the flour reserves. Marama and a few of the other women retrieved their instruments and celebrated their arrival at the lake. Though the tents and sleeping mats were still clammy when the tribe retired for the night, the little celebration had revived the tribe members. As many of the men and women began to make love, Gloria felt sick. She had to leave.

Gloria slipped out of the tent, wrapped in her blanket. The sky above the lake was a deep black, but snow still blanketed the tops of the mountains. She looked up and tried to become one with everything as Rongo had advised her. With the sky, lake, and mountains all around, it was not difficult. With the tribe, however, she would never really succeed.

She startled when she heard steps behind her. Wiremu.

"You can't sleep?"

Gloria didn't answer.

"In the beginning it was hard for me too. When I came back from the city, that is. But I loved it as a child." She heard in his voice that he was smiling. "We would crawl from one woman to the next. Their arms were always open."

"My mother did not want me," Gloria said.

Wiremu nodded. "I heard about that. Kura was different. I hardly remember her."

"She's beautiful," Gloria said.

"You're beautiful." Wiremu stepped closer to her and raised his hand to touch her face, but she shrank back.

"*Tapu?*" he asked softly.

Gloria could not make jokes about it. She backed up toward the tent.

"You can turn around if you want. I won't attack you from behind. Gloria, what's wrong?" Wiremu approached and put his hand on her shoulder, but Gloria's reflexes could not separate a friendly touch from a hostile one—especially not at night. Before she even knew what she was doing, she'd reached for her knife. Wiremu ducked when he saw it flash, threw himself to the ground, and rolled away. He sprung back to his feet and looked at her.

"Glory."

"Don't touch me. Never touch me again."

Wiremu heard the panic in her voice.

"Gloria, we're friends, aren't we? I didn't mean to do anything to you. Look at me. I'm Wiremu, don't you recognize me? The would-be medicine man?"

Very slowly Gloria's composure returned.

"I'm sorry," she said quietly, "but I, I don't like it when people touch me."

"You only needed to say that. Gloria—I accept *tapu*, you know that." Wiremu smiled again, raising the palms of his hands in a gesture of peace.

She nodded shyly. Side by side, but without touching, they reentered the tent.

Tonga saw them walk in. He lay back down content.

Though the weather at the lake was better than in the plains below, it nevertheless rained a great deal. But there were fish and game in abundance, and they enjoyed themselves. Gloria accompanied Rongo in search of medicinal plants. She learned to work flax and listened to Marama's stories of Harakeke, the god of flax, a grandson of Papa and Rangi. The women told stories about the gods of the lake and mountains, describing the travels of Kupes, the discoverer of Aotearoa and his battles with giant fish and land monsters.

Sometimes they met with other tribes, organizing a protracted *pohiri*—an elaborate greeting ceremony—and celebrating afterward. Gloria danced with the others and blew the *koauau* for the women's war-*haka*. She forgot her constant fear of doing something wrong. Marama and the other women did not chide their students, explaining patiently instead. Squabbles among the girls never became as acrimoniously drawn out as at boarding school, in part because the adults never took sides. Gloria learned to differentiate the Maori girls' good-natured teasing from the merciless ridicule of her former classmates, and eventually could even laugh along when Pau teased her that her self-made *poi poi* ball looked like the egg of some strange bird. Because she could not make it properly round, it wobbled in peculiar ellipses while she danced, and when it struck Ani in the head, she declared it to be a new magic weapon.

"It's just a little soft, Glory; you need to try to make them from *pounamu*."

They looked for these in a stream, and in the evening Rongo showed them how to whittle the stones into small god figurines that they wore as pendants. Gloria and Ani gave each other their *hei-tiki,* which they wore proudly around their necks. Wiremu later surprised Gloria with one, saying he hoped it would bring her luck. Though the other girls gossiped about it, she trusted Wiremu. He was nothing but a friend.

Although Gloria began to enjoy her days in her new family circle, she still found the nights in the communal tent painful. As often as the weather allowed, she slipped outside and slept under the stars, even if every noise gave her a start. Sometimes, Wiremu appeared. He sat at a distance from her, and they talked. Wiremu told her about his time in Christchurch. How alone he had felt at first and how he despaired when the others teased him.

"But I thought you liked it!" Gloria said, surprised. "You even wanted to stay and study more."

"I liked school. And I'm a chieftain's son. I was big and strong, and I taught fear to the *pakeha* boys. *Mana*, you know how it is." He smiled.

Gloria understood. He had won influence in his tribe.

"But you were lonely," she said.

"*Mana* always makes a man lonely. A chief has power but no friends."

Later, Wiremu continued, he had earned respect in the *pakeha* high school through his scholastic achievements. Matters only escalated at university, where he met students who had never become acquainted with his fists. He had, by then, become "too civilized" to thrash them.

Gloria spoke little of her adolescence in England but told him a bit about Miss Bleachum and her interest in plants and animals.

"Miss Bleachum said I should study natural history. Then I could have stayed in Dunedin. But I know so little. We only ever played music or painted and looked at strange pictures."

Over the next few days Wiremu often brought her examples of interesting plants and insects, and one night he carefully woke her to show her a kiwi. They followed the flightless bird's shrill chirping, eventually discovering the shy animal under a bush. There were many nocturnal birds on Aotearoa, particularly in the foothills, but seeing a kiwi was something special. Gloria trusted Wiremu entirely as she followed him. Wiremu invited her on more short walks at night, but he never touched her.

The tribe eventually left the lake and headed further into the mountains toward Aoraki, the island's high mountain, which they considered sacred.

"A few *pakeha* climbed it some years ago," Rongo reported, "but the spirits did not like that."

"Why did they allow it then?" Gloria asked. She knew the mountain as Mt. Cook, and she had heard about the successful expedition.

Rongo gave her standard reply: "Don't ask me. Ask the mountain."

As they pressed into the McKenzie Highlands, Gloria mustered the courage to tell the story of her great-grandfather James around the campfire. In the long, convoluted style of the Maori, she told of McKenzie's encounter with his daughter, Fleur, and how John Sideblossom had hunted him down and drove him into exile in Australia.

"But my great-grandfather returned from the great land beyond the sea where the earth is red as blood and the mountains seem to glow. And he lived long."

Gloria's listeners applauded enthusiastically, and Marama smiled at her.

"You'll be a *tohunga* yet if you keep it up. But that's no surprise. Your father, too, speaks beautifully—even if he makes strange use of his talents."

Given wings by Marama's praise, Gloria practiced her rhetoric. She worked intensively on her *pepeha*, the personal introduction speech that each Maori can recite when a ceremony demands it. In it one named one's *tupuna*—ancestors—and described the canoe and the details of the journey that had brought them to Aotearoa. Marama helped Gloria name the tribe the travelers then formed and showed her the places they had inhabited. Especially fascinating was a valley that formed a natural fortress. Now it was *tapu* because some people had once battled there. The men of the tribe feared setting foot in the place, but Rongo and Marama led Gloria there and meditated with her by the fire. Gloria wove a detailed description of the rock fortress into her *pepeha*.

Describing the *pakeha* branch of her family was more difficult, but Gloria gave the name of the ship on which Gwyneira had traveled, used Kiward Station as the destination, and labeled the Wardens as her *iwi*—her tribe. As she described the area where she was born, she felt something almost like homesickness. The Ngai Tahu had been traveling for three weeks. And although Gloria felt accepted for the first time in years, she often sensed that she was leading someone else's life. She was succeeding in her role as a Maori girl, but was that what she really wanted to be? As she practiced handling medicinal plants, learned to weave and understand the meaning of the weaving patterns, and prepared the meat the men brought, she realized that the women of the tribe did nothing more than what Moana and Kiri did in the kitchen back home. Yes, they worked under the open sky, but that was the only difference. Gloria, however, had always enjoyed working with the sheep and cattle. She missed the animals.

Though the Maori did not stop her from hunting and fishing with the men—all the women were allowed to, and every Maori girl learned how to survive alone in an emergency—it was rare for them to do so. If a girl did join the men, it was often mistaken as an attempt to get closer to someone, and Gloria did not want to take the risk. The one time she convinced her friends to go hunting with her, it soon devolved into uninhibited flirting with the boys.

So she mostly stuck to the fire and only occasionally accompanied Wiremu fishing. Though it would have been more enjoyable to share in the men's duties than to sit around the fire with the women, who discussed her relationship with Wiremu as they braided reeds and twigs, Gloria soon realized that she did not want to kill every day for her sustenance. She hated taking the birds or small strangled rodents out of the traps. She missed the work of a breeder, who kept animals for many years, contemplating the best pairings of ewe and ram, mare and stallion, and celebrating birth rather than death. She liked taking care of animals, not hunting them down.

So she was not especially disappointed when the tribe started toward home. Tonga would have liked to continue the migration, but the sheep would soon need to be herded out of the highlands on Kiward Station, and there was good money to be made for the men. Besides, the seeds the women had planted before the migration would be sprouting. The families could survive the winter off the harvest and the money earned from the *pakeha*—without undertaking arduous treks and hunting expeditions in the rain and cold. Tonga could object as often as he liked that this was not the traditional way and made them dependent on the whites. A warm fire and a little luxury in the form of *pakeha* tools, cooking pots, and spices were more important to the people than any tradition.

Not that this meant that they took the direct route back to the Canterbury Plains. The return stretched out over several weeks and included visits to sacred sites and other tribal villages. Gloria could now have performed the ceremonies blindfolded. She sang and danced with the other girls without inhibition and recited her *pepeha* when their hosts wondered about her foreign appearance. In this she always received great acclaim; her descriptions of the *pakeha*'s voyage from far-away London across the *awa* Thames and their sojourn over the mountains of their new homeland inspired her listeners' imagination. Gloria's *mana* in the community grew. She walked upright and proud among her friends when the tribe finally set foot on the land of the *pakeha* again. Wiremu smiled at her occasionally, and she did not shy from doing the same.

"Don't you want to go home today?" Marama asked, looking with puzzlement at Gloria's Maori festival clothing. The tribe had settled back into the village, and Gloria was cleaning the meeting hall with several other girls in anticipation of the approaching festivities. Marama, however, had assumed her granddaughter would want to go home.

"Gwyn will hear that we've arrived. She'll be expecting you."

Gloria shrugged, though in truth she was torn. On the one hand she wanted to celebrate the return with the tribe; on the other, she yearned for her comfortable bed and the privacy of her room—and even for her great-grandmother's embrace, her scent of roses and lavender, and dinner served by Moana and Kiri. A proper table. Proper chairs.

"What is this talk of home, Marama?" Tonga asked. He had just entered, followed by his sons. Wiremu entered last. "Gloria is at home here. Do you mean to send her back to the *pakeha*?"

"I'm not sending anyone anywhere, Tonga," Marama said calmly. "Gloria must know herself what she's doing and where and with whom she wants to live. But it would be proper for Gloria to at least visit Gwyn and show her that she's well."

"I . . ." Gloria began, but the elders bade her be quiet.

"I think Gloria has already proved where she belongs," Tonga said grandly. "And I think she should complete this connection to her tribe tonight. For months we have observed Gloria and Wiremu spending time together. The time has come, in the presence of the tribe, here in the meeting hall, for them to sleep together."

Gloria was taken aback. "I . . ." she began again, but her voice failed her. All her education as a *whaikorero,* or artful speaker, had not prepared her for this situation. "Wiremu," she whispered helplessly.

Wiremu had to say something. Though she was trying hard to protest, she was almost relieved that she was speechless with panic. If she refused him here in front of everyone, Wiremu would lose face in front of his tribe. It was up to him to stand up to his father.

Wiremu looked from one to the other.

"This, this comes as a surprise," he said stuttering. "But I, well, Gloria . . ." He approached her.

Gloria looked at him imploringly. Evidently, he found it difficult to admit to the others that nothing had ever happened between them. Gloria cursed his male pride. And her old rage began welling up inside her. Tonga had put his son in an impossible situation. And he'd done the same to her. It did not exactly increase a chieftain's son's *mana* to get turned down in front of the entire tribe. He had no right to propose on his son's behalf.

"I, uh." Wiremu was still searching for words.

Gloria began to find this alarming. Wiremu should have been able to manage a simple "No, I don't want to" or, if it had to be, a stall: "Give us time."

"Gloria, I know we've never discussed it. But as far as I'm concerned, I'd welcome it. That is, I would happily . . ."

Gloria looked at him in disbelief. This man she had trusted was betraying her.

"We could do it merely as a formality," he whispered to her in English. "That is, we would have to have our wedding night in front of the whole tribe." Wiremu had enjoyed enough of a *pakeha* education that this last sentence was embarrassing for him as well.

"Then it's decided. We'll celebrate it tonight. Gloria, you will be greeted in this *wharenui* like a princess," Tonga beamed.

Unsure how to proceed, Wiremu shifted his weight from one leg to the other. The *pakeha* in him was expecting the bride's formal "I do."

Once again something burst inside of Gloria. Frenzied with rage, she ripped the flax band with Wiremu's *hei-tiki* from her neck and threw it at his feet.

"Wiremu, you were my friend. You swore never to touch me. You told me a Maori girl got to choose. And now you want to sleep with me in front of the whole tribe without even asking me what I want?" Though no one threatened her, Gloria drew her knife. Standing among men who were armed with spears and war axes—ritual weapons, to be sure, but sharp nonetheless—she knew that it was a ridiculous thing to do, but she needed to feel the cold steel in her hand.

In that moment Gloria would have gone up against an army. She no longer felt any fear, only rage—a searing white-hot rage. But for the first time, her rage no longer left her speechless. She neither held her peace nor flailed about with words. Suddenly she knew what she had to say. She knew who she was.

"Tonga, you think I need to secure my ties to the tribe? That I could only be part of this land if I belonged to the tribe? Then listen to this, my *pepeha*. Gloria's *pepeha*—not that of the daughter of Kura-maro-tini, nor that of the great-granddaughter of Gerald Warden. Not she of the Maori, not she of the *pakeha*." Gloria stood upright and waited until all of those present had gathered around her. Not long ago, a crowd that size would have robbed Gloria of her voice. But she had long since passed that point. The shrinking violet of Oaks Garden no longer existed.

"I am Gloria, and the stream a mile south of here runs to the land that anchors me in the here and now. The *pakeha* call it Kiward Station, and they call me heiress. But this girl, Gloria, has no *tupuna*, no ancestors. The woman who calls herself my mother sells her people's songs for fame and money. My father never granted me my land—perhaps because his father once drove him from his own. I know not my grandfather. The story of my predecessors is soaked in blood. But I, Gloria, came to Aotearoa on the *Niobe*. I crossed an ocean of pain and traveled on a river of tears. I landed on foreign shores; I crossed a land that burned my soul. But I am here. *I nga wa o mua*—the time that will come and has passed—finds me in the land between the lake and the circle of stone warriors. In my land, Tonga. And don't you dare ever challenge me for it again. Not with words, not with deeds, and certainly not with trickery."

Gloria glared at the chieftain. When the tribe spoke of this performance later, they spoke of an army of raging spirits whose souls had given her strength. Gloria herself needed no spirits. And she did not wait for a reply. With her head held high, she left the *wharenui* and her tribe.

She only began running once the door had shut behind her.

Peace

Dunedin, Kiward Station, and Christchurch

1917–1918

1

Jack McKenzie stared out at the horizon. A white mist was slowly becoming visible. New Zealand—land of the long white cloud. The South Island looked as it had for the first settlers from Hawaiki. When it had been announced that they were approaching their destination, anyone who could walk or be pushed in a wheelchair had come on deck. All around Jack, people laughed and cried. For many Gallipoli veterans, it was a bitter homecoming—and not one was the same man who had left.

Jack looked out over the water, but the waves made him dizzy. Depressed by the sight of the men, he considered heading down below deck. All these boys who had gone into the war singing, laughing, and waving were returning with arms and legs shot off, blind, lame, sick, and dumb. And it had all been for nothing. A few weeks after the last offensive, when Jack had been wounded, they had pulled the troops out of Gallipoli. The Turks had paid for their victory with blood, but they had won. Jack felt a leaden heaviness. He still had to force himself to make any movement; he had only hauled himself up on deck because Roly had insisted on it. At the first sight of home, Jack thought of Charlotte. A shiver went through him.

"Are you cold, Sergeant McKenzie?" Roly O'Brien wrapped a blanket around Jack's shoulders. "The nurses are coming with hot tea. The men are going to stay on deck until the land really comes into view. It's exciting, Sergeant McKenzie. Do you think it will be long until we dock?"

"Just Jack, Roly," Jack said wearily. "And yes, it will be hours before we dock. The land is still miles off. You can't even see it yet."

"But it will show up soon, Sergeant McKenzie," Roly chirped optimistically. "We're coming home, and we're alive. Lord knows there were days I didn't believe it would happen. Now cheer up a little, Sergeant McKenzie."

Jack tried to muster some joy but felt only exhaustion. Perhaps it would not have been all that bad to sleep forever. But then he chided himself for his own lack of gratitude. He had not wanted to die. Just put God to the test. But he had reached a point where he no longer even cared about that.

Jack McKenzie owed his survival to a chain of fortunate circumstances but most of all to Roly O'Brien and a small dog. Roly and his rescue brigade had used the time between two attack waves to retrieve the dead and wounded from the battlefield—or rather, out of the no-man's-land between the opposing trenches where the Turks shot the ANZAC soldiers like rabbits. The assault had been doomed to fail from the beginning; Jack and all the other veterans of the Turkish offensive could have told the high command that much. Earlier in the year they had used the onrushing Turks for target practice—in August the position was reversed. After the first wave, the plains had been strewn with casualties, and even a tenth or twentieth wave would have perished in the enemy fire—as long as the Turks had enough ammunition. And the reinforcement lines to Constantinople had functioned flawlessly. It was only out of kindness that the Turks left the rescue troops unmolested.

Jack would not have survived if anyone but Roly had found him. During battles such as that one, resources were extremely limited and rescue troops had to decide which of the wounded could be saved and which to leave behind with a heavy heart. Shots to the lung belonged in the latter category. Even when the staff doctor could operate in peace, only a small percentage of victims survived. In the chaos behind the front lines, the chances of making it were practically nil.

Roly had been unwilling to accept that. Although his men shook their heads, he had insisted that Jack McKenzie be placed on a stretcher and carried out of the line of fire.

"Best you hurry," he had pressed the men, "and don't just unload him in the trenches. He needs to be on the operating table right away. I'll take him to the beach."

Roly had known he was overstepping his authority, but he didn't care—the young man knew he owed Jack for saving him from a court-marital. So he waved the medics with Jack's stretcher over to the ambulance in one of the support trenches, where another decision was made. Only those who had a real chance of surviving were taken to the beach. Someone saw to the others later if it was still possible. Roly and his men lined up with the stream of medics who were carrying stretchers through the trenches, past the deathly pale young soldiers waiting in the reserve trenches for their turn. By then they knew what awaited them.

"You can let him down here," Roly had said, breathing heavily. Once they had reached the open country at the beach, he had driven his men at a jog. As they entered the field hospital, another selection took place as the doctors determined who went on the operating table first.

Roly had felt Jack's pulse and wiped the foamy blood from his mouth. He was alive—but wouldn't be for long without a miracle.

"I'll be right back. Hold on, Sergeant McKenzie.

"Commander Beeston," Roly called, running through the tents.

But before Roly found the doctor, Paddy had found Jack.

Dr. Beeston had been operating for hours, and Paddy was not allowed in the operating tent. The little dog yapped helplessly by the door and then crawled inside, only to be thrown back out again—until he finally picked up a scent he knew. Whining, Paddy nuzzled Jack McKenzie's hand, which hung limp from the stretcher. Yet Paddy's old friend made no motion to stroke him. In any case, something was not right. Smelling blood and death, the little dog sat down next to Jack and let out a heartbreaking howl.

"What's wrong with that mongrel? I can't stand it." One of the young caretakers cast a glance at Jack and reached forward to open his jacket, but Paddy growled at him.

"Great, now the cur means to bite too. What's the commander thinking, letting him run around like this? Dr. Beeston," the young man called to the doctor, who had just come out of the operating room. He looked around, utterly exhausted, at the unending flood of new cases. Dr. Beeston gave up the idea of having a sip of tea between patients.

"Commander Beeston? Your mongrel, er—" The young caretaker stopped, realizing that the doctor could send him directly to the front if he said something wrong now. "Could you, er, remove your dog, sir? He's impeding our work."

Dr. Beeston walked over, irritated. He had never heard complaints about Paddy before. Granted, he might be in the way a little now and then, but . . .

"The dog won't let me close to the wounded man, sir," the nurse reported. "I could . . ." He reached again for the buttons on Jack's jacket, but Paddy snapped at him.

"What's this about, Paddy? But wait a moment, that's . . ."

As soon as the doctor recognized Jack, he ripped his shirt open himself.

"A punctured lung, sir," the young corporal said. "It's a mystery to me why anyone brought him here. It's hopeless."

Dr. Beeston glared at him. "Thank you for your professional opinion, young man. Now into the OR with him. Quickly now. And keep your opinions to yourself."

Roly had fallen into a panic when he could not find Jack after giving up his search for Dr. Beeston in frustration. But Paddy was still saving Jack's place and whined when he saw Roly.

"Now where could he have gone off to, Paddy? Could you find him? Our Sergeant Jack? Well, aren't you good for nothing?"

"Who are you looking for, Private?" asked the young corporal in passing. "The punctured lung who was here? He's in the OR. Personal orders from Beeston. Now the pets decide who ends up on the chief's table."

Roly did not return to the front, but he assuaged his guilt by making himself useful in the hospital until Beeston finished his operation. Dr. Pinter, an orthopedic specialist, noticed the experienced nurse and ordered him to his own operating table, where he worked on men whose limbs had been shredded by hand grenades and mines. After the fifteenth amputation, Roly ceased counting. The wounded kept coming. Jack's fate was out of Roly's hands. He would have to wait for a break and then look for him.

The shooting had not died down until late in the night, and morning had already begun to light the sky by the time Dr. Pinter sent the last invalid to the hospital.

"They won't be attacking again, will they?" the doctor asked a captain who had his arm in a sling. He looked at Dr. Pinter with empty eyes.

"I don't know, sir. No one knows anything. Major Hollander was killed yesterday. The high command is still taking counsel. But if you ask me, sir, this battle is lost. This whole damn beach is lost. If the generals have even a spark of reason left, they'll call this off."

Roly had expected the doctor to upbraid the young officer, but Dr. Pinter merely shook his head. "Don't ask for trouble, Captain," he admonished gently. "You'd do better to pray."

The prayers of the doctors and soldiers on the front had not been answered, however.

Shortly before daybreak, the first machine-gun salvos boomed. New attack waves began—and new dead. The Battle of Lone Pine, as the August offensive was later called, after the most hard-fought-for trench, didn't end for another five days. Though the official communiqué relayed that the ANZAC's advance several hundreds of yards into Turkish soil had been a success, they had paid for it with nine thousand dead.

Roly had found Jack on the morning of the second day. He could easily have spent hours searching for his friend among the hundreds of men lying in dense rows had Paddy and Dr. Beeston not been at his bedside, where the doctor was inspecting his wound. Jack was unconscious, but he was breathing and no longer spitting blood.

"O'Brien?" Dr. Beeston asked as Roly approached. The doctor's face had looked almost as pale and sunken as his patient's. "Does he have you to thank for still being alive?"

Roly nodded guiltily. "I couldn't leave him lying there, sir. Naturally I know that—I'm prepared to accept the consequences."

"Oh, forget that," Beeston sighed. "If it makes you feel better, I overstepped my authority as well—or stretched it. We have our guidelines. We shouldn't try and play God."

"Wouldn't we have been doing that if we'd left him lying there, sir?"

"Not in this sense, O'Brien. Then we'd have been sticking to the rules. God—and feel free to take it as blasphemy—knows no rules."

The doctor carefully covered Jack. "Take care of him, O'Brien. Otherwise he'll get forgotten in this chaos. I'm going to arrange for him to be evacuated on the *Gascon* tonight."

The *Gascon* was a well-equipped hospital ship.

"To Alexandria, sir?" Roly asked hopefully. Transfer to the military hospital in Alexandria for a wounded man generally meant the end of the war for him.

Beeston nodded. "And you'll accompany him. That is, you'll accompany the transport. Someone's played God with you too, O'Brien. Someone with good connections. Your marching orders back to New Zealand came yesterday with the reinforcements. Apparently an invalid in Greymouth who's very important to the war effort can't live without your care. It seems that New Zealand coal production would grind to a halt without you."

Despite the circumstances, Roly could not suppress a grin.

"That's too much of an honor, sir," he remarked.

"I dare not make any judgments. So pack your things, soldier. Take care of our friend, and for heaven's sake, stay out of the line of fire, so nothing happens to you now. The *Gascon* is leaving at fifteen hundred hours."

Jack had been considerably closer to death than life when the hospital ship arrived in Egypt, but he was tough. Roly's intensive care had contributed significantly to his survival. There were far too few medics for the number of heavily wounded men, and some of the soldiers died while still on the ship, others shortly after arriving in Alexandria. Jack held on, however, and eventually regained consciousness. He looked around, registering the suffering around him and that he had survived, but he had become a different person. He was not stubborn or grouchy like many other survivors, and he politely answered the doctors' and nurses' questions. But beyond that he seemed to have nothing to say.

Jack had requited Roly's jokes and encouraging words with silence—and made no effort to overcome his weakness. He slept a great deal, and when he awoke, he gazed silently, first at the blanket on his bed and then, much later, when he was allowed to sit at the window, out at the sky. As Jack listened to the call of the muezzins over the city, he thought of what Roly told him Dr. Beeston had said: "God doesn't stick to rules."

Jack's convalescence had stretched out over many months. Although the wound healed, he lost weight and suffered from chronic exhaustion.

Roly had remained by his side throughout. He ignored his marching orders, and the staff doctors in Alexandria did not mention them. The hospital was hopelessly overcrowded, and every caretaker was needed. Besides, the urgency of his return home had lessened markedly since Tim Lambert had learned that Roly was out of the line of fire.

In December 1915, the British leadership had evacuated the shores of Gallipoli, which had come to be known as ANZAC beach. As they left, they blew up the trenches.

Roly had told Jack breathlessly about the successful action.

"They hit the bastards one last time. A whole bunch of Turks went up in the explosion."

Jack sank his head.

"And for what, Roly?" he asked quietly. "Forty-four thousand dead on our side—more on the Turks', they say. All for nothing."

That night Jack had dreamed again of the battle in the trenches, of thrusting his bayonet and shovel into the bodies of his opponents over and over. Into forty thousand bodies. When he woke up drenched in sweat, he wrote to Gloria and described the withdrawal of the ANZAC troops. He knew she would never read the letter, but it was a relief to write it down.

A persistent cough had plagued Jack that winter. Seeing how thin and pale Jack was, a doctor diagnosed him with tuberculosis and ordered his transfer to a sanatorium in Suffolk.

"To England, sir?" Roly inquired. "Can't we return home? There are sure to be tuberculosis sanatoria there too."

"But no military facilities," the doctor said. "You, Mr. O'Brien, can return home."

"But I haven't officially been demobilized," Roly objected.

"No, you just have six-month-old marching orders. Do what you like, O'Brien, but get out of here. We can smuggle you on the ship to England, but you should leave your unit before someone sends you to France."

Roly had sought work on a farm while Jack lay in the wan sun of an English spring staring into a matte-blue sky. He visited Jack as often as he could, and when the sanatorium's services were expanded to include invalids from the war, he found a job as a caretaker. Tim Lambert approved his leave of absence but asked for regular news about Jack. Jack's mother, Tim wrote, was very concerned. Roly could imagine. Jack, however, did not respond when Roly suggested that he dictate a letter.

Jack saw the grain in the fields ripen; he heard the songs of the harvesters, observed the way the fall painted the leaves yellow. In the winter he stared into the snow but only saw the bloody sand of Gallipoli. Another year passed during which his health did not improve. Sometimes he thought of Charlotte, but Hawaiki was far, even farther than America, or wherever Gloria might be.

"Three and a half years, and we're still at war," Rory had mumbled as he flipped through the paper that lay on the table next to Jack's recliner. It was an unusually warm day, and the nurses had taken the convalescents into the garden. "How is it supposed to end, Sergeant McKenzie? Will someone win, or will we keep on fighting and fighting?"

"Everyone's already lost," Jack said quietly. "But naturally the end will be treated as a big victory, whoever celebrates it. I also have cause to celebrate. The doctors are sending me home."

"We're going home?" Roly beamed.

Jack smiled weakly. "They're assembling a transport of disabled vets. All the men with amputations and the blind who can or want to be sent home right away."

"Then I can come with you. They'll need caretakers, won't they?"

"They're looking for volunteers among the nurses," Jack said.

Roly's whole face had shone. "It's strange," he said. "When it began, I wanted to go to war so that no one would tease me about being a male nurse anymore. But now I'd even throw on a dress to get to go home as a nurse."

After all that time away they were finally almost home. Jack knew he should be thankful. But he only felt cold as she stared out at the breathtaking view of the fog-enshrouded land. The ship would anchor in Dunedin. Jack wondered whether Roly had informed Tim Lambert of their arrival and, if so, whether the Lamberts had informed his mother. If they had, his family would surely be waiting for him at the quay. Jack dreaded that. But there was a good chance that was not the case. Because of the war, mail was even slower than usual.

During his last days in Alexandria, Jack had learned that in light of his bravery at the Battle of Lone Pine he had been promoted again and granted a medal. He had not even looked at it.

"Do you want it?" he asked when Roly chided him about it. "Here, take it. You've earned it more than I have. Show it to Mary; put it on when you get married. Nobody is going to ask you for the certificate."

"You don't mean that, Sergeant McKenzie," Roly said with a covetous look at the velvet jewel case. "I couldn't."

"Of course you can. I hereby grant it to you," Jack said, opening the case. "Kneel, or whatever it is you're supposed to do in these situations, and I'll consign it to you."

Roly proudly stuck the medal to his lapel as the ship entered Dunedin's harbor. Many other men likewise decorated themselves with their trophies. They might be missing arms or legs, but they were heroes.

The crowd who greeted them at the docks was considerably smaller than the one at their departure. It primarily consisted of doctors, nurses, and family and friends, who cried at the sight of the wounded men. The sanatorium in Dunedin—a repurposed girl's school, they said—had sent three vehicles and a few attendants.

"Is it all right with you if I leave you here, Sergeant McKenzie?" Roly asked. He hoped to catch the night train to Christchurch, and then continue on to Greymouth. "Are you sure you don't want to come? After all, Christchurch is . . ."

"I still haven't even officially been demobilized, Roly," he said, dodging the question.

"Bah, who's going to look into it, Sergeant McKenzie? We'll deregister you, and they'll send you the demobilization forms later. That's what I'm doing."

"I'm tired, Roly," Jack said.

"You can sleep in the train. I'd feel much better if I could drop you off with your family."

"I'm not a package."

Roly finally gave up and left Jack so he could gather their things. Jack watched the nurses help the men on crutches and in wheelchairs onto land. Eventually a young woman in a dark dress and apron approached him. She was not wearing blue like the professional nurses, so she was probably a volunteer.

"May I help you?" she asked.

Jack found himself looking into clever, pale-green eyes hidden behind thick glasses in a narrow face framed by austerely combed-back hair. The woman blushed at his probing gaze. But then a vague recognition sparked in her eyes as well.

"Miss Bleachum?" Jack asked tentatively.

She smiled but could not completely hide her shock at the sight of him. The strong, perennially cheerful foreman of Kiward Station rested on a reclining chair, pale and thin, covered by a blanket even though it was not cold, too exhausted to set foot on his homeland without help. Suddenly embarrassed at his weakness, he sat up and forced himself to smile. "It's nice to see you again."

2

When Roly came back with his and Jack's bags, he found Jack chatting with a young woman.

"Sergeant McKenzie, I would not have thought it possible," he laughed. "We've hardly reached the dock, and you already have a woman at your side. Miss." Smoothing his frizzy hair, Roly bowed formally.

Sarah Bleachum smiled shyly as Jack introduced her.

Roly looked relieved when he heard she worked at the Princess Alice Sanatorium.

"Then I can rest easy leaving Sergeant McKenzie to your care. Do you happen to know if there's still a train to Christchurch tonight?"

Sarah nodded. "I can arrange a seat for you as well, Mr. McKenzie," she offered, "in the sleeping car even. If I call your mother, she'll send someone from Kiward Station to meet the train. You really should be examined first, but the Princess Alice Sanatorium is only a transition facility for this transport. All the men are slated to return home."

"I'm sorry, Miss Bleachum, but I'd like, I'm just tired, you see." Jack blushed on account of the lie. He did not feel any weaker than before, but the thought of returning to Kiward Station filled him with fear. He could not face the empty bed in the room he had shared with Charlotte. Gloria's empty room. His father's empty seat—and his mother's sad eyes, in which he might only see pity. He would have to face it all eventually. But not yet.

Sarah exchanged a look with Roly, who shrugged.

"Well, I'll be going then. I'll be seeing you, Sergeant McKenzie." Roly waved and turned to go.

Jack felt he owed Roly at least a hug, but he could not bring himself to do it. "Roly, could you just call me Jack?"

Roly laughed. Then he dropped his duffel bag, approached Jack, and, leaning over, drew him into a bear hug. "Take care, Jack!"

Jack smiled as Roly left.

"A good friend?" Miss Bleachum asked, taking Jack's duffel bag.

"A very good friend. But you don't need to take my things. I can manage."

"No, let me. I have to make myself useful."

Jack followed her, walking slowly down the gangplank. A doctor was moving from one veteran to another, greeting the newcomers before they were helped into the vehicles. Jack thought he recognized the man. He noticed Sarah's face light up as the man approached them.

"This is Dr. Pinter," she said, introducing the man with a radiant smile on her face. The doctor smiled, but turned serious when he looked at Jack.

"Dr. Pinter, this is . . ."

"We've met before, haven't we?" Dr. Pinter asked. "Wait a moment, I remember, Sergeant McKenzie, right? Gallipoli, the man who was shot through the lung who was saved by Beeston's dog." He smiled bitterly. "You were the subject of much conversation in the field hospital for a few days. I'm happy you survived it."

Jack nodded. "And you were a captain?"

Dr. Pinter shrugged. "Major. But who cares about that now? We all waded through the same blood. God, it's rare for us to still be getting veterans of Gallipoli. Most of them are coming from France now. You weren't sent back to the front, were you?"

"No, Mr. McKenzie was treated in England," Sarah interjected, having already pulled Jack's charts out of a stack of papers to give to Dr. Pinter.

"How about you?" Jack asked. He was not really interested in the doctor's story, but felt he should make conversation. "I mean, you were a staff doctor, and we're still at war."

Dr. Pinter bit his lip. Jack recognized the traces Gallipoli had left there. He, too, was thin and pale, his still-young face lined with wrinkles. The doctor raised his hands and held them in front of him. They shook uncontrollably.

"I could no longer operate," Dr. Pinter said quietly. "It's yet to be diagnosed, perhaps a nervous palsy. It began in Gallipoli, on the last day. They had already evacuated almost all the troops. Only the last patrols were still in the trenches. It was supposed to appear as if they were still fully manned. Well, a few of the boys took it too far. They wanted to give the Turks a show battle, but the Turks had heavy artillery behind them. The men were torn to bits. What was left of them was placed on my table. I saved a seventeen-year-old, if you can call what I did saving him. Both arms, both legs. All gone. But I'd rather not say more. After that this trembling began."

"Perhaps you just need to rest," Sarah said. Though she spoke quietly, she finally said aloud what she'd thought before.

Dr. Pinter lowered his gaze. "I need a few new memories. I'd like to not see blood anymore when I close my eyes. I'd like to not hear shots when it's quiet around me."

Jack nodded. "I see the water. The beach, my first view of the beach before we landed. It was a beautiful beach."

Then both men fell silent. Sarah wanted to say something, but this was not a moment for small talk. She looked over, almost enviously, at the other nurses chatting and joking with their patients.

Jack shared a room with a grumpy older man who clutched a whiskey bottle. Where he got it was unclear, but he was not prepared to give up a single sip.

"Medicine against headaches," he grumbled, pointing to a nasty scar on left side of his face.

"Bullet's still in there," the man said. Then he drank in silence. That was fine with Jack, who sat staring at the garden outside their window. It was raining. Jack thought vaguely of the haying on Kiward Station, but it was all very far away. Gallipoli was close.

Jack woke feeling his usual leaden exhaustion and cold. Sensing that Sarah would not leave him in peace, he had slowly dressed himself and was sitting at the window watching the rain when she appeared.

"The next train to Christchurch leaves at eleven. Shall I have you taken to the station?"

Jack bit his lip. "Miss Bleachum, I'd rather, I'd like to recover a little first."

Sarah Bleachum pulled the other chair up to the window.

"What's wrong, Mr. McKenzie? Why don't you want to go home? Did you have a fight with your mother? Bad memories?"

Jack shook his head. "No, my memories are good. Too good. That's the problem. Gallipoli hurts, but I know someday it will fade. Happiness, on the other hand, that you never forget, Miss Bleachum. That leaves an emptiness behind that nothing will fill."

Sarah sighed. "I don't have many happy memories. I was rarely properly unhappy, though. I like teaching, and I like my students. But nothing that big."

"Then you're one to envy, Miss Bleachum," Jack said curtly and sank back into silence.

"Would you like to talk about it? That's what I'm here for. I mean, Kiward Station is such a lovely place." She looked at Jack searchingly. "And yet you shy from it like a horse. Just like . . ."

"It's an empty place," Jack broke in. "I feel Charlotte there. And my father. And Gloria. But it's like a house after a big party. The smoke of cigars and the scent of candles linger in the rooms. You think you can hear the echo of laughter, but there's nothing there. Just emptiness and pain. I thought I'd come to terms with Charlotte's passing. And my father, he was old. His death followed the rules."

Sarah frowned. "The rules?" she asked.

Jack did not explain.

"But Gloria, ever since Gloria disappeared, I can't bring myself to do it, Miss Bleachum. I can't bring myself to look into my mother's eyes, where I know I'll see nothing but questions. And the only answer is that God does not stick to any rules."

Sarah reached for his hand.

"But Gloria is back, Jack! I thought you knew. Didn't Mrs. McKenzie write you? Well, you were probably already at sea. But Gloria is back. She was here, here with me!"

Jack looked at her in a daze. "Where is she now?"

"Mrs. McKenzie picked her up. As far as I know, she's at Kiward Station."

Jack's hand clenched hers. "Can I still make the train? Will you call my mother for me?"

Gwyneira McKenzie was happy—but she also had an unsettling feeling of déjà vu as she welcomed Jack on the platform. The thin, pale young man who stepped much too slowly and ponderously off the train was a stranger to her. His face had wrinkles that had not been there three and a half years before, and his chestnut-colored hair was sprinkled with strands that were almost white. Too early, much too early for his age. But it was his wooden hug that scared her most of all. It was just as it had been when she had fetched Gloria from the train station at Dunedin—though Jack was polite enough to pretend to return Gwyneira's embrace.

Jack likewise seemed not to want to talk. He answered questions, even tried a smile, but initiated no conversation. He had locked up the past few years tightly within himself. Just as Gloria had. Gwyneira dreaded the prospect of seeing the two silent, withdrawn figures at the dinner table. Gloria was still traveling with the Maori, and despite all the tension, Gwyneira missed her and worried about her. Not that Gloria was in any danger with the tribe, but worry had been such a constant companion to Gwyneira these last few years that she no longer could fight it. And now Jack too.

As Gwyneira drove them home, she complained about the poor hay harvest and the fact that they had to herd the sheep out of the highlands earlier than usual.

"And we had a cold summer, so the grass down here isn't as abundant as it usually is. I've already thinned the number of cattle—better to have fewer that are nice and round than a big scrawny herd. I'm so happy you're back, Jack! It's been difficult doing everything alone." Gwyneira put her hand on her son's shoulder. Jack did not respond.

"Are you tired?" Gwyneira asked, trying desperately to draw some reaction from him. "It was a long day, wasn't it? A long trip."

"Yeah," Jack said. "Sorry, Mother, but I'm very tired."

"You'll recover quickly here, Jack," Gwyneira said optimistically. "We'll have to put some meat back on your bones. And make sure you get some sun. You're awfully pale. What you need is a little fresh air, a good horse, and we have puppies, Jack. You should pick one out. What day is today, Jack? Tuesday? Then you should call him Tuesday. Your father always named his dogs after days of the week."

Jack nodded, exhausted. "Is Nimue still around?"

"Of course. But she's with Gloria—discovering her roots." She snorted. "Nimue would have to travel to Wales to find hers, but Gloria is exploring her Maori heritage at the moment. She's migrating with Marama's tribe. If you ask me, Tonga is making marriage plans. Before she left, people were gossiping about Gloria and Wiremu."

Jack shut his eyes. So an empty house after all. Nothing more than the echo of voices and feelings in abandoned rooms.

Then again, Jack was astonished to realize that he felt something. A twinge of anger—or jealousy. Once again someone was attempting to take Gloria away from him. First the Martyns, now Tonga. He always arrived too late to protect her.

"I don't know what to do. He just holes up in his room. It's almost worse than with Gloria. At least when she first returned she went riding."

Gwyneira refilled Elaine's cup with tea. Elaine had made her annual trip to Kiward Station to breathe a little country air with her youngest sons.

"You mean he doesn't do anything on the farm?" Elaine asked. She had just arrived and had yet to see Jack. His friend Maaka had insisted he go see a few animals meant for breeding. The foreman was desperately trying to get Jack to take an interest in Kiward Station again, but since his return Jack had still not settled in. Gwyneira knew exactly how it would go. Jack would ride out, glance at the animals, and say a few noncommittal words. Then he would excuse himself on account of his fatigue and barricade himself in his room anew.

"But he used to be foreman here," Elaine said.

Gwyneira nodded sadly. "Yes, he had it all under control. And it was in his blood, you know. Jack is a born farmer and husbander—and dog trainer. His collies were always the best in all the Canterbury Plains. But now? He tolerates the whelp I gave him, but nothing more. He's not training her, doesn't go out with her. She just keeps him company while he looks out the window. When she gets bored of that, he lets her out; then she follows me around or goes to the stables. I'm at my wits' end."

"Maybe the boys and I can get him to come out," Elaine pondered. "He does like children."

"Try it," Gwyneira replied, "but Maaka has tried practically everything. He works so hard at it; it's touching. I had been worried it might come to wrangling over who's in charge since Maaka's managed the farm for the last three and a half years, but he would have gladly turned the rudder over to Jack if only he had wanted it. But he keeps running into a wall."

"Maaka didn't join the tribe for their migration?" Elaine asked.

"No, thank God. I wouldn't have known what to do without him. Especially during this awful summer. The cold stunted the grass, and the hay harvest was disastrous; the rain spoiled half of it. And if things continue like this, we'll have to herd the sheep back into the hills early. Hopefully the tribe will be back by then."

"If not, I'll do it with my two cowboys," Elaine said, looking out the window. Her boys were enjoying themselves in the pasture with two cob mares. Frank Wilkenson was trying his luck as a riding instructor. "And do you know what? I'd like a new collie. Callie's been gone so long now, but I'm still always looking around for her. I need a new shadow. I'll ask Jack to help with its training. He has to show me how to do it. Then he'll thaw."

Jack appeared an hour later, sweaty and drained from the ride. A short outing like that would never have been a strain before, but it was clearly too much for him. He drank some tea and exchanged a few polite words with Elaine. What interested him most was Roly.

"Roly's doing well; he's finally getting married," Elaine told him with deliberate cheer. Jack's thinness and paleness had shocked her. "I was told expressly to invite you. Aside from that he's very busy. He's taking care of Tim again, of course—which is doing Tim good. He gets along fine on his own, but it's tiring. Roly also has a new patient, Greg McNamara—the boy who went off to war with him. You know, the poor fellow lost both legs. And his family is completely helpless. Until Roly returned, Greg just lay in bed all day. His mother and sisters couldn't lift him, and his small pension is only enough to survive. We gave them Tim's old wheelchair as a start, and our pastor wants to see to it that they receive donations for his care. Greg would like to work, but that doesn't look likely. Mrs. O'Brien could give him a job in the sewing shop, but Roly doesn't dare make the offer. It would look too much like charity."

Jack's frowned. "All the male nurse jokes," he said, remembering Greg's teasing.

"Like I said, it's tragic," Elaine replied. "You were lucky, Jack."

"Yes, I was," he said softly. "Would you excuse me? I should go wash."

In a certain sense, Elaine's plan worked. Jack politely agreed to help train her dog, and he showed up punctually every morning to work with them. Tuesday likewise benefited. She learned quickly and adored her master. Unlike Shadow, however, she did not get to enjoy a walk or ride afterward. Jack always retired immediately after the training session. He no longer appeared to derive any joy from working with the animals as he once had. When he praised the dog, he did so kindly, but his eyes did not light up, and there was no smile in his voice.

"He behaves impeccably," Elaine informed Gwyneira, "but it's as if something inside him is dead."

3

Have you heard anything from your lost children?"

Gwyneira had been so preoccupied with her own troubles that she did not ask about Lilian and Ben until late in the visit. She was driving her granddaughter to Christchurch in the chaise. Elaine planned to visit Elizabeth Greenwood for a night before returning to Greymouth.

"Contradictory things," Elaine replied.

Gwyneira frowned. "What should I take that to mean?"

She was not expecting any big news, as Elaine would have reported that without prompting. She gave Gwyneira regular updates about the young couple in her letters, so Gwyneira knew about her first great-great-grandson, whom Lilian had named Galahad for incomprehensible reasons.

"According to Caleb's sources, the professors at the university, that is, they're doing well. According to George Greenwood's private detective, they're doing *very* well."

Jeremy and Billy were out of earshot, proudly riding two horses alongside the carriage. Otherwise Elaine would never have talked so openly. She kept what she knew about Lilian and Ben to herself—just as Caleb Biller did with his family. Caleb relied on his connections to Ben's university, and twice a year Elaine received reports from a detective George Greenwood had hired for her.

"What's the difference?" Gwyneira asked.

"Well, they moved to Wellington recently. Ben has a teaching professorship there. Caleb is bursting with pride. Normally they place men that young in an assistant position at best. Ben was always a high achiever—though I never noticed it, that doesn't mean anything."

"And?" she asked.

"Well, a teaching position means a small income. So Ben doesn't need to work on the docks anymore or whatever else he was doing to feed the family. He could afford a small apartment and just be able to make ends meet if Lilian pinched pennies. Or gave some additional piano lessons."

"But?" Gwyneira was getting impatient.

"But in reality they live on the edge of town in a darling house with a garden. In the morning a nanny pushes little Galahad around in a stroller—a very expensive stroller, the detective thinks. Lilian wears nice dresses, and whenever there's a theater performance or a concert, they attend."

"How do they pay for that?" Gwyneira asked, surprised.

"That's precisely the question."

"I hope Elizabeth Greenwood might be able to tell me more. George has put the detective on the case again."

"Do you suspect anything illegal?" Gwyneira asked.

Elaine laughed. "Hardly. The thought that Ben Biller could rob a bank has frankly never occurred to me—though that would certainly make him more interesting. But from all I've heard about him, he's simply a nice bore. Very much like his father."

"Why does Lily find him so interesting then?" Gwyneira asked. "She's such a lively girl herself."

"The charm of the forbidden," Elaine sighed. "If Florence and Tim hadn't gotten so angry, everything would probably have worked out differently. But they didn't even learn anything from their children running away. In fact, war is brewing between the Lambert and Biller Mines right now. Each of them is trying to snatch shares from the other. Florence went deep into debt for her own coke furnace and is now trying to lure away our customers by lowering her prices. Tim wanted to do the same, but Uncle George advised Tim to wait it out. While the Biller's furnace is busier than ours at the moment, it's not profitable and should simply run itself into the ground over time. We just hope Florence doesn't ruin herself with it. The whole business is absurd. But I'd just like to see my grandson at least once. And I miss

Lily. Though he would never admit it, Tim does too. We absolutely have to think of something."

"Have you heard of this?" Elizabeth Greenwood asked, pushing a book across the table toward Elaine.

Gwyneira had just left, and the two women were having tea. Elaine took the book with furrowed brow. She wanted to ask about Lilian and Ben, but she tried to be patient.

"Well, have you?" she asked again.

Elaine flipped through the book. "*The Mistress of Kenway Station.* Yes, I read it. Very exciting. I like stories like that."

"And?" Elizabeth asked. "Did anything stand out to you?"

Elaine shrugged.

"About the story, I mean. The farm at the end of the earth, the scoundrel who more or less keeps his wife prisoner."

Elaine blushed. "You mean me. It should have reminded me of Lionel Station?"

Elizabeth nodded. "I couldn't help noticing."

"It wasn't all that similar. I can't remember the heroine, well, her . . ."

"No, the heroine is saved by a childhood friend," Elizabeth agreed. "The ending wasn't the same. But then came this." She produced a second book, *The Heiress of Wakanui.*

Elaine read the jacket text: "'Since the death of his beloved wife, Jerome Hastings has become a difficult, withdrawn man. He manages his farm, Tibbet Station, with a hard heart, and his enmity with the Maori chieftain Mani threatens to plunge the entire region into war but for Ahu, the chieftain's daughter, who secretly loves him.'"

"What am I missing here?" Elaine asked.

Elizabeth sighed.

"In the end they have a baby," she helped.

Elaine reflected. "Paul and Marama Warden. Kura-maro-tini. Isn't that a bit of a stretch?" She looked at the jacket. "Brenda Boleyn. I don't know a Brenda Boleyn."

"And is this just a coincidence too?" With a grand gesture Elizabeth revealed a third book, *The Beauty of Westport,* and read the jacket text aloud:

"'Through no fault of her own Joana Walton loses her position as a governess in Christchurch. Fleeing the cruel Brendan Louis, she ends up on the West Coast—an unforgiving place for an innocent girl. But Joana remains true to herself. She finds a meager income as a piano player in a bar—as well as new love in Lloyd Carpinter, who owns shares in a railway line. But will he stay with her when he learns of her past?'"

Elaine went pale. "I will kill whoever wrote this."

"You no longer believe it's a coincidence, do you? In any case, I've made inquiries."

"I sense something is afoot."

"The books are published by a press in Wellington, and there's some connection between it and the newspaper Ben Biller has occasionally written for over the last few years."

"Abbreviated BB, right? I saw it in the detective's dossier. But he can't have made much from that. The boy has no talent. The last thing I read of his was some doggerel about flowing hearts."

"I've started having the newspaper sent to me. BB writes very moving short stories. In the same style as Brenda Boleyn."

Elaine shook her head. "I can't picture it. The boy was completely incapable of writing such a thing, and this book"—she indicated *The Mistress of Kenway Station*—"may not be great literature, but it's still very polished."

Elizabeth grinned. "And it's not about the Biller family. Not to mention that this person masquerading as Brenda is likely a woman."

Elaine stared at her. "You mean, he's not the one doing the writing? You mean . . . Lily?" She stood up and began pacing the room. Elizabeth could only just save a costly Chinese vase from being knocked over. "Damn it, I'm going to bend her over my knee. Or I'll hold her so Tim can. He's wanted to do that for some time now. How could she?"

"Now don't get so worked up. One would have to know your family story quite well to pick up on the similarities. I wouldn't even have figured it out after the first two books if the hero of the first hadn't been named Galahad."

"She named her son after him?" Elaine had to smile.

"Galahad represents her dream man," Elizabeth remarked drily. "I don't know Ben Biller, but he would have to be a rare beam of light to come close to the hero in the book. So, what should we do now? Any ideas?"

"First, I'm going to write an admiring letter to Brenda Boleyn. And ask carefully about the details of my family history. Perhaps she's some long-lost cousin making a proper mess of the Kiward Station line of succession. We'll see how Lily responds."

"A very diplomatic solution—and one that flies elegantly over Tim's head. Then you'll probably tell him that Brenda is an old friend from school, right? But you're going to have to work this out, Elaine. It really is a farce to have two families at war over nothing."

"But an original one," remarked Elaine, "the Montagues and Capulets thumping each other on the head while Romeo studies Polynesian and Julia makes money off her family history. Not even Shakespeare would have thought of that."

Dear Brenda Boleyn,

Having just had the opportunity to read your third literary work, I'd like to express the greatest admiration and esteem for your talent as an author. Rarely does a writer succeed in enthralling me with her imagination the way you have.

Yet, a question if I may: to my astonishment I've found remarkable parallels in all of your books to the history of my family. At first I thought it to be a coincidence, then perhaps a spiritual affinity. A person as sensitive as you undoubtedly are may well possess medium-like abilities. But why is it my family of all families that your presumptive familiar spirit describes to you? These thoughts have led me to the conclusion that perhaps you might be a hitherto unknown or lost family member who has knowledge of my family history through a much more mundane channel. Should that be the case, I would be very happy to make your acquaintance. Until then, I remain, with admiration,

Yours,
Elaine Lambert

Lily startled at first when she saw the handwriting on the envelope, but she received so much reader mail that she didn't think much of it. As she read the first lines, however, she turned red, only to begin giggling.

She reached for her typewriter, but then changed her mind. On some perfumed stationery she treasured, she wrote these words: *Dearest Mummy.*

4

Gwyneira McKenzie had never been a particularly patient person, and her advancing age had done nothing to change that. The summer had made the greatest demands on her forbearance: first Gloria's return and rejection, then her leave-taking for the migration with the Maori, and now Jack. Though Elaine's visit had lifted Gwyneira's spirits a bit, Jack continued to slip like an aggrieved ghost through the house, and Gwyneira had heard nothing from Gloria.

Her feelings finally caught up with her on the day the Maori returned from their migration. Kiri and Moana asked to leave early after preparing a simple dinner for Gwyneira and Jack.

"Tribe back. We celebrate," Moana declared happily.

Gwyneira waited for Gloria to appear. As morning gave way to afternoon and there was no sign of her, Gwyneira knocked on the door to Jack's room. When no one answered, she ripped the door open. Her son lay on his bed staring at the ceiling. He seemed not to have heard her knocking. Tuesday, who had been lying near his feet, sprang up and barked a greeting. Gwyneira motioned her away.

"I don't know what you're up to that's so important in here," she roared at her son, "but you'll have to interrupt it for a couple of hours to ride down to the Maori village. The tribe is back. And I'd like—no, I insist—that Gloria make an appearance here before the day is over. That's not asking too much, damn it all. She's had the whole summer to herself. But I want to know she's well, and I'd like to hear what she's done over the last few months. Even if it's no more than 'It was fine, Grandmum.'"

Jack got up slowly. "I don't know, shouldn't we wait until she . . ."

He did not know what he was feeling. He had been longing to see Gloria since Maaka had announced that morning that the tribe was returning, but he was afraid of how Gloria might react to the sight of him. Would she be startled like most people? Would she be sympathetic? Contemptuous? Jack condemned himself sometimes for his weakness, and he saw deprecation in the eyes of other men as well. That young shepherd, for example, Frank Wilkenson, still believed in the glory of Gallipoli. He had wanted to hail Jack as a hero, but when he saw what the war had made of him, he thought Jack a worthless coward.

"No, Jack, no, I won't wait any longer," Gwyneira said, pacing the room. "And if there's a wedding taking place over there, be so kind as to drag the bride away and bring her here before she lies down with that Wiremu in the sleeping lodge."

Jack almost had to laugh. His mother had never been a prude, but he had never heard her speak so explicitly.

"I'd be happy to try, Mother, but I'm afraid Tonga will run me through for it. Besides, he would have invited you. There's no way he'd pass up that opportunity."

Gwyneira snorted. "He would have bade me come tomorrow," she said melodramatically, "to see the blood on the sheets."

Jack didn't bother reminding her that most Maori girls had long since ceased to be virgins by the time they selected a husband. If Gloria had decided to marry Wiremu, surely he was not her first lover. Jack felt anger and a flash of sadness at the thought. Jealousy? He shook his head. That was nonsense. Gloria was a child. And he ought to be able to grant her happiness should she find it in Wiremu's arms.

Jack's horse, Anwyl, was waiting in its stable. Tuesday danced enthusiastically around him.

"Should I saddle him for you, Mr. McKenzie?" Frank Wilkenson asked with barely concealed contempt. Over the past few months Jack had occasionally taken him up on the offer. Now he was ashamed of that.

"No, I'll do it myself." He overcame the wave of weakness that washed over him as he lifted the heavy saddle.

"I'm riding to the Maori village," he said curtly. "I should be back in two hours." Then he chided himself for announcing his departure like a girl going out for a ride alone. He would never have done that before. But before he had been invincible.

"Understood, Mr. McKenzie; round up the lost daughter." Frank Wilkenson grinned insinuatingly.

Jack briefly thought about firing him, but could not summon the energy.

As Jack approached the village, he saw people dressed for a festival gathered in front of the meeting hall. Jack alighted to call out the ritual greeting and request an invitation to enter the *marae*. Normally the Maori would have long since noticed his arrival, but today all eyes were focused on the meeting hall. Suddenly a girl broke away from the group and began to walk calmly away. At first Jack supposed her to be a priestess performing some ceremony, as the girl was wearing the traditional hemp skirt and woven torso covering in tribal colors. Once she had rounded the corner, however—and could no longer be seen from the *wharenui*—she began to run toward the sparse woods that Jack had just emerged from—and almost right into Jack and Anwyl.

When the young woman saw the man and horse, she stopped in her tracks, startled. Her eyes flashed as she looked up at him.

Jack found himself looking into a wide face that was nonetheless narrower than that of most Maori women. The artfully painted *moko* made the girl's eyes appear larger, and he immediately noticed her blue eyes. Jack stared at the woman. She was young, but no longer a child; she had to be around twenty.

"Let me past!" The girl displayed no fear or recognition—simply naked, seething rage.

Jack was shocked when he saw a knife blade glint in her hand.

He raised the palms of his hands defensively, then uttered a single word.

"Gloria?"

The girl trembled. Then she appeared to calm down and took a moment to look at him.

Jack waited, searching her eyes for any signs that she recognized him. For sympathy, for shock, for rejection. But Gloria's face merely showed exhaustion and weariness.

"Jack."

Jack looked at her more closely. Ten years had passed since that little girl, face streaming with tears, had exacted that impossible promise from him: "If it gets really bad, will you come get me?"

"I'm supposed to take you home," he said quietly.

"You're late." She remembered.

"You managed without me. And you, you're . . ."

He did not know how to put his impression of her into words. Gloria's Maori and *pakeha* features came together not in an ethereal whole as with Kura but in a seeming tension between cultures. And a strange expression filled Gloria's eyes. As old as the world—and yet rebellious, combative, young.

"Do you want to come along?" he asked.

Gloria nodded. "I was on my way."

"In that outfit . . . Don't get me wrong, you look beautiful, but . . ."

"I'll change at home."

Determined, Gloria started off.

"Don't you want to ride with me?" Jack asked—and was suddenly aware of the awkwardness of his words. Gloria was no longer a child whom he could let sit behind him on the horse's croup. Let alone with bare legs in that short skirt. Then again, nothing had prepared him for the wild, almost panicked look in Gloria's eyes.

"That, that wouldn't be proper," she finally said, regaining her composure.

Jack suppressed a bitter laugh. The old Gloria would never have considered what a lady ought to do.

"Then ride alone," he replied. "Sitting like a lady. You still know how, don't you?"

Gloria gave him a mocking look. "When you can't ride anymore, you're dead."

Jack smiled and gave her Anwyl's reins as he dismounted. Once she'd mounted the horse, he began walking alongside her. It was a long way, but Jack did not feel tired. On the contrary, he felt more energized than he had in a long time.

"You have a horse on Kiward Station," he said after a while. "Do you want to ride again?"

"Of course," Gloria said.

It did not sound like she intended to continue living with the Ngai Tahu. Jack considered whether to ask her about Wiremu, but he decided against it. Behind them there was rustling in the bushes. Jack started, wheeling around ready to defend himself—and noticed that Gloria did the same. Both of them laughed apprehensively when Nimue burst out of the shadows. She greeted Jack enthusiastically, Tuesday somewhat less so. They walked along in silence for a bit.

"I'm happy you're here, Gloria."

"It's my land," she said calmly.

Her confidence disappeared, however, when they reached Kiward Station's stables and Frank Wilkenson took the horse. He had been drinking whiskey with a few other shepherds in the next room, and they all ogled Gloria's short skirt. She blushed. Jack took off his jacket and gave it to her.

"We should have done that earlier," he said. Now they could only slip in through the kitchen and hope to evade Gwyneira.

However, she was waiting in the passage to the supply rooms. She was still wearing her housedress from that afternoon and looked beleaguered. Jack had never seen her looking so old. He thought he could detect traces of tears on her cheeks.

"What have you brought me here, Jack?" she asked with a hard voice. "A Maori bride? I didn't mean it seriously. You didn't have to steal her away. She'll just run back to her tribe at the next opportunity." Gwyneira turned to her great-granddaughter. "Couldn't you have at least invited me, Gloria? Couldn't we have celebrated it here? Do you hate me so much that I had to learn from the cook that my great-granddaughter was getting married?"

Jack frowned. "Who said anything about getting married, Mother? Gloria wanted to take part in a dance. But then she changed her mind. She was on her way home when I found her."

"You've always lied for her, Jack. So, Gloria, how it is this supposed to work? Do you want to live with Wiremu here? Or in the camp? Are you going to raze this house when the tribe takes it over? Naturally Kura would have to agree since the land still belongs to her."

Gloria stood tall before her grandmother, and her eyes flooded with rage again.

"It belongs to me! Me alone. My mother shouldn't dare try to take it from me. And it will belong to no one else. I'm no one's bride. And I will be no man's wife. I am . . ." She seemed to want to say more, but then changed her mind, turned around and ran off, just as she had already done once that day.

Jack suddenly felt tired.

"I, I'd like to retire," he said stiffly.

Gwyneira fixed him with a wild look. "Yes, why don't you all just retire?" she roared at him. "Sometimes I get sick of it, Jack. Sometimes I just get sick of it."

Neither Jack nor Gloria appeared for breakfast the next morning. Gwyneira was embarrassed after her outburst. She learned from Kiri that Gloria was in her room and seemed to be busy smashing all her handmade Maori goods to pieces. Jack had left on horseback to spend the day at the circle of stone warriors. Kiri and Moana informed Gwyneira what had really transpired in the village.

"Tonga wanted marriage with Wiremu and Glory. Had told whole tribe. Only not Glory and Wiremu. They did not want marriage," Kiri said.

"Wiremu did," Moana corrected her.

"Wiremu wanted *mana*. But he coward," Kiri explained. "Glory very angry because he not sleep with her but he pretend."

Gwyneira cursed her mistrust. She should at least have given Gloria a chance to tell her version of events. When the girl appeared at dinner that evening—in the spinsterish outfit she had worn to greet Gwyneira in Dunedin—she expressed her remorse.

"I was afraid, Glory. I thought you'd fallen for Tonga's tricks. Kura was close to doing that once."

"I'm not Kura," she said angrily.

"I know. Please, I'm sorry."

"It's all right," Jack said appeasingly. The tension between the two women almost scared him. Gloria seemed to hold Gwyneira responsible for all her troubles, and he wondered what had happened to the girl. Just how long had she traveled alone? What had she done to earn her passage back to New Zealand? He had gleaned one thing from her reaction to the rustling in the bushes: Gloria had lived through her own war.

"No, it's not all right," she yelled. "Don't speak for me, Jack. It's only all right when I say it is." She paused. "It's all right," she said stiffly.

Gwyneira sighed with relief.

After dinner she stopped the girl, who wanted to go straight back to her room.

"There's something for you, Gloria. A package from your parents. It came a few weeks ago."

"I don't want anything from my parents," she said angrily. "You can send it back to them."

"But they're letters, child," Gwyneira replied. "Kura wrote that she was sending you your mail. Kura's agent collected it all and gave it to her in New York."

"Who would have written to me?" Gloria asked testily.

"I don't know, Glory. I didn't open the package. Why don't you have a look? Then you can burn them if you want."

Gloria had built a fire in front of the stables that afternoon and thrown her Maori dress into it.

Gloria nodded.

Back in her room, she opened the envelope. The first letter that fell out had been opened. Her mother must have read it. Gloria looked at the sender: Private Jack McKenzie, ANZAC, Cairo.

Dear Gloria,

I'd hoped to be able to write to you on Kiward Station. After all, you finished school and Mother was so full of hope that you'd finally come home. But now she's told me about an American tour with your parents. No doubt a very interesting experience you'll prefer to our old sheep farm. My mother is very sad about it, but it's only for a few months.

As you've surely heard, I have decided to leave Kiward Station for a while to serve my country as a soldier. After the death of my father and my beloved wife, Charlotte, I wanted to do and see something else. As for the seeing, I'm definitely getting my money's worth. Egypt is a fascinating country. I'm writing you from the shadow of the pyramids, so to speak. Tombs that rise up like castles to hold the dead fast. But what sort of immortality is that, if you wall up the soul and carefully hide the body in a burial chamber beneath the earth to protect it from corpse robbers? Our Maori would not understand, and I, too, would prefer to picture Charlotte in the sun of Hawaiki than in eternal darkness.

Gloria let the letter fall and thought of Charlotte. Gloria could hardly remember the Greenwoods' youngest daughter. What had suddenly inspired Jack to write her such a long letter? Or could it be that he'd always written? Had her school intercepted his letters? Why? And who would have done that? Gloria scanned the rest of the envelopes in the packet. Aside from a few missives from Grandmum

Gwyn and two cards from Lilian, they were all from Jack. She eagerly opened the next envelope.

. . . Modern Cairo is considered a great city, but it lacks government buildings, squares, and palaces. People here live in closed-off, boxlike stone houses, and the streets are narrow alleys. The life and goings-on in the city are hectic and loud. The Arabs are exceedingly business minded. During maneuvers there's always a swarm of men dressed in white offering refreshments. It drives the British officers crazy. Apparently they're afraid that even during combat we'll be counting on there always being a melon seller nearby. In the city the natives try and sell us antiques that are supposedly from the burial chambers of the pharaohs. Given the quantity of these objects, that's unlikely. The country could not have had that many rulers. We take it that they simply carve the idols and sphinxes themselves. It sends a shiver up my spine to think of people actually robbing the dead—the custom of burying people with goods is a strange one. Sometimes I think about the little jade pendant Charlotte wore around her neck. A hei-tiki *carved by a Maori woman. She said it would bring luck. When I found Charlotte at Cape Reinga, she did not have it anymore. Maybe her soul is wearing it to Hawaiki. I don't know why I'm telling you all this, Gloria—apparently Egypt's not doing me any good. Too much death all around me, too much past, even if it's not my own. But we're being relocated soon. It's getting serious. They want to attack the Turks at the entrance of the Dardanelles.*

Gloria involuntarily reached for her own *hei-tiki*, but then she remembered she had thrown it at Wiremu's feet. Better that way; let him take her Maori soul elsewhere.

. . . I will never forget the beach, how it looked in the very first light of morning. A small bay, surrounded by rocks, ideal for a picnic with a woman you love. And I will never forget the sound of that first shot. Though I've heard hundreds of thousands of shots since then, that first one destroyed the innocence of a place that until that moment God could only have looked upon with a smile. We changed it into a place where only the devil laughs.

Gloria smiled wearily. There was no doubt the devil had a lot of fun in this world.

Suddenly she had no desire to continue reading. But she carefully hid the letters beneath her laundry. They belonged to her, and no one else was to find them—Jack least of all. He might not think it right for her to read them now. After all, he hadn't spoken of his experiences at Gallipoli. And besides, Jack had written to a different Gloria. He must have had a child in mind when he colorfully described how he had ridden camels and chastised big, heavy men for letting themselves be carried through the desert on tiny donkeys. On the other hand, some sentences seemed only too pointedly directed at the woman Gloria now was. Marama would probably have said that the spirits had guided Jack's hand.

Gloria lay down but could not sleep. It was not dark yet, and she stared at the bare walls of her room. She stood up and retrieved her old drawing pad from the furthest corner of her chest of drawers. When she opened it, she found herself staring at a colored picture of a weta. Gloria ripped the page out. Then she drew the devil.

5

"You didn't go out to herd the sheep back with the others?" Jack asked.

He hadn't thought he'd see Gloria at the breakfast table that morning. The shepherds had set out before dawn to herd the sheep in the highlands together and then back to the winter pastures. Almost four weeks sooner than usual, as a cold and rainy fall had followed the wet summer. Gwyneira was afraid of losing too many sheep, and of an early onset of winter.

"All alone with that horde of wild rascals?" Gloria asked him sullenly in turn.

Jack bit his lip. No, of course they couldn't send Gloria off into the highlands with the shepherds, though it occurred to him that she may have gone if he had ridden out too. He looked over at his mother and saw the silent accusation in her eyes. Gwyneira felt he was shirking his duty by not going—as did the *pakeha* shepherds. What the Maori thought, no one knew. But his mother and her men did not accept his continuing weakness. He was healthy. He could ride if he wanted. And Jack knew that too. But he could not bear to think of the tents, the campfires, the men's pompous speeches, which would bring back memories of the laughing, overly confident boys who had died at Gallipoli. And a little of Charlotte, too, who had ridden along during the herding once or twice and managed the food wagon. They had shared a tent, retired early, and lain in each other's arms while the rain beat down on the tent or the moon shone brightly.

Gloria hadn't given any thought to whether Jack was participating in the herding. She was too distracted by her own dilemma. When she had shown up at the stables offering to work with the cattle and the sheep on the farm, the men had proved stubborn. No one gave her any tasks or was willing to work with her. Gloria now understood that migrating with the Maori had been a big mistake—returning in native clothing all the more so. The *pakeha* among the workers laughed behind Gloria's back and called her Pocahontas. Her instructions were not followed, and her questions answered curtly. She could no longer count on their respect.

The Maori shepherds were not much better. Though they had certainly gained respect for Gloria—speeches like the one she had given in the *wharenui* impressed the tribe—the men pointedly kept their distance. Passive resistance against their often overzealous chieftain was one thing, but screaming at him and throwing a statuette of the gods at his son's feet was taking it too far. For the Maori of Tonga's tribe, Gloria was *tapu*, and people avoided her.

Though Gloria was used to being ostracized, it gnawed at her, and she did not know how to occupy herself. When she tried to train the whelps in the yard, she made mistakes and heard the men laughing when a little collie did not obey her. It was no different with the young horses. She cursed the years she'd lost studying art instead of learning farmwork.

Increasingly, she returned to her room in the afternoon and opened Jack's old letters.

We're digging in. You should see the trench system here. It's almost like an underground city. The Turks across the way are doing the same. You could go crazy thinking about it. We just sit here, each lying in wait for the other, hoping that some idiot on the other side will get too curious and take a peek over the wall. We then blow that guy's head off—as if that would change the course of the war. A few of the better heads in our ranks have developed a periscope. With the help of a pole and two mirrors, we can now look out without any danger. They're also at work cobbling together a shooting contraption.

But the Turks have the upper hand. They hold the high ground in the mountains—if their weapons had more range, they could shoot right into our trenches. Fortunately that's not the case. But how we're supposed to conquer this country is beyond me.

These days I think a lot about courage, Gloria. A week ago the Turks risked an assault with completely unbelievable bravery. We mowed down thousands of them, but they still kept leaping out of their trenches and trying to storm ours. In the end two thousand Turks were dead. Can you imagine, Gloria? Two thousand dead men? We eventually stopped shooting—I don't know whether someone ordered it or if our humanity compelled us. As soon as the Turkish rescue troops had fetched the dead and wounded from no-man's-land, another assault wave began. Is that courage or idiocy, Gloria? Or desperation? After all, it's their land, their home they're defending. What would we do if our homeland were at stake? What are we doing here?

Gloria's heart beat wildly as she read those lines. Would Jack perhaps understand what she had done to make it back to Kiward Station? To distract herself, she once again took up her drawing pencil.

After the sheep had been herded back, Kiward Station was full of life. Animals stood everywhere in their paddocks, which were constantly being cleaned out and restocked with food. Gwyneira worked on an elaborate plan to make use of available pastures as she watched the meager stockpile of hay dwindle. Both Jack and Gloria remained locked away in their rooms.

In desperation, Gwyneira brought the matter up with Maaka, who merely said he did not need the girl.

"She'll only scare off my men," he said. Gwyneira did not press the issue with him. She tried to talk to Gloria about it but once again showed little tact. Instead of asking Gloria about the incidents Maaka was alluding to, she made accusations. Outraged, Gloria rebuffed her and ran to her room. Gwyneira had no idea that Gloria was in there crying in anger and helplessness. Gloria needed support, but her great-grandmother always seemed to side with her opponents.

Gwyneira sometimes thought she might go mad. She still insisted on family dinners, but Jack and Gloria merely cloaked themselves in silence when she brought up the hay shortage or her concerns about the animals. When Gloria had offered a few suggestions early on, Gwyneira had rebuffed her ideas.

"The land around the circle of stone warriors isn't *tapu*," Gloria said. "If there's a scarcity of fodder, the sheep could graze there; it's almost five acres. Naturally it would be nicer if the sacred site stood on untouched land, but the grass will grow back. The gods don't care, and Tonga should not act as if they did."

The idea had outraged Gwyneira—after all, she had been granting the Maori their sacred sites for decades, and she did not want to rock the boat. Gloria, however, felt betrayed anew and held her tongue.

Shortly after Christmas, Jack surprised his mother and Gloria by announcing that he was planning a trip to Greymouth for Roly's wedding. Jack was dreading visiting the town where he had celebrated his honeymoon with Charlotte. But he owed it to Roly. After spending a few days learning to operate Gwyneira's car, he rumbled off to Christchurch and caught the train to Greymouth. Elaine and her sons greeted him radiantly at the station.

"You look good, Jack. You've put on some weight. Watch out, I'm going to fatten you up."

Jack informed her that he would rather stay in a hotel than impose on her hospitality. Elaine seemed disappointed, but she quickly recovered her good spirits and teased him.

"Just not the Lucky Horse, Jack, I won't be held responsible if you stay there! Roly is insisting on celebrating his wedding there, of all places. Tim and the rest of their regular group are thrilled, but a night there would put your virtue to the test."

Jack ended up taking a room in one of the upscale hotels on the pier and spent several hours staring at the waves before Roly and Tim came for him.

"Bachelor party." Roly laughed. "Farewell to the single life. We're going to have one more good go of it, Sergeant . . ." He grinned. "Beg your pardon, Jack! Sorry, Mr. Lambert."

Tim Lambert laughed. "Roly, what you call my—how are we related again, Jack?—in any case, what you call Jack is none of my business. Besides, if this night goes as festively as planned, we'll all end up on a first-name basis anyway."

Jack liked Elaine's husband and tried to make a joke himself. "I believe Elaine is my niece. But don't worry, Tim, you don't need to call me uncle."

Greg McNamara bore his fate with more composure than Jack had imagined he would. At least he did that evening when the whiskey flowed in streams. As a wounded veteran, Greg enjoyed hero status. While it was visibly embarrassing for Jack and Roly when the first glass was raised to the heroes of Gallipoli, Greg beamed and never tired of recounting the adventures at Cape Helles that had cost him his legs. Much later in the evening, a girl appeared who took a seat on Greg's lap.

"This is really a brothel," Jack observed, confused, to Tim, who was chatting with Madame Clarisse, the owner of the establishment.

"He figured it out." She laughed. "Where'd you round this one up, Tim? The last sheep pen in the Canterbury Plains? I thought you'd been to war, Mr. McKenzie. Didn't you ever, well, let's say, seek distraction with one of the heroines of night?"

Jack blushed. He would not admit it, but he had not so much as embraced a woman since Charlotte's death.

"Hera, why don't you come see to this man?"

Hera was a stout Maori girl with brown eyes and long, black hair. Jack managed to exchange a few friendly words with Hera before retiring early.

"Tired already?" the girl asked, surprised. "Well, it's smart not to drink yourself into oblivion the night before the wedding. Someone should say a kind word to the groom on the subject. But we have beds here too." She smiled invitingly.

Jack shook his head and took his leave. He slept fitfully in his luxury room, dreaming of Charlotte and Hera, whose faces merged into one. In the end, the girl he kissed was—Gloria.

Since the O'Briens and the Flahertys were all Catholic, the long-suffering pastor of the Methodist church once more had to summon all his tolerance and open his little church in Greymouth to a Catholic colleague from Westport.

Madame Clarisse showed up with her girls, and all of them were glared at by the highly respectable mothers of the bride and groom. The men looked completely hungover and the women somewhat peeved about that, but in the end all the women present cried when Roly and Mary said "I do."

Jack thought about his and Charlotte's wedding and could hardly hold back his tears. Greg, next to him, cried like a baby. It was unlikely he would ever marry. The girl he had been seeing before Gallipoli had left him after his return. And how was he supposed to support a wife?

After the ceremony, the guests convened at the Lucky Horse. Jack sat with Elaine and Charlene, Matt Gawain's wife. Jack's gaze followed Hera, who was dancing with one man after another. "Go on and bring the poor thing to our table, Mr. McKenzie," Charlene said. "She could use a break."

"The poor thing?" Jack asked. "Yesterday she gave the impression she was having fun."

Charlene snorted. "That's part of the job, Mr. McKenzie. Would you pay for a whore who was always whining?"

"I've never paid for a whore, but if the girls don't have fun, why do they do it?"

Elaine and Charlene—neither of whom was entirely sober by then—groaned theatrically.

"Sweetheart," Charlene said in a smoky voice. "There are several reasons. But 'fun' has never been one of them."

Jack looked at her uncertainly. "You worked here, didn't you?" he asked awkwardly.

"That's right, sweetheart." Charlene laughed.

Jack did not know how to respond.

"If you have something against former whores then you should avoid the West Coast," she said angrily.

"I don't have anything against former whores," Jack said. "I was just thinking a girl always has a choice."

"You could always starve honorably," Elaine said.

Charlene laughed bitterly. "Our Madame Clarisse never forces anyone, of course, but in most establishments, the men have the final say. Little Hera was sold before she was even ten years old. Her mother was Maori, let herself be lured away from her tribe by some bastard. He dragged her to the South Island from the North, and she had no way to get home. When he didn't find any gold in his pan, he sold her—and later her daughter. No one asked them, Jack."

"And I had a friend in Queenstown who did it to pay for her passage from Sweden," Elaine said.

Jack saw his chance to contradict them. "But Gloria came over as a cabin boy. She didn't have to."

"As a cabin boy? All the way from England to New Zealand?" Charlene asked.

"From America," Jack corrected.

"And that cabin boy never once took his shirt off? Not to mention his underpants? I was still a child when we came over, but I remember well how hot it got on the Pacific. The sailors worked with their shirts off."

"What, what are you trying to say?" he asked, an aggressive note in his voice. Elaine laid her hand on his arm.

"She's trying to say that if that's the case—and I only know what Grandmum Gwyn told me—then at least one or two of her shipmates must have been in on it."

"One or two?" Charlene scoffed. "Since when do cabin boys sleep in rooms with two beds? Lord, Lainie, they sleep in boxes of six or ten. A girl would stand out."

"OK, fine, so there were coconspirators," Jack said, pouring himself another whiskey. His hands shook.

"And you think they kept the fact that Gloria wasn't a boy to themselves without compensation?" Charlene asked. "Take the halo off the girl before it starts to pinch."

"You should go dance, Jack," Elaine said. She saw that Jack had clenched his fists so tightly around his glass that his knuckles had turned white. "Hera . . ."

"Hera is welcome to drink with me. I don't care for dancing." Jack took a few deep breaths. He did not tend toward fits of rage. Least of all when someone was only telling the truth.

"And maybe you, too, Charlene." Elaine signaled to her friend to make herself scarce. "Grab Matt and give him a little exercise. And send Tim over when you get a chance. He's been standing at the bar too long."

Jack drank half a bottle of whiskey in silence. First alone, then next to Hera, who sat there waiting. Eventually she took him upstairs, and he fell asleep in her arms.

The next day he forced her to take the money for a full night.

"But nothing even happened," the girl protested. "You should know that much."

Jack shook his head. "More happened than you can imagine."

For the first time in his life, Jack McKenzie paid for a whore.

6

The following evening, Jack was on the platform waiting to board the night train to Christchurch when a tall, slender man approached him.

"Mr. McKenzie? Caleb Biller. We've met, awhile back. I had a few rather interesting conversations with your wife when you were here before."

Jack offered his hand. "Nice to see you again, Mr. Biller. You're aware that Charlotte . . ."

Caleb Biller nodded. "Your wife passed a few years ago. I'm deeply sorry; she was a brilliant researcher."

"Yes," Jack said quietly. He wondered what Biller wanted from him. Surely he had not come to the train station to express his condolences years after Charlotte's death.

"I don't mean to disturb you, Mr. McKenzie, but it would interest me to know how you managed Mrs. McKenzie's estate. The articles of hers that I've read led me to believe that she gathered Maori myths, and then recorded and translated them."

"She wrote down hundreds of them," he said.

Caleb's eyes brightened. "I thought as much. But what interests me is where her records are. Have you offered your spouse's papers to any institute?"

Jack frowned. "Institute? Who would be interested in them?"

"Any of the better universities, Mr. McKenzie. You didn't throw her writings away, did you?" The thought seemed to fill Biller with horror.

Jack no less so.

"Throw them away? What are you thinking, man? After Charlotte poured so much of her heart into them? Naturally I still have them! Perhaps I should . . ." Jack thought guiltily of the many folders filled with Charlotte's clear handwriting. He should have looked through them by now.

Caleb Biller sighed with relief. "I had hoped as much. Mr. McKenzie, as much as I respect your feelings, Charlotte did not undertake research just to have the results sit in a desk drawer. Surely you could appreciate the need to make them available to other researchers and therefore to posterity. Could you bring yourself to do that?"

"If you think someone would want her documents, should I send them to you?" He shouldered his duffel bag. The train was pulling into the station.

Caleb Biller hesitated. "I'm not the best person to talk to," he replied. "It's really something for a, well, a more linguistically oriented researcher. I concentrate on native art and music, you see?"

Jack did see but did not find that very helpful. "Well, Mr. Biller, I have to board now. Tell me what you have in mind."

"In theory, to any university you want."

"Mr. Biller! Which one?"

"How about Wellington? They've recently acquired a professor who . . ." Caleb Biller began, shifting his weight from one foot to the other.

"That's fine, Mr. Biller. Wellington. As soon as I find the time to go through the material, I'll send it off. Is there someone in particular I should address it to?"

Biller suddenly turned red. "It's undoubtedly a great deal of paper. The university might want send someone to look over it himself."

Jack wondered what he was getting himself into. But then he recalled another connection to the Biller family.

"Tell me, didn't your son elope with my grandniece Lilian?"

Biller turned scarlet.

"That young fellow who compares Polynesian dialects or something like that?"

Biller nodded. "My son would be better able to evaluate your wife's records than anyone," he explained.

Jack grinned. "Undoubtedly. And perhaps you could turn it into a family reunion while your son is reviewing the materials."

"I still haven't told Elaine anything. Nor my wife or Timothy Lambert. They don't know anything about the children. In all honesty, the idea hadn't even occurred to me until yesterday when I heard you were here. But it's not just a selfish idea, Mr. McKenzie. Your wife's research . . ."

"I'll write to Wellington. I promise," he said amiably. "As soon as I pull myself together. You understand I have to look through her papers myself first."

Caleb raised his hand in farewell. "Thank you, Mr. McKenzie. I hope you find time soon."

Jack forced himself to smile. Time was not the problem. The problem was in entering the room they had shared, breathing in Charlotte's scent, and touching the things she had touched. But Caleb was right. Charlotte would have wanted it. Jack felt a pain in his chest and suddenly saw the pharaohs' tombs in Egypt. Souls walled up with a plethora of worldly goods, chained to the here and now, far from Hawaiki. Charlotte would have hated that. Jack determined to take on her room the very next day.

Tense and exhausted, Jack finally reached the farm the following afternoon. He drove the car into the garage and decided to enter through the kitchen door, hoping to avoid his mother and get some sleep before dinner. Then he would be better prepared to recount the wedding—and face Gloria. But he spotted Gloria in the corral near the stables with a young collie.

"Sit," she commanded in a slightly impatient voice, tugging on the dog's collar. Nimue, who was waiting outside the corral, took a seat. But the little dog in front of Gloria remained standing, its tail wagging enthusiastically. Jack saw how she was struggling to maintain her composure. To Jack she looked very young—and very attractive.

Jack stepped closer. "You're giving contradictory signals. He doesn't know what he's supposed to do."

"But I can't do more than show him," Gloria replied unhappily. She pressed the puppy's rear to the ground with her hand, but he stood back up as soon as she let go. "I taught Nimue how to do it ages ago. Maybe this one's just dumb."

Jack laughed. "Don't let my mother hear that. A dumb Kiward collie—that would be like a sheep giving birth to a checkered lamb. No, it's just that you've forgotten the technique. Here, watch."

Jack slipped into the corral and greeted the little dog with a friendly pat. Then he took the leash and tugged on it while giving a curt command. The whelp's rear plopped onto the ground.

"Why won't he do that for me?"

"You're making one small mistake," Jack explained. "Right when you give the command and tug on the leash, you bend over. So he comes to meet you, tail wagging. Which is good. It would be much worse if he were afraid of you and wanted to back away. But if he thinks you're flirting with him, he'll want to respond in kind. Now, watch how I do it."

Gloria observed how Jack kept his upper body straight when he gave the whelp the command to sit. The pup raised its head—and plopped down on its rear again.

"Let me try." Gloria imitated Jack's posture, tugged on the leash—and the collie sat. Both Gloria and Jack praised him effusively.

"You see?" Jack smiled. "Not such a dumb dog, just . . ."

"Just a dumb Gloria. I can't do anything right. I think I'm going to give up." Gloria turned away. Normally she would never have let those words escape her, but that day had once more pushed her to her limits. She and Gwyneira had gotten into a tiff that morning over some sheep that had wandered onto tribal land, which had angered Tonga. Fearful of offending Tonga and losing her much-needed Maori workers—since so many of the white shepherds had joined the ANZAC—Gwyneira had taken Tonga's side, infuriating Gloria, who had insisted that Tonga needed to be put in his place and that the workers wouldn't quit, because they needed the money. Gloria had retreated to her room, but she was in no mood to read Jack's letters that day and she wasn't inspired to draw. Finally she had gone out to train the dog—and suffered another defeat. Gloria had had enough and for once she gave voice to it.

"You're not dumb," he said. "You just didn't know the trick. What's wrong with that?"

"Do you know more tricks like that?" Gloria asked reluctantly.

"Hundreds. But today I'm too tired. How about I show you tomorrow?"

Gloria smiled, and it almost took Jack's breath away. He had not seen her smile candidly since his return home. But as her eyes brightened, he saw a glimmer of the trust that Gloria had felt for him as a child—and the admiration.

"All right," she said quietly, "but somewhere where no one will be watching."

Working with Gloria and the collies was a welcome excuse to put off going through Charlotte's papers. Though Jack did not quite understand why they had to work in secret, he heeded Gloria's wish and met her in already grazed sheep paddocks and a few times even in the circle of stone warriors.

"Is it true what you said then?" he asked her as they rode home over the wintery brown grassland. "That there's no *tapu* at all on the land here?"

"Of course. You can read the story yourself. Rongo Rongo says she told it to your wife."

"Yes," Jack said quietly, "Charlotte gathered thousands of stories."

"This one is a few hundred years old, and everyone tells it differently. But there was some duel in the stone circle. Two men with strong *mana* fought over something."

"Over a woman?"

"Rongo Rongo told me about a fish. A talking fish perhaps; I can't recall. Maybe even a spirit in a fish. But it had to do with who would receive the honor for having caught it. It would have made the *mana* of the fisherman even stronger. The whole thing ends bloodily, with both men dying. Their battlefield has been *tapu* ever since. That's not unusual; many holy sites were once theaters of war."

Jack nodded and thought of Gallipoli. It would be a good idea to leave that beach untouched for the rest of time.

"Within the stone circle we're . . . the Maori aren't supposed to eat or drink. It's a place of contemplation and for thinking about the spirits of the ancestors. Strictly speaking, no one should have been allowed to be buried there. But that's how Tonga is—he interprets every *tapu* however it suits him in the moment. Nothing happened outside the stone circle. Whether a few sheep graze there or not is irrelevant to Maori beliefs."

"I take it the Wardens didn't keep sheep there so that they didn't accidentally wander into the stone circle," Jack said.

"That's probably how it started, but regardless of what Tonga says, it wouldn't be sacrilege to simply fence in the stone circle to keep the sheep out. It's true that praying while surrounded by barbed wire isn't particularly attractive, but . . ."

"No one would come here in this weather anyway."

"And it just would be for a few weeks, to spare hay. Which is down to the dregs. Maaka has already asked around on other farms. Unfortunately, no one has anything to sell. I have no idea how she means to solve the problem."

"She's over eighty," Jack said in an effort to excuse his mother. "She doesn't have any more taste for confrontations."

"Then she should give up managing the farm," Gloria said coolly.

Jack bit his lip and tried to suppress his feelings of guilt. His parents had transferred the management of Kiward Station to him years before. When he had lived with Charlotte on the farm, he had been foreman. Gwyneira could have long since retired if he had not gone to fight in that senseless war. Jack thought of Maaka's attempts to hand the farm's management back to him. He should pull himself together and at least look at the books, inspect the hay stores, and then have a word with Gwyneira about Tonga's land claims. But he could not even summon the energy to put Charlotte's affairs in order. Only the hours he spent working with Gloria did not seem to cause him stress. He had even begun to look forward to them.

"Well, the land around the stone circle wouldn't save us either," he said finally. "We'd maybe gain a week or two."

"Jack, the stone circle is just one example. I can show you four or five more pieces of land we don't graze out of consideration for the Maori. Usually it's not necessary, but in most cases the claim is invalid."

"By right and by law it is," Jack replied. "The land was rightfully acquired from the Wardens; even Tonga acknowledged that in the end."

"The claim is invalid in every respect. It's not as though every speck of land on which two Maori youths bloody each other's noses instantly becomes *tapu*. The whole thing is Tonga's invention. He's just playing rather mean games with Grandmum."

"The shearing companies are coming tomorrow," Gwyneira said to Jack and Gloria at dinner. It was now the middle of September, and the weather had improved.

"Already?" Jack asked. "We've never shorn before October in the past."

"We don't have any more hay. We have to herd them early. If the weather holds, the ewes can head to the mountains in the middle of October."

"But that's madness," Gloria said, dropping her fork and glaring at her great-grandmother. "That's much too early. We'll lose half the lambs."

Gwyneira was just about to argue back when Jack made a conciliatory gesture with his hand. "The weather can turn at any moment," he said calmly.

"It can, but it won't," Gwyneira insisted. "After that awful summer and rainy winter, it has to stop raining sometime."

"On the West Coast it rains three hundred days a year," Gloria said angrily.

"It will undoubtedly stop eventually," Jack said. Gloria was right—his mother was about to make an egregious mistake. "But not before spring really begins. And not necessarily right away in the mountains either. Mother, you know what kind of weather they're having now."

"We don't have a choice. The weather has to play along. What about the shearing sheds? Would either of you like to oversee one of them? Number three still isn't taken unless I do it myself."

Gwyneira looked searchingly from one to the other. She would never have admitted it, but she was desperately hoping for help.

Gloria was torn. She was dying to oversee one of the shearing sheds. Having spent her childhood recording the results of the shearers on a blackboard, she knew how to do it, and she was eager to take on the responsibility herself this time. But she knew the men would not make it easy for her.

"I'll do it," Gloria declared, glaring at Gwyneira in warning. She knew that her grandmother had been hoping that Jack would volunteer.

Gwyneira did not appear happy about Gloria's decision and gave Jack several meaningful looks, but he pretended not to notice. He knew he ought to offer to give Gloria a hand. But the thought of the noise—the men's voices, the laughter, and the natural, raucous camaraderie—made him shudder. Maybe next year.

"I need to see to the things in Charlotte's room," he said by way of excuse. "I wrote to that university and . . ."

Gwyneira had learned to handle her son with care. So she simply sighed quietly to herself.

"Very well then, Gloria," she said, "but please be sure to count properly and not to let yourself be influenced by anything. The contest between the shearing sheds has nothing to do with vanity. It only serves to motivate the shearers to work faster. So don't let yourself get carried away."

"And counterfeit the numbers? You can't be serious."

"I'm only giving you advice."

"I won't listen to another word," Gloria yelled, frustrated by Gwyneira's implication that she might not be able to handle the job. "If you think I'm too dumb or too vain to keep a list, then you'll have to do it yourself. Otherwise I'll be at shed three tomorrow at eight."

Gloria created a small scandal by coming to work in breeches. The men from the shearing companies who arrived around midday stared at her in amazement—and were then informed by the shepherds during the first break of all the scandals surrounding Gloria Martyn.

As if that were not enough, Frank Wilkenson was also assigned to shearing shed three. Gloria assumed that Gwyneira had done that on purpose. He was next in line for the position of assistant foreman, and he was probably supposed to keep an eye on her.

In truth, however, Wilkenson was simply there to shear sheep like all the other men from Kiward Station who could be spared and who had command of the technique. It was quite common for the farmworkers to assist the shearing companies, and good shearers from the farms competed with the professionals in the shearing contests. In shed three, Wilkenson and the fastest worker from the shearing company were soon neck and neck. Though Gloria could hardly keep up with noting the results, she felt she had a good grip on the work—until Frank Wilkenson and his men challenged her scoring.

"Come on, Pocahontas, that can't be right. That was sheep two hundred, not one ninety. You miscounted."

Gloria remained calm. "That's Miss Martyn, if you please, Mr. Wilkenson. And the count is correct. Mr. Scheffer has two hundred, and you are ten sheep behind. So you should hurry up and get back to shearing instead of causing trouble."

"I saw it too, though," said Syd Taylor, Wilkenson's friend and favorite drinking buddy. "I was counting along."

"You don't even know how to count, Syd," one of the other men teased him.

"You could hardly count and shear at the same time," Gloria remarked, "but perhaps that's why you only have eighty-five sheep."

"Now don't get fresh, chief's daughter."

Syd Taylor towered over Gloria. She felt for her knife, but knew that was not the right approach. Gloria took a slow, deep breath.

"Mr. Taylor," she said calmly, "that's unacceptable. Get out of here; I'm dismissing you. The rest of you, please keep working."

Gloria sighed with relief when Syd Taylor moved toward the door.

"I won't take this lying down," he said. Gloria thought she had won—until Frank Wilkenson looked up from his work and grinned at his friend. "I have to win this contest first, Syd, but afterward I'll clear this up with Mrs. McKenzie, don't you worry."

Keeping her cool, Gloria reprimanded him once more. She had learned that fits of rage accomplished nothing. But fear gnawed at her the rest of the day.

Her fear proved not unfounded. Frank Wilkenson proved himself to be the fastest shearer not only in shed three, but on Kiward Station.

Gloria saw him in Gwyneira's office when she came home after work, dirty and tired.

"She just tends a bit toward overreaction, and Syd, well, he can't help teasing girls."

Gloria knew she should go in and set things straight. But recalling her last confrontation with Gwyneira over Tonga, she let it go. She crawled into bed.

At dinner Gwyneira revealed that she had rehired Syd Taylor. Gloria stood up without a word and went to her room. After she had cried her eyes out, she sought refuge in her stack of letters. By then she had read most of them. The one she had in her hand was dated August 6, 1915. Jack must have been wounded shortly thereafter. Gloria unfolded the letter.

Today two thousand men died in a feint attack. Only to distract the Turks. Tomorrow it's supposed to get serious. We're to leap out of the trenches and run screaming into enemy fire. The new troops seem to be looking forward to it. Tonight I'll sit with them at the fire and listen as they dream of becoming heroes. I'm beginning to hate this campfire bliss. The men with whom I drink tonight might be dead tomorrow. This battle can't be won.

Gloria knew exactly how Jack had felt. She spent half the night drawing.

7

Jack McKenzie had never fought as fiercely with his mother as he did that night.

"How can you give her oversight over a shed and then undermine her authority? Gloria was probably completely in the right. Syd Taylor is a son of a bitch."

"We all know he's no choirboy," replied Gwyneira, folding her napkin, "but Gloria has to learn to ignore a little teasing. My lands, when I was that young they even made advances on me. They're men, after all. And they've never taken etiquette lessons."

"And what if the story unfolded completely differently? Why is Frank Wilkenson stepping in for the fellow? Did he not maybe have something to do with it? You should at least have listened to Gloria's side of the story. And even if she made the wrong decision, she was in charge of the shed, and her word was law. It's always been that way. Either you trust her or you don't." Jack thought of Gloria's face, which no longer expressed anger—just pure desperation.

"That's just it, Jack. I don't know if I can trust her," Gwyneira replied. "She's so contrary, so angry at the whole world. She doesn't get along on the farm, or with the Maori apparently. Something's not right with the girl."

Jack did not know how he should tell her. In fact, he could not tell her. He would be betraying Gloria if he did. True, she had not told him her story. What he thought he knew had come to him thirdhand. But who was he to say aloud what Gloria could not even bring herself to say?

The next morning Jack rode out to the shearing shed. He had no idea what he could do to help Gloria. After all, it would be no less mortifying if he took over. But he had to do something. When Jack pushed open the door to the shed, he was almost knocked down by the noise of the protesting sheep and the men yelling out their tallies to Gloria, who stood at the board in the middle of the room, looking small and vulnerable. Frank Wilkenson and Syd Taylor were working in the front row.

"Jack." Gloria did not seem to know if she should be happy or annoyed. Had Gwyneira sent Jack here to relieve her of her authority?

Jack smiled weakly. "I wanted to see if I can still do it," he said, loud enough that Wilkenson and the other first-class shearers could hear it. "Would you start a tally for me?"

A few of the older sheepshearers applauded. Jack McKenzie used to be among the best.

Gloria knew that too. She gave him a heartrending smile. "Are you sure?"

Jack nodded. "I don't think I can win. But I'll give it a shot." He took out his shears and looked for a workstation. "We'll see how much I've forgotten."

Jack reached for the first sheep and turned it on its back. Naturally he had forgotten nothing. He had done this ten thousand times. His hands flew over the animal's body. By noon, Jack was worn out, but he was ten sheep ahead of Wilkenson. In the general competition, however, the professional Rob Scheffer had taken the lead.

Jack did not like to leave Gloria alone, but he knew he would fall behind if he continued. His lungs burned, and he was exhausted. So he excused himself by saying he needed to go work on Charlotte's papers.

"And don't give your boss any grief," he said with a sharp look at Wilkenson. "Miss Martyn may be doing this for the first time, but she'll be taking over the farm soon enough. I think she'll tap an extra keg on her first day if you all win."

Gloria gave him a thankful look as he made his exit.

That evening Gloria changed for dinner, though she had no desire to face Gwyneira. Probably she would have defended herself in some way. After Jack had left the shed, Wilkenson had tried once more to challenge Gloria's tallies, but this time the whole shearing company had opposed him. Gloria didn't completely understand why, but Jack's entrance had won her respect.

As she left her room, she was surprised to find Jack waiting for her. It seemed as if his whole body ached: he looked sore after the unaccustomed work, his eyes watered from the dust in the shed, and he was fighting back a cough.

"I'm not used to a good day's work anymore," he joked as Gloria looked him over, concerned. "I hope you're hungry for grilled meat. Oh, and grab a jacket. We're eating with the shearers tonight. Mother's providing mutton, and we're taking a keg of beer. It's time we made our appearance at the fire."

"But you . . ." Gloria did not finish her thought. She may just have been imagining that Jack had been avoiding the society of men since Gallipoli.

Jack took her hand. Gloria was startled but fought back against her aversion. Jack closed his fingers gently around hers. "I'll manage," he said. "And you will too."

Gloria sat at the men's fire, replying to their japes monosyllabically, but that did not stop the sheepshearers from lauding her for donating the keg. The oldest among them still recalled Gloria from when she was a child on the farm, and they teased her about her high-class English boarding school.

"Be nice to the young lady," one advised the younger men. "Otherwise she'll run away again. We didn't think you'd ever come back, Miss Martyn. We thought you'd marry a lord over there and live in a castle."

Gloria actually managed a smile. "What would I do with a castle and no sheep, Mr. Gordon?" she asked. "I'm right where I want to be."

She found herself in rare high spirits when Jack accompanied her back to her room. As she thanked Jack, she pushed her hair out of her eyes in a futile effort to keep it under control.

"You should just cut it off," Jack said, smiling. He did not understand why Gloria suddenly went pale.

"You think I'd look pretty if I . . . ?"

Jack was thinking of the pictures of modern young women with short haircuts and hadn't intended anything by it. But Gloria saw only the faces of all the men who had been excited by her bald head—and made her do things that still made her blood run cold.

"I always think you're pretty," Jack replied, but Gloria didn't hear him. She fled into her room, profoundly horrified, and slammed the door behind her.

Two days passed before she could look at Jack again. Jack, who did not understand, apologized several times. Only later did she realize that he might have been referring to the close-cropped hair she'd had as a child. She chided herself for her stupidity but did not know how to explain herself to Jack. So they simply ignored it and moved on.

The sheepshearing continued without further incident, and shed three won. When the men tried to lift their boss up on their shoulders and carry her once around the shed during the celebrations, she initially panicked, but Jack intervened and diplomatically held his horse's stirrups for her. Rob Scheffer, the overall winner, was permitted to lead Anwyl around the shed while the others sang "For She's a Jolly Good Fellow." Jack watched, relieved, as Gloria laughed along and celebrated with the men.

The euphoria died down once the shearing companies had moved on. It was raining again, and Jack and Gloria stood in front of the naked sheep in their pens. Gwyneira had given directions to herd the sheep into the highlands once this—according to her view, final—patch of bad weather had passed.

"They're so thin," Gloria worried. "They're normally not like that, are they?"

Jack agreed. "They're scrawny. The ewes in particular are giving everything to their lambs. But the situation still isn't dire. After a few weeks in the pastures, they'll be plump again."

"We need to get to the pastures first," muttered Gloria. "It looks like they're freezing."

Jack nodded. "They were already thin, and now they don't have their wool. It was too early for shearing, and it's definitely too early for the highlands. What does Maaka have to say about all this?"

Gloria snorted. "He's only thinking about his wedding. It suits him fine if the sheep are gone. Then he doesn't have to feel guilty about leaving Grandmum alone with the sheep and that unspeakable Wilkenson. That rat is simply after Maaka's job. But she isn't *that* dumb."

"Gloria! Your Grandmum is not dumb."

Gloria raised her eyebrows doubtfully.

"What if we were to herd them out onto the rest of the pastureland on Kiward Station? Without regard to Tonga's *tapu*. Would that improve things?"

"Of course. They'd stay warmer than in the foothills, and we could keep a closer eye on them during lambing."

"Jack, why don't we just make Tonga and Grandmum accept it after the fact? With Nimue and the four little dogs, we could have all the sheep up to the circle of stone warriors and the other pastures before morning."

Jack considered this. "There would be a lot of trouble."

"Jack, think of all the lambs. They'll freeze to death up there. If we let them pick Kiward Station dry first, we'll gain four weeks. The weather will be better by then."

"All right, Glory. We'll do this on our own. We'll herd this group to the empty cow stables near the Maori village first. They can warm up there. And if it doesn't rain tonight, we'll take them out. Go call the dogs."

After slipping out of the house and retrieving the horses from the stables, they were on their way. Gloria found she almost enjoyed riding next to Jack beneath the starry sky. It had cleared up, and they had a little moonlight.

"That's the Southern Cross, do you see it?" Gloria asked, pointing upward. "Miss Bleachum showed it to me once. It helps sailors navigate."

"Did it help you in Australia?" Jack asked quietly. "There were people at Gallipoli from the Outback. They said it was incredibly beautiful but vast and dangerous."

"I didn't think it was beautiful. This is beautiful."

The circle of stone warriors rose up before them, and the dogs were driving the sheep briskly ahead. The ride had hardly taken an hour, and now the ewes spread themselves out, feasting around the stone circle. Jack secured the sacred site with a roll of barbed wire he had brought.

"Do you think Grandpa James's spirit is really here?" Gloria asked, helping him stretch the wire between the monoliths. Though the shadows of the stone warriors looked a little eerie in the moonlight, she was not afraid.

"Of course. Don't you hear him laughing? He would have taken a devilish pleasure in all this. Just now he's recalling how he herded the sheep away from the bog farms at night while the shepherds played cards in their barracks. Regardless of what Mother says tomorrow, James McKenzie would be proud of us."

Gloria smiled. "Hi, Grandpa James," she called into the wind. Jack had to hold himself back from putting his arm around her.

The grass seemed to rustle in reply.

By morning the two of them had distributed some five thousand sheep across various pastures. Jack collapsed dead tired into bed, falling into a deep sleep during which he dreamed of neither Charlotte nor Gallipoli.

Gloria slumbered restlessly. She expected to be pulled out of bed and scolded at any moment, but nothing happened, even though the missing sheep must have stood out to the stockmen that morning.

The workers, however, did not report the missing sheep to Gwyneira right away, turning instead to Maaka. He knocked on Jack's door late that morning.

"I found the sheep," Maaka said, "and I just wanted to tell you that I didn't tell Tonga. I already suggested herding the sheep out there three months ago. Not just to Mrs. McKenzie. I also spoke with Tonga and Rongo Rongo. Rongo didn't have any misgivings, but Tonga was outraged at the idea of even a single sheep nibbling on sanctified grass. You're best off just ignoring him. If you're lucky, he won't notice until I'm gone in a couple of days, and then he won't be able to do anything. He can't herd the beasts back alone, and these *pakeha* fellows are pretty helpless without direction. Wilkenson, of course . . ."

"Wilkenson's only waiting to take over your position," Jack warned.

Maaka grinned. "Again, the last thing Tonga wants. A Maori foreman suits his plans much better. When are you going to come back, Jack? The farm needs you."

Jack frowned. "I'm here, aren't I?"

Maaka shook his head. "Your body is here, but your soul is stuck on two beaches, one on the North Island and the other in that country—I can't even pronounce the name. In any case, either is a bad place for your soul. Just come home, Jack."

In order to distract himself, Jack began looking through Charlotte's things. It was torture opening her drawers, taking out her clothing, and arranging it in boxes for charity. Jack found her letter paper—and a letter to the University of Otago she had begun. As he read it, his eyes filled with tears. Charlotte was offering her research to the linguistics department. Caleb Biller had been right. She had wanted to pass on her records. And she had sensed that she would not be coming back from that trip to the North Island. What she could not have known was that Jack would not organize her papers until years later.

In the furthest corner of her desk, he came upon a packet.

Jack.

Jack read his name in Charlotte's large handwriting. He trembled as he opened it. Out of it fell her small jade pendant. So she had not lost it in the sea. She had set it aside. For him. For the first time Jack looked at it more closely—and realized the jade stone depicted two figures intertwined in one another. Papatuanuku and Ranginui, the earth and the sky before they were torn apart. Jack unfolded the page in which the amulet had been wrapped.

Remember that the sun could not shine until Papa and Rangi separated. Enjoy the sun, Jack.

With love,

Charlotte

That afternoon Jack wept for Charlotte for the last time. Then he opened the window and let the sun in.

8

Gwyneira McKenzie had dozed off over her papers in the office. She had always hated paperwork and could no longer give it the attention it required.

"Mrs. McKenzie?"

Gwyneira shot up from her slumber and found herself face-to-face with a fully armed Maori warrior. Naturally she recognized Tonga as soon as she got a second look, but before she could express her anger, she had to calm her wildly beating heart.

"Tonga? What the devil are you doing here?"

"It's less your devil than the spirits of our dead that led me here," Tonga said with a gravelly voice.

Gwyneira felt an old anger rise up within her. Who did this impertinent brute think he was to break into her house with his clan and scare her to death?

"Whoever led you here, you could easily have waited for Kiri or Moana to announce you. It's sheer impudence to simply to show up here and . . ."

"Mrs. McKenzie, it's an urgent matter."

Gwyneira's eyes flashed.

"What is it then? Did you discover a way to bring the spirits back to life by scaring an old woman?"

Tonga frowned. "Do not mock me. I'm sorry that I woke you."

Gwyneira sat up with a dignified air. "So, what do the spirits say?" she asked impatiently.

"You are flouting our agreement, Mrs. McKenzie. The sheep of Kiward Station are desecrating the sacred sites of the Ngai Tahu."

Gwyneira sighed. "Again? I'm sorry, Tonga, but we don't have enough grass. The animals are hungry, and that makes them resourceful. We can't even patch the fences before the beasts are out again. Where are they hiding this time? We'll send a man to herd them back."

"Mrs. McKenzie, we're not talking about a few dozen sheep. This is about thousands of sheep purposely driven onto our land."

"Your land, Tonga? According to the governor's decree . . ." Gwyneira was exhausted.

"Sacred ground, Mrs. McKenzie. And a promise you've broken. You'll remember that you assured me back then."

Gwyneira nodded. Tonga had asked for a few favors when he had allowed James's burial in the stone circle. Since Kiward Station had pastureland in abundance, Gwyneira had been happy to promise to leave a few more supposed Maori holy sites alone. Over the last few years, however, the number of sites had grown.

"I'm sure it was an oversight, Tonga," she sighed. "Maybe one of the new hires."

"Maybe Gloria Martyn!" thundered Tonga.

"Do you have any proof of that?" She was angry at Tonga, but if Gloria had really defied Gwyneira's explicit instructions . . .

Tonga looked at her coldly. "I am sure that proof can easily be furnished. Just ask around your stables. Surely someone heard or saw something."

Gwyneira glared at him. "I'll ask my great-granddaughter herself. Gloria won't lie to me."

Tonga snorted. "Gloria is not exactly known for her straightforwardness. Her deeds contradict her words. And she has no respect for *mana*."

Gwyneira smiled cruelly. "Did she contradict you? Now I am awfully sorry for you. In front of the whole tribe, as I understand it. Is it true that she did not want to marry your son?"

Tonga straightened himself up to his full height and started to turn around. "The last word on the inheritance of Kiward Station has not yet been spoken. So far Gloria has not chosen a *pakeha* either. Who can say what the future will bring?"

Gwyneira sighed. "Finally, something I can agree to without reservation. Well, let's wait and cease making plans, Tonga. As far as I know, that's what all your spirits would advise. I'll see to the sheep."

She dismissed Tonga. But he did not go before having the last word.

"I hope so, Mrs. McKenzie. Because until the situation is corrected, no man of the Ngai Tahu will be seen on Kiward Station. We'll feed our own stock and cultivate our own fields."

He walked proudly out through the manor house's main entrance.

Gwyneira called for Gloria.

"It doesn't matter what your intentions were or what is or isn't *tapu*," Gwyneira said angrily to Gloria and Jack, who stood before her like children being scolded. "You're not to simply ignore my directions. Tonga appeared here, and I knew nothing about it. What was I supposed to tell him?"

"That in an emergency you had to deviate from a promise given under very different circumstances," Jack explained. "That you're sorry, but it's your right."

"I have not deviated," Gwyneira said with dignity.

"But your great-granddaughter and heiress did. After consultation with the local spiritual authority, if I can put it that way. Rongo Rongo gave her blessing."

"This isn't about Rongo Rongo's blessing but mine," Gwyneira informed him. "Gloria has no authority in these matters. And you've abdicated your position as foreman, Jack! So don't try to give me orders. Tomorrow you'll herd the sheep into the highlands. Or no, actually you two will remain home. Who knows what else you'll think up."

"Are we grounded?" Gloria asked importunately.

"If you want to call it that. You're acting like a child. So don't complain when people treat you like one."

"We should have approached it differently," Jack said as they watched Maaka and the remaining *pakeha* stockmen herd the sheep together and head west. "She's not entirely wrong. We should have acted openly."

Gloria shrugged. "She was wrong. And it doesn't have to do with the sheep or the *tapu* anymore. It went exactly like we planned it. The supposed sacrilege had long since taken place; the land was no longer untouched. And if Tonga had not sent her more workers, well, then we would not have had enough men to herd the sheep from the *tapu* land. Grandmum could have hanged him with his own rope. But she didn't want to do that. She didn't want to hang Tonga but, instead, me."

Gwyneira wondered how everything had derailed. Though she loved Gloria with every fiber of her being, the girl did nothing but fight with her. Gwyneira simply could not bear the hatred in Gloria's eyes.

Gwyneira could not stand it in the house that day. Gloria was ensconced in her room, and Jack was bringing box after box of Charlotte's personal belongings downstairs. Gwyneira thought of the time when Jack and Charlotte had lived there happily, when the house had been full of laughter and the hope for grandchildren. Now there was only sadness and anger. Gwyneira wandered through the deserted stables and sheep pens. The men were all in the highlands; only the handful of *pakeha* that huddled sneeringly around Frank Wilkenson had stayed behind. Fortunately Maaka was still there; he defied his chieftain and appeared for work like he did every day. He had tried once more to make Gwyneira change her mind.

"Mrs. McKenzie, the weather looks fine at the moment, but that could change. It's only the beginning of October. And the sheep are freshly shorn; they won't survive two weeks in the highlands if there's a cold snap. Let Tonga protest. He'll calm down again."

"This isn't about Tonga," Gwyneira repeated. "It's about my authority. I keep my promises, and I expect my directions to be followed. So, be on your way, Maaka, or should I ask Wilkenson to lead the herding?"

So Maaka had shrugged and left. Gwyneira felt more alone than she ever had in her life. She went over to the horses and tossed them some hay. Gloria would have to take over the feeding. Hopefully she would do it. The girl had been smoldering in her room since their last confrontation, but the horses were close to her heart.

Gwyneira scratched Princess, the riding pony, on her forehead, lost in thought. It had all started with her. Gwyneira cursed herself for having ever allowed Gloria to play the wild tomboy on the pony. She was still convinced that that was what had first alerted the Martyns to her failure to raise the girl into a lady. And then her second mistake. Gwyneira remembered Gloria's expression only too well when she had asked about Princess's foal. Jack had promised her that horse. How could Gwyneira have given it to Lilian? Though a new foal would soon be born, Gloria had yet to show the slightest interest.

Gwyneira stroked the horse. "It's all probably my fault," she sighed. "It's not yours, anyway."

She could not know then that just a few days later Princess would spark the next commotion.

The men were back, and it was raining again. A warm, spring rain, but no less irritating for that. The farmworkers stayed in the barns and played cards. Jack was supposedly still seeing to Charlotte's estate, though in all likelihood he was just sitting in the room they had shared and brooding dully.

Gloria tried to stick to a certain routine. If she stayed inside, filling one drawing pad after another with her gloomy pictures, she would go mad. Hence she dutifully trained the dogs and took Ceredwen out on rides. She was just heading out one afternoon when she glanced over at the muddy paddocks and saw that Princess was thrusting out her back and shivering. She called on the first farmworker she came across in the stables. Frank Wilkenson appeared, apparently on his way back from the privy to the circle of card-playing men in the barn.

"Mr. Wilkenson, would you please be so kind as to bring Princess inside and give her some oats? I'm going to give her a blanket; it looks like she's freezing."

Wilkenson grinned disdainfully. "Horses don't freeze, Miss Martyn." He emphasized the "Miss" as if the polite address did not suit the girl. "And we don't have any fodder to spare. It's being rationed."

"Your farm horses and Welsh cobs don't. But Princess is largely Thoroughbred. These horses soak through if it rains long enough. So, please bring the horse inside."

Wilkenson laughed, and Gloria realized that he had been drinking. From the looks of it, the other men who were now looking over at them from the barn weren't sober either.

"And if I do it, Miss Pocahontas? What do I get out of it? Will you come back in a grass skirt?"

Laughing, he reached for Gloria's wet hair and twisted a strand between his fingers.

Gloria felt for her knife, but she'd forgotten to take it out of the pocket of her old leather jacket and stick it in her raincoat. Gloria cursed her lack of foresight. She had just begun to feel safe. A mistake.

"Get your hands off me, Mr. Wilkenson," she said, in as stern and composed a tone as she could—but her voice trembled.

"Oh, and what if I don't? Will you cast a curse on me, my little Maori princess? I can live with that." With lightning speed he clasped her arm. "Come now, Pocahontas, one kiss, and I'll fetch your little pony."

Gloria bit at the man as he laughingly pushed her onto some straw bales. Nimue and the young dogs barked, and Ceredwen pawed the ground anxiously, first with one hoof then the other. The men in the barn hooted.

Suddenly the door was ripped open from the outside. Jack McKenzie stood in the entrance, Princess prancing on a lead rope. For a fraction of a second, he stared at the confusion in the stables. Then he dropped the rope, crossed over to Gloria in two strides, spun Wilkenson around, and landed a perfect right hook.

"You'll get nothing," he said. "You're fired, effective immediately."

Wilkenson seemed briefly to consider striking back. But he held back and grinned.

"Who's to say that the little honey didn't want it?" he asked.

Jack struck again. So quickly that he surprised Wilkenson a second time. Gloria reached instinctively for the knife that hung near the barn door for the purposes of opening the hay bales. A strange gleam filled her eyes. She turned to Wilkenson as he was struggling to his feet.

"Hey, sweetheart, we can talk about this."

Gloria seemed to be miles away. She slowly approached him with knife drawn as if on a sacred mission.

Jack saw the expression in her eyes. It was all too familiar. Men had leaped out of the trenches with that same fanatical yet empty gaze—with no other thought than to kill.

"Gloria, Gloria, this scum isn't worth it. Gloria, put the knife down."

Gloria did not seem to hear Jack. And Jack had to make a decision. Gloria knew how to throw a knife. Jack had watched her practice. He had to stop her. But he didn't want to fall into her hands, nor under any circumstances to be the next man who attacked her or touched her without her permission. Jack stepped between Gloria and Frank Wilkenson.

"Gloria, don't do it. It's Jack. You don't want to do anything to me."

For the length of a heartbeat, he thought she didn't recognize him. But then her eyes made it clear she registered Jack.

"Jack, I . . ." Gloria sank into the hay bales, sobbing.

"Everything's all right," Jack spoke softly, but he still did not dare to touch her.

Instead he turned to Wilkenson.

"Taking your time? Get your ass up, and get off this farm."

Wilkenson did not seem to have fully appreciated the danger. He was still staring angrily at Jack. "If I go, I'll be taking at least three men with me."

He turned to Taylor and his other drinking buddies.

"Do you mean those bastards? Don't even bother. I'm letting them go too, you see. I heard their cheers. Now get out, all of you. Help your fearless leader up and onto his horse. Then away with you."

Jack waited for the men to get up, grumbling.

"Come on, we need to catch Princess," Jack told Gloria. "She's run off."

Gloria trembled.

"I, first I have to unsaddle Ceredwen," she whispered.

"I'll fetch Princess then. Will you be all right alone?"

Gloria grasped the knife and looked at him. Then she said quietly, "I was always alone."

Jack once again fought the urge to take her in his arms. The lost child—and the woman of shame. But Gloria would not want that. Jack did not know what she saw when she looked at him, but he knew that she still didn't trust him.

9

You were brave," Gloria said to Jack on the way back to the house. They were soaked through. Jack was exhausted after bringing all the horses into the stables, feeding them, and caring for the remaining sheep and cattle. And now he had to break it to his mother gently that he had just let go most of her remaining workers. Only a few *pakeha* had not belonged to Wilkenson's clique, and he hoped they would show up for work the next day. Maaka was in Christchurch. Tonga's people were boycotting Kiward Station, and it was raining buckets. Jack did not even want to think about the storms in the foothills. Despite all that, he felt satisfied, almost happy. Walking along beside him, Gloria was quiet but appeared to have relaxed.

"I was at Gallipoli," he reminded her with a crooked smile. "We're heroes."

Gloria shook her head. "I read your letters."

Jack blushed. "But I thought . . ."

"My parents forwarded them to me."

"Oh." Jack no longer remembered every word he'd written, but he knew that he would be embarrassed by a few passages. He'd still thought of Gloria as a child when he'd written them.

"I didn't even send the last letters," Jack said, relieved. Those last letters—from the hospital in Alexandria and then from England—were the worst. Gloria had been missing for months by then, and he had written them to a girl he believed to be dead.

"No?" Gloria asked, astounded. She only had two unopened letters left, which she had put off reading after his last report from Gallipoli. But they had stood out to her because the handwriting on the envelopes was in another hand. Less fluid, rather awkward. Roly must have addressed and stamped and sent them. Gloria was suddenly in a hurry to get to her room. She had to read those letters.

Dearest Gloria,

It's senseless to write you since I know you'll never get this letter. But I cling to the hope that you might still be alive and thinking of me. At least I now know that you thought about all of us, even if in anger. I've since become sure that you never received my letters to you in England. Otherwise you would have called for help. And I, would I have come? I lie here, Gloria, and ask myself what I could have done differently. Would anything have saved Charlotte? Would it have saved you if I had not forgotten one love over another? I wanted to believe that you were just as happy as I was, and in doing so, I betrayed you. And then, after Charlotte's death, I ran away. From myself and from you, into a foreign war. I fought and killed men who did nothing but defend their homeland and, in doing so, I betrayed my homeland.

As I write, I hear the muezzins calling to prayer. Five times a day. The other patients say it's driving them crazy. But for the people here it makes life simpler. "Islam" means "submission." Take things as they come; accept that God does not stick to rules.

She dropped the letter and picked up the next.

England—now I've ended up here, too, and I think of you, Gloria. You saw the sky here, the green of the meadows, the giant trees unknown to us. They say I have consumption, though a few doctors have their doubts. But it's certainly not entirely wrong since I do feel that I'm being consumed, that I want to be, that it might be easier to die than continue living. I now fear nothing more than returning to Kiward Station, into the emptiness after Charlotte's death and your disappearance.

You've been gone so long now, Gloria, and even though my mother won't give up and keeps hoping you'll turn up on Kiward Station, they say that "as far as anyone can tell" you are no longer alive. The police in

San Francisco have given up the search anyway, and none of the detectives my mother and George Greenwood have hired picked up even the smallest lead. Perhaps it's senseless, even stupid to write this letter, almost as if I wanted to reach your ghost. Only the thought that God is taking "as far as anyone can tell" ad absurdum gives me strength.

Gloria held the letters in her lap and cried. More than she had since that night in Sarah Bleachum's arms. Jack had written to her in England. He had always been thinking of her. And he was ashamed too. Perhaps he had done worse things than she had.

Gloria hardly knew what she was doing. As if in a trance she ripped her drawings from her pad and placed them in the last collection of Charlotte McKenzie's notes on the mythology of the Ngai Tahu. Before migrating with the Maori, she had read all of Charlotte's writing, and the last folder still lay on her bookshelf. Jack knew she still had it, so he was sure to go looking for it eventually.

Gwyneira paced fretfully in the salon, listening to the wind and rain outside the window. She dared not think about what it looked like in the highlands. She regretted her decision to have the newly shorn sheep herded out there, but nothing could be done now. She would not be able to find capable men on short notice to bring the sheep back, especially without the help of Frank Wilkenson.

Gwyneira nevertheless cursed herself for not having let him go long ago. Jack had been right to fire him without notice, but she should have recognized herself the way he tormented Gloria. She would never be able to look Gloria in the eye again. Gwyneira poured herself a whiskey and mulled over where she'd gone wrong.

The piercing ring of the telephone interrupted Gwyneira's gloomy thoughts. The operator announced a call from Christchurch, then George Greenwood's voice came on the line.

"Mrs. McKenzie? Actually I wanted to speak with Jack, but could you please just tell him that Charlotte's records need to be ready soon? The expert is coming from Wellington the week after next."

George's voice sounded cheerful. "And guess who he's bringing with him? I don't think much of all this secretive business, so I'll just tell you. The university is sending Ben Biller, and Lilian will accompany him. The boy has no idea about the family connection. Lily is leading him just as blindly as Elaine is Tim."

Gwyneira's mood brightened somewhat. "You mean Lily is coming here? With little—what's his name again?"

"Galahad," George replied. "Strange name. Celtic, right? Well, anyway, yes, she's coming. And most likely Elaine and Tim. So you'll have a full house."

Gwyneira's heart leaped with joy. A full house. A bouncing baby, Elaine and Lilian's teasing. And Lily had always managed to make even Gloria laugh. It would be wonderful. Perhaps she should invite Ruben and Fleurette as well.

"Oh yes, and I have something for you to tell Maaka as well," George continued, though now in a more businesslike tone. "You should send out Wilkenson right away to herd the sheep back. The meteorologists and Maori tribes in the highlands are predicting heavy storms. Why did you even send the sheep out, Mrs. McKenzie? It's so early in the year."

Gwyneira's high spirits were instantly extinguished. She said good-bye to George and drank another whiskey. Then she did what she had to do.

Jack knocked on Gloria's bedroom door. He had not been able to find Charlotte's last folder, and he knew that Gloria had been the only one to look at the notes.

And perhaps Gloria would be amenable to a short conversation. Jack felt lonely after the unpleasant talk with his mother. Gwyneira had appeared understanding, even guilty, about having let Frank

Wilkenson stay on so long, but she also looked old and overwhelmed by the sudden lack of help.

Gloria only opened the door a crack.

"Do you have Charlotte's last folder?" Jack asked gently.

She handed the folder to him through the narrow opening, hardly letting herself be seen. Jack caught only a glimpse of her flushed face. Had she been crying?

"Is something the matter, Gloria?" Jack asked.

She shook her head. "No. Here's the book."

Gloria shut the door before he could ask more. Jack left, shaking his head. He took the book with him to his room, opening it in the light of the new electric lamp.

What he saw made him shiver.

A dark city towering in front of a starless sky. In the gaps between the buildings, the devil laughs—and a ship is leaving harbor. It is flying a flag with a skull and crossbones, but in the place of the skull is a naked girl. A boy is standing on deck, staring at the devil, who appears warlike, sure of victory. Tears flow from the dead eyes of the girl on the flag.

Then a girl in the arms of a man—or is it actually the devil from the previous picture? The artist did not seem able to decide. The man holds the girl tight, possessively, but she does not look at him. The couple is lying on the deck of a ship, and the girl's gaze is directed out to sea—or at an island in the distance. She is not defending herself, but she is also not enjoying the man's company. Jack blushed at the sight of the oversized member stabbing between the girl's legs like a knife.

And another city. Different from the first. Among a sea of low buildings is what looks like a teahouse. The man is drinking with the devil. And between them, prepared like a fish on a platter, lies the girl. Knives lie at the ready beside her. The devil—easy to recognize this time—is pushing money over to the man. This time the girl is not naked, but her short, revealing dress makes her look even more defenseless. Her expression is uncomprehending, frightened.

After that the images reflected naked horror: the girl chained in hell, surrounded by dancing devils plaguing her from every direction. Jack blushed at the sometimes shocking details. Some pictures had been crossed out, while others showed evidence of where the pen had broken through the paper. Jack could feel her rage.

Finally, after a seemingly endless row of harrowing drawings, the girl is lying on a beach. She is sleeping; the ocean lies between her and the devil. But on the other side of the beach new monsters await. The next pictures depicted yet another odyssey through hell. Jack was shocked when he saw the girl's shaved head, which increasingly resembled a skull from one picture to the next. In the last few, the girl's face has been reduced to bones and empty eye sockets. The girl, represented as a skeleton, is wearing a dark outfit with a pale high-necked blouse. She is finally boarding a ship and looking again toward the island that was discernible in the first picture.

Gloria had taken Jack on her journey.

"You're crazy." Gloria's voice was echoing shrilly through the salon when Jack came downstairs the next day.

Gwyneira stood across from Gloria in riding clothes. She had some saddlebags draped over one shoulder.

"She intends to ride into the highlands," Gloria announced when Jack walked in. She was so worked up that she did not even remember the pictures, nor did she take note of his eyes, which were bloodshot from lack of sleep. "Your mother intends to ride into the highlands to bring back the sheep."

Gwyneira looked at the two of them majestically. "Don't call me crazy, Gloria," she said calmly. "I've ridden into the highlands more often than the two of you can count. I know exactly what I'm doing."

"You plan to ride alone?" Jack asked, taken aback. "You want to go into the foothills alone and herd five thousand sheep together?"

"The three remaining *pakeha* shepherds are coming too. And I was at Marama's last night."

"You rode all the way to the Maori village last night and spoke with Marama?" Jack could hardly comprehend it.

Gwyneira glared at him. "Fine, once more: I spoke with Marama, and she's sending her three sons. She doesn't care what Tonga has to say about it. It's possible others will join. I've offered double pay. But I'm going now. I'm taking Ceredwen, Gloria, if that's all right with you. She's the best trained horse we've got."

Jack looked as though he was in a trance. "She's right; you are crazy." He had never spoken to his mother like that before, but Gwyneira's plan was appalling. "You're over eighty years old. You can't lead a herding expedition."

"I must do what I can. I made a mistake; now I'm going to fix it. Snowstorms have been reported, and the sheep have to come back. Since no one else wants to or is able . . ."

"Mother, stop it. *I'll* ride," Jack said. A moment before, he had still felt tired and depressed, but Gwyneira was right: you did what you had to do. And he could not let his parents' life work—and Gloria's inheritance—go down in a snowstorm.

"I'll come too," Gloria said without hesitation. "With the dogs we'll each do the work of three men. And the sheep will be falling over each other to come home."

Jack knew that was not the case. The animals would be disoriented by the bad weather and considerably harder to manage than usual. But Gloria would realize that soon enough herself.

"Are the packhorses saddled?" he asked his mother. "And don't bother arguing. The matter is settled. We'll ride, and you'll prepare everything here. Look for someone in Haldon to help you—you should be able to do that by phone. And make sure you order oats and wheat. The sheep will need to regain their strength after coming through the storm. We'll herd them into the shearing sheds and the old cattle stalls. We'll discuss what happens after that later. Look through the saddlebags, Gloria. Mother, tell her what she needs. A great deal of whiskey, in any case. It will be cold, so the men will need something to warm their insides. I'll go to the stables and see to the men."

Jack had not said so many words in a row since getting wounded, especially not in that tone. Sergeant McKenzie had died at Gallipoli, but Jack McKenzie, foreman of Kiward Station, was suddenly back.

10

Marama's three sons were waiting in front of the stables. Tane, the youngest, had just turned fifteen and was looking forward to the adventure. Two Maori shepherds had joined them, both experienced men with a lot of *mana* who dared to defy Tonga. A third caused Jack to furrow his brow: Wiremu.

"Have you ever worked with sheep?" Jack asked reluctantly. He could not think of a reason to turn Tonga's son away, but he did not know how Gloria would react.

Wiremu shook his head. "Only as a boy. Then I was sent to town. But I can ride. And I think you need all the men you can get." He lowered his head. "I owe it to Gloria."

"Then we'll let Gloria decide. Men, you all know this will be a hard ride, and it's not without danger. We should set out as soon as possible. If we're to believe the warnings, the weather will only be getting worse. So get yourselves a horse."

In the stables Jack met the three remaining *pakeha*, all young, untested boys who barely knew three commands for the dogs. He sighed. He had never ridden out on a herding expedition with such a motley crew before—or on such a dangerous ride. It went against his principles to take young Tane with them. But like Wiremu said, they needed every man they could get.

It was pouring as they rode off, eleven riders and five packhorses. The mountains, normally such an exhilarating backdrop beyond the plains, were barely visible behind the curtain of rain and looked more like ominous shadows.

After moving slowly through a morass of mud all morning, they finally reached more solid ground around midday. Able to make better time, Jack set a brisk pace, while trying not to overtax the horses. That evening they ran into a flock of young rams that were clearly on their way home on their own.

"Clever little fellows," Jack said. "We'll take them with us for now. Tonight we'll stay in the watch station hut at Gabler's Creek. They can graze there. Tomorrow Tane will ride home with them."

As they rode on, he steered his horse alongside Gloria's. He had seen her wince when he had mentioned the hut. "We can set up a tent for you," he said, "or you can sleep in the stables. Though I don't like the idea of leaving you alone there."

"I'd be alone in a tent too," Gloria remarked.

"But my tent would be between your tent and the hut," Jack said. He tried to meet her gaze, but she would not look him in the eye.

Though he dreaded the idea of setting up tents in the rain, like Gloria, he balked at the prospect of sleeping communally in the hut.

"In that case"—Gloria kept her head lowered and spoke quietly—"you could sleep in the stables too."

The hut was a small, solid structure with its own fireplace and alcoves. The men lit a fire in the fireplace as soon as they arrived and offered Gloria one of the beds.

"Miss Martyn would prefer to sleep in the stables," Jack refused for her, "but for the moment please make room at the fireplace, so she can warm up. Who's cooking?"

Wiremu suggested that the men sleep in the stables, and the others reluctantly agreed. But Gloria shook her head. "Then we won't have any room left for the horses. And I don't want any special treatment. If I don't want to share the common sleeping area, that's my business."

That night, Gloria slipped into her sleeping bag and curled up near Ceredwen in the straw, which kept her sufficiently warm. Nimue and two other young dogs curled up against her and would have contributed more warmth if they had not been soaked to the bone themselves. Self-conscious and anxious, she watched Jack spread out his sleeping bag—on the other end of the stables, directly next to the door to the cabin.

He sighed with relief when he heard Gloria's even breathing shortly thereafter. He still remembered how he had listened to it when she was a child. Back then she had often crawled into his bed, telling him about her dreams, especially when she had nightmares. That night Jack was glad she did not want to talk—not yet.

The next morning the weather broke briefly. Tane departed for Kiward Station with the rams, while the rest of the group continued the expedition. They made good time, and by midday they came upon another flock of sheep. After herding them together, they pushed on. It began to storm, and their pace slowed. Toward evening they reached the valley where the men of Kiward Station traditionally pitched their camp. Gloria knew it from migrating with the Maori. It was a caldera covered with grass and bordered on two sides by high cliffs, which made it easier to keep the sheep together. From here they would head out the next day to look for and gather the rest of the sheep.

Although the rocks offered some protection, the wind gusted and flurries of snow began to whip around the men as they struggled to put up their tents. The ice-cold air burned Jack's lungs and made it difficult for him to breathe, and he was damp with sweat under his thick clothes.

"Two ewes are giving birth," Wiremu said, as if there were not already enough to do. He had done a good job of setting up the tent he was sharing with Marama's oldest son. Lambing, however, was beyond him.

Jack fought through the storm to the first animal, while one of the experienced Maori saw to the other. Fortunately, both births went smoothly. They only had to help one of the lambs.

"Let me reach in," Gloria said. "I have smaller hands."

"But you haven't done it in years," Jack yelled over the storm.

"Nor have you," Gloria said. Then she reached into the sheep and pushed the stuck lamb's crooked foreleg into position. With a splash of amniotic fluid, the lamb slid into the world.

"I'll take him in with us, Mr. McKenzie," said the old Maori as he shoved the weakly protesting animal into his tent and out of the wind.

Jack staggered toward the confusion of tarps and poles of which his own tent still consisted. He should have ordered someone to put it up while he cared for the sheep, but by now everyone had retired to their own shelters. Except Gloria. She joined in without a word, but again and again the wind ripped the tarp and ropes from their hands. Jack held the poles tight, wheezing, while Gloria fixed them in the ground. When the tent was finally standing, he let himself fall down on the seat of his pants. Gloria dragged in the sleeping bags and sat down in a corner, completely exhausted. Only then did Jack realize that her own tent still lay in the snow, a mess of tarps and poles.

"I can't build another one," Jack whispered. "We'll have to ask a few of the men."

The workers had long since crawled into their tents. No one would willingly go back out into the storm just to set up Gloria's tent. The girl looked in panic at the narrow space, half of which was taken up by Jack's camping bed. It was not fair. He had promised.

Then she heard how his breathing rattled.

Jack lay with eyes closed on his blanket trying to breathe more steadily, but when the air finally grew a little warmer, he had to fight the urge to cough.

"I'm sorry, Glory. Maybe, maybe later, but . . ."

Gloria knelt next to him when he began to cough. "Wait," she said, rummaging in her saddlebags. Gwyneira had supplied them with some medicine, and she had added to the collection.

Gloria produced a small jar of *kohekohe* syrup. "Take a sip." She put the jar to his lips when he did not respond.

"You have a fever," she said.

"It's just the wind," Jack whispered, but Gloria saw that he was shaking. She opened his sleeping bag, and Jack barely managed to crawl inside. Gloria helped him close the sleeping bag, but even then he did not stop shivering.

"Should I see if the others could somehow make some tea?" she asked.

Jack shook his head. "No fire will burn in this storm. Glory, I, I won't do anything to you; you know that. Just make your bed and try to sleep."

Gloria was indecisive. "What about you?"

"I'll sleep too."

"You need to get those wet clothes off."

He looked at Gloria skeptically.

"It won't bother me," she said. "I know you're not going to do anything to me."

She fished a dry flannel shirt and denim pants out of his saddlebags and kept her back turned while Jack peeled off his wet clothing. He was shivering so violently that he had difficulty pulling on the dry clothes, and the effort caused him to begin coughing again. Gloria crouched in her corner, concerned, and looked over at him.

"You're sick."

Jack shook his head. "Go to sleep, Gloria."

Gloria extinguished the lantern. Jack lay in the dark, trying to warm himself and listening to her breathing. Gloria lay there, tense, listening to his. Jack wheezed and shivered for what seemed like hours. Finally Gloria sat up and scooted over to him.

"You have a fever," she said, "an ague."

He did not respond, but his shivering body spoke for itself. Gloria wrestled with herself. Without a source of warmth, he would not be able to sleep and would be worse off the next day. She knew there was something wrong with his lung. He could die.

"You won't touch me, right?" she asked quietly. "Just don't touch me." Then she opened his sleeping bag with trembling fingers and slipped inside. She nestled up to his slender body to give him warmth. Jack's head sank onto her shoulder, and he finally fell asleep.

Gloria wanted to stay awake, under no circumstances to lose control, but then the labors of the day demanded their tribute from her as well. When she awoke, she was curled up the way she always slept, and Jack had laid his arm around her.

Panicked, Gloria wanted to extricate herself, but then she realized that he was still asleep. And he hadn't grabbed her. His hands were open; his arm seemed merely to form a sort of protective nest. Nimue lay on her other side, Tuesday on his. Gloria almost had to smile. Jack awoke as she carefully removed herself from his embrace.

"Gloria."

Gloria froze. No one had ever spoken her name so gently, so tenderly. She swallowed and cleared her throat.

"Good morning. How, how are you?"

Jack wanted to assure her that he was doing well, but his head hurt and he was fighting back a cough.

Carefully Gloria put her hand on his forehead. It was burning. "You have to rest."

Jack shook his head. "A few thousand sheep are waiting out there," he said, with an effort at cheer, "and it doesn't seem to be snowing anymore."

Some of the men had already started fires outside their tents.

"We should see that we get some hot tea. And then set out as quickly as possible." Jack attempted to stand, but he grew dizzy as he sat up. Breathing heavily, he fell back into bed.

Gloria laid another blanket on him. "You're going to stay right here. I'll handle the sheep."

"And the men?" Jack asked quietly.

Gloria nodded with determination. "And the men."

Without waiting for him to contradict her, she pulled on another sweater and her raincoat and left the tent.

"Everything all right, boys? Restful night?"

Gloria's voice sounded cheerful and confident. If she was afraid, she hid it well. But looking out over the camp gave her strength. The men squatted, frozen, in front of their tents—no one there had any intention of taking advantage of her. Gloria waited for somebody to make an allusion to her and Jack, but the Frank Wilkensons and Syd Taylors of the shepherds were not there, thank God. That gave Gloria the courage to tell the men what she said next.

"We're going to drink our tea and then ride out to herd as many sheep as we can. The weather we had yesterday could return anytime.

Mr. McKenzie is sick, so he has to remain in the tent. Wiremu, I'll need you to look after him."

Wiremu gave Gloria a pained look. "I'm not a doctor."

"You studied medicine for a few semesters and used to help Rongo Rongo. Every summer—she told me. And we can do the herding without you." Gloria cut off any further discussion by immediately turning to the other men. "Paora and Hori, you'll make a team with Willings and Carter and ride through the areas where the sheep usually gather. Anaru, you'll go with Beales. Have you ever been herding before, Anaru? No? But you went on the migration, of course, so you know the area. Let Paora tell you where you're most likely to find big flocks. Rihari, you'll ride with me."

Rihari, Marama's middle son, was a good rider and tracker and had a mutt that had proved its worth on the hunt. "We're going to head further into the mountains for lost sheep. Kuri and Nimue should be able to sniff them out. Paora and Hori—you have your own dogs. Anaru, Willings, Carter, and Beales, each of you take one of the young dogs."

Jack nodded to Gloria appreciatively when she entered the tent with a cup of tea. "I would have given the same orders, Glory," he said softly. "But I wouldn't have sent you alone into the mountains. Are you sure?" He warmed his hands on the hot clay cup.

"I'm not good for anything down below. Neither Rihari nor I know the valleys where the flocks usually are, but if we ride up into the passes, we could save dozens of animals."

"Be careful," Jack said, stroking her hand with his fingers.

Gloria smiled. "And you be good and listen to Wiremu, all right? He won't admit it, but Rongo thinks he'll be a *tohunga*. He's just bitter because it didn't work out at the *pakeha* university. He plays the hunter and trap layer instead of doing what he can and wants to do."

"It doesn't sound like you hate him," Jack said, both teasing and serious.

"If I were to hate all the cowards in the world . . ." Then she left.

Jack lay there, feeling pride and fear for Gloria by turn. The mountain passes were not without their dangers, especially during sudden winter storms. But then Wiremu came over, and Jack hardly found time to think. The young man lit a fire in front of the tent, heated some stones in it, and then laid them around Jack in order to warm him. A short while later he was bathed in sweat. Wiremu applied herbal poultices to his chest and had him inhale their hot vapors.

"A lot of lung tissue was destroyed when your lung was wounded," he said after a brief inspection of the scar. "It's a wonder you survived. The organ can't take in as much oxygen as normal, which is why you tire quickly and don't have much energy."

"What does that mean?" Jack wheezed. "That I should stay at home like a girl?"

Wiremu grinned. "The Warden girls do not tend to stay at home," he observed. "And it's no good for you either. Normal farmwork won't be a problem. But you should avoid heavy physical exertion in weather like yesterday. And you need to eat more. You're too thin."

Wiremu poured him some tea and more of Gloria's *kohekohe* syrup. "No one who sees the hocus-pocus surrounding its harvesting believes it, but it's very effective. Rongo does three dances before she harvests the leaves." Wiremu sounded contemptuous.

"She shows the plants how much they mean," Jack remarked. "What's wrong with that? A lot of *pakeha* say a prayer before they break bread. You must have had to do that in boarding school."

Wiremu grinned again. "*Pakeha* hocus-pocus."

"Wiremu, what did Gloria say?" Jack asked abruptly. "Back then in the *marae*. To Tonga. I saw from a distance that she spoke in anger, but I couldn't hear what it was."

Wiremu blushed. "It was her *pepeha*, her introduction of herself to the tribe. Do you know how that goes?"

"Only vaguely. Something like 'Hi, I'm Jack. My mother came to Aotearoa on the *Dublin*.'"

"Normally you name the canoe on which the ancestors of your father came first," Wiremu corrected him. "But that's not so important. More important is the meaning. With the *pepeha* we remind ourselves of our past because it determines our future. *I nga wa o mua*, you understand?"

Jack sighed. "The words themselves. To understand the concept, you would have had to come to Aotearoa on the first canoe. So what was so awful about the ships on which the Wardens and Martyns traveled here?"

Wiremu repeated Gloria's speech to him.

11

Gloria rode through the mist, hoping either that it would burn off or that the steep path into the mountains would eventually lead her above it. She wondered how Rihari, who was riding ahead of her, could find the way with such confidence. The dogs had herded together a flock of almost fifty sheep, mostly rams that were reluctant to let themselves be herded into the group by Nimue. They had all been going it alone or in small groups. Outcasts and rebels, Gloria thought, and had to laugh.

When they finally emerged from the fog bank, an expansive panorama revealed itself. The snow-covered mountain peaks seemed to float above the clouds, and the horses strode over barely visible fairy bridges between the valleys and chasms. Gloria could hardly get enough of the breathtaking landscape, but she also knew that they had a long descent ahead of them—with many detours in search of more sheep.

"Do you think we'll find more sheep up here?" Gloria asked.

"No. I only rode up this far to check on the weather." His voice sounded strangely hollow. "To check on that." Gloria had been looking south toward Mt. Cook, but Rihari pointed west.

The cloud formation gathering there was likewise a natural spectacle. But instead of getting lost in its beauty, any halfway knowledgeable observer would have trembled at the sight.

"Oh, Rihari, what is that? The next storm? Or is the world coming to an end?" Gloria asked, gazing with horror at an opaque mass of black and gray clouds that flashed ominously with lightning. "Is it coming this way?"

Rihari nodded. "Can't you tell?"

The front had already pressed closer while they talked.

Gloria took up the reins and squared herself. "We have to return to camp and warn the others. If that's as bad as it looks, Rihari, it'll rip our tents away."

Gloria turned Ceredwen and whistled for the dogs. Rihari followed her. The horses were in a hurry to get back to camp and took up a fast pace. Gloria often had to rein in her mare. The danger of slipping and falling into a chasm was too great. Rihari tried to control the sheep but was forced to leave that to the dogs. The animals grew panicked as the storm front advanced. The wind blew the mist away—a bad sign—and then it began to rain.

"Gloria, we can't stay here on the pass. If there's a snowstorm like yesterday, it'll blow the horses right off. We wouldn't even be able to see our hands in front of our faces."

"So where should we go instead?" The wind tore the words from Gloria's mouth.

"There are caves in a valley very near here."

"And why," Gloria asked angrily, "aren't we there? We could have used them as a camp."

"They're *tapu*," Rihari yelled over the wind and lashing rain. "The spirits, but you know Pourewa. Weren't you there with Rongo once?"

Gloria thought for a moment. Suddenly she saw a rock fortress in her mind. A valley surrounded by mountains. A volcano crater or glacier had created a sort of fort there thousands of years ago.

"The spirits will have to prepare for a visit," Gloria declared. "Rihari, where is it?"

Rihari hesitated. He did not seem to want to desecrate the land, but the storm was fast approaching.

Gloria ignored Rihari's indecisiveness. "Lead us there now, and we'll fire off our rifles," she said. "Perhaps the others will figure out to look for us there. We'll light the flares."

Determined, Gloria pulled Ceredwen ahead of the clearly reluctant Rihari and spurred her horse on energetically. As the rain gave way to snowfall, Gloria wrapped her scarf around her face, limiting her vision. She almost rode past the entrance to the crater, but Rihari stopped her.

"Wait," he yelled. "I think it's here."

Gloria peered through the driving snow. It was almost as if the spirits were masking the entrance to their valley, which in summer was hard to miss. Despite his obvious scruples, Rihari steered his horse unerringly toward two rocks, which formed a sort of gateway—the gate to the Pourewa of the spirits.

Gloria did not hesitate. At her whistle the dogs piloted the sheep through the stone gate. When she entered, she was greeted with a sight that enthralled her, just as it had when she'd been here with Rongo. The rocks at the entrance gave way to a small valley formed by steep, soaring cliffs. A poet would have compared the spacious rooms to a cathedral or a knight's hall. But Gloria just saw sufficient shelter for her sheep. People and animals alike would be protected from even the most savage storm here.

Sparse grassland spanned the space between the rocks around a small lake.

Gloria wrestled with herself. She had the perfect shelter—not only for the few dozen animals she had but for everyone, including Jack and his men.

Should she ride down and retrieve the others? That would be best, but she didn't know whether she could manage it before that savage storm unleashed its full fury. Or should she fire off the flares and hope Jack saw them and understood her signal correctly? But what if he interpreted the flares as a call for help? Then he might only send a search team. The group would be separated, and everyone would end up more helpless against the storm. The men must have seen the storm front by now. If Jack had his wits about him, he would have them break camp.

"Do the others know about this place?" Gloria asked.

Rihari tried to nod and shake his head at the same time.

"Wiremu perhaps, but not the others. I only know this valley because I accompanied Rongo Rongo here once. If you herd the sheep here, the spirits will be very angry, Gloria."

"A harmless earth spirit could hardly be angrier than Tawhirimatea is showing herself to be now," she replied. Tawhirimatea was the god of weather. "Listen, Rihari, you wait here and mind the sheep. I'm going to ride down to camp and get the others before the storm gets any worse. I'll take Kuri with me; he'll lead me on the way back if I get lost."

"You won't make it," Rihari said. "You don't even know where it is."

Gloria snorted. "I've always loved to race. And I'll find the camp. On the way back, I'll just ride uphill until I get my bearings. Keep firing off the rifles. That'll help me find the way back. Maybe the others will even meet me halfway. Hopefully Wiremu has enough of a brain to forget *tapu* and lead everyone here."

Rihari chewed his lower lip. "I don't know, I—shouldn't I be the one to ride? I promised Mr. McKenzie to look after you."

Gloria glared at him. "I can look out for myself. And I'm ten times the rider you are."

As if to prove it, Gloria spurred her reluctant mare, making her spin around on her hind legs. Accompanied by Nimue and Kuri, Gloria raced down the mountain at a gallop. She had never been afraid on a horse before, but that day she was rigid with fear. Ceredwen could not be allowed to notice that, though. Gloria relied on the mare's sureness of foot but maintained secure contact with the reins to give the horse as much support and help as possible. Sometimes the animal slipped on the scree, and Gloria felt her heart miss a beat. But Ceredwen always recovered. Nimble as a cat, she leaped over ledges and flung herself around narrow hairpin turns. Further down in the foothills the snow turned to rain; the storm had yet to reach its full strength here. Gloria finally exhaled when, spread out beneath her, she saw the circular valley where they had put up their tents the day before. It was full of sheep. Over the course of the day, the men had herded thousands of them together.

It looked like all of the shepherds had returned; they were hastily taking down the tents. Clearly they had been ordered to hurry. Gloria looked for Jack and finally recognized him at one of the fires. He sat, leaning on his saddle, a blanket around his shoulders, apparently giving directions. Occasionally, he glanced nervously to the west. Gloria bit her lip. He must still be sick if he was making the men work instead of helping them. Hopefully he would be able to ride.

Ceredwen tugged impatiently against the reins, but Gloria made her slow to a walk as they approached the camp. Gloria dismounted and led the mare past the last few sheep. Jack's pale face brightened when he saw her. He stood up with a bit of a struggle and walked toward her.

"Gloria, oh God, Gloria! I wouldn't ride back down until I'd found you." As Jack pulled her into an embrace, Gloria suddenly felt a leaden tiredness. She wanted to fall to the ground, and she longed for Jack's warmth in a tent.

But then she pushed him away. "Not back down," she said breathlessly, "upward and to the west. I know it sounds crazy, but there's a valley."

"But it's *tapu*," Wiremu remarked.

Jack gave him a stern look. "Maori hocus-pocus?" he asked.

Wiremu lowered his eyes.

"I wanted to ride back to the cabin," Jack said indecisively. "I sent Hori and Carter ahead with part of the flock that way around midday."

"Then they should make it before it gets serious. But we won't, Jack. It's a day's ride from here. We'll be at the caves in an hour or two."

Jack reflected a moment. Then he nodded.

"We'll follow Gloria," he said, turning to the men. "Hurry up. We need to be faster than the storm."

"But we'll be riding into it," one of the men objected.

"Then we'll need to ride that much faster."

Wiremu brought Jack his horse.

Gloria turned to him while Jack mounted. "Will he make it?"

"He has to. Whether uphill or down, he can't stay here no matter what. We'll be done for on open ground. That's not just any storm, and it came out of nowhere."

"The fog hid it," Gloria yelled against the wind. "Now come on. I'll ride ahead. The less confident riders should hold on tight. We're going to move fast, and the path is uneven. But not that dangerous except for one or two places."

The newborn lambs were unlikely to be able to keep up with the brisk pace, but they could not make allowances for that now. She tried to take the first few uphill miles at a gallop because the terrain was not yet that difficult, but they did not make progress as rapidly as Gloria had hoped. The horses shied at every little thing, and they did not want to move toward the darkness. All the animals wanted to flee the storm, and the dogs had to work very hard.

The rain first gave way to snow, and then to hail, which pelted their faces like arrows. Gloria looked at Jack and the less experienced riders with concern. The latter were keeping up their courage and clinging fast to the manes of their tolerant horses. Jack, however, looked completely exhausted. Though she was tempted to stop and look after him, she pulled herself together and spurred Ceredwen onward. Jack had to push through it. There was nothing she could do for him until they reached the safety of the valley.

Jack rode doubled over Anwyl's neck, with his scarf wrapped around his face. He fretted over his decision to follow Gloria's suggestion. If the worst of the storm caught up to them before they reached the valley, they would all die.

Gloria was having the same fight with herself. She was getting increasingly worried as the storm raged more violently and they moved forward more slowly. The route that had seemed so short to her on the descent seemed to be dragging on for hours. The riders' coats were long since covered with snow and ice, but Gloria did not have time to think about the cold. She was working feverishly to find the right path despite the limited visibility. Kuri, however, seemed to know where he was and, more importantly, where he wanted to go. Gloria clung to the leash that prevented the dog from running off.

Suddenly a rifle shot sounded over the roar of the storm. The men behind Gloria gave a yell. They spotted a weak flash of light behind the curtain of snow. Rihari was firing the flare rounds. They were close.

"There it is," Gloria screamed against the storm. "Do you see those rocks? Ride along them, and there'll be an opening."

Kuri was barking; she dropped his leash, and the dog ran to his master. The men and their animals pressed into the valley.

Rihari had thought of Gloria and the men, chilled to the bone from herding, and Jack. He had gathered brushwood and dry grass that the wind had blown under the rocks and even broke the last *tapu* and slaughtered a sheep, an old ram that would probably not have survived the trek anyway. Its meat was roasting over the fire as the exhausted men arrived. Jack slipped from his horse and gratefully accepted a cup of tea.

With an iron will, Gloria held out in the storm until the last sheep had crossed through the stone gate. Only then did she ride into the valley herself. The caves were warm and almost completely sheltered from the wind. Gloria risked a head count while she warmed her frozen hands on a cup of tea, which had been reserved from the first pot—for "the boss," as they all now called her.

"Is it bad?" Jack asked quietly. Wiremu had unsaddled his horse, and Jack now sat at the fire leaning against the saddle on the ground.

Gloria pursed her lips. "We didn't lose as many lambs as I thought. Probably because the horses were moving so slowly. But still, it will be a poor year to have been born. At this point we have no more than two-thirds of the mature animals. The rest are out in the storm. We'll see how many survive. How are you?"

"Good." Though Jack's lungs burned with every breath and he was frozen to the bone, his reply sounded honest. During the last few hours he had not thought he would survive the storm. He had only ordered the descent to the cabin in the hope that the men might reach the calmer land below before the worst of the storm hit. But Jack would not have ridden with them anyway. Not without Gloria. Now he felt profound gratitude.

Wiremu brought him and Gloria meat and fresh tea, which he had spiked with a generous shot of whiskey. The men sat at their own fire, drinking it straight from the bottle and toasting their "boss." They also raised their glasses to Rihari—and to spirits, as they got more drunk.

"They should put up the tents before they're too drunk," Gloria said. She had retreated to be near Jack, who sat near a smaller fire. "Will we be able to get the stakes in the ground? Or is it stone?"

Wiremu sat down with his meat next to the two of them.

"You can't eat anything here," Gloria reminded him spitefully.

Wiremu smiled. "I eat where I want. I'm leaving the tribe, Gloria. I'm going back to Dunedin."

"To continue your studies?" Gloria asked. "Despite . . ." She pointed to her face as if tracing invisible *moko*, the designs painted onto the skin.

Wiremu nodded. "I don't belong here or there, but I like it better there. I'll reformulate my *pepeha*." He looked at her. "I am Wiremu, and my *maunga* is the University of Otago in Dunedin. My ancestors came to Aotearoa on the *Uruau*, and now I cross the land on the bus. In my skin the history of my people is written, but my story, I will write myself."

Wiremu set up Jack's tent and helped him inside. He had heated stones again to warm him, and after a new herbal poultice, Jack's breathing became more regular. Wiremu accompanied Gloria on a final inspection of the animals. It took a while as three sheep lambed. One ewe didn't survive.

Jack awoke as Gloria slipped into the sleeping bag next to him. This time she was the one trembling with cold. Jack would have liked to pull her close to him, but scrupulously avoided touching her.

"Was there no one to put up your tent?" he asked.

"Wiremu is sharing it with two abandoned lambs. He's going to be a good doctor someday. But I don't think he'll be specializing in birthing. When the ewe died, his face turned green."

"So we lost another sheep?" Jack asked.

Gloria sighed. "We'll lose a few more. But not all of them by a long shot. It's a hardy breed."

"Not just the animals," he said softly.

Gloria curled up, once again with her back to him.

"You looked at the pictures?" she asked quietly.

Jack nodded, but then remembered that she could not see him. "Yes. But I already knew."

"You, how? How could you know?" Gloria turned around. In the glow of the lantern Jack saw that first she blushed, then turned deathly pale. "Can you tell just by looking at me?"

Jack shook his head. He could not help himself; he raised his hand and stroked the hair from her face.

"Elaine," he said. "Elaine knew. Or rather, she had a feeling. She couldn't have known the details, of course. But she said that no girl in the world could have done it any other way."

"She didn't"—Gloria wrestled for the words—"sell herself."

Jack arched his eyebrows. "If I understood her correctly, she only owes her virtue to the circumstance that the local madam was looking for a pianist more than another prostitute. If you had been given the choice, you would have taken the piano too."

"No one would have wanted to hear that," Gloria whispered in a moment of gallows humor.

Jack laughed, and then dared to put a hand on her shoulder. Gloria did not protest.

"Grandmum?" she asked breathlessly.

Jack stroked her reassuringly. He could feel her bony shoulder under her thick pullover. Another person who needed to eat more. "My mother doesn't need to know everything. She believes the story about you making it as a cabin boy. That's better for her."

"She'd hate me if she knew."

"No, she wouldn't. She wanted more than anyone else for you to come back. She'd save her hate for the bastards who did that to you. And for Kura-maro-tini."

"I'm so ashamed."

"I'm ashamed too," Jack said. "But I have much more reason to be. I occupied a foreign beach, disfigured it with ugly trenches, and beat its rightful owners to death with a shovel. That's much worse."

"You had orders."

"You too," Jack said. "Your parents wanted you to stay in America. Against your will. Saying no was the right thing. You can look in the mirror, Gloria. I can't."

"But the Turks shot at you," Gloria said. "You didn't have a choice."

"I could have stayed on Kiward Station counting sheep."

"I could have stayed in San Francisco ironing my mother's clothes."

Jack smiled. "You need to get some sleep. May I put my arms around you?"

That night Gloria leaned her head on Jack's shoulder. When she awoke, he kissed her.

12

Timothy Lambert avoided the train whenever he could. Even in first class, the compartments were so narrow that he could not sit comfortably after he removed his leg splints. And though the train passed through gorgeous landscapes, the jolty ride through mountains and valleys caused him excruciating pain.

George Greenwood, however, had not backed down. For whatever reason, the people from the University of Wellington who wanted to introduce some groundbreaking innovations in mining to them insisted on meeting in Christchurch.

Tim shifted his weight for the umpteenth time and looked over at his wife. Elaine would not hear of his going without her. If they were going to be in Christchurch anyway, she had argued, they could also visit her family on Kiward Station. She looked particularly attractive that day. A simple visit to her grandmother's seemed to bring her to life. Her eyes were shining, and her face was slightly flushed. She'd made a real effort. Her red locks were tied into a new coiffure. Her green dress hugged her still slender figure, and her skirt was shorter than usual.

She noticed his gaze and smiled. As if to entice him, she pulled her skirt a little higher, though not without making sure that Roly was fast asleep in the opposite corner of the compartment.

This little bit of flirting had a considerable enlivening effect on Tim, and Elaine sighed with relief. She had observed with concern as he shifted around in a desperate search to get comfortable. She was glad when the train reached Arthur's Pass, and the passengers could get out and stretch their legs. Tim only managed with Roly's help, a sign that he was doing really poorly. The opportunity to stand up and walk a bit seemed to provide him some relief, however, and Elaine smiled when he put his arm around her and admired the mountain vista. Though the weather was clear, dark clouds were gathering behind the steep mountain massifs, making the snow-covered peaks glow almost unnaturally, and the air seemed electrically charged. The calm before the storm.

Just then, Elaine saw Caleb Biller approaching them. His presence was no surprise to her—but could he not have stayed in his compartment? It was a childish thought. Even Tim felt no enmity toward Caleb. After exchanging a few friendly words about the weather, the group reboarded the train. Caleb came to sit with them, and bored them with tales of Maori musical research until the train finally pulled in to Christchurch. George Greenwood was standing on the platform with his wife, Elizabeth, who was enthusiastically rocking a toddler in her arms.

Tim frowned when Elaine leaped up so quickly after the train came to a halt that she knocked his crutches to the floor. She was among the first off the train. Even Caleb stared eagerly at the platform and looked impatient to get off.

"Which of the Greenwoods still has such young children?" Tim asked grumpily as he left the compartment. Roly shrugged.

Elaine descended nimbly from the train and greeted George with a few words. Then she turned to Elizabeth and the baby. A red-haired little boy.

Tim did not know what to make of it. Elaine was a good mother, but she had never shown much interest in strangers' babies.

"Hi, George," Tim said, giving Greenwood his hand. "What sort of progeny do you have here? Elaine's crazy about him." Tim took a closer look. "Almost looks a little like her."

George grinned. "Actually, I think he looks more like you."

Tim furrowed his brow. But it was true. The little boy had his angular face and a decidedly dimpled smile.

"He certainly didn't get anything from Florence." That was Caleb Biller, and he sounded very pleased. The inkling that had been budding within Tim crystallized.

"George," he said severely. "Tell me the truth. There are no researchers from Wellington. This is a conspiracy. And this is . . ."

"Galahad," Elizabeth purred. "Say hello to your grandpa, Gal."

The boy looked indecisively from one person to another. Then he smiled at Roly, who was making a face.

Tim suddenly found it difficult to maintain his balance.

"There is a researcher from Wellington," George said. "You know I would never lie to you. He even knows a little bit about mining, if you count the mining of *pounamu* at Te Tai Poutini, whose history and reverberations in Maori myths he presented to me in a long, impressive dissertation over breakfast this morning."

Elaine suppressed a giggle, to which Galahad responded with a chortle. Elaine took him from Elizabeth.

"Oh yes, there's even a *haka* . . ." Caleb seemed to want to add a thing or two to his son's presentation. But then he recalled his duties as a grandfather. He produced a tiny *putatara* from his pocket and held it out to Galahad. "It's made from conch shell," he explained to the boy, "from a variety found on the beaches of the East Coast. The bigger the shell, the deeper the sound."

"Caleb," Elaine sighed. "Just blow into it."

All of the adults covered their ears, but the boy squealed with delight when Caleb drew a piercing note from the instrument.

Tim suddenly felt like an idiot. He needed to give the child a present. Just then, Roly pressed a toy train into his hand.

"You?" Tim was about to scold Roly, but Roly merely pointed at Elaine, who was lost in play with the baby. Tim wanted to be mad at her but could do nothing but grin broadly at her. When Galahad discovered the train, he let out a sound of rapture.

Elaine gave Tim an apologetic look, but Tim did not want to discuss Elaine's secret plot just then.

"Fine, fine," he grumbled. "Where's Lilian? And how did the child get a name like Galahad?"

Elaine and Lilian, like Caleb and Ben, could hardly leave each other's side. While mother and daughter chatted endlessly about life on the North Island, father and son discussed the visual representation of myths in Maori art. They almost came to blows over whether the representation of Papa and Rangi in the natives' jade and wood carvings should be called "static" or not. Tim conversed a bit stiffly with George and Elizabeth, sipped some whiskey for his pain, and finally went to bed, taking with him Lilian's latest novel—*The Beauty of Westport*. A half hour later Roly brought him the rest of the bottle.

"Mrs. Lambert will be coming a little later. She's taking Lily home and is helping put Gila—Galo—er, the baby to bed." The Greenwoods had placed their guest room at the Lamberts' disposal; the Billers were staying at a nearby hotel. "But she says you could use the rest of this bottle, and that you should look at the funny side of all this."

Tim gave him a pained look. "Go to bed, Roly. We have a big day ahead of us tomorrow. You're going to help me bend my daughter over my knee."

"I'd love to keep you here, of course," George Greenwood said during breakfast. "But it's better that you drive to Kiward Station today. I'm worried about Gwyneira; she was rather beside herself on the telephone earlier. If I understood rightly, she's completely alone on the farm except for a Maori boy who's helping her with the animals. Jack and Gloria are in the highlands trying to herd the sheep. In that storm. Your grandmother is terribly worried. And not without reason; they're expecting the very worst kind of weather."

Tim and Elaine nodded. They had feared as much when they had seen the dark clouds and strange light at Arthur's Pass. But what were Kiward Station's sheep doing in the mountains so early in the summer?

Lilian did not say anything. She hid behind the strands of hair that had stolen out of her very adult-looking chignon. Tim had brought her book downstairs that morning and placed it next to his plate with a telling expression. Lilian turned red as a tomato. She was not exactly hoping for a catastrophe to distract him from her book, but she was not opposed.

"We can talk about it in the car," Tim remarked sternly. "You'd better consider how to explain what you were thinking. George, can you lend us a car, or can we rent one? A large one, if possible. I need a little legroom."

After the train ride, his legs still hurt, and he would have liked to lie down in bed with another of Lilian's books. Naturally it was trash—and moreover a scandal exposing the Lamberts' family history—but nothing had ever so completely distracted him from his pain before.

George nodded. "Come with me, Roly. We have several company cars."

Lilian saw her chance. "No, I'll drive. Oh, please, Uncle George. I've always chauffeured my daddy."

Elaine sighed. "Act like a lady now and then, Lily, and don't steal Roly's work."

"But I'm much faster," she declared. "Roly won't feel unnecessary, will you?" She gave Roly a pleading look, which, as expected, left him wrapped around her little finger.

"Of course not, Mrs. Biller," replied Roly. "I'll keep an eye on the baby. What's his name again?"

When the travelers reached Kiward Station, Gwyneira hardly noticed her great-great-grandson. For the first time in all her years there, she was completely undone.

"They're going to die up there," she repeated again and again, "and it's all my fault."

Elaine saw to it that Moana and Kiri made tea for everyone. They seemed to be in a similar state of unrest, muttering something about a fight between Marama, Rongo Rongo, and Tonga that was shaking up their world as much as the storm was Gwyneira's.

Moana muttered, "Marama say, if die Glory and Jack, then Tonga's fault, and Rongo say spirits would be angry."

"No one's dead yet," Tim said, as Elaine poured him some tea. "And if my eyes were working properly in the car, the first sheep are back, aren't they?"

Gwyneira nodded. Tane had indeed come home safe and sound with the young rams. The animals had already broken out again, however. The paddock into which Tane had driven them was not very secure.

"If someone tells me where the tools are, I can repair that," Roly said, wanting to make himself useful.

"Mostly it has to do with the lack of fodder," Gwyneira said. "Nothing's left in the paddocks, and if we herd them to the last grassy areas . . ."

Tim and Elaine listened to her story with a frown and tried to comprehend the confusion around the promise, *tapu*, and spirits.

"One minute, do I understand this correctly?" Tim finally asked. "This circle of stones does belong to your land, right? But in exchange for permission to bury Grandpa James, the chief demanded the right to exclusive use of other land that did not belong to him either?"

"They don't actually use it," Gwyneira said.

"And what is all this about *mana*?"

"*Mana* denotes a man's influence within his tribe. But there are spiritual aspects as well. You increase it by . . ." Ben set himself up for a longer lecture.

"Extorting an old woman, among other things," Tim stated. "Seriously, though, that's what this is about. The man wants to impress his people by controlling the local *pakeha* and exerting influence on the land use and labor market. You need to put a stop to it. Herd those sheep where the grass is growing, and if he gets worked up about it, we'll just have to give his *mana* a jolt. It would be interesting to see what kind of effect it had on the spirit world if you threatened to drive his people entirely from your land. Tell him you'll tear down the village by the lake."

Gwyneira looked at him, horrified. "People have been living there for hundreds of years."

"And the coal in Greymouth has been lying under the ground for thousands of years. But I'm hauling it out. And so far no spirit has gotten worked up about it."

"Now, don't exaggerate," Elaine chided him. "Besides, the sheep have just been shorn, and it's storming outside. Do you really not have any more hay?"

"Just what's left for the horses. Jack thinks I should order concentrated feed. But the seller is located in Christchurch and doesn't want to deliver it."

"What? Where's the telephone?" Tim asked.

He came back a few minutes later, snorting with rage. "The rat tells me that he can't come before next week because of the weather! As if it's never rained here before. I told him we'll send a wagon and get the feed ourselves. Can we assign a man to that?"

Gwyneira shook her head. "We don't have anyone here except for Tane. And we couldn't possibly send him to Christchurch alone."

"Then I'll drive," Lilian offered. "Do you have a covered wagon? We have to cover the feed. What horse should I yoke? Naturally a car would be better."

"Take Ben with you," Tim ordered, "even if unloading sacks isn't exactly your specialty."

"You're wrong there, sir." Ben grinned at him, rolling up his sleeves and showing his considerable biceps. "Before Lilian began writing her, er, books, I worked nights on the docks."

For the first time Tim felt respect for his son-in-law. Until then he would never have believed Ben capable of supporting his family with the sweat of his brow. Ben was not Caleb. His son-in-law was a man.

"If Ben would like to go and Gwyneira doesn't have anything against it, you can pick up his father afterward," Tim grumbled conciliatorily. "If Caleb sits alone in Christchurch, he won't see any of his grandson."

Gwyneira's spirits rose as she accompanied Lilian and Ben to the stables and pointed out a cob team and a box wagon. Elaine joined them and immediately began organizing the stables.

"These need to be cleaned out. Tane can do that. Or do you need him for repairing the fence, Roly? Oh, you know what? Forget the fence. We'll drive the sheep into a shearing shed. And the other sheds should also be prepared since Jack and Gloria are bringing back loads more sheep."

Elaine borrowed an old-fashioned riding dress and a waxed jacket from Gwyneira, and by the time she had locked the rams in the first shearing shed with Tane's help, she was soaked to the bone.

"Is it worth riding after Jack and Gloria? What do you think?" she asked Tim while she crouched shivering in front of the fireplace. Tim had just been on the phone with George Greenwood, who was going to provide an extra delivery wagon. The delivery team would remain at the farm temporarily to help care for the animals.

"We won't get the sheep down here before the storm strikes. But maybe someone could warn them?"

"It could hardly be done in time," said Gwyneira. "Normally it's a two-day ride. Well, a very fast horse with a good rider could perhaps do it in a day."

"Impossible, it's got to be snowing already up there," remarked Tim. "And where would the rider look? They could be anywhere."

"I know where they are. I . . ." Gwyneira made a motion to rise.

"You stay where you are," Elaine commanded. "Don't get any dumb ideas. It looks like we'll just have to wait and trust Jack's experience with the mountains and the weather."

Gwyneira sighed. "You can't really count on Jack much anymore."

Roly O'Brien, who was likewise warming himself on the fire after spending the entire day straightening up the stables, glared at her. "You can always count on Sergeant McKenzie. If he has to, he'd bring your sheep back from the gates of hell."

Gwyneira looked irritated for a moment. But then she looked the young man over closely.

"So you're the Roly I've heard about," she said finally. "You were there with Jack. Would you tell me about the war, Mr. O'Brien?"

Roly had never spoken in such detail about Gallipoli before, and it was not only thanks to the excellent whiskey with which Gwyneira loosened his tongue but also her animated sympathy. The old lady with the tired eyes listened in silence, but the longer Roly spoke, the more life came into her gaze, and the more they reflected her sorrow and horror.

The delivery truck with the feed arrived the next morning, and everyone went straight to work getting things ready for the herd's arrival. There was more than enough work to keep everyone distracted all day, but the mood on Kiward Station that evening was palpably depressed. With the storm now raging over the Canterbury Plains too, everyone's thoughts were on what was happening in the mountains. Lilian tried to distract Gwyneira with Galahad, but the baby was tired and fussy. In the end she took the infant to bed and joined her parents in silence. The only ones engaged in any kind of enthusiastic conversation were Ben and Caleb.

"It will be very helpful to be able to consult Mrs. McKenzie's records," Caleb remarked, once more praising Charlotte's contributions.

Gwyneira, happy to be able to do something useful, stood up.

"My son has laid out her things. If you'd like, I can go get them."

She did not normally enter her son's room without asking, but she had seen Charlotte's folders on his desk. And if her worst fears came to pass, she would soon have to clean up this room anyway. She took a deep breath as she stepped inside, inhaling the same air he had breathed, and was suddenly dizzy. She sat down on Jack's bed and pressed her face into his pillow. Her son. She had not understood him. She had not grasped any of it. In her heart she had believed him a coward. And now he might never come back to her.

Finally she collected herself and reached for the folders. One lay next to the rest of the stack. When Gwyneira picked it up, a pile of pictures fluttered to the floor. Gwyneira sighed, turned the light on, and began gathering the pictures together. She was startled when a skull grinned back at her.

Gwyneira had spent the night before in Gallipoli.

Tonight she would be traveling on the *Mary Lou* and the *Niobe.*

By the next day the storm had abated, but it was still freezing. Elaine and Lilian shivered as they saw to the sheep and horses. Roly and Ben and the new helpers were just carrying a load of water when a veritable torrent of wet, freezing sheep descended onto the farm. Hori and Carter had arrived with the first flock. They had suffered only a few losses and even reached the watch hut before the storm.

"We thought the wind would blow it away, but it's still standing," Carter reported. "Have you gotten any word from Mr. McKenzie or Miss Martyn?"

"You didn't ride back up to look for them when the storm subsided?" Elaine asked severely.

Hori shook his head. "If anyone is still alive up there, Mrs. Biller, he, or she, will manage without us. And if no one is still alive, at least we managed to save these sheep."

Like most Maori, he thought practically.

Elaine went in search of her grandmother to give her the news about the sheep. The night before, Gwyneira had been pale as death when she'd returned to the salon and silently handed the folders to the Billers. After that she had gone to bed and had not appeared that morning. But Elaine found her grandmother sitting by the fireplace. She was playing with Galahad, but it was obvious that her thoughts were elsewhere. She looked like she had aged several years.

"The men brought back two thousand sheep, eight hundred of them with lambs. The lambs that were born yesterday have mostly been lost. They couldn't survive the snowstorm. But a lot of them are giving birth today, and Jamie is truly working miracles."

"Who is Jamie?" Gwyneira asked absently.

"The new shepherd Lilian hired. And four or five more Maori have come. Tim had a few harsh words for them over the business with Tonga. Told them if they pulled that again, they wouldn't be hired back," Elaine continued her report.

Gwyneira sensed that the farm was slipping away from her. It was not a bad feeling.

13

Gloria did not return Jack's kiss, nor did she pull away. Before she lowered her eyes, she looked at him in surprise and confusion.

A thin layer of snow lay in front of the tent. Even far under the rocky roof, the wind had blown snow inside, and it was so cold that it did not melt. Snow blanketed the valley between the rocks, but the pond had not frozen. It was a sickly blue, reflecting the blue-gray sky. A few dirty gray sheep drank from it, standing in snow soiled with dung. Most of the animals seemed to have survived, and the lambs bleated out of the next tent. Unhappy, but very much alive. Curses could be heard from outside. Wiremu and Paora had seized one of the ewes and were now trying to milk the half-wild animal for the orphaned sheep while it protested violently. Other men were busy relighting the fire. Rihari was bringing water in from the pond.

Jack had hoped he would be able to ride again that day, but after the forced ride the day before, it was hopeless. He still had a fever and was fighting dizziness as Wiremu helped him to the fire. He squatted, exhausted, and tried to make sensible plans for the day.

"Well, what do you all think? Shall we ride back and bring ourselves and the animals to safety, or should we try and find the rest of the sheep?"

"You can't ride, Mr. McKenzie," Willings said. "You could barely hold on to your horse yesterday. You need to stay here until you're doing better."

"It's not about me," Jack retorted gruffly.

"We'll gather the rest of the sheep," Gloria decided. "Assuming that a few survived. The beasts spend every summer up here. They probably know all kinds of shelters like this one."

"But we should send someone to Kiward Station," Paora responded. "Mrs. McKenzie will be beside herself with worry."

"I can't spare anyone for that," she said impatiently. "The sheep have to be found quickly now and herded back. For the flock here, the grass in the valley will be enough until tomorrow. They can brush the snow away. Besides, they need to recover after that storm. Then a team can descend with them tomorrow while we gather the rest of the animals and follow the next day, weather permitting. What do you think, Rihari?"

The Maori pathfinder and weather watcher looked searchingly at the overcast sky. "I believe Tawhirimatea's anger has dissipated. It looks like rain, maybe a bit more snow, but the storm seems to have passed."

"We'll move camp again. Early tomorrow," Gloria said, looking around the rock-walled valley. "And by next summer, when the *tohunga* come to speak with the spirits, the grass will have grown back and the valley should look as it always has."

Gloria did not say whether this decision was out of respect for the *tapu* or whether she simply did not want to anger Rongo. She wondered a little at the fact that no one challenged her, but the magic of the hidden sanctuary had touched the soul of even the last *pakeha*.

That evening Gloria slipped quite naturally into Jack's tent and crawled into his sleeping bag. She lay next to him without looking at him. He felt her body stiffen, but he did not mention it; just as she had not said a word about the kiss that morning. They exchanged a few forced remarks about the sheep—Gloria and the men had tracked down almost a thousand animals that day. Jack kissed Gloria gently on the forehead.

"I'm proud of you," he said. "Sleep tight, my Gloria." He wished more than anything to take her in his arms and break through her defenses, but that would be a mistake. And Jack did not want to make any more mistakes. Not with the woman he loved.

He forced himself to turn his back to Gloria and fell asleep while waiting in vain for her to relax. When he awoke, he felt her warmth. She had snuggled against him, her breasts against his back, her head leaning on his shoulder. Her arm lay over him as if she wanted to hold him tight. Jack waited until she woke up. Then he kissed her again.

That morning Gloria sent Paora, Willings, and Rihari on to the watch hut with most of the flock. Jack was still not strong enough to be very useful, but, with Tuesday's help, he managed to keep the remaining sheep together while Gloria, Wiremu, and two of the Maori shepherds searched through the highlands once more for lost sheep. Wiremu enjoyed a surprising success that afternoon. In a hidden valley he discovered what they thought were the remaining sheep, about six hundred ewes in all. Many of them had lost their lambs, but almost all of the valuable adults had survived.

Gloria was overjoyed, and when she sat at the fire that evening, she nestled lightly against Jack. In the tent she allowed him to kiss her again, but lay stiffly on her back. This time Jack did not turn away, but he still did not touch her. In truth, he did not really know what to do. He detected no fear from Gloria's tense body, just acquiescence to the seemingly inevitable. Jack found it almost unbearable. He could have worked around fear, but the surrender appeared to be a desperate form of self-preservation.

"I don't want to do anything you don't, Gloria," he said.

"I do want to," she whispered. To his horror, it sounded almost apathetic. Jack shook his head. Then he kissed her temples.

"Good night, my Gloria."

It did not take as long for her to relax that night, and he felt her warmth on his back as he fell asleep. The next morning they would ride to Kiward Station. It would probably go no further between them right away. But Jack could be patient.

The next day Maaka arrived first. The young foreman had decided that the rest of his wedding celebrations could wait. Instead of welcoming his beautiful young bride formally into his tribe's *marae*, they spent their first night at Kiward Station in the manor, where it was more crowded than it had been for many years.

Tim Lambert was relieved at Maaka's arrival, having come to fear that his adventurous wife and his even more impetuous daughter might plan a rescue operation for the missing shepherds in the highlands on their own.

As soon as he had an opportunity, he took Maaka aside.

"Now, tell me honestly," he asked, "is it possible that someone is still alive up there?"

"Absolutely, sir. There are any number of caves, valleys, and even isolated woods that offer shelter. As long as they weren't surprised by the storm and they know the area."

"And? Does Jack McKenzie know the area?"

"Not as well as the Maori men, sir. The tribe often spends the whole summer up there, so Marama's sons probably know every rock."

"What do you think about the idea of a search party?" Tim inquired.

"What for?"

"Well, to rescue them! Something must have happened or else they would have been here by now. What could they still be doing up there otherwise?" Tim exploded.

"Herding the sheep together," Maaka answered curtly.

Tim was taken aback. "Do you think that anyone would just manage to survive a once-in-a-lifetime storm and then not come directly home but instead continue gathering sheep as if nothing had happened?"

"Probably not anyone, sir. But a McKenzie, yes." He paused for a moment. "Or a Warden. I'll see to the preparations in the old cow stalls, sir. So that the sheep can go somewhere dry when they arrive."

The stalls were clean and being strewn with straw and the fences checked and repaired when the first group of men and sheep arrived. Smiling, Marama put her arms around Rihari. Elaine sighed with relief when they assured her that the rest of the company would be coming down the next day.

"Couldn't you have sent someone ahead?" Gwyneira asked between laughter and tears. She had brought the wet and tired men into the house, poured them generous quantities of whiskey, and had them recount their adventures.

"We suggested it, but the boss, Miss Martyn, said we needed every man."

When Elaine and Lilian came downstairs to dinner a little too early, Gwyneira was sitting at the fire turning a glass of whiskey between her fingers.

"They never called me boss," she said, lost in thought.

Lilian giggled. "Well, times change." She smiled. "And to think she used to be so shy. That seems to have passed."

Jack, Gloria, and her men spent the last night in the watch hut. Wiremu insisted that the two of them sleep in the main room this time. Jack was still unwell and had to lie down somewhere warm after the ride. But then Gloria sprung a surprise on them. "We'll all sleep in here," she decided. "The lambs will be in the stables, and with all that bleating, no one would get a wink of sleep." She glanced at the men as she spoke. With the exception of Wiremu and Jack, no one knew what a hard decision that must have been for her. The Maori were used to sharing the communal sleeping lodge; it would never have occurred to them to harass young women in that manner. Especially not when she belonged to someone else.

Jack hoped Gloria would come to him again, but she remained in her alcove, barricaded behind the thickest sleeping bag. Jack took the second bed in the cabin without protest; the ride through the cold and damp had affected him badly. He patiently drank the infusion Wiremu brought him.

"I don't completely understand it," Wiremu said. "She shared a tent with you, but here . . ."

Jack shrugged. "In the hut, Wiremu? Wouldn't that be taking it a little far?"

"Won't you be getting married?" Wiremu asked. "I thought . . ."

Jack smiled. "It's not up to me. And I don't want to receive the same rebuff you did."

Wiremu grinned painfully. "Watch out for your *mana*," he responded.

The following evening they reached Kiward Station with thousands of sheep. Lilian and Elaine rode out to meet them.

Gloria looked bewildered when she saw her cousin again.

"Didn't you disappear to Auckland?" she asked, looking Lilian over. She had hardly changed since she'd seen her last and still had the same mischievous, jaunty laugh.

"*You* were the one who disappeared," Lilian replied. "I just eloped." She, too, looked Gloria over, but she saw a completely different person from the heavyset, anxious, and grumpy girl from Oaks Garden. As Gloria sat self-assured in the saddle, her face flushed and marked by the hardships of the adventure, Lilian realized she had rarely seen such an interesting face. She should take note of it for her next book. A girl who travels half the world in search of her love. A new version of "Jackaroe." But she had the vague feeling Gloria would never tell her the whole story.

Lily happily told Gloria about her life in Auckland and her baby, and Elaine gave them an update on Kiward Station. Jack and Gloria looked at each other silently, occasionally casting proud looks at the animals they herded ahead of them. When they reached the yard, the men were waiting to divide the sheep into the pens. Maaka was there to coordinate everything, but the men who had been part of the herding expedition only looked to Gloria. And Gloria looked to Jack.

"All right, good job, boys," Jack said. "It's nice to be back. We can all congratulate ourselves—Paora, Anaru, Willings, Beales. That was good work. I think we'll talk to the boss about a little bonus."

Jack looked at Gloria. Gloria smiled.

"I take it you've kept the shearing sheds for the ewes. We'll herd the rams straight to the greens behind Bold's Creek. And I don't want to hear the word *tapu* anymore. If it stays dry, the sheep that have had their lambs can go to the circle of stone warriors tomorrow."

As Jack calmly gave orders, Gloria and some of the men were already whistling for the sheepdogs to separate the flock.

"Maaka, will you take over? I'd like to say hello to my mother. By the looks of it, we've got a full house," Jack said.

"A bath would be a good idea," Gloria remarked as she dismounted. "I'll take the horses to the stables, Jack. You go on ahead and warm up."

As she led Ceredwen and Anwyl to the stables, Gwyneira flung open the door to the stalls from inside. Jack had been expecting his mother to be in the house—when they had visitors, she rarely found time to get things done around the stables. Gwyneira was wearing an old riding dress, and her face looked more youthful than Jack had seen it in years.

"Jack, Gloria." Gwyneira ran toward them and hugged them both at the same time. She took no notice of the fact that Gloria embraced her stiffly and Jack only politely. All that would change with time, and there was time. In any case, their immediate response paled in comparison to what had just happened in the stables, which for Gwyneira was still a wonder after all these years.

"Come in, there's someone who wants to say hello," she said mysteriously, pulling them over to Princess's stall. "He was just born," Gwyneira said, pointing into the stall. Jack and Gloria pressed forward against each other.

Next to the riding pony stood a chocolate-colored stallion. A tiny white snip stood out between his nostrils, and he had a star on his forehead.

Gloria looked up at Jack. "The foal you promised me."

Jack nodded. "It'll be waiting for you when you finish washing up."

Kiward Station had rarely seen such a large dinner party as on that evening. Jack greeted Roly with unusual heartiness and then sat down next to Gloria. Gwyneira sat beaming at the head of the table, holding her first great-great-grandson on her knee. Galahad drooled on her nicest dress and ruined her hair by pulling on it, but that sort of thing had never bothered Gwyneira. She looked at Gloria, pleased. The girl was wearing the pants outfit she had bought her in Dunedin. Lilian could hardly contain her excitement.

"It looks good on you," Lilian said. "But the new fashion in dresses would too. I'll show you some magazines."

Gloria and Jack were quiet as usual, but it was not a quiet that provoked uneasiness. They did not seem to mind all the company. When they spoke, it was about Princess's foal, who naturally reminded Lilian of Vicky.

"Unfortunately I had to leave her in Greymouth, though it would have been so much more romantic to flee on horseback. I'd love to have her at home. Can you take horses on the ferry, Daddy? Or do they get seasick?"

To Gwyneira's great surprise Jack spoke up. In a quiet voice—as though he were no longer used to talking—he told them about the cavalry's horses on the sea journey to Alexandria. "Once a day the ship would turn and sail against the wind in order to ease the heat. Even back then I thought they shouldn't do that. That the horses had no business being at sea—and least of all in the war."

"Maybe we'll move back to the South Island," Lilian considered. "It doesn't matter where I write, and Ben has his pick. The University of Otago would go crazy for him." Lilian gazed proudly at her husband.

Tim rolled his eyes, but Elaine caught him and shook her head admonishingly.

Gwyneira smiled benevolently.

Later they all gathered in the salon. Caleb and Ben were involved in yet another conversation about Maori myths. At one point, Ben pointed to Charlotte's notes to make his argument—and Jack recognized with alarm that it was Charlotte's last folder. His heart contracted. Could Gloria's drawings have ended up in this stranger's hand? Why had he not hidden them somewhere?

Ben Biller noticed his shocked gaze and interpreted it as disapproval.

"Do forgive me, Mr. McKenzie. Naturally we didn't want to take the papers without your permission. But your mother did us the favor."

Gloria followed Jack's gaze.

Jack then turned to Gwyneira, who looked up and saw the horror in Gloria's face.

"You two should come right over here," Gwyneira said quietly. "Not to worry. Everything is safe. You don't have to say a thing. I'd just like to give you both a hug. Now that you're back."

Before retreating upstairs for the night, Gloria kissed her great-grandmother on the cheek, something she had not done since she was a little girl. Gwyneira was moved to tears.

14

Gloria quietly pushed open the door to Jack's room. She did not knock. She had never knocked as a child. Back then, she had worn a nightshirt and curled up with her protector so that she could go back to sleep without nightmares. Tonight, however, she threw off her bathrobe and slipped naked beneath the blankets. She trembled, and Jack thought he could hear her racing heartbeat.

"What do I need to do?" she asked quietly.

"Nothing at all," Jack said, but she shook her head. Gloria pulled back her freshly washed hair; Jack raised his hand at the same time. Their fingers met and sprang apart as if electrified.

"I've already tried 'nothing at all,'" Gloria whispered.

Jack stroked her hair and kissed her. First on the forehead, then the cheek, then on the mouth. She did not open her mouth for him but only held still.

"Gloria, you mustn't do that," Jack said softly. "I love you. Whether you sleep with me or not. If you don't want to . . ."

"But you want to," Gloria murmured.

"That doesn't matter. If it's love, both partners have to want to. If only one of them enjoys it, it's"—he could not find a word for it—"it's wrong."

"Did Charlotte like it the first time?" Gloria asked, relaxing a little.

Jack smiled. "Yes, even though she was a virgin when we married."

"Even though?" Gloria asked.

"To me you're a virgin, Gloria. You've never loved a man before. Otherwise you wouldn't ask how it works." Jack kissed her again, letting his lips wander over her throat and shoulder. Cautiously he stroked her breasts.

"Then show me," she said quietly. She was still trembling, but grew calmer as he kissed her arms, her wrists, her rough hands, and her short strong fingers. He guided her hands over his face, encouraging her to stroke him too. He touched her gently and tentatively, as he would a shy horse.

Gloria's fear expressed itself in the form of resignation. She did not stiffen—she must have discovered that the pain was more bearable when she relaxed her muscles—but Jack had to guard against her becoming a limp doll in his arms. He talked to her, murmured sweet nothings between caresses, and tried to touch her in a way that those men had not. When he finally pushed into her, she pressed her face to his shoulder and kissed him. He made love to her slowly, caressing and kissing her while he was inside her. Before he came, he rolled over and pulled her on top of him. He did not want to collapse on top of her like one of those lustful johns. She fell down beside him and curled against his shoulder as he caught his breath. Finally she dared a question. Her voice sounded anxious.

"Jack, is the reason you're so slow, is it because you've been sick? Or that you are sick?"

Jack was completely taken aback. Then he laughed quietly.

"Of course not, Glory. And I'm not slow either. I just take my time because, because it's nicer that way. Especially for you. Wasn't it nice?"

"I don't know. But if you do it again, I'll try and pay attention."

Jack pulled her close. "It's not a scientific experiment, Glory. Try not to pay attention to anything. Except you and me." He tried to think of an image to explain love to her, and suddenly he had Charlotte's tender last note before his eyes.

"Think of Papa and Rangi," he said softly. "It should be as if heaven and earth were becoming one—and did not want to separate again."

Gloria swallowed. "Could I maybe be the heavens this time?"

For the first time she did not simply lie under a man but moved on top of Jack, kissing and stroking him as he had done for her. And then she did not pay attention to anything anymore. Heaven and earth exploded in pure ecstasy.

Gloria and Jack awoke wrapped tightly in each other's arms. When Jack opened his eyes, he found himself gazing into two cheerful collie faces. Nimue and Tuesday had curled up at the foot of the bed and were clearly happy that their masters had woken up.

"We can't make a habit of that," Jack remarked with furrowed brow, motioning the dogs out of bed with a movement of his head.

"Why not?" Gloria mumbled drowsily. "I really liked it the second time."

Jack kissed her awake and made love to her once more.

"Does it get better every time?" she asked afterward.

Jack smiled. "I try. But as for it being a habit, Gloria, could you see yourself married to me?"

Gloria snuggled closer to him. As Jack waited on pins and needles, she listened to the sounds of the waking house.

Jack and Gloria wanted a small wedding, but Gwyneira seemed disappointed when she heard that, and Elaine also protested heavily. She obviously felt she had been robbed of a big celebration for Lilian and now wanted to be included in the planning for Jack and Gloria's wedding.

"A garden party," Gwyneira decided. "The nicest wedding celebrations are always garden parties, and summer is right around the corner. You could invite everyone in the area. You have to anyway. After all, the heiress of Kiward Station is getting married. People will be expecting a big to-do."

"But no piano music," Gloria insisted.

"And no waltzes." Jack was thinking of his first dance with Charlotte.

Gwyneira thought about her first dance with James. "No, no orchestra at all. Just a few people who can fiddle and play the flute. Maybe someone will even dance another jig with me."

Ever since she had heard about Gloria and Jack's engagement, Gwyneira looked years younger. She was as excited as a young girl about the wedding.

"And we won't wait forever," Jack said. "No six-month engagement or anything."

"But we need to get the sheep to the highlands first," Gloria said. "So not before December."

One source of anxiety for Gloria was her wedding dress. She never had thought she looked attractive in a dress. And all the guests would compare her to Kura, whose simple silk gown and long, silky hair adorned with flowers had been described to her many times as a child. Gloria would have much preferred to walk down the aisle in riding pants.

Lilian came to the rescue. A lecture position had materialized for Ben in Dunedin, and she had planned a trip to the South Island to look around for a house. That was the official reason anyway. In reality, she went straight to Kiward Station and oversaw all the wedding-related details that her mother had not already claimed for herself. The revelation that there was still no wedding dress threw her into the greatest state of excitement.

"We're going to Christchurch tomorrow to buy a dress," Lilian said decisively. "And I already know exactly what you need." She produced an English women's magazine from her pocket and opened it to a page she had marked. Gloria cast an astounded eye over the loose flowing gowns made of light fabric, some of which were decorated with sequins and fringes that reminded her a bit of Maori dancing skirts. The new dresses only reached to the knee and had a flattering drop waist.

"It's the latest fashion! There's a new dance you do in them, the Charleston. And your hair needs to be just a touch shorter. Look, just like this girl. In fact, we can do that right now. Come with me."

Lilian's scissors flew so quickly and skillfully over Gloria's rebellious head of hair that it reminded her of the men from the shearing companies. When Lilian had finished, Gloria could hardly believe the transformation. Her thick hair no longer stuck out from her head but flatteringly framed her face and emphasized her high cheekbones.

"Outstanding," Lilian said. "I'll handle your makeup for the wedding. And tomorrow we'll buy that dress."

This plan ran aground, however, because there was no Charleston dress to be found anywhere in Christchurch. In fact, the salespeople were shocked at the pictures.

"Shameless," declared one piqued matron. "Something like that will never take off here."

Gloria grew increasingly discouraged as she tried on a few other dresses.

"I look terrible."

"The dresses are terrible," Lilian declared. "My word, it's like there was a contest to see which tailor could sew the most flounces onto a wedding dress. You look like a buttercream cake. No, something has to be done. Does anyone on Kiward Station have a sewing machine?"

"You don't mean to sew it yourself, do you?" Gloria asked in horror.

Lilian giggled. "Of course not."

Gloria told Lilian that the closest sewing machine was in Marama's possession. It had been one of her son-in-law William's last presents to her, and she had put it to good use sewing simple breeches and shirts for her sons.

"Wonderful," Lilian cheered. "That model will wake some of Mrs. O'Brien's old memories. She conjured up my mother's wedding dress on a machine just like it. Can I place a quick call to Greymouth?"

Mrs. O'Brien, Roly's mother, took the train for the first time in her life, arriving in Christchurch two days after Lilian's call for help. After initially registering the same shock as the salespeople in the shops, she accepted the challenge and went about selecting the material she would need.

By the time Gloria actually got to try on the dress, Mrs. O'Brien did like it. And Lilian desperately wanted a similar one since she was to be the matron of honor. The dress transformed Gloria into a whole other woman. She looked taller and more grown-up, but also softer and more alluring. For the first time, she saw herself as slender, and she twirled around—as well as she could in the high-heeled shoes Lilian had insisted on.

"And instead of a veil, you need a hat like this with feathers," Lily said, pointing to another magazine. She had been nervous about making this suggestion, but Gloria proved enthusiastic. "Can you manage that, Mrs. O'Brien?"

Jack grew increasingly quiet as the wedding day approached. Elaine and Lilian's enthusiastic preparations reminded him too much of all the trouble Elizabeth and Gwyneira had gone to over his wedding with Charlotte. While Charlotte had enjoyed all the fuss, Gloria fled to the stables whenever she could.

"We should have eloped," he remarked the evening before the wedding. "Lilian and Ben did it the right way: up and done with a signature from the civil registry in Auckland."

Gloria shook her head. "No, it has to happen here," she said in an unusually soft voice.

A letter from Kura and William Martyn had arrived the day before, a response to Gloria and Jack's engagement announcement and invitation to their wedding. They could not attend, of course—and expressed pique that no one had taken their tour schedule into account when planning the event. Originally Gloria was annoyed by the letter, but Jack took the missive out of her hand, scanned it briefly, and laid it aside.

Gloria had stiffened from simply having touched Kura's letter, so Jack pulled her to him.

"I would never have dared to love you in this way," he said into her hair, lost in thought.

Gloria broke away and looked at him in confusion. "What do you mean?"

"If they had not sent you to England," Jack said, "were you to have remained here and never grown up in my eyes, I would have loved you, but like a little sister."

"I understand. I would have been *tapu* for you. That might be. But am I supposed to get down on my knees now and thank my parents?"

Jack laughed. "At least don't be so mad at them. And you should read the postscript." He picked up the letter and placed it in her hand.

Gloria looked uncomprehendingly at the few words tacked on to the letter: Kura Martyn planned to ask Gwyneira to have a deed drawn up. She intended to sign over Kiward Station to her daughter for her wedding. Gloria wanted to say something but could not summon any words.

"Aren't you afraid now that I'm just marrying you for all those sheep?" Jack asked with a smile.

"That could still work," she replied. "Think of Grandmum. She's lived a long and happy life with her husband's sheep." Gloria smiled and reached for Jack's hand. "Now come, we'll let her know. She'll have her first really good night of sleep in decades."

The wedding took place on a radiant summer day. Although Elaine was heartbroken that she didn't get to play the bridal march at the wedding—Gloria was adamant about no pianos—Marama paid tribute to *pakeha* tradition by playing Western music on the *putorino* flute and sang Maori love songs in her ethereal voice.

"That was beautiful," said Miss Bleachum, who had been one of Gloria's bridesmaids. She appeared happy and looked youthful in a fashionable pale-blue dress. Dr. Pinter had accompanied her to the wedding and was the obvious reason for her joyful state. He had put on weight, and his strained wartime demeanor had given way to a relaxed and serene manner. He informed Jack that he was operating again.

"We're opening a children's hospital," Miss Bleachum told him. "Robert inherited a little money, and I've saved mine. We bought a gorgeous house that's wonderfully suited to the work. The children can't go straight back to school after their operations, so I can teach them. It would have been hard for me to give up my profession."

She blushed as she spoke these last words.

"You're getting married then?" Jack asked. He knew it, of course, but he still enjoyed make her blush. "And here we'd hoped you'd soon be returning to us."

Gloria helped her get over the awkwardness by introducing Dr. Pinter to Wiremu. Unlike Tonga and the tribe's other dignitaries who had shown up in traditional Maori clothing, Wiremu was wearing a suit.

"Wiremu studied medicine. Perhaps you need an assistant in your hospital?"

Dr. Pinter's gaze fell on Wiremu's tattoos. "I don't know. He might scare the children."

"Nonsense," Sarah responded, beaming. "On the contrary. He'll give them courage. A big, strong Maori warrior on their side. Children need that. If you're interested, you're more than welcome."

Sarah held out her hand to Wiremu. Dr. Pinter did the same.

Tonga watched his son with every sign of disapproval. Finally he joined Gwyneira.

"I can congratulate you once again," he remarked. "First Kura, now Gloria."

"I didn't choose either of their husbands," she replied. "And I never wanted to play this game. Kura was always different. You would never have held on to her, even if she had married a Maori. Just as I couldn't hold on to her. But Gloria came back. To me and to all of you. She belongs to this land. Kiward Station is . . . what do you call it? Her *maunga*, right? You don't need to bind her to the tribe. Her roots are here. And Jack's too." She followed Tonga's gaze to his son. "And Wiremu. Perhaps he'll come back at some point. But you can't force him."

Tonga smiled. "You're getting wise in your old age, Mrs. McKenzie. Well, tell the couple that they should come to the *marae* at the next full moon. We'll carry out a *pohiri*—to greet the new member of the tribe."

"The new member?" Gloria did not understand.

"Not a brand-new one," Rongo said. "There'll be plenty of time for that. But Jack as Gloria's husband."

"So how did things go with Florence?" Elaine asked.

Tim Lambert had only arrived on Kiward Station that morning and had not yet had a quiet word with his wife amid all the preparations. Now they sat together with Elaine's parents and Gwyneira at a quiet table far from the dance floor where Roly and Mary were twirling about.

Tim regarded his wife with an almost anguished expression. "Well, we're still not friends. But I think she understood where we stand—she's first and foremost a businesswoman. She'll agree to our suggestions."

Ben and Lilian's visit to Greymouth had not gone off without some tension. Lilian had hoped that Florence Biller would fall for her baby's charm just as her own parents had, but Ben's mother was cut from a different cloth. She looked at little Galahad with more suspicion than admiration. Almost as if she were already weighing whether he would be as much of a failure in her eyes as his father and grandfather. On the other hand, she had to accept the facts. Gal was one of the heirs of her mine—as well as one of the heirs of Tim's. In any case, Florence had to give up her ruinous rivalry with the Lamberts and close her coke furnace. In exchange, Tim had suggested that they open the planned briquette factory on her property.

"The rail connection is much better, and the land has already been reclaimed. We wouldn't need to clear any more forest, which makes everything cheaper. And Greenwood Enterprises can invest in you as easily as in me. We'd need certain assurances, of course—which absolutely excludes any family feuds."

They had sealed the agreement with a glass of whiskey, which Florence gulped down a bit too hastily. But she held it, Tim observed, like a man.

"That all sounds very good," Elaine said, looking over at Lilian and Ben. Ben was conversing with Wiremu while Lilian chatted with Gloria's former governess. Florence crossed the room to greet them, and just as she was out of earshot Elaine added, "We can't complain about Ben. He seems to really love Lilian. If I only I had the slightest idea what she saw in him!"

"Enlighten me if you ever figure it out," Tim responded, "but I'm afraid you'd do better solving the riddle of the pyramids."

"Now even Miss Bleachum's getting married," Lilian said, laughing. While Ben was chatting with Wiremu and Jack was forced to drink whiskey with a few neighbors, Lilian and Gloria sat down at the family table. Lilian was in high spirits.

"Will she still have children too? She's not exactly young anymore. And Dr. Pinter, well, it's a mystery to me what she sees in him."

"What do you see in Ben?" Gloria asked casually. She just wanted to shield her beloved Miss Bleachum from any gossip. She did not notice that all the other women at the table were holding their breath in anticipation.

Lilian furrowed her brow. She seemed to be considering the question.

"I always thought you would marry someone like one of your heroes, the ones in all those songs and stories and all."

Lilian sighed. "Oh, well, all those adventures are wonderfully romantic when you read about them, but in reality, it's no fun to be as poor as a church mouse, without a proper home, and no idea where to go."

"Oh really?" Elaine asked, amused. "Who would have thought that?"

Elaine's mother, Fleurette, and Gwyneira both fought back a laugh, and even Gloria made a face. Lilian, however, did not seem to notice the irony at all.

"No, really. Terrible things are always happening to heroes. If Ben were to take to the sea or something, I would worry about him all the time."

"And what does that have to do with what you see in him?" Gloria asked. She could not always follow Lilian.

"Well, I never need to worry about Ben," Lily said blithely. "In the morning he goes to his library and studies South Sea dialects—and the most exciting thing he has planned is an excursion to the Cook Islands."

"And what about the lovely South Sea island women?" Elaine teased her. "He does know 'I love you' in at least ten different dialects."

Lilian giggled. "But first he would need to exhaust the topic of the principle of couple formation out of emotional impulses in individual cultural groups, and research its possible practical or mythological roots and discuss pictorial depictions of sexual relationships in the geographical area in question with other researchers. By then the girl would be so bored, I'd have no reason to worry."

The others laughed openly, but Lilian did not seem to take offense.

"And you don't get bored?" Gwyneira asked. Her eyes flashed vivaciously.

"When I get bored, I have Galahad. And Florian, and Jeffrey. The new one is named Juvert."

She listed the protagonists of her books. "And when I have to continue writing at night because my hero is trapped somewhere or has to save his girl from some horrible calamity, Ben doesn't mind if he has to cook."

"Real heroes shoot the rabbit for dinner too," Gwyneira teased. She thought of James and the happy times when he had fished and hunted for her and then roasted his prize on the fire.

"And afterward they leave the intestines lying all over the place," Fleurette remarked drily. "I know what you mean, Lily. Your Ben is the greatest."

At midnight Elaine's sons set off fireworks. The guests, most of them already tipsy, greeted them with cheers.

Gwyneira, however, headed to the stables. She knew that the horses were locked in. She would not find James there hurrying to bring in the mares before the noise scared them. Nor would anyone be playing the fiddle near the barn, as there had been on her own wedding night. Back when Gwyneira had first gotten married, the shepherds had twirled the maids to the music of an accordion, fiddle, and tin whistle while a string quartet had played for the guests in the festively lit garden. Gwyneira could still see the fire before her and James's beaming face as she joined the men and granted him a dance. She had almost kissed him then.

But even now a couple was kissing in the stables. Jack and Gloria had fled the commotion and were holding each other close while thousands of artificial falling stars lit the sky.

Gwyneira did not say a word. She simply slipped away into the darkness and left them to each other. They were the future.

"This is my last wedding on Kiward Station," Gwyneira said nostalgically. She had declined the sparkling wine and was sipping some whiskey. She drank to James. "I won't live to see the next generation."

Lilian, the wine having bubbled to her head and so quick to get teary, embraced her great-grandmother. "Nonsense. Look, you've already got a great-great-grandson." It sounded as if she counted on Galahad getting married the next day. "And besides, we could really stand to get married again, Ben. It was pretty sad at the civil registrar's in Auckland. This was so much better. Especially the fireworks. Or we'll do something different and marry according to Maori customs. Like in *The Heiress of Wakanui*—that was so romantic." She beamed at Ben.

"Dear, Maori tribes don't have romantic weddings." Ben looked afflicted; he had probably given this lecture to his wife several times before. "Most formal marriage ceremonies have a function in dynastic alliances whereby a clerical union is also assumed." He wanted to go on but noticed that his audience was no longer listening. "You simply invented the ritual in *The Heiress of Wakanui*."

Lilian shrugged. "So? What's wrong with that? At heart it's always just about a really good story."

Afterword

Even a historical novel needs a good story, but a serious author should steer clear of Lily's carefree approach to history and mythology. I have worked hard to embed my fictional characters' story in a well-researched web of facts. In the case of the Battle of Gallipoli, that was relatively easy. The story of the ANZAC troops can be found in countless forms—from eyewitness accounts to narratives for young people to stories on the Internet. However, the suffering of the men in the trenches is almost invariably painted in a heroic light.

The reinterpretation of this catastrophic military blunder and subsequent defeat into a heroic epic hardly has its equal. Gallipoli was one of the bloodiest battles of the First World War, and the only credit to the high command lies in the successful withdrawal of their troops with an astoundingly small blow to morale. Though a few critical journalists asked piercing questions about the sense of the battle back then—thereby perhaps shortening the disaster—all that gets celebrated now is the heroism of the soldiers who were mercilessly delivered up. One exception is Eric Bogle's song "And the Band Played Waltzing Matilda," which impressed me much more than all the parades on the annually celebrated ANZAC Day.

I have tried to represent the mood and the course of the struggles at Gallipoli as authentically as possible. The characters of the soldiers and their superiors are, however, fictional. The medical officer Joseph Lievesley Beeston and his mixed-breed dog so disinclined to military discipline, Paddy, are the only exceptions. Their adventures can be read on the Internet. Beeston's war journal provides a great deal of information, as well as the background for my story. Unfortunately no pictures of the two have survived. Thus I had to use my imagination, although in the case of Paddy, the image of my own, also largely discipline-resistant dachshund mix, imposed itself. Thanks, Buddy, for constant inspiration.

The Maori tribe on Kiward Station played a role in my previous books, but this time I had Gloria delve deeper into their ideas and way of life. Research of Maori culture is not easy—in part because there is no such thing as a unifying Maori culture.

Every tribe had and has its own customs and *tapu*. They can vary greatly and depend largely on the community's circumstances. For example, the South Island was much poorer in resources and more thinly populated than the North Island, so there were far fewer military confrontations between the tribes there—laws, *tapu*, and concepts of value therefore have been much less marked by militarism.

Only the pantheon and aspects of the mythical world are held in common by practically all the inhabitants of the North and South Islands. With almost all the better universities in New Zealand offering Maori studies now, academia serves as a good source. Academics tend to study certain aspects of Maori culture in order to try then to fit them into the larger whole, where possible. Less serious publications pick and choose what seems to fit neatly into their view of Maori culture or whatever can be easily marketed. A German alternative healer, for example, devoted a whole book to tea-tree oil as a supposed panacea among the Maori, while official Maori organizations do not even mention the *manuka* tree as a medicinal plant.

Mystics have also begun tapping into the apparent wisdom of the Maori. This at least sets their previously preferred target—the Aborigines of Australia—free. After all, the Aborigines do not show much enthusiasm for the miracle powers ascribed to them by delusional Westerners. Rather than crude publicity, they would have preferred greater acceptance, better educational opportunities, and higher paid jobs. In principle it can be said about all publications on Maori culture (not to mention that of the Aborigines) that reasonable doubt is more than appropriate. Since the authenticity of sources is hard to verify, I have largely limited my research for this book to the testimonies and publications of Maori or Maori organizations. Though that does not guarantee absolute authenticity (understandably one tends to leave the darker aspects of one's own culture off of the "About Us" page), it nevertheless avoids risky speculation.

It must also be noted here that on the subject of the study of Maori culture, I have skipped ahead a little in time. There was not yet a Department of Maori Studies in Auckland in the early twentieth century.

The gulf between Maori and *pakeha*, however, was never as deep as that between natives and colonists in other parts of the world. This is especially true of the South Island. There were never notable confrontations between the Ngai Tahu—to which not only my fictional tribe but also practically all *iwi* of the South Island belong—and the immigrants from Europe. According to the testimony of a Maori culture researcher who was kind enough to converse with me on the subject, the tribes willingly adapted to the Western way of life because, at least at first glance, it offered a higher quality of life. Only later did doubts about that emerge, and in that sense, Tonga, too, is a little ahead of his time. Today there is a strong movement among Maori, particularly those on the North Island, that pushes for a return to their own culture and encourages young *pakeha* to engage with it as well.

As for Lilian's story, the reader may ask whether the story of her wedding is credible. In fact, one could and still can take one's vows spontaneously in New Zealand—as long as one has a passport and has reached the minimum age. The written approval of the parents for those under eighteen was, and remains, a formality.

The *Auckland Herald* did indeed exist in Lilian's day. The paper was owned by the Wilson family. However, Thomas Wilson, my relaxed editor in chief, is fictional—unlike the medium Margery Crandon, who was world famous in her day. Whether the lady took her nonsense to New Zealand, though, is doubtful, at least during the war years, when she was making herself useful driving an ambulance in Boston. Though Crandon did wrap Arthur Conan Doyle around her finger, the great magician Houdini shared Lily's estimation of the medium and revealed Crandon to be a fraud. It did no harm to her reputation as a mystic. It does not always have to be a good story.

Acknowledgments

As always, I would like to thank my friends and editors for advice and help with the production of this book, especially my miracle-working agent, Bastian Schlück. Klara Decker did the test reading as usual, and Eva Schlück and Melanie Blank-Schröder contributed to the discussion of the often somewhat unwieldy character of Gloria. It is undoubtedly a little unusual for the heroine of a novel to get in her own way as often as Gwyneira's great-granddaughter does, and the girl even got on my nerves occasionally. But that is just how she was: a human in a story about humans.

Rob Ritchie helped me with information about the life of British soldiers and even checked the whole Gallipoli chapter for accuracy. It surely took him many hours. The authentic feeling of being shot at unexpectedly I owe to those modern, rather undisciplined hunters I once encountered on a stroll, to whom, however, I am not really grateful.

As I worked on the first chapters, my border collie Cleo, who lent her inspiration again and again to the first volumes of this trilogy, was still sitting beside me. Then she took her leave, after twenty years, with the spirits to Hawaiki.

As far as heaven, Cleo, and a few stars beyond.

—Sarah Lark

About the Author

Photo © Gonzalo Perez, 2011

Sarah Lark's series of "landscape novels" have made her a bestselling author in Germany, her native country, as well as in Spain and the United States. She was born in Germany's Ruhr region, where she discovered a love of animals—especially horses—early in life. She has worked as an elementary-school teacher, travel guide, and commercial writer. She has also written numerous award-winning books about horses for adults and children, one of which was nominated for the Deutsche Jugendbuchpreis, Germany's distinguished prize for best children's book. Sarah currently lives with four dogs and a cat on her farm in Almería, Spain, where she cares for retired horses, plays guitar, and sings in her spare time.

About the Translator

Photo © Sanna Stegmaier, 2011

D. W. Lovett is a graduate of the University of Illinois at Urbana–Champaign, from which he received a degree in comparative literature and German as well as a certificate from the university's Center for Translation Studies. He has spent the last few years living in Europe. This is his third translation of Sarah Lark's work to be published in English, following *In the Land of the Long White Cloud* and *Song of the Spirits.*